A FAINT REFLECTION OF RIDDLES BOOK ONE

THE WOOD BETWEEN THE WORLDS

A Jake Moriarity Novel
by
R.G. Ryan

"There's blood on the wood between the worlds..."
Bob Ayala

COPYRIGHT © 2019 by R.G. Ryan.

All rights reserved. This book or parts thereof may not be reproduced in any form, stored in a retrieval system, or transmitted in any form by any means—electronic, mechanical, photocopy, recording, or otherwise—without prior written permission of the publisher, except as provided by United States of America copyright law.

This book is a work of fiction. Names, characters, places and incidents are products of the author's imagination. Any resemblance to actual events or persons, living or dead, is purely coincidental.

Published by Dream Chasers Media Group
Las Vegas, NV

Library of Congress Control Number:2019911156
ISBN 978-1-7333949-0-1

Edited by Cheryl D. Gollner
Cover Design by Sarah Wagner

JAKE MORIARITY NOVELS

Watercolor Dreams

Finding Wonderland

The Secret Of Gaspard

The Haunts Of Cruelty

A Faint Reflection Of Riddles
Book One: The Wood Between The Worlds

PROLOGUE

Jerusalem, AD 33

The Centurion viewed the uneven road lined with wooden monuments to the ultimate form of public execution—the Roman cross. That very morning in one of their rare conversations, his father had opined that it was a corridor of agony.

He was correct.

The process of crucifixion produced a level of suffering previously unknown to man. So great was the victim's agony that the guardians of the Roman tongue had coined a new word that was gaining in popular usage. *Excruciating.* It meant, "From the cross."

A measure of callousness was necessary for one in his line of work. After all, human suffering was his stock in trade. He caused it, considered himself—and was considered by others—to be one of the best. And yet there were still specific things about the poor wretches assigned to him and his fellow practitioners of pain that always caught his eye. Typically, he would search their faces, alert for the moment when the true self was revealed.

It always happened.

Oh, there were many who would come before him resolved to endure to the end with dignity, but it didn't matter. The intricate system of reduction gradually stripped away their resolve just as the flagrum stripped away their skin. Ultimately, the experience pressed every victim, regardless of race or social strata, to that place where they yielded all to the torment. And it was that passage for which he waited. He didn't know why. Call it satisfaction for a job well done; call it pride in one's craft. Whatever the case, it was that and little else that kept him going.

As he approached a grouping of three crosses on a lonely hill, he slowed to gaze dispassionately upon the limp, broken shell that had once housed the spirit of the man in the middle. Like everyone else, he'd heard the rumors, but he hadn't believed any of it. Walking on water; turning water into wine; bringing dead people back to life. He considered it to be nothing more than fodder for the fertile imaginations of the Jewish populace.

Nevertheless, there had been something about the man. The way he had endured the torture. In his fifteen years of experience, he had never seen the likes. He had gained no satisfaction in the mutilation of this man. Throughout the whole ordeal, he hadn't been able to shake the notion that the man had pitied him.

Pitied him!

Stopping a few paces away, he observed the men engaged in the gruesome process of releasing the victim from the patibulum. One appeared to be a man of some means and was at the moment engaged in a heated conversation with the soldiers regarding the disposition of the body. He watched as the man produced an official looking document that evidently bore the seal of Pilate. The soldier examined it closely while the men began preparing the body for transport. The Centurion had decided the situation warranted his involvement and had actually begun to move forward when someone called his name.

"Hello, Justus. Come to admire your work?"

So great had been his concentration, the greeting startled him.

"Well, Caleb," he replied, turning his attention toward the man who had spoken. "I've always believed that one should give one's best to whatever it is that one has chosen to do."

The fact that a Roman Centurion would even speak to

a Jew was unheard of. It was therefore a social absurdity that over the years Justus and Caleb had become friends of a sort.

Caleb laughed.

"You don't fool me, old friend. If you were offered a chance to join the Praetorian, you would accept without hesitation."

Justus thought for a moment before answering.

"The Praetorian—yes, yes I would. But that doesn't translate into dissatisfaction in my current duties."

With his son's assistance Caleb finished hoisting a bloody and splintered patibulum onto his old cart. The one hundred and ten pound timber to which the victims of Roman crucifixion were nailed had run its course and was being retired. Fitting, Caleb thought, that its last victim had been the crumpled and mutilated form of the man on the ground.

"That will have to be the last one for this trip, father," Caleb's son Phillip remarked, mopping his brow on the sleeve of a tattered robe.

"Very well, go ahead and tie down the load while I talk to Justus."

Watching his son, Caleb thought once again about his good fortune in being the principle supplier of wood for the Roman army. The position had alienated him from the Jewish community, but it provided a good living, as well as an elevated social standing, and was therefore acceptable.

Besides, someone had to do it.

"How old is the boy, Caleb?" Justus admired the young man's strong frame and had thought more than once that he would make a fine soldier.

If only he were a Roman.

"Phillip is, let's see…twenty-nine. Although the passage of years seems to have somehow escaped my notice. Why, I remember just like it was yesterday when he and Jesus used to…" Caleb stopped, fearing to complete the sentence lest he offend his friend.

"Jesus?" Justus was momentarily confused, convinced

that he hadn't heard clearly. Pointing to the body which now lay ignobly on the ground at the foot of the staticulum, he said, "Surely you're not referring to this criminal?"

Caleb searched his friend's eyes before replying.

"Yes, Justus. You see, when his father, Joseph, was alive I delivered wood to his carpenter shop. Joseph was a good customer and when Jesus and Phillip were children they played together whenever I made my deliveries."

"I see." Justus looked once more at the brutalized remains before continuing. "I just realized something, Caleb. I never consider the fact that the men I put to death were ever any more than the miserable criminals they have become."

"And this concerns you?"

Justus turned his head slowly to gaze into Caleb's eyes.

"Oddly enough, I find that it does. Take this man, for example. I heard him called by many names today—King of the Jews; the Messiah; teacher. I even heard one of the other Centurions pronounce that he was the 'Son of God.'"

"And what if he was?" Caleb prodded.

"What if he was…what?"

"What if he was the 'Son of God', the Messiah? How else do you explain what happened when he died—you know, the darkness…earthquake?"

Justus noticed that Phillip had walked up to stand behind his father.

"And you, young Phillip, what do you believe?"

Phillip looked at Jesus' body as the men carefully, somberly wrapped it in a burial cloth.

"Well, from the time we were children playing together I always knew there was something different about him. I heard all the rumors, but to me he was just my funny, kind friend who knew all the places to hide from our fathers so we wouldn't have to do any work." Phillip smiled at the memory. "Then after Joseph died we quit delivering wood to the shop and we sort of lost touch."

Justus smiled before asking, "So, who was he, Phillip?"

Phillip looked at Jesus' body, then back at Justus.

"I...I believe that the man you crucified today was the Son of God."

Justus stood perfectly still as he pondered Phillip's pronouncement. He truthfully didn't know what to say in reply, so he said nothing.

"Well, Justus," Caleb said after a moment or two. "We'd better be moving along if we're going to get this wood put away before dark."

Justus held up his hand.

"Wait, don't leave just yet." Turning his gaze to Phillip, he said, "Young man, you will be wise to keep that belief to yourself. Most of my colleagues are not as lenient as I, and many people have been arrested for far less blasphemy than what you have just uttered."

"But, sir...you asked me to state my beliefs," Phillip replied quickly, as beads of sweat began to form along his brow.

"Indeed I did. But you don't need to tell everyone *all* of what you believe. In fact, I strongly urge you to tell no one from this day forward. It would not sit well with me if one day I found you in my courtyard awaiting my scourge."

Caleb and Phillip, shaken by the exchange, turned silently to leave, pushing the cart bearing the wood soaked in the blood of Phillip's former friend.

As Justus watched them go, he shouted after them, "Son of God, indeed! The only *god* I know is enthroned in Rome and pays my wages. And I guarantee you that this man wasn't *his* son."

Phillip and Caleb exchanged frightened glances as they pulled their cart past the spot where Jesus' body was being hoisted to waiting shoulders, each lost within their own private thoughts.

As for Justus, the conversation had left him in a foul and yet contemplative mood. Walking toward the men who held the body aloft he shouted, "You there."

They stopped at his command and awaited his approach.

Pulling the burial cloth away from the bloody swollen face, he stared hard as if attempting to see beneath what remained of the dead man's skin.

After a few seconds examination he muttered, "Even if you were God's son, he's not much of a father to have let you die so horribly."

Turkey, AD 1200

The sound of the battle filled the misty coolness of the night as the two warriors ran for their lives through streets that only yesterday had echoed with the happy voices of children engaged in childish pursuits. Now, broken bodies lay mingled with the shattered remains of the city in a macabre living portrait depicting the horror of war. A "holy war," they called it, although at this point there was nothing holy about it.

"We must hurry—they're almost upon us," Everard called over his shoulder to Renaud as the walls of their temporary refuge came into view.

Only another hundred feet or so and they would gain the relative safety of the battlement. Sanctuary—home to them both for the past two, torturous years.

"I can't, Everard. I can't run any further," Renaud gasped as he fell headlong at Everard's heels.

Pierced by an assailant's sword through his liver, the wound had cost him too much blood. His strength was gone. Refuge or no refuge, he knew that his time had come—time to meet the One for whom he had lived this life of austere discipline.

"I won't allow this." Everard bent, pulling his friend up, preparing to hoist him over his shoulders. "You will not die here in the street like a common man. That is, if you die at all."

"Oh, I'm dying, old friend. Of that you can be sure. Leave me. Leave me, Everard, and save yourself." Renaud's eyes reflected a mixture of pain and desperation.

"Listen to me, stubborn old goat," Everard wheezed as he bent under his load and resumed his now stumbling flight. "We are in the business of saving, you and me. No one should be left behind. Remember?"

The credo of The Brotherhood—*no one should be left behind.* It had been written, recited and reflected upon daily since they had entered the knighthood together many years ago. Two young men filled with visions of a life given to service of their Lord and of his King.

His voice bouncing in time with Everard's labored steps, Renaud gasped, "So, I'll not be allowed to die a glorious death?"

Everard merely laughed as he climbed the seven steps leading to the ornately carved wooden doors of the compound.

"Not today, brother, not today."

Pounding on the thick wood produced a loud hail from above.

"Away! Away with you or face the wrath of God!"

"Open," he shouted in return. "Open in the name of the Lord and of his King."

In the street behind them the surge of the battle had carried the few remaining Christian soldiers into view. Badly beaten, they now sought the only refuge that remained.

"Everard? Is that you, brother?"

"Yes, and Renaud. He's wounded. Open quickly or we perish."

The massive doors swung open effortlessly as two heavily-armored men emerged to relieve Everard of his burden.

"Take him to the chamber. Pass him through the portal," Everard intoned gravely.

Knowing glances were exchanged and the two knights half-carried, half-drug their suffering comrade toward a small structure set back along the northeast wall of the compound.

With the doors shut and barred, Everard quickly made

his way toward the Sanctuary and the reliquary located three levels below. It didn't take a wise man to know that this battle would be lost. But all would not be lost—he would salvage what he could. If it cost him his life, he would salvage the remnant, for it was the cornerstone of their faith.

CHAPTER ONE

Present day

Early Friday morning. Not quite "Oh-dark thirty", but close enough that it felt that way.

6:00 a.m., to be precise.

Aaron and I were beginning the last set of triceps presses at the new gym we had decided to try out. The machine, made by a company called Hammer Strength, mimicked the motion of parallel bar dips, with free-weights as the resistance instead of one's own body weight. It was our favorite machine in the gym. If you want to know the truth, the reason we had abandoned our former gym is that the management brain trust had determined that they needed more room for their *CrossFit* exercise area and had gotten rid of our beloved triceps machine without even polling the membership as to their preference. Had they taken the time to do so, they would have discovered that there were no less than forty members who disagreed with the decision as evidenced by the rapid termination of their memberships. It's not that I have anything against *CrossFit* and its devotees; it's just that they could have found another way to accommodate one without eliminating the other. Just saying.

At present, Aaron was moving smoothly through a set of ten reps with approximately the weight of a bull elephant stacked in front of him. Well, that may be overstating a bit, but five forty-five pound plates per side comes out to about five hundred pounds when you add in the starting resistance of the machine. I maxed out at four plates per side, an impressive amount of weight, or so I've been told, but not even close to Aaron's ability. And when I say ten reps, that's ten reps without breaking a sweat. The man could've easily popped off twenty had he been so inclined.

Along about rep number six, he asked casually, "So, where we gonna have breakfast after we're done?"

I stared in disbelief.

"How do you do that?"

"Do what?" he replied, while blowing past ten and moving on to eleven and twelve.

"Carry on a conversation in a perfectly normal tone of voice while hoisting that much weight?"

He glanced at the clanging plates.

"What...this? Ain't no thang, baby."

Eighteen, nineteen, twenty...

"Okay, stop! Just stop!"

He grinned, eased the apparatus back into place and stood.

"Come on now, Jake, not everybody can be blessed with superior strength. Besides, you're no weakling yourself."

"I know," I said jealously. "But it's disturbing to see you banging those reps out with no apparent effort."

"Who says there was no effort?" he replied around a frown.

"No *apparent* effort, is what I said, apparent being the operative word."

"Look, if it makes you feel any better, those last two were beginning to push me a little bit."

I was about to come back with a caustic retort, when my phone started buzzing. I pulled it out and saw that it was my friend, Elliot Spencer.

Elliot and I go back ten or twelve years or so to when he had called me to find some missing family heirlooms for his parents over in London. I should probably mention that Elliot is a Brit. During the search for the missing items—which were found, of course—Elliot and I hit it off and have remained pretty good friends over the years.

Dr. Elliot Spencer and his colleague, Dr. Werner French,

are associate deans over the department of anthropology and archeology at Northwest Pacific University in Seattle, Washington. They make quite a pair. Werner is a shade over six-six, and Elliot is maybe five-seven in shoes. Werner weighs around three-fifty and Elliot goes about a buck-forty after a big meal. Werner's hair is long, red and untamed, with skin that bears witness to the years spent at numerous archeological digs around the world. Elliot, by contrast, has baby-fine blonde hair with a creamy complexion that looks as if a razor has never touched it.

Like I said, quite a pair.

But, between them they comprise one of, if not *the* most respected and highly acclaimed archeological teams in the world. To the extent, that when they speak…the archeological community listens.

"Elliot," I said in cheerful greeting. "What a surprise. Haven't heard from you in a while."

"I know, I know," he stammered. "I am quite terrible when it comes to staying in touch. By the way, is Aaron there with you?"

"Yes, he is. We're just finishing a workout."

"Well, please greet him for me and tell him that my parents are still raving about the tickets he graciously provided earlier this year for his London concert."

I turned to Aaron, "It's Elliot Spencer. He said to thank you for the concert tickets you gave to his parents."

Aaron said, "It was my pleasure. Any time I'm in London, they will have free tickets."

"Did you hear that?" I asked.

Elliot replied, "I most certainly did. And I will make sure to thank him in person."

I had been hearing something in Elliot's voice—like barely contained excitement, or, perhaps stress bordering on panic.

"Okay, Elliot…why are you calling me. I know it isn't just to catch up."

I could hear him take in a deep breath on the other end of the call.

"Jake..." he began. "Werner and I have stumbled upon the most amazing discovery."

If Elliot Spencer and Werner French were dubbing a discovery, "amazing", then it must be something incredible.

"Okay," I replied. "You have my attention. What's going on?"

His answer came out in a rush as if he couldn't stand to wait another second.

"Jake, we've found the remnant of the true cross." He kind of paused like he was waiting for me to say something. After a few seconds he said, "Hello?" like he was afraid the connection had been broken or something.

"I'm still here, Elliot."

"Oh, well, when you didn't say anything I thought perhaps the line had gone dead," he said after another few seconds of silence.

"Sorry," I replied, taking a seat on a nearby weight bench. "It's just that I'm not sure I'm following you."

I meant it. If you want to know the truth, I was pretty confused by the statement.

"Jake, the cross—*the* cross that Jesus of Nazareth died on. We know the location of the remnant." His voice had raised an octave in his excitement.

If what he said was true, I could certainly see why these guys were so worked up. Of all the relics that had been taken from the Holy Land during the Crusades, no one had ever recovered this one. Sure, there had been rumors and legends through the years, and even today some pieces were purported to exist. But there had never been an actual, verifiable piece of the cross.

Never.

"Congratulations, Elliot," I said. "This could remove any doubt that you guys are at the top of the archeological heap, so to speak."

"Thank-you, Jake. And while I'm sure you are correct, there's...umm...a bit of a problem."

He sounded worried.

"All right. Tell me about it."

"We know *approximately* where it is. Not precisely."

"I see. And just how *approximate* are we talking?"

"Well," he replied. "We know it's somewhere in south central Turkey."

"That certainly narrows it down."

"I know, I know...but it's there. We know it's there. We just need you to go find it."

"Listen, Elliot," I said wearily. "I've just wrapped up a case that left me, well, played out and was really hoping to have a bit of down time before I jump into something else. Especially something of this magnitude. So...I don't know."

"Right." His tone dripped with disappointment. "It's just that this is...well...urgent, Jake. We need to move right away or the window of opportunity will close and this...this treasure will be lost."

"Lost to you, or lost permanently?" I asked.

He started to reply, but stopped and blew out a long breath of air.

"Look, I won't beat about the bush. This is huge, it's the most important archeological find in modern history. If we don't find it, someone else will. And that *someone* will have a prominent place in the history books. For me, for Werner—and by extension for the university—this is a game changer, Jake. Right now we have a leg up on everyone else."

"And how did that come about?"

"We are in possession of historical documents that we've recently re-translated and deciphered. The net result being that we've gained a whole new understanding of something that has been right under our noses for decades—perhaps even centuries."

I said, "And this *something* is the location of the cross?"

"Yes. But, others have these same documents, or at least

copies thereof. If we figured it out...so could they. That's why time is of the essence."

"Well, I don't technically have anything else to do so—"

"You'll do it?" he asked hopefully.

"Okay. I'll do it."

He suddenly burst into excited, unintelligible babble directed, I assumed, at Dr. French.

After much hooting and hollering, he came back on the line.

"When do you think you can get here?"

Long story short—which, for the record never results in a shortening of said story—I agreed that I'd book the first flight available and meet him at SeaTac the next morning.

As Aaron and I collected our things and exited the gym, I tried to wrap my mind around the import of what Elliot had purportedly found. My mind was filled with a certain kind of awe as I reflected on what I had agreed to do. Aside from being the most important find in the history of the Church, it was something that had the potential to rock the archeological community.

It was huge!

It suddenly felt as if I were faced with a task for which I was completely unprepared. Finding the remnant of the true cross—the wood between the worlds.

CHAPTER TWO

Aaron sat with his nose buried in the restaurant menu. And, for the life of me, I couldn't understand why. We were in a small diner that specialized in breakfast—the same diner we patronized every single day following our workout. The menu wasn't elaborate. In fact, it was a mere three pages not counting the cover. Straightforward, good old American cuisine. Burgers, hot dogs, meatloaf, simple salads and breakfast items that consisted of eggs any style, hash browns, sausage, bacon, pancakes and waffles.

That's it.

And yet, he sat for a full five minutes every single time just staring at the menu as if trying to determine what to order. And every single time, he wound up ordering the same thing.

"Why are you staring at the menu?" I finally asked in frustration.

He lowered the folder so he could peer over the top edge.

"Because I'm trying to decide what to order. Typically when one is going to order food in a restaurant, one consults the establishment's menu and orders whatever looks good."

I rolled my eyes so far back in my head that I nearly went back in time.

"You've got to be kidding me."

He frowned.

"Why would I be kidding you about food, bruh? There are many things in life toward which I adopt what some may consider a cavalier attitude. Food is *not* one of them. I take food very seriously."

"But...dude...you order the same damn thing every time we come in here. And we come in here every flippin' day. Okay, look, I'll prove it to you." I turned and hailed our server. "Brittney, can you come over for a sec?"

Brittney, our cute, perky waitress by day, pre-med student by night, hustled over, a friendly smile lighting up her pretty face.

"Yeah, what's up, Jake?"

I cleared my throat.

"What is Aaron going to order?"

She frowned, and turned her head slightly, looking at me out of the corner of her eye.

"Is this a trick question?"

"Nope. Just tell me what the man is going to order."

She shrugged, holding her hands out to the side.

"Uh, the same thing he orders *every* single time you two come in."

"And what would that be?" I inquired.

"Three eggs over medium; six slices of bacon; hash browns extra crispy; four buttermilk pancakes with enough butter, and I quote, 'to hurt me.'"

"And..." I prompted.

"Oh, yeah...a large glass of whole milk in a frosty glass."

I turned to Aaron, a triumphant smile fixed to my gloating countenance.

"Well?"

"Well, what?" he growled.

"You always order the same thing. So why are you staring at the menu for five minutes?"

"Might want something different," he replied in a surly tone.

"Great," Brittney said, whipping out her order booklet. "What'll you have?"

He sat still for a full ten seconds before slamming the menu on the tabletop and waving his hand at her as if swatting away a fly.

"You know!"

"Right," she replied, drawing the word out dramatically. "And how about you, Jake?"

"Same thing."

She raised her eyebrows, "Oooh, the man is a madcap. Coming right up, guys."

As she walked away Aaron said, "You did that on purpose."

"Did what on purpose?"

"Ordered the same thing as me."

"So?"

"So, you always get the same thing too. Why you wanna change it up today if not to just rub it in my face, or something?"

"I wasn't rubbing it in your face," I protested. "When she was going through your order, it all sounded so good that I couldn't resist."

He grinned.

"Why you think I always get it? Some things a man just can't resist."

"You got that right."

After a pause to sip his coffee, he asked, "So, you think this cross thing Elliot is talking about is legit?"

"All I know is that Elliot Spencer is completely legit, and he believes this to be genuine."

Aaron was silent for a beat, and then said, "So, why hasn't someone found it before now?"

"It's complicated, but according to Elliot, the signs have been there for anyone to follow. It's just that no one has figured it out."

"Until now?"

"Yeah, which means that if Elliot and Werner figured it out…someone else can as well."

"So, what 'chu gonna do?"

"Well, I told Elliot that I'd come up tomorrow morning

and meet with him and Werner…and then see what develops."

"Tomorrow, huh?"

"Yeah. You want to come?"

He sighed and shook his head slowly.

"Can't…remember? Me and Muriel are heading to DC on Sunday for that Kennedy Center thing with the President and a bunch of other luminaries."

"So," I said. "You're saying that you'd rather play for the President of the United States instead of helping me out on a case?"

"I know, right? My priorities are all messed up." As Brittney delivered our food, he suggested, "Why don't you see if Cassie wants to go? Seems to me she needs some distraction."

I said, "You're right. The more I can keep her moving forward, the more quickly life is going to regain some equilibrium."

Six months previously, Cassie's husband, Michael James Harvey—novelist Charleston Hawthorne to his millions of devoted readers—Aaron and Aaron's fiancée, Muriel Palmer, had been involved in a horrific traffic accident.

It was one of those days that had started out horribly, and then degenerated from there. I had just rescued Cassie from the monster known as Paul Morgan and was bringing her back to the FBI command center at a hotel in Henderson, Nevada. Aaron was driving my Land Rover with Muriel in the front seat next to him, and Michael seated directly behind her. They had stopped for a red light, waited it out, and had just pulled into the intersection, when a drunk driver traveling at a high rate of speed t-boned them, striking the vehicle on the right-hand side just behind the front door…right where Michael was sitting.

The force of the impact had shattered Muriel's femur, requiring a titanium rod to be inserted, but she was now fine. Michael, however—a strapping 6'7" giant of a man, had been rendered a paraplegic with a barely functioning left hand.

Aaron said, "Every time I go over to their place in Carlsbad, I still expect to see him to come loping through the house like he used to with that big, goofy grin on his face. Instead, he's in that wheelchair contraption he had custom built for himself after the accident."

"It's amazing, isn't it, how one moment can change your life forever."

"Tell me about it," Aaron said quickly. "One minute I'm driving your car to come and pick you and Cassie up, the next minute that drunk son of a bitch turns Michael into a paraplegic and leaves Muriel scarred and messed up."

I thought about the accident, now six months past, and the extent to which it had altered the trajectory of all our lives.

"I guess I still haven't settled it."

"Don't know how you could," he replied while digging into his stack of buttermilk pancakes. "But, all things considered, Cassie seems to be on top of it."

I shoved the eggs and hash browns around on my plate and said, "I think I'll call her. She did dabble in archeology for a bit her junior and senior year of high school. I even sent her on a dig once in Arizona."

"Huh! I never knew that. So, there you go. She'd be perfect."

He was right. And yet, there was a subtle resistance nagging at me, just there at the fringes of my consciousness. Something telling me not to do it. But, I told whatever it was to go away and let me make my own decisions. After all, it was just archeology.

What could possibly go wrong?

CHAPTER THREE

We finished up our breakfasts and drove home.

Together.

We live right next door to each other. Been that way for nearly twelve years now. Our houses are in the type of neighborhood in which you'd expect the world's most highly decorated jazz pianist to reside. And me? Well, let's just say that I've been equally, surprisingly successful in my own endeavors over the years, which makes it possible to own the house right next door to Mr. Perry. Not bragging. I'm very grateful actually.

After parking my Land Rover in the garage and bidding Aaron a good day, I decided that since I was no longer a solitary man—having given my heart part and parcel to the fair Gabriella Marcus, or Gabi to those she loves—I should most likely give her a head's up on my situation before proceeding with my call to Cassie.

So, I walked straight into my den and plopped down in my favorite chair. I called up Gabi's name under the favorites section on my phone and waited for the miracle known as cellular service to do its thing.

"Hey there, mister," came her sultry, dusky-hued answer to my call.

You have to understand that with Gabi, the whole "sultry" thing isn't something for which she strives. It's just her. She has this voice that sounds like raw honey mixed with bourbon when experienced in front of a warm fire on a cold winter's night.

Or something like that.

"Hey yourself. What are you up to today?"

You may be wondering why, if the fair Gabriella and I are so much in love, we live in separate domiciles. Well, I will tell you. Years before meeting me, Gabi purposed in her great big, wonderful heart that she would never spend the night in a man's house unless there was a ring on her finger. Antiquated? Old-fashioned? Puritanical? Who the hell cares! It's what she desires and I support her convictions.

"Oh, just taking care of a few loose ends."

"With work?"

She holds a very prominent and lucrative position as administrative assistant to one of the largest venture capital firms in Las Vegas. Due to the abject and out of control nepotism on the part of the principle partner, she is strongly considering resigning. Honestly, she doesn't need the money. First of all, her grandmother is, as my very southern mother would have said, "Well off." And, secondly, she has, well…me.

"Yes," she said. "They aren't making it easy to leave."

"In what sense?"

"Well, my boss, in what I am sure was a fit of desperation, offered to raise my salary by—get this—fifty thousand a year."

"Wow! Fifty grand! That is *not* an inconsequential amount."

"No," she said behind a sigh. "It isn't."

"And what did you tell him?"

"I said that if he made it a hundred thousand, I'd consider it."

"And…" I prompted.

"He said he'd think about it."

I laughed.

"And what happens if he agrees?"

"Then I will be independently wealthy."

Hidden within our casual, jocular banter was the incontrovertible fact that Gabriella Marcus is the real deal. Companies all over the Southwestern United States have been vying for her services for a number of years because she is an incredibly wealthy person…and I'm not talking about money. Wherever she goes, she makes whatever situation she happens to be involved in better. In short, her "wealth" is her own unique self. Companies recognize that—covet it—and are willing to pay very well to be associated with her.

"At which point you won't need me, I suppose?" I teased.

"Oh, I will always need you, Mr. Moriarity."

"And I you."

"So…I sense something's afoot."

"Seriously? Afoot?"

"I have no explanation. It just sort of slipped out."

I said, "Well, it definitely demonstrates a particular prescience on your part."

"I knew it. So, what's happening?"

"So, you remember me talking to you about my friend, Elliot Spencer?"

"Is he the archeologist up in Seattle?"

"*Professor* of archeology to be exact."

"Yes, I do. Why?"

"Well, just as Aaron and I were finishing up our workout, he called me."

"Okay," she replied. "I'm guessing that it wasn't a social call?"

"No, it wasn't. It seems that he and his colleague, Werner French, have found what they believe to be the greatest archeological treasure in history."

"Wow! That sounds…well, if I'm being honest…it sounds suspicious. What is it?"

"They believe they know the location of a piece of the cross."

She paused before saying, "The cross, as in *the* cross? Like, the cross that Jesus was crucified on?"

"That's the one."

She was silent for a few seconds.

"That's…" she began. "That's…or I should say, that

would be amazing. I mean, being that I'm a Jew I have very conflicted feelings about the whole Jesus and the crucifixion/resurrection thing. But for the worldwide Church, it's—"

"The biggest archeological find in history."

"Right. So, what do they want from you?"

"Well, it seems that they know approximately where it is but not precisely."

"And you being a near savant when it comes to finding lost things..."

"...could be very helpful in securing it, if, in fact, it actually exists."

She said, "Yeah, about that...haven't there been countless claims throughout history from people purporting to have a piece of the cross? I mean wasn't there some something about a nail from the cross forming—what was it...the Iron Crown of Lombardy?"

"Exactly! Lots of claims about this and that throughout the centuries. Even to this day there are places in the world where those claims are still in force."

"Then...what makes this any different?"

The question of the hour.

"Well, I suppose that knowing Elliot as I do—and to a lesser extent, Werner French—if anyone could find such a unique and exceptional thing, it would be them."

"So, you're going to help them?"

"Yeah, I am."

"Well, I wish you luck, good sir. When are you leaving?"

I said, "I'm going to try to get a flight first thing in the morning."

"I see. Do you think you could spare an hour or two to have lunch or dinner with your best girl?"

"I was thinking both, actually."

"Well, then. I guess I'd better smart me'self up a bit. What time is it, anyway?"

I checked my watch.

"Just a little after 7:30."

"And, when did you want to fetch me?"
"Well, high noon?"
"Hmm...that doesn't leave me much time."
"For what?"
"Making myself presentable."
"Oh, please. You could roll out of bed and throw on a pair of sweats and look better than ninety-percent of the women in Las Vegas."
"Only ninety-percent?" she said with a well-practiced pout in her voice.
"Ha! Ha! I will see you at noon, little missy."
"Don't be late, Mr. Moriarity."
"Wouldn't think of it."

I ended the call and thought about the relationship that had developed between us. And while I fully embraced the nearly overwhelming feelings of love and affection I had for this woman, there were still moments when the memory of Abby—my first wife, dead these long years from pancreatic cancer—saturated my mind like jasmine scented mist. I remain quite conflicted about the hereafter and all things related to the Deity, but one thing I know for sure is that Abby has given me tacit permission to move on.

I know it.

I feel it.

I'm fine with it.

Mostly.

I shook my head and said out loud, "It's just that sometimes I miss you so much, babe, that I can hardly stand it."

In the ensuing silence, a clip of memory from our first year together rattled through my mind, purring along like an old 16mm film. We were standing at the end of the Municipal Pier in Santa Cruz, California. It was after sunset and to the south, the lights from the Boardwalk danced across the waters like sprites beckoning us to come join the fun. To the north, we could see a few brave surfers finishing up a sunset session at Steamer Lane.

Abby laid her head against my shoulder and said, "Do you think heaven will be like this, Jake?"

"You mean, like Santa Cruz? Or like this moment of contentment where everything seems right?"

"That one."

"Well…if nearly two thousand years of Christian doctrine is to be believed then, yes. I believe we'll be quite content in heaven."

"But," she said. "My contentment is based entirely on the fact that I'm with you and you're with me. I can't imagine living without you and feeling anything quite like this."

And there it was. The issue that had kept me single throughout the intervening years. Twenty, if you're counting. But, as my dear friend Gaspard Ducharme had once told me, "Monsieur, we have a saying in France: *Qui n'avance pas, recule.* It means, 'who does not move forward, recedes.' In other words, there is no standing still, mon ami. You either evolve, or you devolve. I believe that nowhere in life is this more true than in love. Perhaps life is telling you that it is time to move forward."

It was great wisdom from a man who has lived enough of life for his opinion to matter. And yet, there were times—now would be one—when my heart felt as if it were going to explode and my brain dissolve into useless paste due to the hesitation I still battled. All these years of clinging to that one moment frozen in time where I'd had something so perfect, so special…

I gave my head a sharp shake and stood and began peeling my clothes off on the way into my bedroom. There would be no answers forthcoming on this day.

CHAPTER FOUR

I had just gotten out of the shower and thrown on some clothes that had managed to pass the sniff test, when my phone started playing, "She," the theme song from the movie, *Notting Hill.*

It was, and had been for a long while, Cassie's ring-tone. I've raised Cassie—or, Cassandra if you want to be technical—as my own child since she was orphaned at the age of seven when my sister, Alicia and her husband Ben were killed in an automobile accident. I don't mind telling you that Cassie is the light of my life. She's twenty-six now and has been through enough to reduce most humans to the state of emotional cripples—including being trafficked for sex at the age of eighteen and, most recently, a kidnapping that ended in her husband Michael becoming a paraplegic.

"Hey, little girl."

"Hi, Uncle. I got your message on my machine."

The tone of her voice carried some urgency, as I had imagined it would when I had left the message for her to call an hour before.

"And…?" I prompted.

"You can't be serious."

"That was my first reaction too when Elliot told me."

"But, the cross. This is huge. You think it's legit?"

I could hear the awe in her voice.

"Well, it's like I told Aaron…Elliot is legit; Werner is legit; therefore, by association, I would deem anything those two are involved in to be legit as well."

"I'd have to agree." She waited a second before asking, "Is Aaron going with you?"

"Not this time. He and Muriel are going to DC for that Kennedy Center thing for the President."

"Oh, yeah. That's right. So…you'll be by yourself?"

"Well, I was actually wondering if you wanted to go with me."

She gasped, "Really?"

"Sure. Why not?"

"Well…I don't know. I suppose I do have a little experience in the field."

"Right. So, do you have anything else going on?"

She drew a breath in preparation to speak, but ended up just blowing it out.

"Is something wrong?" I inquired.

"No, not really. It's just…well, I'm having a pretty rough week. And…"

The sentence was left unfinished, hijacked by a marauding sob.

"Tell me what's going on, sweetheart."

"Well, it's Michael."

"He driving you nuts?"

"Yes, he is. I mean it's not bad enough he's in a wheelchair from that damned car wreck. He's…I don't know…trying to prove something. Like, 'I can still be America's favorite novelist even from a wheelchair.' But I feel like it's just sucking whatever life he has left right out."

I said, "I assume you've discussed this with him?"

"Discussed it? And, when would that be? He wrote his last best-seller in six weeks. Now, it's like he's out to top that. There is no time when he's available for anything except writing, sleeping and eating. All that to say…I actually would welcome the diversion. So…I'm in. Truthfully, he won't even know I'm gone."

"Are you sure?" I asked hesitantly.

"Without question. I'll bring Vanessa along and we'll—"

"Hold it!" I said. "I don't recall Vanessa being invited to the party."

Vanessa is Vanessa Phillips...my soon to be adopted daughter.

"Besides," I continued. "Isn't she supposed to be starting a new term at Morgan Sommers Dance Academy?"

"That's not for two more weeks. In fact, she told me this morning that she was, how did she put it? Oh, yeah, 'As bored as a blind guy watching a silent movie.'"

That made me laugh.

"That's pretty bored. Still..."

"Look, I'm sorry to get all fierce on you, Uncle, but Vanessa comes with me or the offer is withdrawn."

I said in my best Humphrey Bogart voice, which, as attested by folks far and wide, is not very good at all, "You drive a hard bargain, sweetheart."

"You know," she replied. "I hear they have therapy for that."

"Oh, come on. It's not *that* bad. I mean...right?"

"Terrible. So, we're in?" she said excitedly.

"I know I'm probably going to regret this, but...all right, you're in."

Cassie let out a victory whoop on the other end of the line.

"Yes. Vanessa isn't going to believe this."

"That will make two of us."

"Oh, come on, you want us to be there and you know it."

"Maybe," I hedged while pulling up the Alaska Airlines website on my desktop computer. "I'm checking Alaska Airlines because they typically have better flights into the Northwest. So...San Diego to Seattle...I'm seeing a 9:30 a.m. flight arriving at 12:31."

"That'll work. That way we can go straight to lunch from the airport."

"Well, hang on. I have to see what's available from Vegas." I re-entered the search parameters. "So...okay, this is just about perfect. There's a 9:37 a.m. flight arriving at 12:11 p.m. That'll give me time to rent a car and be back by the time you've got your luggage."

"Yes. So, lunch is on."

"You know…for such a slender young woman, you seem overly fixated on food," I teased.

"Right? It's like lately I'm either eating or planning my next meal. I have no explanation."

I loved how suddenly and drastically her mood had changed. It made me laugh.

"What?" she prompted.

"Oh, it's just good to hear the excitement in your voice."

"Well…I mean besides getting to hang out with my second favorite person on earth, this seems like it could potentially be a pretty big deal."

"Yes, it does. It could also be potentially dangerous."

She said, "Really? How?"

"Think about it: If, in fact, they have actually stumbled upon a piece of the true cross—and especially if it happens to be the last remaining piece—do you really think that's something that they will be able to keep secret? And if others learn of its existence, don't you think they will want to, at the very least, co-opt it or, worst case scenario, steal it?"

"Well…" she mused. "When you put it that way, I get it. But our part is just going to be in the finding, right? We should be long gone when and if any of that other stuff happens."

"That's the plan. So…see if Pete can give you a ride to the airport and let me know so—"

"Uncle!" she said, interrupting me. "You don't have to keep doing this, you know?"

"Doing what?"

"Being in charge of my life. I'm a big girl. I can make my own arrangements."

I chuckled, "Yeah, you are and you can. I just forget sometimes."

"Sometimes?"

"Okay, okay. You're on to me."

"I love you, Uncle."

"I love you too, little girl. See you tomorrow."

I shoved the phone back into my pocket, and thought through all the reasons I had just given Cassie as to why the situation could possibly turn deadly. A sudden, insistent feeling that I had just made a horrible mistake in inviting my two girls to accompany me rolled through my soul like a frozen mist.

Maybe instead of giving them a ride to the airport, Pete needed to come with us.

CHAPTER FIVE

"Mr. Moriarity, sir, it's good to hear from you. How you doin' this fine morning?"

It was a constant source of amusement, and borderline consternation, every time I heard Pete Tolles' good 'ol boy tone of voice and viewed his "aw shucks" mannerisms, for they belied the unassailable fact that he was a 6'3", two hundred and fifty pound package of utter lethality. A former FORECON, or Force Reconnaissance Marine, and part-time bad guy for hire, he had become an official part of our little family and a trusted associate.

"I'm doing well, Pete. How's it going with Eddie?"

"Eddie" was Edwina Madison, a wee slip of a girl I had also rescued from Paul Morgan during Cassie's kidnapping.

And, by the way, that would be the *late* Paul Morgan, thank you very much.

Eddie was now living with Muriel and working with Cassie in managing Michael's business affairs.

In short, she was blooming. Obvious to all was the fact that much of the credit for her recovery belonged to Pete and the way he had simply showered her with tender love and affection.

"Well, now," he said in answer to my question. "That right there is a matter of some debate, if you don't mind me saying so."

"Oh, and how's that?"

"Well, sir…that there little woman is a conundrum."

I laughed.

"Using the words 'woman' and 'conundrum' in the same sentence could rightly be judged a redundancy, my friend."

"Boy howdy! You got that right. For example...last night we was fixin' to go to dinner and—"

I cut in, "Let me guess...you asked her where she wanted to eat and she suggested that you pick a place."

"If that don't beat all. Yeah, that's exactly what happened."

"And, of course, every single place you suggested she slapped down like Shaq guarding the paint."

"Exactly. After about five minutes I finally told her to just pick a place and you know what she said?"

"Yes, I do. Because it's exactly what happens with Gabi every time we go out to dinner. In fact, it's gonna happen later on this morning because we're going to lunch. Oh, *and* dinner."

"So, Eddie winds up saying..." he pitched his voice up into a falsetto range, "'Oh, I don't care where we go.'"

We both laughed.

I said, "Bro, file that under 'the same thing happens every time.'"

"So, what's on your mind, Mr. Moriarity?"

In spite of my best efforts to dissuade the practice, Pete insists on calling me Mr. Moriarity. He claims that it's his way of showing honor and respect.

"Well, I know that this is sudden, but I've got something I could use your help on."

"All right..." he prompted.

I briefly laid out the scenario to him, or at least as much as I knew about it.

He said, "So, let me get this straight. These two fellas up in Seattle claim to know the location of a piece of the cross that Jesus was crucified on?"

"That's what they say."

"But, they need us to...what...go and fetch it?"

"Well, pinpoint the precise location and...you know... now that I think about it, Elliot didn't mention anything about fetching it."

"But, what would be the point of finding something like

that, and then leaving it in place? If it's the genuine article, don't you think they'd want it where it would be safe and people could come and look at it—pay money to look at it? I mean, hell's bells, look at all the fuss that's made over that there Shroud of what's-it. People would go crazy to get a peek at the cross."

He was right.

"Yes, well…so…I suppose that *fetching* would definitely be part of the bargain. Anyway, I could use your help."

"Well, sir…I don't rightly know how I could turn something with this much potential down. But there's one thing my daddy always told me that I believe applies to what lies ahead."

"Okay. What's that?"

"Son, if you climb into the saddle…be ready for the ride."

I said, "Words of wisdom, my friend."

"So, when do we leave?"

"Umm…tomorrow morning?"

He laughed his good 'ol boy laugh.

"Well now, as it turns out, Eddie is gonna go to DC with Aaron and Muriel, so I'm available. Anyone else invited to the party?"

"Cassie and Vanessa are going to come along. In fact, give me a second and let me check their flight and see if I can get you on it as well." I pulled up the website and went to the booking page. "Not only is there space available, but for an extra fifty bucks each, I can get all three of you bumped into first class."

"That right there is good news for a long-legged fella like me. What time?"

"The flight leaves at 9:30 a.m."

"Okay. I'll give Cassie a ring and arrange to pick her and Vanessa up. How are we gonna deal with appropriate armaments?"

"With my FBI creds I can take my pistol on the flight

with no problem and you and Cassie can check your unloaded firearms in locked cases inside your luggage as long as they are declared."

"I thought it was something like that, but that's good to know. All right, then. I will see you tomorrow in Seattle."

"Yes sir. And, thanks for this, Pete."

"It is my pleasure, Mr. Moriarity, sir. My pleasure."

As I disconnected the call, I thought about his comment regarding climbing into the saddle and being ready for the ride. It wasn't so much that I wasn't ready for the ride…I would just have preferred to know in advance where the "ride" was going to take me and how rough it was going to be.

I supposed I'd find out soon enough.

CHAPTER SIX

Hidden safely away within the frozen reaches of the jagged Swiss Alps, a group of nine men sat around a raging fire in secret conclave. The chalet—dating to the late sixteenth century—did not exist on any maps, couldn't be seen from any direction, nor was it accessible by any mode of transportation other than helicopter or skilled mountaineering.

Among the men, only the one called Primus knew the identities of The Nine. For here they had no names, only a number. They had been summoned from five countries: three from Italy, two from Turkey, two from Spain, one from the United States, and Primus himself from Austria.

"And how did Delilah sound?" Primus addressed Number Six as he accepted a fresh cup of coffee from his personal assistant, Gérard, who bore a striking resemblance to the French actor, Jean Reno.

"She sounded confident—excited, Primus."

Primus nodded his overly large, hoary head.

"Wonderful. And in her excitement did she happen to mention anything concrete?"

"Only that the manuscript is on the premises and that she has succeeded in establishing an emotional connection with Dr. French."

"Does that mean that she's slept with him already?" Number Three asked, backed by a chorus of laughter from the others.

"Gentlemen!" Primus shouted, capturing and holding the gaze of each man present. "Please restrain yourselves. This is not a men's club. We have serious business to which we must attend. You may continue, Number Six."

"Thank-you, Primus. Now as I was saying, Delilah has established an emotional connection with Dr. French and is confident that she will gain his full cooperation quite soon."

"Whatever does that mean?" Number Four asked while taking another languid sip of his rare cognac.

Number Three added, "Yes, I'd like to know that myself."

Number Six, having had a lifetime aversion to pressure, was feeling way too much of it at present.

"Well, I suppose it means that the young lady has captured the good Doctor's fancy and expects to be in possession of the manuscript before the end of the week."

Number Four rolled his eyes—an annoying affectation derided privately by all present.

"Is that what she *said*, or is this purely supposition on your part?"

Number Six didn't really care for Number Four and had made no effort to hide his dislike over the years. That the feeling was mutual was an accepted fact in the circle.

"My dear Number Four, as we all know, what a lady *says* and what she means are two quite different propositions. I heard what she *said* and may I hasten to add that I also *know* what she means."

This brought a smile, however brief, even to the face of Primus.

"Thank-you, Number Six, for sharing that report. Now, we must move on."

"Primus?" Number Eight sought his attention.

"Yes?"

"Well, it's just that..." He looked around the circle at the other members as if seeking support. "It's just that I retain a measure of uneasiness about this Delilah woman. I mean, how can we be sure that she is trustworthy?"

"I am intrigued that you have waited until now to ask a question of this gravity, Number Eight. It leads me to believe that something is afoot of which I have not been made aware."

Primus turned the full force of his displeasure on Number Eight who shrank visibly under the onslaught.

"Primus, I think he is merely stating the obvious," Number Two remarked in a valiant effort to rescue his struggling colleague.

Primus turned.

"The obvious? And would you care to enlighten me as to what that might be?"

"No, let me speak for myself." Number Eight had prevailed over his initial intimidation and now stood to address the group. "Gentlemen, I think we are all aware that this young woman, Delilah—or whatever her real name happens to be—is carrying out this assignment purely at the good pleasure of our esteemed leader. I don't recall the merits of this decision having ever been discussed in this—"

"Discussed?" Primus roared. "Since when am I required to discuss my decisions with you, sir?"

Trembling with emotion Number Eight nevertheless found the courage to continue his assault.

"But that is the very issue I raise, brothers. We have no voice other than what amounts to a sniveling approval of Primus' pontificating decisions."

Seven sets of eyes tracked back and forth between Primus and the oddly contentious council member as seconds ticked heavily by.

Primus finally broke the silence.

"So, you would all like to have something to discuss?"

Number Eight looked back and forth between Primus and the rest of the council.

"I think I speak for the majority when I say, yes. Yes we would."

Primus gave only a slight nod to Gérard and the knife flew from his hand more swiftly than any in the circle could have believed possible, imbedding itself in the neck of the unfortunate Number Eight who collapsed to the floor gurgling in the blood that erupted from his ruined throat.

"So...now you can discuss that," Primus said matter-of-factly as he looked around at the stunned faces of his colleagues.

Number Eight thrashed a bit on the floor and then was still. Apparently unbidden, Gérard effortlessly hoisted the body to his shoulders, and carried it out of the room without a sound.

When the door had closed Primus said lightly, "Now then, shall we continue?"

CHAPTER SEVEN

Saturday Morning

The pilot had just announced our final approach into the Seattle-Tacoma International Airport, or SeaTac as it is commonly known. I had always taken issue with the term "final approach", as it sounded so needlessly morbid. I agree with a comedian I once heard at some point in the distant past when he pointed out that for those who struggle with an innate fear of flying, having to begin the experience at a "terminal" was disheartening. But then, they up the ante by announcing, "final call" before the flight's departure. It's enough to put you right over the edge.

My seatmate on the flight from Vegas had been the oh-so-talkative Bonnie Metcalf. Among the myriad pieces of information Bonnie shared with me over the course of two hours is that she is thirty-three and single (a fact which she mentioned ten or twelve times during the flight); works as a buyer for Nordstrom's Department Store; hails from Melbourne, Australia; doesn't care for American sports *or* food; and were it not for her employment, considered it highly unlikely that she would ever travel to the States. But, she was cute, in an overdone and over-the-top way and didn't really require any investment in the conversation on my part aside from the occasional, "Oh really?" "You don't say?" "No kidding?"

You get the picture.

As the pilot banked the plane hard to port, Ms. Metcalf said, "I can just about get through the flight…but the landings always freak me out a little. In fact…I'm terrified of landings!"

I wasn't a big fan of landings either.

Or flying, for that matter.

Or anything having to do with height in general.

"What specifically about the experience troubles you?" I inquired, not fully understanding my seeming need to prolong a conversation that had begun upon her taking possession of seat 3A next to my 3B and had continued virtually unabated right up until that present moment.

"Oh...I don't know, Jake."

Apparently we were now on a first name basis.

Lucky me.

She continued, "I suppose it's that weightless feeling one gets right before the wheels touch down. Know what I mean?"

I did. But, being the manly man I perceived myself to be, I wasn't about to give chatty Ms. Bonnie the satisfaction of knowing it.

The plane bounced through a pocket of turbulence prompting her to grab my arm while exclaiming, "Oh God," and screwing her eyes shut. "Please just tell me when it's over."

I wasn't accustomed to having strange women—or strangers of any gender, for that matter—grab onto my person. And I found the experience unsettling. On a couple of levels. Not the least of which was the familiarity factor involved. I mean, really? Would you just grab a total stranger like that?

I said, "I'm thinking you will know one way or the other. Either we'll roll smoothly into our gate, or the plane will crash and...well, you get the picture."

Her eyes flew open and she turned her pretty head to regard me suspiciously while slowly withdrawing her hand.

"That...that is incredibly and needlessly morbid."

She was right. But, it quieted the conversation and succeeded in getting her to unhand me.

My lunch and dinner dates with Gabi had gone about as well as one could expect, given the uncertainty that always accompanied my departures. In short, my chosen profession was something with which Gabi struggled. Having been placed in mortal danger herself as a direct result of said profession on two separate occasions, I could understand her point. And yet...what I do and what I *am* seem to be inseparable. Therefore, moving forward we seem to be at an impasse regarding how to address her concerns.

She is mostly fine with it, believing that what I do is essential in order to maintain a healthy balance in the universe, or something like that. I just know that given a preference, she would prefer that I do something that carried with it a lesser chance of being routinely shot, punched, stabbed and subjected to general mayhem committed against my person. But...it's what I do and I intend to continue doing it as long as I can.

Or until Gabi persuades me to do otherwise.

I am not a stupid man.

Much to Bonnie's relief, the pilot brought the plane down with a barely perceptible bump and we began taxiing toward our gate, which we learned, to our utter chagrin, was blocked by another plane that had been held up due to a ground stop in San Francisco.

Probably fog.

I mean isn't it always the fog in San Francisco?

So we hung out on the tarmac for about three hours. Okay, it was probably more like twenty minutes, but felt like three hours to me given Bonnie's resurgent conversation. But, the other aircraft finally cleared out and at long last we were able to access our gate.

After deplaning—okay, I've got to tell you that every time I hear that word, all I can think of is that little bitty guy who used to be in the opening scenes of the old Fantasy Island TV series who would point to the sky and exclaim excitedly, "De plane! De plane!"—anyway, after deplaning I did my business at the first men's room I came to and headed down to baggage claim, where I bid a relieved and final farewell to Bonnie.

Standing by the conveyor and watching the luggage and its slow parade before anxious passengers, I heard a familiar voice muttering, "I say," in a most proper British accent.

I turned around and was surprised to see Elliot Spencer standing there watching Bonnie walk away, pulling her luggage behind her. She was very good at it—the walking away thing.

"That about covers it," I replied.

"What…you didn't find her fetching?"

"Uh…no."

"My, my," he said with a smile. "Things must have changed considerably since we last met."

I laughed and pulled him into a bro-hug.

"What are you doing here, Elliot? I told you I was renting a car."

"I know, I know," he said. "But, I figured that I might as well rent the car for you, and then after Cassie and the others arrive we could all go to lunch and then head over to the university."

"That was very thoughtful, thank you."

"Oh, it is my pleasure, Jake," he replied as I returned my gaze to the conveyor just in time to see my bag seemingly pick up speed and jet past me.

I thought about giving chase, but that would have meant executing a move tantamount to a USC running back plowing through the entire Notre Dame defense.

Not worth it!

I checked my watch.

"Pete, Cassie and Vanessa should be here within fifteen or twenty minutes."

"Perfect. I'm really looking forward to seeing Cassie. The last time I saw her, she was in pretty bad shape."

The occasion he referenced had been seven years previous when my sweet Cassie had only been about three weeks on the other side of me rescuing her and Muriel from Paul Morgan. At the time, Elliot only lived about a mile or so from the hospital and, true to his kind and generous heart, he had not only put me up for the two weeks of Cassie's treatment, but had also gone with me every day to see her. And on the days when she wasn't doing well, he would simply sit by me to help bear my grief...that is, when he wasn't fussing over Muriel, for whom he had developed an instantaneous and lasting infatuation.

But, she had been so out of it at the time that she had barely noticed. If you want to know the truth, when it came time to leave and Elliot was driving us to the airport, she only knew that he was my friend and that he had helped us out during the hospital stay. It wasn't until much later that I had told her of Elliot's deep and smoldering passion—a revelation that she found to be at once both threatening and compelling. Threatening because of all she had suffered at the hands of cruel and heartless men, and compelling because what had stood out from the little she *did* know of Elliot was that he was caring and gentle.

Genuinely so.

Even though he tried valiantly for the next year to win Muriel's heart, she was simply too broken. And when at long last Aaron had come along...well...it was, as they say, a done deal.

Elliot took it as well as any broken-hearted, lovesick fool can take such a thing and has remained good friends with her in spite of it all.

"I don't suppose..." he said, "...that Muriel will be joining you at some point."

"No, I'm afraid not. She's heading back to DC with Aaron. He's playing for one of those Kennedy Center things they do with the President on occasion."

He nodded and replied wistfully, "Well, it would have been delightful to see her."

I suddenly saw my luggage approaching and was just beginning to reach for it when a pair of over-zealous, school-aged brothers lunged in front of me in an unsuccessful attempt to snare a suitcase that looked as if the plane had drug it all the way from Vegas. While they planted themselves directly in my path and engaged in an impassioned debate as to which one was to blame for the precious cargo eluding their grasp, I somehow managed to bypass the conflict and retrieve my things just as I heard a couple of familiar shrieks coming from the escalator.

    My girls had arrived.

CHAPTER EIGHT

Cassie and Vanessa bounded down the remaining segments of the escalator and sprinted toward me with Pete following along at a much more pedestrian pace. To the casual observer the resulting reunion would have appeared to be taking place between people who hadn't seen each other in months if not years. In reality, it had only been a matter of a couple of weeks.

But, what can I say...we miss each other.

After introductions were made between Elliot, Pete and Vanessa, we moved on to another carousel to fetch their luggage.

I said to Cassie, "How'd you present this trip to Michael?"

"Oh, I just told him that you needed me on a case and that I would be gone for an indeterminate amount of time. He just looked up at me from his keyboard and muttered, 'And?'"

I didn't like the sound of that.

"So," I replied. "You're saying that he was indifferent to your absence?"

"No, not exactly. It's just...I don't know. I have trouble explaining it. It's just that his focus is so completely on this new novel—and being as task oriented as he is—it's virtually impossible to distract him."

"I suppose that's a blessing and a curse."

She nodded wearily.

"Yeah, you could say that. Mostly it's good. But there are times like this when I'd prefer a different response."

"Were you able to secure a temporary assistant?"

"Oh, sure. He's going to have three different in-home

nursing assistants around-the-clock, plus his publicist is sending over someone during business hours to help out with scheduling and clerical stuff."

"Sounds like everything is covered." As we moved to join the others at the baggage carousel, I said, "Any issues with declaring your firearms?"

"None whatsoever. We just did the locked, hard-sided case thing inside our luggage and were good to go."

"Good. I wasn't exactly sure how it would go, so it's good to hear."

Elliot asked, "Don't you check your weapon, Jake?"

"No. Since FBI is Federal, we are actually required to fly with our weapons."

"I say…I did not know that. What about other members of law enforcement?"

"It gets a bit complicated, but with few exceptions, state and local officers cannot be armed."

"Well," Vanessa said. "With everything that has gone on during my lifetime, I feel a lot better knowing that there is someone onboard who could take down a bad guy if necessary."

"Most definitely," Cassie agreed. "The whole issue of gun violence and everything that goes along with it—you know, the hyper-politicization and constant wrangling over gun rights, et cetera—kind of obscures the fact that there are times when someone *having* a gun is better than them *not* having it. Poorly stated, but, do you know what I mean?"

"I do, indeed," Elliot replied. "And while I am a huge proponent of stricter gun laws, I realize that the issue is far more complex than merely carping the same tired slogans every time there is a mass shooting. What I'm concerned with is what happens in the spaces *between* the shootings. What about when all the rhetoric cools, the conservatives go back to hiding behind the second amendment and the liberals are, once again, back to their pet projects?"

Pete smiled his good ol' boy smile and said, "Well sir, I

hear you. But I have to say that I grew up in a small, Central Texas town where everyone and their sister had a gun. And we basically had no crime. Why? Because the bad guys knew that virtually every house they'd try to invade, or every pickup they'd try to hijack—hell, every liquor store they'd try to rob —everybody was packin' and they'd likely be shot all to hell and gone if they tried anything. So they just moved on elsewhere."

"With all due respect, my good man, that sounds like a middle-America, idyllic fantasy unattainable in the real world."

"Yeah...well...it was *my* world and it was about as 'real' as it gets, old son. Besides, I think what Cassie was tryin' to say was, it's much better to have a gun and not need it, than it is to need a gun and not have it."

"So, you don't believe in gun control?"

Pete smiled widely.

"Oh, yes sir, I do. That's why I use both hands when I shoot."

That brought a laugh from everyone, including Elliot.

While it was obvious that Pete and Elliot were polar opposites on the topic, there was no rancor. Just a civil exchange of ideas. Which was good because were Pete to get, as he was fond of saying, "riled up", I feared for Elliot's safety.

Vanessa asked, "Speaking of gun control, doesn't Chicago have the strictest gun control laws in the US and gun violence is *still* out of control?"

Elliot replied wearily, "Why do people always bring that up!"

I said, "Possibly because a particular political party is overly fond of using Chicago as an example of a city that has enacted very strict gun controls."

We finally found their assigned carousel and formed up in a ragged circle to await the arrival of the luggage.

Cassie said, "I think it's a fair point. But, if stricter controls are the answer, wouldn't there be empirical evidence to back up the contention?"

Elliot smiled.

"Very well stated, young lady. As to your point, I offer Japan, Australia, my homeland of Great Britain and Germany."

"But isn't Japan the only one of the four with outright bans on gun ownership?" Cassie inquired.

I said, "That's true. In fact, Germany has one of the highest per-capita ratios of gun ownership in the world. The last statistics I saw from the FBI were something in the range of five and a half million legal weapons in the hands of about a million and a half private individuals. Add in another twenty million illegal weapons, and the saturation is impressive."

Elliot shook his head in confusion.

"What is your point, Jake? I thought we were talking about gun control."

"My point is that even with all of those guns, Germany—unlike the US—actually enforces their gun laws. I attended an FBI seminar on the topic a couple of years back, so I'm not just making this up. So, to my knowledge, Germany is the only country in the world where—and I'm paraphrasing—anyone under the age of twenty-five who applies for a gun license is required to submit to a psychiatric evaluation—including personality and anger management segments—with a trained counselor. Additionally, even experienced hunters, including those who only shoot for sport, who are *over* the age of twenty-five can be called in for psychiatric tests if they display certain types of behavioral tendencies, such as drunk driving. As a result, Germany's homicide rate due to gun violence is among the lowest in Europe. We're talking about a death rate of .05 per one thousand people, compared with 3.34 in the US. And, based on recent statistics, the rate has actually been declining."

Elliot said, "While I'm not prepared to concede the argument, you make a compelling point."

"Compelling enough for you to buy us lunch?" Cassie said, with a flutter of her eyelids.

"Of course, dear friend. Win or lose, that was never in question."

The luggage suddenly materialized, having escaped from *Baggage Land,* the mysterious world hidden away behind the vertical strips of acrylic—a world of consummate mystery to the average person. After the luggage was collected, we followed Elliot out of the terminal toward the SUV he had rented on our behalf.

Walking to the car I said, "Elliot, I need you to tell me something straight up."

He looked at me in that way of his—totally open countenance, clear eyes with not even a trace of guile or deceit. I'll tell you the truth, some people try real hard for it, but it's something that can't be faked.

"All right, Jake. I'll certainly try."

"You think we have any chance at all of finding this remnant?"

He took a quick breath as if to answer, then he held it and stared off into the distance. When he exhaled it was long and slow. He turned back to me.

"Jake, old friend, I do, I really do. It's why I called you. I know in your ears this thing must sound like some sort of misguided scavenger hunt or something." He stopped walking and caught everyone's gaze for effect. "But I assure you, it is not. This is the real thing."

I could see that he believed this. It was in his eyes and I could hear it in his voice. It was good enough for me.

"Okay. Let's go talk to Dr. French," I said as we resumed walking.

"After lunch, of course," Cassie insisted.

It took Elliot a moment to respond, but he finally said, "Right," and followed after us.

CHAPTER NINE

Lunch was a hastily implemented affair at a trendy little restaurant in Seattle's U District, the choice of which had less to do with its stellar cuisine than it did with its proximity to Northwest Pacific University and the fact that we were all hungry—or, "starving" in the case of Vanessa and Cassie.

Which brings to mind something I may or may not have mentioned on a previous occasion: Girls, in general, are never merely hungry, they are always starving; never cold, but freezing. I'm afraid my contention is inarguable, having reached my conclusion based on years of close, personal observation.

Anyway, regarding our luncheon choice, we went with what was available. There would be plenty of time for lingering, leisurely lunches on another day.

After making the short drive to the university, we parked and entered the building that housed Northwest's department of anthropology and archeology, winding our way through hallways sufficient in number to call to mind a rabbit warren. There's something about venerable, old academic institutions that I always find compelling. A particular smell; a certain feel; an atmosphere that makes you want to stop what you are doing and just settle in for a while.

This building had all of that and more.

Elliot picked up his pace, beckoning excitedly with his hand as we neared a tall door that was topped with a sealed transom and a rippled, frosted glass window set into its upper half. Stenciled across the glass in painstakingly applied gold leaf was: *Department of Archeology and Anthropology. Dr. Werner French; Dr. Elliot Spencer.*

Once through the door, we found a reception area flanked by two impressive desks, and behind the desks were two equally impressive coeds, or at least that was my assumption—that they were coeds, that is. Upon seeing Elliot enter the room, they each glanced up from whatever had been the focus of their attention and smiled warmly and affectionately. I understood the emotion. Elliot Spencer seems to draw it out of people.

Elliot briefly introduced us to the two young women, whose names immediately escaped me, before walking through a door on the right bearing Dr. French's name. Upon entering, I saw a room that was maybe twenty by twenty and a ceiling that was all of twelve feet in height. Three of the four walls were lined top to bottom with bookshelves, each crammed with more volumes than it was designed to hold. It was like being in the antiquities section of a library.

Werner French looked up from where he was seated in an ancient leather desk chair behind a massive wooden desk piled high with leather-bound books and yellowed manuscripts.

"You're here," he said exuberantly while standing to greet us.

He was wearing a long-sleeved white Oxford shirt with a button-down collar and blue denim jeans with white athletic shoes. Behind his thick, funky black-rimmed spectacles, his blue eyes looked huge.

He came out from behind the desk to wrap me up in a hug. As I mentioned previously, Werner French was all of 6'6" and north of three hundred and fifty pounds, so being hugged by the man was an intimidating experience.

"Jake, it's good to see you. How long has it been?"

"Let me think...probably five years or so? Maybe that time the three of us got together for dinner when I was on my way to Vancouver, BC?"

"Yes. That's it precisely." Glancing over my head he regarded the other three. "Now, who are these lovely young people?"

I said, "This is my niece, Cassie…"

"Finally," he boomed while stepping forward to hug her, but with a bit less mauling than had been involved in my greeting. "After all this time I get to meet the legendary Cassandra. So good to finally meet you."

"You as well, Dr. French," she replied.

"Oh please," he said, waving off the honorific. "It's Werner."

I continued, "And this is Vanessa, the newest member of our family."

He paused in silent appraisal before hugging her gently.

"I don't know much of your story, young lady, but from what I *do* know…you are incredibly brave and I am humbled to make your acquaintance."

Vanessa actually blushed, saying, "Well…I don't know about the brave part, but thank you anyway."

I continued, "And this is Pete Tolles, our trusted associate."

Even though Werner outweighed Pete by a good hundred pounds, Pete seemed every bit as wide.

Werner extended his hand, saying, "It is an honor, sir."

Pete shook the proffered hand.

"Oh no, the honor's all mine. And, for the record, I really enjoyed your journal on *The Lost City of David.*"

To get an idea of just how weird it was to hear Pete Tolles utter those words, imagine walking into a biker bar, meeting the biggest, scariest, most intense guy in the place and starting up a conversation with him on hidden meanings contained within the 18th Century prose of Jean-Baptiste François Xavier Cousin De Grainville.

Yeah, like that.

Werner stared in open-mouthed disbelief.

"Why…thank you. To be honest, I wasn't sure anyone had ever read that."

As I mentioned previously, Werner French was one of the world's leading medieval archeologists. He had a dozen books in publication and his opinions were often quoted in archeological and historical journals around the world. And yet to me he seemed to be a regular guy who, at fifty, seemed to be uncommonly comfortable in his own skin.

"Oh, yes sir," Pete replied. "I was especially fond of the way you just tore hell out of those fellas who tried to insist that King David was just a minor leader of a small, obscure nomadic tribe." He laughed loudly. "Boy howdy! That was well played, Doc. Well played."

Cassie said, "Pete, is there no end to your ability to surprise me?"

Pete grinned widely.

"Well, Ms. Cassie, I hope not. I surely do hope not."

Werner and Elliot scurried around and produced four chairs that they arranged in a loose semi-circle in front of the desk before Werner returned to his old leather chair that creaked amiably as he eased his considerable weight into it.

"Great chair," I said in admiration.

I have a thing for old furniture. My own house is filled with it.

"I've had this a long time," he explained, running his hands over the arms almost as if he were caressing a woman. "Tried some of those new contraptions down at the back store, but nothing compares to this old girl. Okay, now have a look at this."

He shoved a yellowed manuscript across the desk and stood up to pinpoint a section, his long rusty-hued hair falling across his eyes nearly obliterating his vision.

Absently brushing it back behind his ears with one hand, he tapped the page in front of him and explained, "This manuscript contains eyewitness accounts validating many tales that heretofore had been relegated to the status of myth." He glanced upward briefly to see if we were paying attention. "Of special interest is this story of an obscure village in south central Turkey and an old church that boasts of hundreds—perhaps thousands—that have been healed just by walking through a doorway leading to an inner chamber of some sort. The fact that no one has ever taken the time to investigate the legend is incomprehensible to me."

Elliot added, "The manner in which we stumbled upon this manuscript is quite amazing, really. Twenty-four hours ago, it was in a crate wrapped around a piece of pottery...you know, packing material."

He and Werner looked at each other and shook their heads in obvious amazement.

I said, "So, if I understand you correctly, you're saying that in all your years of investigation, you never heard anything about this village or this church prior to stumbling upon this manuscript?"

"That's right. Absolutely nothing," Werner replied.

"Which is ridiculous," Elliot quickly added, "when you take into consideration the fact that we have been all around this area dozens of times."

From behind us a lilting, feminine voice said, "Excuse me."

A beautiful young woman stood framed in the doorway. She was medium height with short brown hair, cut in a contemporary style. Her hazel eyes were dotted with little flecks of green and she had the chiseled cheekbones of a model.

In short...she was a knockout!

"Emily," Werner said in greeting. "Come in, come in. I want to introduce you to our guests."

She walked forward, coming to a stop beside Werner, a bemused look dancing behind her eyes.

"Emily Young, this is the imminently famous Jake Moriarity, of whom you have heard Elliot and I go on and on about; his two girls, Cassie and Vanessa; and the very large man there is Pete Tolles."

Quite obvious to even the most casual observer was the fact that whatever else she was...Emily Young was the object of Werner's affection.

She smiled and raised a slender hand in greeting.

"So pleased to meet all of you."

Werner hastened to add, "Emily is my research assistant. One of the best in the field and I am quite fortunate to have her."

"Well," she said. "I don't know about that."

After individual introductions were made all around, Werner finally got around to asking Emily if there was anything she needed or if she was merely dropping by to meet us.

She replied, "I know you have a lot of important things to talk about, so I won't keep you. But, I was wondering if you needed me to secure accommodations for Mr. Moriarity and the others?"

Werner looked at me, then at Elliot, and back to Emily.

"Well, I suppose so. That is, unless Jake has already taken care of that."

"No," I replied. "I haven't. So, yes…it would be tremendously helpful."

Emily seemed to hesitate, and then said, "I could definitely book hotel rooms for you all, but here's an option to consider: There are a couple of two-bedroom corporate apartments available in my building that rent by the week and by the month with no contract required. I could check to see if they are available."

Werner said, "Jake?"

I glanced at the others and got noncommittal shrugs in return.

"It seems that we have no preference, so whatever you think is best will be fine with us."

"Great. Let me see what I can stir up and I'll check back in a bit. Anything else I can do for you, Dr. French?"

Werner replied, "I think that will be all for now Emily. And thank-you for your help."

"It was lovely to meet you all," she said sweetly as she backed out of the room and closed the door behind her.

Don't ask me how I knew...but I knew right then and there that there was more to the lovely Ms. Young than met the eye.

Much more.

CHAPTER TEN

We spent the next two hours discussing the challenges associated with finding the remnant, but instead of things becoming clearer, I had a growing sense that I didn't know any more about it than when I had arrived. The best way I can describe the experience is like this: Imagine fighting your way to the center of one of those classic, English mazes. Only when you get there you find yourself in a House of Mirrors—you know, the kind you see in carnivals and beach boardwalks? The ones where no matter which direction you look, you can't tell what's real and what isn't.

If you want to know the truth, the whole thing was starting to make my brain hurt.

I pinched the bridge of my nose between thumb and forefinger and said, "So, Werner, I need to clarify something you said a little while ago."

"All right."

I consulted a few roughly scribbled notes I had made on a small spiral notepad.

"Let me see...you said that the Emperor Constantine's mother—"

"Helena Augusta," he interrupted.

"Right. That Helena went to Jerusalem somewhere around 326, and supposedly came away with not only the wood from the true cross, but four iron nails, the crown of thorns—"

"Along with Christ's seamless robe as well as the flagrums, or scourges used in his torture." He chuckled, "Some even hold that she brought back the plaque Pilate had placed at the top of the cross, along with the remains of the three Magi. Keep in mind, of course, that this is all legend, as is her purported discovery of the precise location of the birthplace of Jesus in Bethlehem."

"If you don't mind me sayin' so," Pete remarked. "That right there sounds like the stuff that sticks to the bottom of your boots when you walk through the steer corral."

Werner replied with a laugh, "Welcome to the wonderful world of forensic archeology, my friend. This is what we do—sorting out fact from, if I may be so bold, bullshit."

"But obviously some of the legends about the cross are true," Cassie said. "Or there's no reason for us to be here, or for you and Elliot to have continued searching all these years."

I added, "And that's what I really want to know. How *do* you separate fact from legend and outright bullshit?"

He leaned back in his chair, clasping his hands behind his head.

"Elliot, tell them what was happening in the world in the fourth century."

Elliot brightened at the prospect.

"Oh, dear, let me think. Okay...Constantine was already pretty much obsessed with everything that had to do with the cross. That, of course, stemmed from the vision he purportedly had of a vertical spear and crossed sword that appeared in the sky with the words, 'in this sign conquer' emblazoned over the top. After that experience he never again went into battle without someone riding at the head of the army holding aloft the spear and crossed sword, i.e. the sign of the cross."

"Wait a second," Pete said. "Are you sayin' that what we call..." he paused to add air quotes, "...the 'sign of the cross' is really from that there vision Constantine had?"

Elliot chuckled.

"That, my dear fellow, is a matter of some dispute. While there are purists who insist that Christ—along with thousands of other Roman criminals—were crucified upon an instrument the design of which exactly matched a lowercase 't', others, such as Werner and myself, hold to the belief that it more closely resembled an uppercase 'T', with two sections: the staticulum, or stationary upright mortise, and the patibulum, or crosspiece. We believe it was the patibulum that was carried by Christ. I believe I can prove our contention through simple human physiology."

"Okay," Pete said. "I'm listenin'."

"Roman law required the condemned souls to carry their cross through the streets of the city to the place of crucifixion—a specific number of steps, actually. In the case of Jesus of Nazareth, the distance was about six hundred and fifty yards. Think about this for a moment. First off, the six-foot-long patibulum alone would have weighed around a hundred and ten pounds. It follows logically that if the staticulum were longer and thicker—and eight feet seems to be the standard—if the entire cross were used, the condemned would have been forced to carry between three and four hundred pounds on their backs. This after having been beaten, caned and scourged for several hours. The blood loss alone would have been sufficient to produce the onset of hypovolemic shock."

"Hypo what?" Vanessa asked.

"Hypovolemic shock. It's a condition brought about by the loss of twenty percent of the blood in a human body."

"Yuck!"

"Right you are. But it gets worse…much worse. The flagrum would have stripped skin and muscle tissue away from the victim's backs and shoulders leaving exposed bone. My point being that even a robust, healthy male would have been hard pressed to perform the act of carrying a four-hundred-pound object that far let alone someone who, had he lived in modern times, would've been remanded to ER."

Pete said, "Sounds to me like that dog just won't hunt."

Elliot screwed up his face and appealed to me for interpretation.

"He means that it doesn't make any sense."

"Oh…right," he replied, drawing out the word. "Now

then, added to that is substantial historical and archeological evidence that suggests the staticulum was permanently sunk into the earth and the condemned would then be nailed through the wrists—"

"Don't you mean the hands?" Vanessa asked.

"Actually, no," Werner answered. "Early anatomists considered the wrists part of the hands, thus Jesus' exhortation to Thomas to 'see my hands.' Anatomically, it is patently impossible that hands could have supported the weight of the body. Crucifixion as a form of execution existed in the Phoenician culture fully a thousand years prior to Jesus' death. But the Romans took it to another level. In their system, spikes would be driven through the wrists and into the patibulum. The patibulum would then be hoisted up and dropped onto the staticulum."

"That's inhuman!"

"Quite right," Elliot said. "It's actually insidiously, ingenuously cruel. The spikes were driven into the wrists in such a way as to miss major blood vessels, but at the same time pierce the median and ulnar nerves. You know the feeling you get when you hit your funny bone?"

Vanessa nodded.

"That's because the ulnar nerve is suddenly and inadvertently triggered. Well, imagine someone deliberately squeezing the ulnar nerve as hard as they could with a pair of pliers for hours on end with no letup."

"Oh, my God!" Cassie exclaimed. "I can't even imagine what that would've felt like."

"But it doesn't stop there," Elliot continued. "While it's possible that, as depicted in most paintings, spikes were driven through the tops of the feet and into a slanted footrest, in Jesus' case—because the Jews wanted the bloody business transacted before Sabbath sundown—many historians, ourselves included, believe that the nails went between the heel and ankle bones and into the outside of the staticulum. The nerve damage in the feet combined with the nerve damage in the wrists would've resulted in the victim suffering from causalgia."

I interrupted, "I know about this from my tactical training. Causalgia is a condition that soldiers experience when a limb has been blown off in battle."

"Right you are, Jake. There are many historical accounts of soldiers begging their comrades to shoot them to end the agony. And…victims of crucifixion would have suffered this in all four appendages."

We all sat for a few seconds in contemplative silence before Elliot continued, "Now, getting back to my original point…when Constantine's mother, Helena, came back with her purported finds, Constantine made sure all of Europe heard about it. It's no wonder that suddenly people began wearing little pieces of wood around their necks that were thought to be fragments from the cross."

Vanessa said, "You mean, kind of like good luck charms?"

"Oh, yes indeed. In fact, it is widely accepted that our expression to 'knock on wood' comes from the practice people had of tapping these fragments, hoping that by doing so it would ward off evil spirits."

Cassie asked, "So, are you saying that some enterprising individuals saw a chance to make money and started chopping up wood and marketing it as holy relics?"

Elliot laughed at a private joke.

I said, "What's so funny?"

He shared a knowing smile with Werner.

"Oh, it's just that John Calvin said if all the relics of the true cross were genuine, there'd be enough to fill a big ship."

Werner added, "There were so many forgeries that Dutch philosopher Erasmus is said to have remarked Christ must have been crucified on a 'whole forest.'"

"Today," Elliot continued. "There are several places that claim to have a piece of the cross, including the cathedral at Notre Dame, the Church of the Holy Sepulcher in Jerusalem,

Balatlar Church in Turkey's Sinop Province—more recently, the church of Hagia Sophia, also in Turkey—and, of course, the Vatican."

"Then, I'm afraid I don't get it," I said. "If a piece of the cross has already been found, then why go to what will undoubtedly be tremendous expense and effort to find another?"

"Because those places that claim to have splinters of the cross are all a part of the myth and legend associated with Helena Augusta," Werner replied wearily.

"Okay, which brings me back to my original question: How do you separate fact from myth and legend?"

Werner leaned forward, allowing the motion of the chair to propel him to a standing position.

"It's simple belief, really."

"Can you explain?"

He walked around the end of the desk toward one of the crowded bookshelves, talking as he went.

"Look, every single piece of wood *rumored* to be a piece of the cross can be traced to the original piece purportedly found by Helena. Now, if you accept as fact that the piece of wood *she* brought back from the Holy Land is indeed a remnant of the true cross, then you can easily believe that splinters from that *original* piece of wood exist today."

"But...?" I prompted.

"The circumstances surrounding her finding of it are so suspect, that one must exercise an extreme amount of faith to accept it as fact."

"Simple as that?" Cassie asked.

He turned his head and smiled.

"Nothing that has to do with antiquities, and especially as it regards religious relics, is ever 'simple', dear girl. All the same, one would be hard pressed to point to anything of substance in our world that hasn't arrived, by and large, as a matter of choice. To be fair, it is often a collective choice, a consensus if you will, but...it is choice nonetheless."

I waited a beat or two before asking, "And the manuscript we've been studying...do you *choose* to believe its veracity?"

Werner returned to his desk carrying a couple of dusty volumes. After sitting heavily in his chair, he looked at me with that penetrating gaze of his and said, "With every fiber of my being, Jake."

Elliot said, "It is our further belief that Helena did *not*, in fact, bring back her alleged relics and that the *actual* patibulum somehow survived. If this manuscript..." he paused to tap the yellowed parchment, "...is to be believed, the patibulum to which Jesus of Nazareth was nailed—and would likely still contain his DNA—forms the doorjamb of that church in Turkey."

I looked back and forth between Werner and Elliot.

"All right, you believe that...and...I choose to believe *you*."

I wasn't sure I meant it, and the triumphant smile shared by the two professors did nothing to alleviate a growing sense of dread hanging over me like a brooding thunderhead.

I couldn't begin to tell you what was wrong, but something was there...just outside the periphery of my consciousness. I only hoped it would be revealed before someone I cared about was hurt.

For some reason, I remembered the "phone a friend" feature on *Who Wants To Be A Millionaire.* I needed some help, but not the kind that Pete or the girls could provide. In the "phone a friend" category, there was definitely someone I could call —someone who had been a close friend and mentor to me through the years.

Paddy Quinn, one of the toughest sons of Ireland to ever wear NYPD brass.

At his retirement ten years ago, he had been a Detective Sergeant assigned to homicide. His closed case files ranked among the highest in department history.

We had begun as enemies and ended as friends. And I knew, from his own insistence, that if ever I needed anything, all I had to do was call.

As to why I needed him specifically, it had to do with sheer toughness—for at seventy-two he could still take down most anything that walked on two legs—but it also had to do with a mind that had the unique ability to consider all sides of an issue simultaneously. In short, he had the best bullshit filter of anyone I had ever known.

I excused myself, walked through the outer office, into the hall and dialed his number.

CHAPTER ELEVEN

The floor was sticky.

How that fact had managed to escape Paddy Quinn's attention until now was a mystery. Of course, when one was on one's hands and knees, rooting around for one's dropped cheaters, i.e. reading glasses, the condition of the flooring tended to become disgustingly self-evident.

"Retirement Living," the gaudy sign had trumpeted on the day he'd visited the housing facility ten years ago with his late wife.

Late.

Wife.

Two short words. So much unspoken between the spaces. She had been his world. Everything. Everything that mattered, anyway.

The retirement community wasn't great, but it was what they could afford on his detective's pension. He had no complaints, for the provision was generous enough. It was just that living expenses and the sickness that had stolen the life of his one great love exceeded his income. Thus, the humiliating job three days a week at the convenience store down the street.

It wasn't how he'd imagined living his life. Then again… life without his Maggie was no life at all, only existence. Add to that the sheer worthlessness he felt at having been "put out to pasture", as he called it, fully three years before his time should have been up, and most days, he found himself trying to figure out what the point was.

Of living, that is.

The young man who was first in line called out, "What'd you lose down there, pops, your brain?"

The other customers chuckled uncertainly.

"Be with you in a minute, young fella'."

What was he doing here anyway—a man of his age and stature—crawling around on the filthy floor of a convenience store doing a menial job for minimum wage?

Shaking his head slowly in frustration, Paddy stood to his full 6'2" height, realizing that what he had at first considered a temporary condition in his right knee had now been proven conclusively to be permanent.

"Now then, what can I be doin' for ya', lad?" he said pleasantly in his deep, Hell's Kitchen Irish brogue.

More quickly than Paddy's aging eyes could follow, the kid pulled a gun from the waistband of his pants and stuck it in his face.

"What you can do for me, old fool, is give me all the money in that there cash drawer, or I'll kill you where you stand!" the kid shouted.

"Don't resist. Whatever amount is in the drawer is not worth your life," the store manager's words rang in his ears.

The kid shouted to the three other customers, "What are you people lookin' at? Get on the floor. Now!"

The two men dropped to the floor while the other customer, a young girl who looked to be about sixteen, stood trembling in place and sobbing.

The young thug took two steps, grabbed a handful of her hair and screamed, "Shut up, bitch!" before forcing her onto the floor where he stood looming threateningly over her outstretched form.

Paddy observed the scene with a growing conviction—a conviction that compelled him to take some action. But what could an unarmed, seventy-two year-old, washed up detective do against a crazed young man with a nine-millimeter?

"Where's my money?" the punk shouted as he stomped toward the counter.

Wild thoughts raged through Paddy's mind, thoughts of younger days when he would have dispatched this arrogant child without hesitation. Thoughts of what he liked to call the living years, which stood in stark contrast to this slow death.

Suddenly, Paddy's ears heard his mouth say, "What if I don't give you the money, laddie-buck, and instead I take that gun away from you and shove it up your scrawny arse?"

Paddy glanced at the customers on the ground.

They stared back in open horror.

He winked at the girl.

Turning his attention back to the young punk, he said, "What's it going to be, boyo?"

Without saying a word, the young man took careful aim and pulled the trigger.

Once.

Twice.

Paddy Quinn had been shot at numerous times during his twenty-seven years on the NYPD, and he knew full well when a bullet had his name on it. And those two had been close enough for him to not only read his first name, but his last name and middle initial as they whistled by his head.

The kid had missed from point-blank range.

He held the gun up in front of his face and stared at the barrel uncomprehendingly. His attention was so focused on the pistol that he didn't duck the bottle of wine that crashed into the base of his skull.

He dropped like a marionette whose puppeteer had just gone out for a smoke.

The teen girl stood with a broken bottle dangling limply from her hand, staring at the inert form of the would-be robber.

Blood poured from a two-inch gash, pooling under the young man's battered head. One leg jerked spasmodically, tapping out a crazy rhythm on the tiled floor.

One of the men rose to his feet and kicked the gun away

from the kid's hand.

The other man asked, "Is someone going to call the cops or something?"

Expelling a breath he seemed to have been holding for five minutes, Paddy said, "I'll do that just as soon as I find my glasses."

He looked at the young girl and smiled. She dropped the remnants of the bottle and smiled back hesitantly before yielding to a wave of emotion.

Dropping his gaze back to the sticky floor and stepping back a pace, he heard an all too familiar crunch.

"Well whadda' ya' know. There they are."

He was just getting ready to dial 911 on his cell, when it rang. He glanced down at the floor and the shattered remains of his glasses.

"Well, there'll be no help from you," he mumbled before looking up at the man who had kicked the robber's gun away. "Excuse me, sir, but I'm wonderin' if you could help an old fella' out and tell me the name on my screen here. Seems I just stepped on my reading glasses."

"Oh, sure thing," the man replied, holding the phone up so he could see. "It says…Beloved Bastard? That's a name?"

Paddy laughed as he took the phone back.

"It's the name I use for a dear friend. Can you please call 911 for me while I take this call? There's a good lad."

CHAPTER TWELVE

Paddy answered on about the fifth ring.
"Jacob Moriarity, as I live and breathe."
His voice was one of the marvels of human vocalization, in my humble opinion anyway. It started deep in his chest and never quite made it up into the resonance chambers of the facial mask where the treble tones are added. It was all bass. Sonorous and gruff at the same time. Sort of like Michael Keaton's portrayal of Constable Dogberry in *Much Ado About Nothing*. It made you think of a gifted storyteller bellied up to the bar in some ancient pub in County Cork holding his audience captive with merely the sound of his voice.

I said, "Paddy Quinn. How the hell are you?"

"Well, now, there's a question for ya'. A very determined young man just tried to rob the convenience store where I work three days a week to supplement my meager pension."

"Ah, I see. And is the coroner on his way?"

"Now, Jacob, what do you take me for?"

"I take you for the toughest, meanest son of a bitch I've ever known."

"Well, there is that. Fortunately, or sadly as the case may be, the young man is still breathin'."

He pronounced it, "Bray-then."

"Although the young lass who beaned him across the back of his head with that wine bottle was swingin' for the fences, and so she was."

"Do you need to deal with the police, because I can call you—"

"Nonsense. I'll be hearin' none 'o that from you, Jacob. In this neighborhood, it'll take the local constabulary a good ten minutes to arrive, and that young fella on the floor ain't goin' nowhere, if he ever goes anywhere ever again, if you catch my drift. Now then, since I'm fairly certain this isn't a social call... what's on your mind?"

"Well," I said. "I've got something going that I could really use your help on."

I had used Paddy from time to time over the years when cases seemed on the verge of exceeding my ability to produce a positive outcome.

Such as now.

He replied, "Well, now...let me check my calendar to make sure I've got nothin' else goin' on that would pose a conflict. Nope! Nothin' at all. When do you need me and where?"

I laughed.

"I need you now. In Seattle. Although, we might be going to the Middle East."

"You don't say? The Middle East? What part?"

"South central Turkey."

"Sure 'n what'll we be goin' there for?"

I paused a beat and then replied, "We're looking for the remnant of the true cross."

"Jesus, Mary and Joseph!" he exclaimed. "That's borderin' on sacrilege."

"Now, just hear me out, Paddy. There are two professors in Seattle. Very legitimate. One of them is actually a dear friend of mine." I paused and then asked, "Have you ever heard the rumors about the Emperor Constantine's mother bringing a piece of the cross back to Constantinople?"

"Sure, and it now sits where it belongs. In Vatican City!"

I said, "But, what if all of that legend was just that...legend? What if none of it is true?"

"Then somone'll have a bit of explainin' to do, I'd say."

"Well, I'm pretty sure it isn't true."

"How sure are ya'?"

"About as sure as I am that the *real* remnant of the cross sits where it has sat for over a thousand years—in a church in

Turkey."

"Are you suggesting that someone during the Crusades took the cross from Jerusalem back into Turkey?"

"I'm not actually sure *what* I'm saying, Paddy. The only thing I know at this point is that when you consider the issue from an investigative perspective, there certainly seems to be a lot more evidence to support the remnant's existence in Turkey than there is for all of Helena Augusta's claims."

He was silent for a few seconds.

In the background I could hear the sound of approaching sirens.

Finally he said, "As you know, I'm a good Catholic. Always have been. Historically, we Catholic's have been asked to suspend a lot of disbelief when it comes to things such as holy relics. The jawbone of this saint, the finger bone of that one, the skull of another, and so on. And I suppose we've gone along with it all throughout the centuries because it was easier than asking hard questions. Now, being that I've spent my entire life dealing with forensics, I, for one, have always wondered about such things—and especially the myths and legends surrounding the relics brought back to Constantinople in the fourth century. Call it my detective's natural cynicism, call it whatever you like. But the fact remains that I've had an intense curiosity regarding this subject for as long as I can remember."

"Well, you're not alone, old friend. And that's exactly why I need your help."

I heard him say to someone, "Be right with you, officers. The body's right where the lad fell there and the gun was kicked over there under the magazine rack." And then, "Jacob, I've got to go and talk to these young officers. But…I'm in. Just call me later and give me the particulars. When do I leave?"

"On the first flight to Seattle that you can find."

"Okay…well, barrin' the detectives tying me up with questions, I can do that."

"Thanks, Paddy. This means a lot."

"It'll mean a lot to me too. I can use the money."

I laughed.

"Yes, there'll be some of that. I'll call you later."

I returned my phone to its place in my front pocket and walked back into the office, feeling a sudden sense of well-being that hadn't existed ten minutes ago.

CHAPTER THIRTEEN

We quickly wrapped up our meeting and adjourned for the rest of the day around 4:30 p.m. I mean...we had to. My brain was struggling to cope with what I'd already heard and, at present at least, I had no capacity for more.

As it turned out, Emily had, in fact, been able to secure the two apartments on a short-term rental basis. So after agreeing upon a time to meet the following morning with Werner and Elliot, we all headed over to check in to our respective units. I should say that Pete and I checked in. Cassie and Vanessa had a few things to pick up at the store, so they dropped us off and headed off in search of whatever it was they needed.

"Girl stuff," is the only explanation we were given.

The two-bedroom, two-bath unit assigned to us, though sparsely appointed, was surprisingly roomy. Moving in for the two of us amounted to tossing our respective bags into our respective bedrooms and turning the TV on in search of something to occupy our time while we waited for the girls to return.

We are not novices.

We have experience waiting for women.

There are actually only three things a man can do while waiting for a woman: sleep; eat; or watch sports on TV. We combined two of the three...sleeping and watching sports.

We're creative like that.

Actually, on this occasion, I took it to another level and indulged one of my favorite pastimes, which was making lists. It's what I do. I list things that are on my mind—column after column, and page after page. On occasion it gets pretty elaborate. Sometimes I even figure things out by doing this. However, after going at it for better than forty-five minutes, about the only thing I succeeded in doing was adding to my already immense confusion.

When the two girls finally returned—some hour and fifteen minutes later—they stormed angrily into our apartment and plopped down onto the sofa, disgust coloring their lovely faces.

I postulated, "May I assume something happened while you were out that was of an upsetting and off-putting nature?"

"Men!" Vanessa spat bitterly as she slouched.

Cassie said, "Five more minutes with that cretin at the counter and I guarantee you he wouldn't have made it out of the building alive!"

It's not that my niece is a violent individual; she just doesn't have a lot of patience. I blame my end of the gene pool for that.

Pete asked, "So what was the problem? Was the guy slow? Were there a lot of people in line or something?"

Vanessa sat forward, leaning her elbows against her knees.

"I can tell you why he took so long."

"Why's that?"

Cassie interrupted, "No, let me. He spent the entire time with his eyes riveted on a certain part of Vanessa's anatomy."

"Was he hitting on you?" I asked.

Vanessa laughed humorlessly.

"No, just creepin' on me."

Cassie smiled and said, "Tell them what you did."

I could tell Vanessa was a little bit embarrassed.

"Well, when we were *finally* finished paying for our items—a process the guy stretched out for close to five minutes—and were starting to walk away from the counter, I turned back around, walked right up to him, stuck my chest out and said, 'Take a good look, dude, because this is as close as a guy like you will ever get,' and then walked out."

After we all had a good laugh, Pete asked, "So, what'd the guy do?"

"He just stood there staring stupidly and breathing through his mouth, kind of like he'd been doing the entire time."

"Now, maybe he wasn't creepin'," Pete suggested light-heartedly. "Perhaps the boy was just overcome by your beauty—you know, stunned into silence."

Cassie said, "Yeah…no. He was a creep. He kept licking his lips."

"Was he doing the same thing with you?" I asked.

"No, he wasn't. I'm pretty sure I was too old for him."

"So, he was a young guy?"

Vanessa said, "Nope. Probably your age."

"Ahhh, right. Okay then."

"Anyway…" Cassie said, changing the subject. "So, have you two talked any more about the project?"

I said, "Not really. But I've been thinking about a lot of things while we waited for you to get back."

"For instance?"

"Well, first of all…I don't think this is a fake. Something's definitely there. I just don't know what it is yet." I pondered whether I should tell them the rest, then decided on full disclosure. "Cassie, you know that thing—that sixth sense thing you and Aaron always talk about me having?"

"Your 'Spidey Sense?'"

"Well, it's really going off on this one, but not in a good way." I looked at each of them before continuing. "I think there's an unimaginable danger associated with this search."

Cassie said, "Danger is what you're all about, Uncle."

"I know. But I don't want it to spill over and hurt someone I love."

Vanessa got off the sofa and gave me a warm hug, then pulled back, gazing into my eyes with a look of confidence.

"You won't let anyone hurt us."

"While I appreciate the vote of confidence, part of not letting anyone hurt you is all about not putting you in a position where you could be hurt in the first place."

"What are you saying?" Cassie asked.

Pete said, "Well, Ms. Cassie, I think he's sayin' that it might be best if you and Vanessa go on home and sit this one out, because it's not just about finding this here relic. It's about finding it before someone else does, and that someone else might not play nice."

"Very well said, Pete," I affirmed. "That's exactly what I've been thinking."

Vanessa asked, "Do you have any idea who?"

"Not specifically. But just think about this with me in general terms as it regards the implications. From an archeological perspective alone, it'd be the biggest find in modern history." I paused before adding, "Think about what Elliot said before we broke up for the evening."

Before anyone could answer, a soft knock came at the door.

I walked slowly over and bent to look through the peephole.

Emily Young stood on the other side of the portal, her lovely face a mess of tension and worry.

CHAPTER FOURTEEN

I opened the door.

"Ms. Young. What can I do for you?"

She looked around nervously and said, "Can I, uh…can I come in for a minute?"

I swung the door open wide and replied, "Sure. Come on in."

As I stepped aside to let her in, I checked my watch—it was almost 6:00 p.m. and I knew everyone was probably getting very hungry.

I knew I was.

"Thank-you, Mr. Moriarity, and I promise this won't take long."

She hurried past me, an enticing fragrance lingering in her wake. Why do women smell so good?

I closed the door as she walked to the center of the apartment and greeted the others before turning around to face me. She wore no makeup and was dressed in simple athletic pants and an oversized men's flannel shirt worn open over a halter top as if she had just come from, or was just about to begin, a workout. Even without makeup, Emily Young was a stunning young woman.

"I know this is going to seem strange," she glanced down at her attire. "Especially with me dressed like this. And I don't want to give you the wrong impression, but…do you think you and I could speak in private for a few minutes?"

I thought it over for a few seconds before replying, "Pete, why don't you take these two starving young women down to that pizza place we passed on the way here. And perhaps when we're done, Emily can drop me there?"

"Sure thing, Mr. Moriarity. It'd be my pleasure."

Emily added, "Yes, of course. I'd be happy to drop you when we're through."

"Want us to order you something, Uncle?" Cassie asked.

"Oh, you know…something big with every ingredient in the house except anchovies."

"Got it."

After they all trooped out, I said, "Won't you sit down?" and indicated one of the chairs at the smallish table where we sat facing each other in silence.

After a few moments she said, "I don't suppose you have anything to drink, do you?"

"Would the Chardonnay you left chilling for us be sufficient?" I replied as I headed for the refrigerator.

"Perfect."

As I opened the bottle and poured the drinks, she stood and walked slowly around the room.

"I really didn't know how spartan these units were or I wouldn't have suggested you coming here."

I said over my shoulder, "Spartan? Some of the places I've stayed in make this look positively opulent."

"All the same, for someone of your stature, I should have done better," she remarked, returning to her seat.

"Someone of my stature? What's that supposed to mean?"

"Oh, I've heard all about you, Mr. Moriarity."

I glanced in her direction and saw a small smile playing around her mouth.

"Elliot's been talking, hasn't he?"

"Let's just say that your, well, that your fame has preceded you."

"I see. Well, I strongly suggest that you resist believing everything you hear."

I carried the glasses back to the table, sat down and offered a toast.

"Here's to new friends."

She smiled genuinely.

"To new friends."

We clinked glasses and she drained about half of the glass in one gulp.

"So, what's on your mind, Emily?"

She breathed out a big sigh and said, "Well, I was getting ready to hit the gym, and I'd been thinking about something ever since we saw each other this afternoon when I gave you the keys. I knew I wouldn't be able to concentrate on my work-out if I didn't talk to you, so I thought I'd just take a chance and come over." She took another long drink and sat staring at me for the longest time as if she were afraid to speak what was on her mind. Finally, she said emphatically, "You have to talk Dr. French out of going on this expedition."

The stark pronouncement took me by surprise, and I leaned forward on my elbows and said, "Now, why would I want to do that?"

She looked down at her empty glass before finding my eyes.

"Because if he's successful, he and everyone associated with the expedition will almost certainly die."

I held her gaze trying to read something, anything in her eyes.

"And you know this because..."

Her reply was immediate, "Because I work for an organization that is also trying to find the remnant of the true cross."

I sat back in my chair, slowly sipping my wine.

"I thought you worked for Dr. French."

"That's what you're *supposed* to think."

"So that makes you, what, an undercover double-agent?"

"Don't mock me, Mr. Moriarity!"

I smiled and said gently, "I'm not mocking you, Ms. Young. I'm merely trying to get at the truth."

Her anger subsided and she replied, "Okay, fair enough."

After a few moments I said, "Why are you telling me this?"

She stood suddenly and walked over to stand by the window, pulling the blinds aside and looking this way and that.

With her back to me she said, "Because I really admire Dr. French and Dr. Spencer. They're good men and they do not deserve to die."

I sensed that there was more, so I prompted, "And...?"

She turned around to face me.

"And I know more about you than what Elliot told me."

"For instance..."

Her eyes filled with sadness.

"Let's just say, that if you accompany them on this expedition, there's a good chance that someone I care for will die at your hands."

Something wasn't making sense. In fact, nothing was making sense.

"So, this other employer, are they like an archeological group from a rival university or something?"

This made her laugh, albeit humorlessly.

"Mr. Moriarity, the people I work for are not archeologists. Far from it. They are some of the wealthiest, most powerful and pitiless men in Europe. And they will stop at nothing to gain the remnant of the true cross."

Now I was really confused.

"So, if their interest isn't archeological, then what is it?"

She stood, collected her glass from the table and carried it over to the sink where she took her time rinsing it out and drying it.

Turning slowly to face me, she folded her arms and said, "They plan to extract DNA from the wood...and clone Jesus."

CHAPTER FIFTEEN

Nathaniel Prince Epstein sat at his desk in the richly appointed master suite of the chalet pondering the events that had led him to this point in his life—the point where he could take a man's life without so much as a twinge of guilt or remorse. He supposed it could be argued that he had never liked the man and for that reason his death was no more than a trifling nuisance. But he knew the truth, and the truth was that even had the man been a close friend, the icy resolve that now gripped his soul would have remained undiminished.

The intercom buzzed softly.

"Yes?"

"I have taken care of the situation, Primus. What do you wish for Gérard to do now?" Gérard was not only his assistant, but also his bodyguard and the only man on earth whom he truly trusted.

"Keep an eye on Number Two, Gérard. I suspect that he and the unfortunate Number Eight had formed some sort of alliance. In response to Eight's death, he may attempt something foolish."

The low voice rumbled through the speakerphone, "It will be as you wish."

Nathaniel hastened to add, "Nothing drastic, mind you. Just observe for now and report back with anything you see that is worth mentioning."

He didn't trust Number Two. For that matter he didn't trust any of his colleagues—underlings, really, for in his mind he had no equals.

"Very well," came the low reply. "And, Number Five wishes to speak to you."

"By all means. Send him in."

This should be interesting. For Number Five to be requesting an audience so soon after the assassination could only mean one of two things. He was appalled at such barbarism and wished to voice his disapproval, or...he already had someone in mind as a replacement.

He entered Primus' personal space, nervous and sweating as usual—a sign of weakness if Primus had ever seen one.

"Primus," he said ebulliently, extending his hand absently and then withdrawing it as if he had encountered something hot to the touch. "Thank you for seeing me."

"But of course, Number Five. What is on your mind?"

"Right to it, eh? Very well. I feel that Number Eight must be replaced. We have always been nine—neither eight nor seven, but nine. And may I hasten to add that I, for one, am not sorry to see him go. Poor bastard. He knew the risks and his challenge to you was, therefore, based upon an informed choice. Nevertheless, we must move on and we cannot until we find a suitable replacement."

Nathaniel listened to Number Five with feigned interest as he casually swirled his wine.

"I assume, Number Five..." he ventured casually. "That this impassioned speech is but a preamble to the presentation of a personal favorite of yours?"

He sputtered, "I don't know if the man has quite risen to that level, but, yes, I do have a name."

The tiny beads of perspiration around his hairline belied Five's denial.

"Well then, let's hear it."

Nathaniel was all warmth and grace.

Five paused dramatically, and then rushed headlong into his well-rehearsed campaign speech.

"There is a man in Buenos Aires..."

Nathaniel suddenly ceased to listen with his conscious mind, for the mention of this man's name carried him away to another place. It was a place where unimaginable human terror had been face to face with incomprehensible human evil. And this man's roots were sunk down and entwined around the very heart of it all.

The man, if in fact one could lend the designation to such a creature, had been in a position to stop the evil. Instead, he chose silence, and his silence had served to aid and abet. And for that crime—a crime against his own people—he had never been punished. Of course, he had never been accused either, at least not in a formal hearing. The vast numbers of war criminals brought to trial following the Second World War had allowed this insidious weasel to escape and disappear virtually without a trace. And now, here he was being mentioned as a replacement for the recently departed Number Eight.

Perhaps there was a God after all.

Number Five continued his speech, oblivious to the fact that he had lost his audience.

"Now I am fairly certain that were an invitation to be extended, he would at the very least agree to further discussion on the matter."

Nathaniel said nothing.

A full minute passed in silence prompting Number Five to query, "Primus? Did you hear what I said?"

"The call will be made tomorrow, Number Five." Nathaniel had recovered from his stupor with Five being none the wiser. "I must say that to finally meet this man will give me the...opportunity for which I've literally waited a lifetime."

Five brightened at what he perceived as being a vote of confidence from Primus.

"Well then, it's all set."

He stood to leave.

"Number Five?"

Having just reached for the door, Five turned and said, "Yes, Primus?"

"For now, let's you and I keep this matter between ourselves. There's really no need to trouble the others until we have something more concrete."

Five appeared to consider the request.

"Well, I suppose you're right. Although I confess to being just a wee bit anxious to, shall we say, toot my own horn?"

Both men shared a good laugh as Five continued his exit.

When the door had closed, Nathaniel keyed the intercom.

"Gérard, will you come in for a moment, please?"

His reply resonated deeply through the speaker, "As you wish, Primus."

Preparations had to be made. Yes, indeed, many special preparations must be made for this very *special* man.

Gérard entered to find Primus leaning back in his desk chair, smiling. It was an eerie scene, for Primus almost never smiled, and when he did it was usually because someone was going to die.

"Gérard, get my things ready, we'll be leaving first thing in the morning."

As the smile broadened Gérard could only nod his affirmation as he backed slowly out of the room.

"And Gérard?"

"Yes, Primus?"

"Delilah has done what she was supposed to do. And as much as it pains me to give this order..." He paused and continued reluctantly, "Have some of our operatives in Seattle take care of her. But...I don't want her to suffer. Understood?"

"As you wish," Gérard said simply and then closed the door.

Primus felt the rare grip of emotion constricting his throat as he replayed the conversation in his mind. He loved Delilah, after a fashion, and she loved him. But there were things in life that transcended love. He would try to remember that over the coming days when the memories of their times together brought the inevitable pain.

He stood and made his way slowly over to the elegant

wet bar which filled one corner of his hexagonal office. His arthritic hip served as a constant reminder that he was getting old and that time was running out. Refilling his glass with the last of the private reserve cabernet, he sought out his favorite chair, which sat at an angle in front of the hand-carved, Italian marble fireplace.

Allowing his body to ease back into the cushioned comfort, he swirled the wine in his glass, holding it up to catch the light from the fire. It reminded him of blood.

Blood and fire.

As the flames danced in the background, he mused that no two elements so well defined the history of his people on the earth.

CHAPTER SIXTEEN

I'm sure you've had the experience before. The one where suddenly you feel as if all the air has been sucked out of the room and you're left struggling to breathe. I could do nothing but stare at Emily for what seemed like several minutes.

I finally managed to say lamely, "Clone Jesus?"

She walked slowly over and sat once again across the table from me, burying her head in her hands.

When she spoke, her reply came out slightly muffled.

"Sounds crazy, doesn't it?"

"Well, I suppose from a technological perspective, it is theoretically doable. But why would someone want to clone Jesus?"

She leaned back on her hands and said with a sigh, "It's a long story."

"Do you want to talk about it?"

She paused before answering, "It's why I sought you out this evening."

I got up from the table, walked to the refrigerator to retrieve the Chardonnay and refilled our glasses.

"All right. I'm listening."

Emily leaned back in the chair and began to talk. And as her story unfolded, the knot of fear in my stomach seemed to tighten with each line.

"Nathaniel Prince," she said simply at the start.

"What about him?"

"Nathaniel Prince Epstein, to be exact. He's the leader of a group that calls itself, 'The Nine.'"

"Overly self-aggrandizing and dramatic if you ask me,

but…okay. So?"

"Besides being my employer, he's one of the most ruthless men on the planet."

"I've known a lot of ruthless men, Emily. What is there about this man that would cause you to define him in this way?"

She blew out a big breath and said, "There is no life he would not take, no promise he would not annul, and no amount of money he would not spend to achieve his objective."

I smiled and said, "It sounds like the description fits."

"He wasn't always like that," she continued. "There was a noble purpose at one time."

"But…"

"I guess you could say that after so many years of being unable to achieve that purpose, frustration caused him to become ever more narrow in his focus…obsessively so. He told me once, 'Emily, just as chasing a sunset over a hill will never result in gaining the sun, no matter how hard I pursue my purpose it seems to only put it that much further out of my reach.'"

"Was he talking about this cloning thing?"

"Actually, that has only come up fairly recently as technology has continued to advance."

"Then, what is it?"

"I'll get to it, but it's only understandable within quite a large context."

I stood and asked, "Would you care for some coffee?"

She smiled and replied, "So it would appear that we can add mind reading to your considerable set of skills."

I re-entered the tiny kitchen and said over my shoulder, "Go ahead. I'll listen while I get things together."

She scooted around in her chair so she could see me.

"As hard as Nathaniel's purpose has been for him to grasp, money seems to come to him quite easily. Between an enormous inheritance from his father and his natural aptitude for financial management, he is a very wealthy man. And, of course, wealth produces power, which gives him enormous clout in the global business community."

I refilled the coffee maker's reservoir and collected a couple of dark roast K-cups from the cupboard.

"Sounds like quite a guy. What was the source of the family's wealth?"

She laughed humorlessly.

"It's ironic, really, that a Jewish boy from Graz, Austria, is now one of the wealthiest men in Europe thanks in large part to his father's pilfering of the Nazi war chest."

Given my recent experience with Gaspard Ducharme involving taking down a global art cartel dealing in stolen Holocaust art, that piqued my interest.

"So, are you saying that Nathaniel's father stole Holocaust art back from the Nazi's and then sold it for his own profit?"

"No, no, no…far from it. He actually stole the Nazi's *money.*"

I carried two cups of coffee over to the table and sat down, saying, "I've known people who managed to survive the Holocaust, and I can tell you that stealing the Nazi's money was the last thing on their minds. Every waking minute was consumed with just trying to stay alive. How'd he pull it off?"

"I know, it sounds impossible. But somehow between 1939 and 1944, working under deep cover, Nathaniel's father stole close to twenty million dollars right out from under the Nazi's noses while keeping his family out of the camps."

"Even by today's standards that's a lot of money." I said. "Back then it would have amounted to a fortune."

"It was. When his father died in 1962 Nathaniel was twenty-seven, and the family fortune had grown to a little over forty-five million."

"Damn! That'd be somewhere in the range of three hundred million in today's dollars. So, what's he worth today?"

"Nathaniel Prince sits at the top of a financial empire

that, by conservative estimates, is worth close to forty billion euros."

I said, "So, I'm going to guess that this cloning thing isn't about making more money."

"Exactly."

"Then, I don't get it."

She took a careful sip before answering.

"Nathaniel Prince is set on righting a wrong, Mr. Moriarity."

"And that would be…"

The intensity of her gaze seemed to pierce to the back of my skull.

"The Jews of the first century expected an entirely different Messiah than the one they got. They were expecting him to come riding in on a warhorse and lay waste to Rome and all of her armies. Instead, Jesus came riding on a donkey preaching a doctrine of peace. Some, like Nathaniel, have never given up on their version of the Messiah."

"Okay, but what does any of that have to do with this outrageous plan to clone Jesus?"

She blew out a long sigh and continued, "The world is a mess. Nations rising against nations. Famine. War. Disease. In the ancient Jews' idealized minds, the Messiah was supposed to put an end to all of that by establishing a one-world government over which he would be the theocratic head."

"Heaven on earth," I mused.

"Excuse me?"

"You know…the 'Lord's Prayer?' *'Your Kingdom come; your will be done…on earth as it is in heaven?'* There are actually many Evangelical Charismatics who practice what is termed Dominion theology wherein they believe that the purpose of the Church is to hasten the establishment of Christ's kingdom on earth."

"Right. Well, I'm not sure if what Nathaniel Prince has in mind has anything to do with heaven on earth. More like an elite group of men rising up behind Jesus' authority and taking over world governments."

"That is incredibly far-fetched."

"Really?" she replied. "Think about it. At present, conservative estimates put the world's Christian population at somewhere around two and a half billion people. And almost without exception, Jesus Christ is acknowledged as their undisputed Lord and Savior. What do you think those people would do if Jesus were to suddenly appear in the flesh? He *did* promise to come back, you know."

"True," I agreed. "But I'm pretty sure the mode of his return didn't include cloning."

"Fair enough. But if he were to make an appearance—a *Second Coming*, if you will—do you really think Christians would care about the how?"

"That's a good point. However, the Biblical inerrancy folks would have a huge problem if his coming were judged inconsistent with Biblical prophecy. For instance, there's the whole rapture thing—you know, the being caught away in the twinkling of an eye?"

She waved my comment away as if she were swatting at flies.

"Perhaps hardcore exegetes would get their undies all in a twist, but I'm telling you right now that if Jesus Christ walked into, oh…say…what's that huge church in Houston?"

"Uh…Lakewood?"

"Yes. Do you think that if Jesus Christ walked into Lakewood church some Sunday morning, the thirty or forty thousand people in attendance would scratch their heads and say, 'Now, hold on a minute. This isn't the way the Bible said it was going to happen?' Hell no! To a person, they would fall down on their faces and worship the object of their affection and devotion. And the same thing would happen worldwide. It would be a religious tsunami the likes of which has no historical precedent."

She was right. I knew it as surely as I knew the sun would rise and set and the earth spin on its axis.

"All right. Point made, point taken. So, let me get this straight. Nathaniel Prince and his buddies don't really care about the intrinsic religious elements of Christ's return. They're only interested in…what…world domination?"

"Yes. That and one more thing. After Jesus is cloned, and has served his purpose in establishing their absolute control over world affairs, they plan to have him killed. Only, this time, it will be gentiles who kill him and our people will finally be free from the generational guilt…and the Blood Libel!"

CHAPTER SEVENTEEN

I had no idea what she was talking about, so I asked, "What the hell is the Blood Libel?"

She placed her cup on the table, leaned back a little in the chair, and then said, "In November of 1938, the Nazis attacked Jewish synagogues and businesses. They called it, 'Kristallnacht'. Pope Pius XII knew about it and looked the other way."

"I've heard of Kristallnacht, but...I didn't know about the Pope's involvement."

"It wasn't so much involvement as it was a lack of involvement. And he did the same thing when he was informed of Nazi atrocities in Austria, Lithuania, Poland, Spain and the Ukraine between 1940 and 1943—including deportations of Jews to death camps. Just sat back and looked the other way. Nathaniel wondered why there had been no outcry from the church...the same church that claimed 95% affiliation by the very Nazis who were carrying out the Holocaust. And furthermore...why was there no condemnation of Hitler until the war was over?"

"Sounds like a fair question to me."

She hurried on, "Even in the face of overwhelming evidence of Nazi atrocities, Nazis were still allowed to remain members in good standing with the Catholic Church, while in a profound irony, Catholics who supported cremation as an alternative to burial were excommunicated. And when the Allies passed a resolution condemning Nazi war crimes, the Vatican patently ignored it. In fact, the Pope never declared it a sin for Catholics to participate in the slaughter." She paused and then added, "But, it wasn't all just about the Pope. Six million Jews were exterminated by Nazi Germany. How could something of that magnitude have been hidden from the world? The only logical conclusion is that it *wasn't* hidden. The nations of the world knew something was going on, and yet they stood idly by. Why did that happen?"

I said, "Tough questions."

"Right. So in his quest, Nathaniel sort of stumbled upon a historical pattern that originated in the first century—not that he was the first one to do so, but it was significant."

"And what happened in the first century that was so significant?"

"While it's true that the Roman government sanctioned and carried out the crucifixion of Jesus, it was the Jewish religious hierarchy that was the driving force behind the accusations that had stirred up the people. And, as much as anything, that's what ultimately led to his death."

"If I remember correctly, the Roman governor, Pilate, basically resented the hell out of being stuck in what he considered a backwater berg like Palestine while others of his class were living it up in Rome."

She smiled and said, "You know your history, Mr. Moriarity."

"Oh, just enough to get by." I paused to sip my coffee. "So, for a guy like Pilate, the main motivation was probably more about keeping the unwashed masses quiet than in seeking justice."

"Which is exactly why Jesus was expendable. I mean, come on, the man had committed no crimes; spent his life doing good and caring about people, and if the Biblical accounts are to be believed, healing and raising people from the dead. What was there about those actions that could possibly stand as justification for capital punishment? It was all about Pilate attempting to avoid an uprising."

"But in reality...it had the opposite effect."

"You mean the establishment of Christianity?"

"Yep," I said. "What are the chances that such a rabidly loyal core of followers would have been formed had it not been for a galvanizing act like a public execution?"

She nodded her head.

"That's an interesting speculation, and I suppose the world will never know. Anyway...Nathaniel said that in the years following the crucifixion, the men known as Jesus' disciples wrote passionately of their individual and collective contempt of the Jewish religious establishment."

"Kind of like Peter's address on the day of Pentecost?"

She smiled as she took another sip.

"I must say that you are full of surprises, Mr. Moriarity."

"Look, can we dump the 'Mr.' stuff and just have you call me Jake?"

She nodded, "All right, Jake. And the name is Emily."

I hoisted my mug in a mock toast.

"Emily."

"Tell me," she said. "How would a man like you know about the apostle Peter?"

I said wryly, "A man like me, huh? Maybe I need to work on my image."

She laughed, saying, "You know what I mean."

I looked at her for a moment before answering.

"Well, once upon a time, I was a seminarian."

"Emphasis on the *was*?"

"Yeah. Let's just say that the best laid plans of mice and men, etc."

She nodded knowingly and said, "Sounds to me as if there's quite a story hidden away in that sentence."

"There is. It's a story of loving, losing and feeling betrayed by the one being in the universe you had previously believed would always have your back."

"So, you lost your faith?"

"No, to lose something implies that it was inadvertent. I walked away with purpose."

"From God, or religion?"

I smiled and said, "Yes."

The door opened and Pete walked in carrying two large

pizzas with Cassie and Vanessa carrying the drinks.

Cassie said, "Since it was obvious that your conversation with Emily was going to take a while, we decided to bring dinner back to you."

"Oh," Emily protested. "I don't want to impose."

"Nonsense. You're eating with us and that's that."

I said to Emily, "Forget trying to argue with her."

After everyone had a piece of pizza—or two or three in the men folk's case—Cassie asked, "So, what have you guys been talking about?"

I glanced at Emily, seeking her permission to answer receiving a hesitant nod in reply.

"Emily has been filling me in on some very interesting complexities of the case."

Emily explained, "I know things about this case that Jake needs to know before he commits himself any further."

"Like what?" Vanessa inquired bluntly.

Since there were only four chairs at the small table, I sat in the lounge chair.

"Well, so far I've learned that Emily here doesn't really work for Dr. French. She works for a covert group calling itself 'The Nine' who are also seeking the remnant of the true cross. Only their interest isn't historical. They want to extract DNA from the wood and clone Jesus."

Cassie and Vanessa exclaimed simultaneously, "Clone Jesus?"

I looked at the girls and said, "I told you it was complicated. And, unfortunately, it gets worse." I prompted, "Emily?"

She took a deep breath and said, "The Cliff Notes version is that the men who comprise The Nine are among the most wealthy and ruthless men on the continent. All of them are Jews and all of them still cling to the Jew's ancient belief in a Messiah coming to rescue his people and establishing His kingdom on earth."

Pete cut in, "So, are you suggesting that behind those

fellas' desire to clone Jesus is...what...a plan to use him to stir up a global coup of sorts so that they can take over afterwards?"

"Very perceptive, Mr. Tolles," Emily replied. "That's exactly what they anticipate happening."

"Oh, come on," Cassie exclaimed. "No one would follow someone claiming to be Christ who had begun their life as some laboratory experiment."

"No?" I queried. "As Emily has already explained to me, with two and a half billion Christians in the world, were Christ to appear in the flesh—and especially with accompanying signs and wonders, et cetera—there are precious few who would question his legitimacy."

Vanessa said, "It's been a long time since Sunday School, but isn't there something in the Bible about Antichrists, or something?"

Emily replied, "Yes, there is. But think about it: original DNA. This would not be a reproduction or facsimile or cheap imitation. Theoretically, the cloned Christ would be the real thing."

"Only, he wouldn't...not really. Right?" Vanessa turned her head, appealing to me.

"I don't know, sweetheart. This is getting into some pretty sophisticated theo-philosophical-anthro-biological stuff here. When cloning takes place, what part of the individual makes the transfer? For instance, if humans really do possess souls...is that something that makes the transition? Or do they emerge as soulless, zombies devoid of the spiritual characteristics of their DNA counterpart?"

"Even if they didn't," Pete replied. "Seems to me there'd be plenty of people willing to follow even a cloned Christ. And if there was somebody behind the scenes pulling the strings, you could get those folks to do just about anything you wanted them to do."

"And then there's the sub-issue of the Blood Libel," I said.

"The what?" Cassie said.

I gestured for Emily to jump in.

"Well," she cleared her throat. "It will simplify things if I just pick up the story where I left off before you three came in." She drained the last of her coffee before continuing, "I had just finished explaining to Jake that following Jesus' public execution in the first century, his followers—"

I interjected, "And by 'followers', she is referring mainly to the eleven men closest to him."

"Right," she affirmed. "Those men—and Peter in particular—were passionately critical of the religious establishment and everyone else who bought into the rigid laws of Jewish tradition over the teachings of Christ. In fact, Peter went so far as to say, 'you have taken by lawless hands, have crucified, and put Jesus to death.' Although neither Peter, nor any of the other disciples for that matter, meant for the statement to spawn hatred for the Jewish people as a whole, it was that very indictment that gave Constantine permission to do just that."

I asked the group, "You guys keeping up with this?"

Vanessa and Pete simply nodded and Cassie said, "It's fascinating."

Emily continued, "This is where it gets a little interesting. In spite of the disciple's intentions to the contrary, many in the Christian church who had misunderstood the story—resulting in a subtle but growing anti-Jewish attitude—carried this mass indictment forward."

"Excuse me," Pete interrupted. "Mass indictment?"

"She's referring to the implication of the Jews in the death of Jesus," I explained as Pete nodded in understanding.

Emily said, "Right. This misunderstanding led to circulation of the notion that because of the death of Jesus, i.e. the Son of God, the Jews had justifiably been abandoned by God and replaced with a new chosen people, the Christians."

"Replacement theology," I mused. "Widely held to this day."

Emily smiled, "Once again, Jake, very impressive."

"One tries."

"Under this theology," she explained. "The Jews would be subject to God's wrath while at the same time being denied His favor."

"You mean because they were no longer...what...the chosen people?" Cassie inquired.

I said, "I did a fair amount of research into the early church when I was in seminary, and I recall a particularly vile statement from John Chrysostom..."

Emily interrupted, "The Patriarch of Constantinople."

"That's the guy."

"I know the one you're talking about. In fact, as a Jew, I personally found it so chilling that I committed it to memory." She glanced at each of us before continuing, "Chrysostom said, 'Jews are the most worthless of men—they are lecherous, greedy, rapacious—they are perfidious murderers of Christians, they worship the devil, their religion is a sickness. The Jews are the odious assassins of Christ and for killing God there is no expiation, no indulgence, and no pardon. Christians may never cease vengeance. The Jews must live in servitude forever. It is incumbent on all Christians to hate the Jews.'"

CHAPTER EIGHTEEN

Vanessa said quietly, "Holy cow!" as Cassie and Pete just shook their heads in stunned silence.

I explained, "Remember...this guy was in a position to exert a powerful influence on the way people formulated their thoughts and opinions. At the time, society as a whole wasn't as freethinking as it is today."

Cassie asked, "Weren't people actually discouraged to think for themselves?"

Emily replied, "Prohibited would be a more apt description. And as a result of this public ignorance, what began as an earnest criticism of religious hierarchy eventually disintegrated into what I can only call Jewish hatred. By the twelfth century, Jews were not only branded Christ killers, but also as baby killers."

Vanessa exclaimed, "What?"

"In 1144 there was a wild story that started in Norwich, England, about Jews kidnapping a Christian baby and draining it of its blood."

"That's sick! Why would anyone believe something like that?"

"As unlikely as it sounds, somehow the myth took root and spread in a variety of modifications throughout Europe and then on to other parts of the world."

Cassie walked over to the refrigerator to get a bottle of water.

"This is crazy. Did anyone ever stop to ask why Jews would do something like that?"

Emily and I looked at Cassie in silence until she said, "Riiiiight. No thinking."

Emily clarified, "A few popular theories surfaced. Among them, that as punishment for killing Jesus, Jews suffered from hemorrhoids and that drinking blood was the best cure at the time."

"Gross," Vanessa exclaimed with a disgusted expression.

"Another popular theory was that Jewish men, when they're circumcised, lose so much blood that they need to drink the blood of Christian babies to be replenished."

Cassie returned to the table and said, "I still can't believe people bought this stuff."

"My personal favorite is the one that says all Jewish men menstruate and need a monthly blood transfusion, thus the need for blood."

Pete shook his head in disbelief.

"And you're talking about educated people who bought into this—not just the common folks?"

"That's right."

As I walked over to the counter to refill my coffee, I said over my shoulder, "I've heard it said that you can say anything negative about the Jews and people will believe it."

Emily was nodding vigorously in affirmation.

"Let me give you a perfect example of that. I've actually seen medieval documents that talk about someone—supposedly a Jew—stealing communion wafers from a Catholic church, then taking it home and cutting it into pieces. He would then send the pieces to several other Jews and they'd all stab their piece of communion wafer, believing that by doing so the pain of the crucifixion would be perpetuated through the torture of the host bread of the church."

No one seemed to have anything to say and we all just sat in stunned silence waiting for her to finish up.

Emily continued quietly, "History records that thousands of Jews were tortured into confession and then burned alive because of people believing this...this bullshit. And as far-fetched as all this is, nothing, not even the Holocaust, has ever been enough to sway public opinion. And for years Nathaniel, my employer, has sought desperately for a way to reverse the curse, so to speak, and bring this bondage to an end."

She was quiet for a moment, and then she added, "Ultimately, the solution was brilliant in its simplicity: acquire a piece of the true cross, extract the DNA from the wood and clone a new Jesus. And when he is killed—as I explained to Jake that he almost certainly would be—this time it would be the gentiles, i.e. non-Jews, who are to blame for Christ's death, and the Jews will finally be free from their terrible disgrace."

I said, "You haven't yet mentioned why Nathaniel and The Nine have you working undercover, spying on Dr. French."

"Oh, I thought that was obvious. They don't know the location of the cross and are looking to me to steal the documents that contain clues. Barring that…Nathaniel will content himself with allowing Dr. French, and by extension everyone in this room, to lead him to it. At which point…you will all be killed."

We sat in silence, each of us lost in our own thoughts, pondering uncertainly what part we were to play in this madness.

"Well, that pretty well guarantees a sleepless night!" Vanessa finally said numbly.

Cassie added, "No kidding."

The sound outside the window was unmistakable. It was the sound of a round being chambered into an automatic weapon. I caught Pete and Cassie's eye and communicated silently in a way I knew they'd understand.

Danger was present.

Cassie nodded and placed her hands lightly on Emily and Vanessa's arms, motioning for them to precede her into the bedroom. Emily's eyes filled with instant alarm, but she complied quickly and quietly. Vanessa went along with it, because she'd been through this scenario with me a few times before.

In one well-practiced move, I stood, drew my Sig Sauer

P226 Tacops .357 pistol and headed for the door. Once there, I put my ear against the wood and listened carefully while motioning Pete into a backup position.

I heard nothing.

After waiting for another thirty seconds or so, I turned and said to the room more loudly than necessary, "I'm going to run down to the car. I'll be right back."

Once again, I pressed my ear against the door and was rewarded by the sound of scurrying footsteps heading off to my left. I turned and motioned to Pete to wait five seconds and then follow me. I screwed a suppressor onto the end of the Sig. Suppressors are great when you want to keep your killing from becoming public knowledge, and since I was certain that someone was about to die, I deemed it a necessary piece of equipment.

I eased the door open a crack, didn't see anything, and then opened it wider. The walkway was clear. I figured that whoever had been out there was hiding somewhere close by.

Turns out I was right.

I walked through the door and closed it partially behind me. Predictably the lights along the walkway had been put out leaving the area in near total darkness. Holding the Sig by my side I began to walk purposefully toward the parking area. After I had gone about twenty feet down the walkway, a man stepped out from behind a couple of large evergreen trees and stood blocking my passage.

"Something I can do for you?" I said coldly, slowing my progress.

The man looked to be in his thirties, about five-eleven and heavy through the shoulders with that rounded look that weightlifters get. He smiled, thinking foolishly that he had the upper hand.

"Yeah, as a matter of fact there is something you can do for me."

I sensed movement. He looked around me and said to the second man who was now moving up behind me, "Tell him, Geordie."

I heard a raspy voice reply in a thick, working class British accent, "You can go back to wherever you came from and forget all about Emily Young and Dr. Werner French."

I had moved so that my back was against the wall on my left with my gun still concealed behind my back.

"Now, why would I want to do that?" I tried to keep the tone of my voice calm and even.

Tough guy number one—the guy now to my left—said, "Because your health depends on it."

Tough guy number two—the raspy voiced Geordie to my right—thought that was hilarious. He was shorter than the first guy but much broader. He looked to be a little older as well, maybe around my age.

"So, let me make sure I understand what you're saying," I said. "Either I do what you say and go home, or the two of you are going to hurt me. Is that right?"

Geordie said, "Count on it, mate," and took a step toward me.

CHAPTER NINETEEN

I'm pretty sure he meant it as a threatening move, but the only thing it accomplished was to bring him in range of my right hand. I've always been good with my right, especially a right uppercut. I know what these guys were thinking. They were used to their mere presence striking terror in people to the point of paralysis. As a result, when I hit him under his chin with the butt of my Sig, he went down hard and laid there as though dead.

And, for all I knew...he could've been.

"Okay," I said to the other tough guy. "Here's what's going to happen. You are going to return to whoever sent you and tell them to back off, or my associates and I are going to find them and kill them."

He didn't take me seriously—a common mistake made by more people than you can imagine. He chose instead to demonstrate some very fine martial arts moves. I could tell he'd worked very hard perfecting his skills. Unfortunately, Pete came from out of nowhere and had him on the ground in just a shade less than three seconds.

Five seconds after that, he too was unconscious.

Geordie who was, apparently, not dead, hauled himself up off the ground and tried to bull-rush me. I simply sidestepped and hit him again.

This time in the back of the head.

He went down, grabbing the back of his head and moaning loudly.

A concerned, middle-aged neighbor opened her door, stuck her head out and with wide eyes asked, "Is everything all right?"

I smiled, flashed my FBI credentials and replied, "Nothing to worry about, ma'am. Just apprehending a couple of dangerous killers."

Her eyes went even wider and she slammed the door shut.

I grabbed Geordie by the collar and dragged him over to where Pete had the other guy sitting up against the railing, peppering the man with questions. Given that the poor soul couldn't even focus his eyes, I doubted seriously that he was going to be able to summon coherent answers.

"What are we gonna do with these fellas?" Pete asked as I shoved Geordie down beside his mate.

"Oh, I don't know," I said, squatting down so I was at eye level with the men. "Maybe take them inside and make one of them bleed while the other watches?"

Pete licked his lips and smiled so cruelly, that had I not known him to be a kind-hearted soul, I would have feared for my life.

"Now, that right there would be pure pleasure."

Geordie's head appeared to be missing a cervical spine as it was continually weaving side-to-side; front-to-back; and random directions in between.

He wheezed, "You'll get nothing from me or my mate!"

I stood, fearing that if I held that position for much longer I'd have to have Pete help me to my feet. Not exactly the threatening, tough guy persona I was going for.

"I don't know, Pete. I'm thinking that perhaps we should let them both go."

"Aw, hell no!" he replied, playing his part well. "I was already looking forward to having me a little fun, and now you're just gonna take it away from me? That just ain't right, Mr. Moriarity."

Geordie's eyes focused long enough for him to say, "Moriarity? As in, Jake Moriarity?"

I bowed dramatically.

"At your service."

A string of artfully composed profanity issued impressively from his mouth.

"They didn't tell us it was you we was going up against."

I said, "Would that have changed anything?"

The other man replied, "We would've brought more guys, for one thing."

"And…" I prompted.

"I wouldn't have taken the job."

"I have a suggestion," I said.

"Okay…" Geordie replied suspiciously.

"How about we just walk away and pretend this never happened. In other words, no hard feelings between us."

"And?"

"And…you inform your employer that my associates and I are guaranteeing the safety of Dr. Werner French and Dr. Elliot Spencer. And by associates, I'm sure you know who I mean."

He nodded and said, "FBI."

"That's right."

"All right, mate. We'll tell 'em. But I can guarantee that they won't be put off. Not these blokes. That lot will keep sendin' guys at you until they run out…or you're dead."

"Since you apparently know my reputation, Geordie… which of those two possibilities do you think is likely to happen?"

His unfocused eyes stared at me for a few seconds before he answered, "I think they'll run outta guys."

"Pete, help these gentlemen to their feet and point them toward the parking lot. I don't think they'll give us any more problems this evening."

He helped them up after confiscating a Glock 19 and Beretta FS from the two dazed combatants.

After they had stumbled a few steps toward the stairs, Geordie actually turned back around, mumbling a quick, "Thanks, mate," before continuing on his way.

CHAPTER TWENTY

When we got back to the apartment Cassie was standing just inside the door with her pistol in hand.

As Vanessa and Emily emerged from where they had hidden in my bedroom, Cassie said, "Well?"

"We met two gentlemen who strongly urged us go back to wherever we came from and forget about Emily and Dr. French."

Vanessa smiled and inquired, "How badly are they injured?"

Pete returned her smile.

"We was right gentle with them."

"Meaning that they merely have lumps and contusions as opposed to broken bones."

"Are you all right?" Emily was looking me over as if searching for injuries.

Cassie said with a wry smile, "Something you need to know about my uncle Jake, Emily. He always wins."

I asked, "Do you know who these men were, Emily?"

"What'd they look like?"

"One was in his thirties; about five-eleven; looked like he worked out. Sandy colored hair and lots of it. Boston accent. The other guy was about my age; five-eight; built like a power lifter; shaved head and a thick, working-class British accent."

She thought for a moment and then replied, "Those descriptions don't match anyone I know."

"All right. Any idea who might have sent them?"

She responded immediately, "Oh, it was Nathaniel. No doubt about it. He must've somehow got wind of your involvement and sent those men to take you out."

Pete said, "What I don't get is why the man would show his hand and move against us this early in the game."

"What if it had nothing to do with us?" I mused.

"What do you mean?"

I sat down at the table across from Emily and thought over the situation.

"Emily, where is your apartment from here?"

She gestured vaguely toward the left of the door.

"Just four or five units down the walkway. Why?"

"Pete, do you remember the man's surprise when he learned who I was?"

"I sure do. The boy was definitely shocked."

"What does that mean, Uncle?" Cassie asked.

"They may have known someone was working with Werner and Elliot, but they didn't know it was us. In fact, when I told him who I was, he was a bit shaken up."

"A bit?" Pete asked sarcastically.

I started at Emily for a long moment.

"Emily, whatever evil those men had planned for tonight...it was planned for you. Regardless of your former status with Nathaniel Prince, you are no longer an asset."

Her eyes were wide with fear.

"But Nathaniel and I..."

"What about you and Nathaniel?"

She blinked twice, and then sagged as if all the air had gone out of her.

"He and I are...well, close. At least I thought we were. But then, if I'm being honest, I guess I always knew it would one day come to this. I mean it's like I said before, he's a ruthless man. And ruthless people act in ruthless ways, right?"

I thought through what she had told me of the man earlier.

"When you said that Nathaniel is ruthless, did you mean

that he's devoid of pity and compassion?"

She paused for a moment to consider the question and then replied, "Yes...yes, I do. That describes Nathaniel perfectly."

I said, "It has been my experience that highly driven people often cross thresholds in their lives—boundaries they previously vowed they'd never cross. It's like a line in my favorite Beth Hart song, *'I swore to God I'd never be what I've become.'* But when the object of their desire lies just on the other side of that boundary, and they become convinced of their need for said object, then virtually anything can be justified."

Pete added, "Yup. When Mr. Moriarity and I first met up, I was workin' for a man like that. Only in his case, his ruthlessness had made him evil right down to his core. Hell's bells, he was even willin' to kill his own granddaughter to get what he wanted."

The scene flashed vividly through my mind. Harry Olivetti standing there in front of me with his back to the second-floor balcony railing, holding his granddaughter, and Vanessa's niece, Abby in front of him. And then without a word, deliberately falling backward over the railing, not caring whether she lived or died in the process. Thankfully, she lived. Harry lived as well...as a vegetable. It remained in my memory as one of the most craven, selfish acts I had ever witnessed.

I said, "The man you've described, Emily, fits the profile of a classic narcissist: grandiose, entitled, arrogant, manipulative and...ruthless." She was nodding her head, so I continued, "And the one surpassing character trait—or flaw as the case may be—is that they always have to win. At some point in crossing over that threshold I mentioned, everything becomes part of their stuff. Even people. This may be an oversimplification, but if something is perceived as a threat to their..." I used air quotes, "...'stuff', they will do almost anything to eliminate that threat."

"So..." she mused. "My life is in danger."

"You can flat-out count on that, darlin'," Pete replied.

"Look," I said. "I know this is a bit inconvenient, but I want all of us in one place for the rest of the night. Cassie, take Vanessa back to your apartment and collect enough things to get you through the night and Pete will take Emily back to her place so she can do the same."

"So, we're all spending the night here?" Vanessa inquired.

"Yes, we are, even though I doubt that they'll try anything again tonight." I jerked my thumb toward the door. "Especially those two. But once they call in a report to Nathaniel, or whoever dispatched them—"

"That would be Gérard," Emily interrupted with no small amount of disgust, "Nathaniel's private pit bull."

"Right. Anyway, you can bet your last dollar that Nathaniel's not going to be scared off that easily."

"No, he won't," Emily affirmed.

I said, "Pete, we'll split shifts out here and the girls can take the two bedrooms."

"Sounds like a plan," he affirmed.

"Should we be scared?" Vanessa asked hesitantly.

"No, but neither should we be indifferent to the fact that there is a very powerful and determined *someone* out there who means Emily—and by extension, us—harm."

"So, not scared...prepared?"

"Exactly. Now, you should get going. Try to be back here in ten minutes at the most."

"Copy that," Pete replied as Cassie added her agreement.

They had just walked out the door when my phone buzzed.

It was Gabi.

CHAPTER TWENTY-ONE

"Hey, mister. How's it going up there?" she asked, her voice dripping with those dark, honeyed tones.

"Well..."

"Okay...what's up? I know that voice. It means that things are starting to go sideways and you don't really want to tell me because you don't want me to worry."

She was on to me.

"Yeah, that about covers it."

"So what happened?"

"First of all, I think Elliot and Werner are definitely on to something legitimate."

"Okay. That's good. What else?"

"That's just it. The thing that makes me think they're on to something legitimate is that someone just made a run at us. Well, not us specifically, because they didn't really know who we were. But against a young woman named Emily Young, Werner French's research assistant."

She said playfully, "Let me guess...incredibly young and surpassingly gorgeous."

"Nice superlatives, and...yeah, all of that. As it turns out, she doesn't really work for Dr. French."

"Kind of a double agent, like Désirée?"

Her reference was to our friend Désirée—surname unknown—who had helped us save Gaspard Ducharme.

"Exactly like that. She works for a guy named Nathaniel Prince, or Nathaniel Prince Epstein, to be precise."

"Ah, a fellow Jew."

"Indeed."

"And, what's a hardcore Jew doing nosing around a case that involves the cross of Jesus of Nazareth?"

"Well… Nathaniel Prince, and some other very wealthy, very sinister men in Europe calling themselves The Nine—"

"You're making that up," she said, cutting me off.

"No, I'm not. This group is dedicated to finding the wood from the true cross and—get this—extracting DNA so they can clone Christ."

"Come on," she exclaimed. "That sounds like some…I don't know…some comic book movie concoction. That can't be real…can it?"

"I believe the intent is real because operatives dispatched from The Nine tried to kill Ms. Young not more than an hour ago, and would have undoubtedly done so had we not been here. Now, whether or not there is even the slightest possibility of their fantastic scheme succeeding, I haven't a clue."

"But…cloning Christ. From a scientific perspective I can see the logic. I mean if you're going to clone a human being, why not Jesus? But, aside from that, what's the motive?"

"According to Emily, it's all about righting two historical wrongs. First of all, it's an effort to create the Messiah the Jewish people have sought for millennia—a Messiah who will, in contrast to Christ, come bringing a sword to sweep Israel's enemies aside and set up his Kingdom on earth."

"Oh, my God," Gabi exclaimed. "I can see it all now. Every Christian on earth is already expecting and anticipating Christ's return. And if his return came about vis-à-vis cloning, as long as he was here, would anyone even care how it happened?"

"Exactly. The Nine would raise him and, in the process, indoctrinate him with their agenda. By the time he was of age, they would then reveal him to the world and begin the process of setting up, not *his* kingdom on earth…but theirs."

"This is terrifying in its potential to actually succeed. You said The Nine wanted to right two historical wrongs. What's the second?"

"Have you ever heard anything about something called the Blood Libel?"

"As a matter of fact, I actually know quite a bit about it."

"No kidding? So, you're saying you know all about the historical vendetta the Catholic Church has carried out against the Jews for killing Jesus?"

"I don't know if I'd go as far as calling it a vendetta, but, yeah. I know all of the legends associated with it. You know, Jews stealing the bread and stabbing it with daggers to make Christ suffer all over again and other nonsense like that."

"And, do you also know about the complicity of the Catholic Church in the Holocaust?"

She sighed and said, "Only vague references that were never proven. Something about a huge number of Nazis being church members and the Pope basically turning a blind eye to the atrocities committed by Hitler. Why, is any of that stuff legit?"

"Whether it is or isn't, apparently the end game of Nathaniel and his band of merry men is to orchestrate Christ's death."

"Wait, why would they do that when he's the one through whom this…this global empire is purportedly going to be set up?"

"It's because of the Blood Libel. They want him to die, and they want the gentiles to kill him, thus ridding the Jewish people of a centuries-old curse."

She was quiet for a few moments before saying, "Jake, this sounds big. Like, scary big."

"Well, if these guys are as substantial as we've been led to believe, you're right. But, I've gone up against bigger organizations than this before."

"I know. But anytime you throw religion into the mix—especially religion tainted by myths and legends—the resulting brew is the milk of zealots."

I said, "Very poetic, Ms. Marcus."

"I wasn't going for poetic. I just want you to consider

carefully what you're up against."

"Listen, Gabi...I hear what you're saying, but I'm in this and I'm not backing out until I see it through. Besides, I'm not alone. Pete's with me and don't forget who I work for."

"I know, Jake, but this..." she paused as if ordering her thoughts. "My, uh, family story is a bit more complicated than what I've shared with you."

"Okay...I'm listening."

"My dad's brother, my uncle David, was Chassidim, or a member of an extreme sect of Haredim."

"I've heard the term, but I'm not sure what it means."

"People in the West would probably refer to Haredi as orthodox and Chassidim as ultra-orthodox—a term that only applies to about seven percent of the Jewish population, by the way. Haredim means 'one who trembles at the word of God', so the Chassidim think of themselves as being singularly authentic in their practice of Judaism, devotion to Yahweh and strict adherence to Jewish law."

"So, you're saying that uncle David was a zealot?"

"Probably an oversimplification, but...that's definitely how outsiders would view him."

I said, "Let me guess...he died in pursuit of the defense of his religion."

Sighing deeply, Gabi replied, "His death was just so pointless."

"Why do you say that?"

"Because it didn't accomplish anything except him dying. Our family had gone through so much already, what with the horrors visited upon my great grandparents and grandparents during the Holocaust."

"How'd it happen?"

"It was all so long ago, before I was born. And to be quite honest, the family sort of hushed it up. But, from what I've been able to gather over the years, it was just a random argument between uncle David and a few boys from the neighborhood—Zionists. Zionists are despised by the Chassidim and vice-versa. There were four of them against my uncle. The argument grew increasingly heated. Insults replaced argument. Rage replaced insults until finally, violence erupted. Those four boys beat uncle David to death right there on the street, and no one lifted a finger to stop them."

I asked, "Did the police get involved?"

"Involved in what? The same people who refused to help him were the same people who later claimed to have seen nothing when the police interviewed them. Their story was that his body had just appeared on the street, beaten into a bloody mess."

"And the cops bought that?"

She chuckled darkly.

"I can tell that you haven't spent much time around Jewish neighborhoods. To say that they are tight knit would be laughably understated. All of this to say...be extra careful, Jake. These men are zealots and I'm guessing you've never dealt with zealots before."

"While that may be true, they're still bad guys, and bad guys need to be stopped."

"But that's just the thing, Jake. Most bad guys stop when logic tells them they are facing overwhelming odds, or they're wounded, or a leader is put down. Not zealots. You have to kill them to stop them. You have to kill them all."

I had to pause and let that sink in. She was right. But, so what? If someone was coming against my friends—friends who, by the way, were depending on me to do what they could not do, i.e. find the remnant—what was I going to tell them? That I was too scared of zealots to continue?

I heard the apartment door opening and the sound of voices.

"I have to go, Gabi."

"I know."

The silence was strained. I didn't know how to end the call.

She said, "I have a really bad feeling about this, Jake.

Promise me you'll heed my warning."

"I will. I love you, Gabi."

She said quietly, "I love you too, Jake. Talk soon?"

"Yeah. Soon."

And with that, she ended the call and I was left wondering what in the world I had gotten all of us into.

I had a feeling we were about to find out.

CHAPTER TWENTY-TWO

Sunday morning dawned cold and drizzly.
Just another day in paradise.
I tried to count the number of days I had actually seen the sun in Seattle during the many, many times I had visited the jewel of the Pacific Northwest. As one lifetime resident had told me on one of my trips, "Look around you. All that green is there for a reason." I suppose he was right, because I could legitimately count the sunny days on one hand. Still, I loved the town. There was just something about it I found compelling.

And they had great coffee.

I love coffee.

And after the largely sleepless night I had just spent, I had a feeling I was going to require a substantial amount to get through the day ahead.

The sleeping arrangements had worked out just fine for everyone else. The girls had all done their pre-bedtime girl stuff and retired to their respective rooms and I had taken the first watch, which lasted until 2:00 a.m. After Pete took over, I had lain on the sofa thinking through my chat with Gabi and everything I knew about the case thus far, and Nathaniel Prince and The Nine, and the Blood Libel and the possibility of there actually being a remnant of the true cross. All of which conspired to keep me awake until around 5:00 a.m., at which point I fell into a restless slumber dominated by dreams of voiceless, faceless men chasing me through dank, dark serpentine subterranean passages.

When I woke up at 7:30, Pete was drinking coffee and the girls were still asleep. Given that there were three women in residence—and there was no way I was going to let everyone go back to their own lodgings until I deemed it safe—I figured I should perform my morning ablutions while there was a fighting chance to do so. I was surprised by the fact that I was a little stiff from my encounter with the tough guys, so I stood in the shower for a long time just letting the hot water pour over my head and shoulders. It was while so engaged that I realized that I knew less about what was expected of me on this case than any in recent memory. I didn't like that feeling. If you want to know the truth, I hated it.

After about twenty minutes I heard someone knocking on the bathroom door.

"Uncle Jake, you almost done?"

It was Cassie.

"Be out in a sec," I said loudly.

"Please hurry. We're dying out here."

I turned off the shower, dried off, and since I had no need to comb anything, I was ready in about a minute. I opened the door only to find Vanessa planted squarely in the middle of the doorway.

She waggled her finger in front of my face and said, "I don't want to hear one more complaint from you about how long we spend in the bathroom," and then brushed by me, slamming the door behind her.

"And a pleasant good morning to you as well," I called out.

Cassie informed me that I had, indeed, spent a good long while in the bathroom, to which I replied, "But, when I went in, me and Pete were the only ones awake."

"So?"

"So what did it matter how long I was in there when there was no one else desiring to use it?"

"But," she argued. "There was someone. In fact, there were *three* very desperate someone's."

"Not when I went in."

It was an argument that had no satisfactory resolution,

and, therefore, we moved on to other things.

About an hour later, after the girls had all showered, we sat in various positions around the kitchen and living room planning our day.

I said, "First of all, we've got to get over to the University and talk to Werner and Elliot about what happened last night."

"No," Cassie said firmly. "First of all we go back to our apartments and get clean clothes and girl stuff—"

"Then we find food," Vanessa cut in.

"*Then* we go to the U," Emily finished.

"All right," I said. "Girl stuff, food and *then* to the University." I thought for a moment and then said, "You should go do that now, and I'll meet you in the parking lot." I walked them to the door and asked, "How much time are we talking about here?"

Cassie looked to the other girls for affirmation, "What, ten minutes?" They all agreed.

As per the arrangement the night before, Pete accompanied Emily while Cassie and Vanessa headed for their apartment next door.

I closed the door and felt my phone vibrating from its place in my pocket. I answered on the third ring.

It was Elliot.

"Jake, thank God. You've got to get over here right away."

He was definitely worked up about something.

"Take a deep breath, Elliot and tell me what's happening."

He took his time answering, and then said excitedly, "Jake...Werner and I...have found the location of the remnant."

"The specific location or the general location?"

"Well, we know where it was at the start of the thirteenth century."

"Umm, okay. And that's reason to celebrate because..."

He explained, "Because we now have a definite point from which we can trace its path forward."

"How definite?"

"Let's just say that it's a matter of historical record."

"You sound very confident."

"Oh, we are Jake, old boy. We most certainly are."

"Where are you now?"

"I'm home, but I'm just on my way out the door to meet up with Werner at the U."

"Okay, well, Emily and the girls are doing girl stuff—"

"Emily?" he asked, confusion coloring his voice.

"Yeah. I'll tell you all about it when we arrive, but we had some visitors last night; a couple of men who seemed dedicated to doing harm to Emily—"

"Good, Lord!"

"Exactly. So, we all spent the night in my apartment."

"Is Emily all right? Are you all right?"

"We're all fine. Like I said, I'll explain everything when we arrive. After they finish doing their thing we're going to get some food, so…give us about an hour."

"Perfect. Werner and I will be anxiously awaiting your arrival."

CHAPTER TWENTY-THREE

Breakfast was nothing to write home about, consisting of various configurations of bacon/egg/cheese/sausage/muffin/croissant-mac-something-something's from the drive through of a popular fast food joint along with copious amounts of coffee, all of which was consumed in the car en route to the university. Even though it didn't rise to the level of gastronomic delight, it was carbs and protein, both of which we would need before the day was over.

While we were driving, I asked Emily, "Is Nathaniel part of the Chassidim?"

I could see her eyes go wide in the rearview mirror.

"Yes…he is. But how could you possibly know that?"

"My girlfriend, Gabriella Marcus, grew up in an Orthodox Jewish family. One of her uncles was Chassidim. She told me that he was beaten to death by four young Zionists."

"Tragic, but not surprising. The tension between the two groups is historic and has only grown more severe with the passage of time."

"What's the problem, if you don't mind me asking?" Cassie said.

"Basically, the Zionists are secularists, and the Chassidim reject secularism."

Pete said, "Are the Chassidim those guys with the little curly hair things hanging down in front of their ears?"

Emily chuckled.

"Peyos. Yes. It's due to a reference in the Torah prohibiting men from shaving the corners of their head."

"It'd be a good look on you, Pete," Vanessa teased.

Pete laughed, "Well, now, I'll run that idea by Eddie and see what she has to say."

We drove for a while in silence, indecision over what to do with Emily's revelation tumbling around in my mind like bingo balls inside one of those spinning drums. In the end, I decided to hold off and let things play out.

When we got to the university, we hustled through the labyrinthine hallways until we came to Werner and Elliot's office. Once inside, and after we were all settled in our respective seats, Werner immediately launched into a detailed, intensive apologetic of why they now believed what they did about the remnant, most of which was completely lost on all of us.

I finally had to stop him and ask for a step-by-step explanation.

He chuckled and said, "I guess I *am* a bit worked up. Okay, so..." he tapped the yellowed manuscript spread out on the desk before him. "As we explained previously, this manuscript came to us wrapped around a fragment of pottery. Totally random."

Vanessa spoke up.

"But...what if it wasn't?" She immediately blushed and apologized. "Oops, sorry. I just sort of tend to speak what's on my mind."

"It's okay," I replied. "That's a fair question. She's right, Werner. What if the occurrence wasn't random? What if someone meant for the manuscript to come to you?"

He and Elliot stared at each other as if there were some form of mind-meld going on.

Elliot finally said, "Good Lord! I don't believe either one of us ever for one moment considered the possibility. But if it's true, then...who?"

I asked, "Did the pottery come directly to you on its own, or did it pass through a series of other people prior to arriving here?"

Werner replied, "Oh no, it came to the university directly from the archeological dig. I should explain. It was a very well-funded exploration and one that, sadly, neither Elliot nor I were able to participate in. So, we sent some of our graduate students in our place."

"I believe it was Advika Kapoor who actually uncovered the piece and performed the curation in situ," Elliot added.

"In what?" Vanessa asked.

"In situ. It is a Latin phrase meaning, 'on site', and refers to an artifact that has not been moved from its place of, um, deposition. The practice is critical to the archeologist properly interpreting the artifact and gaining an understanding of the culture, i.e. the people who formed it. Conversely, an artifact not discovered in situ would fail to provide sufficient context for understanding an associated culture."

Werner explained, "On site curation involves cataloging, recording, mapping and photographing the artifact where it was discovered, which is exactly what Ms. Kapoor was tasked with doing."

"I feel it necessary to say that labeling something 'in situ' merely means that the object has not been recently moved," Elliot said.

"Right," Werner agreed. "As you can imagine, artifacts that have significant age carry the strong possibility of having been looted from another site—perhaps spoils of conquest, or it was traded, whatever the case—and thus has a cultural origin other than where it was found."

I asked, "So, we're basically talking about establishing provenance?"

"Exactly!" Elliot exclaimed. "Which is why once the in situ curation has been completed the object would be sent on to us to perform a forensic examination that will, hopefully, uncover evidence that was possibly missed in the field."

Vanessa said, "I think I understood maybe about every third word of what you just said."

After we shared a good laugh, Elliot continued, "Okay, okay...I apologize for, how do they say it...nerding out on you.

It's just that this..." he gestured expansively, "...is our world. And our present world is tied part and parcel to worlds of the past. We are every bit as much explorers as any of the great names in history. They discovered things that were yet to be, while we discover things that have already been and attempt to bring understanding."

Cassie said, "What an incredible statement: explorers discover things yet to be, while archeologists discover things that already were and work to bring understanding. Man, if my professors would have explained archeology like that, I may have continued. As it was, I dropped out and...well, we all know things went downhill pretty quickly from there."

"So," I inquired. "Are you saying that your graduate student—Ms. Kapoor—is the only one who handled the artifact following its in situ examination?"

Werner replied, "No, no, no. As you can imagine, we questioned her at length regarding the manuscript, and according to her sworn testimony...prior to walking into this office, she had never laid eyes on it."

"Which means that someone else packed the artifact for shipping?"

"No!" Elliot exclaimed. "She was right there every step of the way to insure its safe transport."

"Then how do you explain the manuscript coming to be wrapped around the artifact?"

"I can't."

Pete said, "There had to be someone who came in after the fact and unpacked the artifact, wrapped the manuscript around it and then repacked it."

"That's the only plausible explanation," I replied. "Unless Ms. Kapoor is saying that once the artifact was in the shipping container that it never left her sight."

Werner was shaking his head.

"That is not the case. She felt that once the packing was done and the shipping company had taken the container away that her responsibility was completed."

Emily, who had been sitting quietly throughout the exchange, cleared her throat and said, "If what Jake and Vanessa are suggesting is true, then there is a third party of interest to be considered." After a pause, she continued, "In other words, we can no longer assume that it is only the university and The Nine who are involved."

CHAPTER TWENTY-FOUR

"The Nine?" Werner asked. "Who, or what, in God's name is The Nine?"

"All in good time, Werner," I replied.

Ignoring Werner's question, Elliot said, "If someone else is interested in locating the remnant, then why do something that would help us?"

"How do you know they are trying to help?" Emily inquired.

It was like a bomb going off in the room.

"Dear girl," Elliot sputtered. "What, what...are you suggesting that..." he tapped the manuscript. "...that this is intended merely to throw us off the trail and that it has no legitimate value?"

She nodded slowly.

"That's exactly what I'm suggesting. I mean...think about it. If Advika didn't place the manuscript around the artifact, someone else did. And that *someone* is executing a classic misdirection—you know, a feint."

Werner was moving a magnifying glass slowly over the yellowed pages of the manuscript spread out before him on the desk.

Sitting back in his chair he exclaimed, "I am simply unable to acknowledge that this..." he gestured toward the paper. "...is fraudulent. There are too many legitimate factors. For instance..."

He beckoned us to join him behind the desk.

"The fourth line from the top, then the eighth, twelfth and so on. Every fourth line up through the twenty-fourth is different."

I prompted, "And that is significant, because…?"

"It's as if the author had some cipher in mind when he composed this account."

Elliot added excitedly, "Which is why we were drawn to this section in the first place."

Werner tapped the manuscript again and said, "So you can see that by taking specific sentence fragments from each line indicated, one can piece together what appears to be a hidden message of some kind."

Elliot nodded enthusiastically, saying, "Go on, now Jake. What do you think it says?"

I started at the beginning of the manuscript and jotted down what seemed to be obvious lines on a notepad.

When I was finished I studied the notes and read the translated words slowly, "All right, it says:

'Crossbeam, blood-soaked wood,

But a remnant;

World Bridge, all are healed,

Who shall find it?"

"Amazing, isn't it?" Werner was positively beaming.

I said skeptically, "And you think this refers to the wood of the cross?"

"What else could it be?" Werner's grin stretched ear-to-ear.

Cassie said, "If it went on to describe a specific location, then *that* would be amazing. As it is, it doesn't indicate where one should even *start* looking let alone reveal where to find it. I'm not sure how this helps make the case for legitimacy."

"Right," Elliot said. "But, if we've found this much of a clue already, why wouldn't there be more clues further in?"

I replied, "I see your point. However, I didn't see anything that even came close to a pattern on the following pages."

Werner returned to his chair, gently moving me aside.

"You are quite right, Jake, quite right indeed. There *is* no further pattern."

Pete, noticing Werner's excitement said, "You seem to be pretty worked up over a non-discovery, Doc."

"Ah, but I said that there are no *further* patterns, I didn't say that I hadn't *found* anything else."

Werner turned carefully to the last page of the manuscript. After finding what he sought, he positioned it so everyone could see and pointed to a sentence in the interior of the second paragraph.

It read, "*Hitherto, I, Renaud, accompanied by my faithful companion, Everard, fled taking what holy relics as could be carried in our arms, longing, praying that our brothers would soon follow us.*"

After reading it several times over, I said, "I give up. What is it talking about?"

Werner turned back a page and pointed to another sentence in the narrative which read, "*Weakened, weary and nearly spent we arrived at Rodosto on the Eve of St. Martin in the year of the Incarnation of Jesus Christ twelve hundred and six.*"

Cassie asked, "Does that mean what I think it means?"

"I believe it does, dear girl. I definitely believe it does."

"Look, it might mean something to you archeological types, but could you fill the rest of us mortals in?" Vanessa implored.

I said, "The 'eve of St. Martin.' Isn't that somewhere around the middle of November?"

"November tenth, to be exact," Elliot replied.

"So, the author of the manuscript is saying that on November tenth of twelve hundred and six, these two men, uh... Renaud and...Everard arrived in this city called Rodosto with the remnant?"

Werner glanced at Elliot for confirmation and said with conviction, "That is what we believe."

"And you can follow the path this remnant took from there?"

"Well...not exactly."

"Then," I said, "With all due respect...if you don't know

where it went from Rodosto, how the hell do you expect to be able to track it eight hundred years removed?"

Elliot paused a beat before replying, "Look, it's like this: If in fact, every single splinter of wood purported to be a piece of the cross can be traced to Helena's acquisition, then this is the first evidence ever uncovered of another source point."

Cassie shook her head in confusion.

"I'm sorry...what did you just say?"

Werner explained, "All of the purported pieces of the cross that have ever been acknowledged—whether from ancient or contemporary documentation—have a single source point."

"Helena?" Vanessa stated.

"Precisely. And this document..." he tapped the manuscript for emphasis. "...is proof that these two men, Renaud and Everard, arrived at a specific location on a specific date bearing a remnant of the cross."

"But, it doesn't say that. It just says relics," Cassie argued.

"Right, but remember what came earlier in cryptic form? *Crossbeam, blood-soaked wood...?*"

After a few moments of silence had passed, I suggested, "Perhaps this is a good time to let them know what's going on with you, Emily."

Emily looked back and forth between the two men, her eyes growing misty.

"I, uh..." she began. "I..." She turned toward me as if appealing for help.

"Just tell them the truth," I prompted, and then added, "I hear it will set you free."

Elliot's face betrayed his anxiety.

"Jake, what is—"

"Just be patient, Elliot. Emily will tell you everything you need to know."

Drawing a deep breath, she blurted out, "I'm not who you think I am. I work for Nathaniel Prince Epstein, the leader of The Nine."

CHAPTER TWENTY-FIVE

Werner rocked back in his chair as if he'd been punched in the face.

"I...I don't understand."

Emily said, "When I came here, it was as an undercover operative of an organization calling itself The Nine."

"But...but..." Elliot replied, unable to summon anything further.

"I know, I know. It's horrible. I *feel* horrible, which is probably why I sought Jake out last night, made my confession and nearly got assassinated in the process."

"Assassinated?" Werner bellowed. "What the hell is going on here, Jake?"

"Be patient, Werner," I said, placatingly. "All in good time."

Elliot asked, "Whoever this organization is...what is their interest?"

Emily glanced at me once again.

I encouraged, "Just tell them."

She nodded and said, "The Nine are a group of incredibly wealthy European Jews. Together, they represent the single largest block of non-state financial reserves in all of Europe. Nathaniel's net worth alone is somewhere north of forty billion euros."

"As impressive as that is..." Elliot replied, "...what does any of that have to do with finding a remnant of the cross?"

"Because once they find it...they plan to extract DNA and clone Christ."

The silence that filled the room was palpable in its intensity.

Elliot finally said, "That's outrageous! Can it really be done?"

"They believe it can and have dedicated vast sums of capital to insuring its success. You see, as I've already explained to Jake and the others, the devout Jews of the world have never given up on the concept of Messiah."

Werner said, "But, they already got their Messiah...and they didn't want him. In fact, they killed him."

"Right. But the Messiah they're looking for is one who will come with military might and restore the Kingdom of Israel to world dominance, which is what they believe all the prophesies in the Torah predicted. And The Nine are dedicated to raising this cloned Christ up as *that* Messiah."

"Good Lord," Elliot breathed as Werner simply sat in stunned silence.

Werner seemed to think out loud, "As far-fetched as that sounds, if Christ were to be introduced to the world—especially a Christ who, like the original, came with signs and wonders—the Christians of the world would follow him en masse."

"Exactly," Emily affirmed. "Along with millions of devout Jews."

"And you knew all this when you came to work for us?"

"In the beginning," she explained, "Nathaniel told me about the position here—and, of course, I'd heard of you both, I mean, who hasn't—and how he felt it would be a good opportunity for me to gain some practical experience in my field. After you hired me, he began expressing a fascination with what he felt were lapses in Helena's storyline regarding her acquisition of cross remnants, which then progressed to talking about the manuscript, which then led to him basically demanding that I do whatever was necessary to extract information from the manuscript and report back to The Nine.

"You see, even with all their money and power, they have no idea where the remnant is located. That's why they went to such extreme lengths, i.e. inserting me undercover, to gain information from that manuscript. You have to understand that in the beginning, I *was* who I purported myself to be—a young, eager research assistant. I never dreamed it would turn into something out of a spy novel."

"And, why are you having a change of heart?" Werner asked suspiciously.

"Because...well, because in the process I sort of fell in love with both of you and...I just couldn't go through with it."

Werner's eyes blinked rapidly, filling with a hopeful light.

"You...fell in love...?"

"Then..." Cassie suggested. "If what you just said is true, doesn't that remove The Nine from suspicion regarding the whole misdirection thing?"

I said, "That would seem a logical conclusion. However, at this point anyway, I'm not sure logic is even a consideration."

"Speaking of illogical, young lady...if you haven't completed your mission, why did The Nine try to kill you?" Elliot asked Emily.

"I don't know," Emily said softly, her voice grown small with worry. "The only possibility I could come up with is that for whatever reason, they now see me as a liability and are sending someone else to deal with the manuscript."

Pete asked, "Do they know about your change of heart?"

"How could they? I haven't spoken about it to anyone outside of this room."

I said, "You know...it wouldn't surprise me in the slightest if they had a double-double agent somewhere just keeping an eye on you, making sure you do what you're supposed to do."

She was shaking her head violently.

"They wouldn't do that."

"How can you be so sure?"

"Because...I just am," she hedged.

"Listen, Emily, we can't help you unless we know everything. So, if there's something you're not telling us, now would be a good time to get it out."

She drew in a sharp breath, started to speak and then held it for a couple of seconds before saying, "Nathaniel is more than my employer. He's my uncle." Off wide-eyed looks, she added quickly, "Not my real uncle. He and my father were best friends since their childhood."

"Were best friends?" Vanessa asked. "Like, past tense?"

"Yes…up until my father's death. When I was a little girl, Nathaniel was always at our house. In fact, there are none of my childhood memories that don't include him. My father always referred to him as 'uncle Nathaniel,' so it just stuck."

I said, "And, have you been close?"

"Incredibly close. Like I said, he was always at our house from the time I was a little girl."

"And did he ever…?" I prompted.

"Oh…oh no!" she said, horrified at my suggestion. "It was never like that. Quite the contrary. He was never anything but kind and generous. Always buying me presents; telling me he loved me; taking me places and introducing me to his friends as his Shayna Maidel. It means, 'beautiful maiden.' Truly, he was always like a second father. I never had to doubt his love. It's why I trusted him so completely."

"And now?"

"This is what makes this so hard. I just can't believe that…uncle Nathaniel would pass down an order to have me killed. I mean why would he do that? It'd be like killing his own daughter."

"If you don't mind me asking…when and how did your father die?"

"It was two years ago…on a climbing expedition."

"I'm so sorry for your loss," I replied as a suspicion began to form. I brushed it away, but it returned with persistence, so I decided to just get it out there. I asked, "Were Nathaniel and your father together when it happened?"

She nodded quickly.

"Yes, and thank God."

"Why do you say that?"

"Because, if Nathaniel hadn't been there, it's highly likely that we never would have found his body."

I said, "How soon after his death did you go to work for The Nine?"

She considered my question, and then answered, "Uh... perhaps six months afterwards."

I shared a quick glance with Werner and replied, "Did you ever consider the chain of events in light of coincidence?"

"I'm not sure I—"

"Not to be insensitive," I said, cutting her off. "But from the perspective of a completely objective observer—and forensic investigator—here's the way it looks to me: Nathaniel has a grand design in mind, i.e. finding a remnant of the true cross. He learns that Werner and Elliot are hot on the trail. He has something with you he feels gives him leverage. Werner, when did you begin searching for a new research assistant?"

"A little less than eighteen months ago."

I continued, "Nathaniel hears of the opening. I assume you have some expertise in archeology?"

She straightened her posture and said with some pride, "I have a Master of Philosophy degree in medieval archeology from Cambridge University and am enrolled in their independent research program for a PhD, thus my work here with Dr. French and Dr. Spencer."

Elliot interjected, "Cambridge is the top program in the world. So, you can imagine our excitement when Emily applied for the position."

I said, "Okay, follow me: Nathaniel hears about the opening here and suggested it to Emily?"

She nodded.

"Yes, he did."

"And, how many others applied, Werner?"

"Oh," he replied, "There were a good number...maybe... forty or fifty?"

"And you chose Emily because...?"

He reddened slightly.

"Well…because…because, she was…" I knew he wanted to say that she was beautiful and he had fallen immediately and hopelessly in love with her, but instead he went with, "…like Eliot said, Cambridge is the top school on the planet for archeology and Emily was imminently qualified and—"

"Someone offered to make a sizeable donation to the program were she to acquire the position?" I suggested.

He stared open-mouthed before replying, "Well, yes, but—"

Emily said, "Where are you going with this, Jake?"

I paused a few beats before replying, "Emily, I believe Nathaniel was responsible for your father's death."

"But—"

"Hear me out. Would your father have ever agreed to you joining Nathaniel's organization?"

"No. He hated what Nathaniel was doing—in fact, hated everything he stood for."

"But Nathaniel needed to get close to Werner and Elliot in order to learn what they knew about the remnant. And what better way to do that than to use you to accomplish his ends?"

"Wait…" she said, her face losing a bit of color. "Are you suggesting that Nathaniel had my father killed so he could pressure me into—"

"I'm not just suggesting it. Coupled with the events of last evening, I believe it to be a near certainty."

"But…my father was his oldest friend."

"What did you tell me about Nathaniel when we first talked?"

Her eyes went cold as she repeated robotically, "That he was ruthless. And that there is no life he would not take, no promise he would not annul, and no amount of money he would not spend to achieve his objective."

"Is it me you're talkin' about now," said a booming voice behind us.

I turned to see the hulking, beaming figure of Paddy Quinn filling the doorway.

CHAPTER TWENTY-SIX

"Paddy," I said, jumping up to greet my friend. "How did you find us?"

"Well, as it turns out, I'm a detective. It wasn't hard, you know."

In response to everyone's confused looks, I explained, "This is Detective Sergeant Paddy Quinn, formerly of New York's finest, now retired to a life of blissful ease."

"Blissful, my arse," he snorted. "But...pleased to meet you all."

"How you doing? Flight okay?"

"Well, I'm feelin' a mite knackered. Old fellas like me aren't used to keepin' these sort of hours. But I'll live."

After introductions were made all around, I said, "I asked Paddy to come and give us a hand on the case. In all seriousness, nobody in the history of the NYPD has more closed case files than Paddy. He was without question the best at what he did."

"I'll be thankin' ya' to not lay it on too thick, Jacob. No sense gettin' these fine folks' hopes up."

Elliot left the room and returned with a chair for Paddy.

"Here you go, sir."

"Now, young fella, if we're to be gettin' along, there'll be none 'o this 'sir' business. It's just Paddy."

"Fair enough. And in return, we don't run on formalities around here, so we can dispense with Dr. French and Dr. Spencer."

Paddy gave his large head a quick nod.

"Duly noted. So, what were you sayin' before I made my grand entrance?"

I said, "In brief…" I gestured toward Emily, "Emily had just finished telling us about her relationship to Nathaniel Prince Epstein, the leader of a shadow organization calling itself The Nine. He's the one responsible for her working here in the department of archeology. Her purpose was to find out everything she could about the contents of the manuscript open there on Werner's desk and report back."

"I sense a big 'but' comin'."

I nodded.

"But…last night she had a change of heart and decided to not go through with it. At the same time she was telling us about who she really was, two operatives tried to assassinate her. We believe the men worked for The Nine."

He looked at Emily; at Werner; Elliot; the two girls and Pete, and then back to me.

"Pardon me for askin', but if Emily here didn't get 'round to tellin' you all of this until last evenin', then how in blazes did The Nine, or anybody else for that matter, know about it in time to hire the operatives, give them orders, and send them on their way to carry out those orders?"

I started to answer and then realized I had nothing of substance to say.

Paddy continued, "Who else have you told, darlin'?"

Emily's eyes grew wide.

"No one, absolutely no one. I mean who *could* I tell?"

"I see. And did you make a phone call, send a text or email dealin' with the subject?"

"No, nothing like that either. It's almost as if they were reading my mind."

"Or, like you suggested earlier," I said. "For reasons known only to Nathaniel, he decided that you were no longer an asset, gave the order to have you removed and has sent someone else to finish the job."

"Any idea who that might be?" Pete asked.

"Yes. It can only be one person. Gérard—he is Nathaniel's personal assistant. At first I believed that he was merely the one who organized the hit on me. But now, I believe that he will carry out the rest of Nathaniel's plan."

"It is of no importance," I said.

She shook her head violently.

"You don't understand, Jake. Gérard is the worst man I have ever met. He is cruel. Evil. Plus, he is highly skilled in all manner of fighting. If you should have to face him, I fear for you."

Paddy said, "Now, darlin', you obviously don't know Jacob very well, or you wouldn't be worryin' your pretty head. If it came to that—and I hope it doesn't, and so I do—'tis this poxy bastard that would be wise to be afraid...not Jacob."

"He's right," Cassie affirmed. "My uncle has never lost."

"But, he's never faced anyone like Gérard," Emily argued.

I said, "If I had a dollar for every man of whom that was said, I'd be a wealthy man."

"Sure 'n you're already richer 'n Croesus," Paddy growled.

"Be that as it may...I am accustomed to going up against men who are the best in their field. And, Cassie is correct...I have never lost and I don't intend to start now. Besides, we've also got Cassie, Pete and now Paddy with us. You couldn't possibly have any way of knowing this, but with those three beside me, there are very few circumstances I can think of that would give me even the slightest concern." After a brief pause, I asked Werner, "Now, if you are absolutely convinced of this manuscript's authenticity—"

"And I am," he replied.

"Then I suggest we begin putting a plan together to go fetch the remnant."

"But, what about the misdirection thing?" Vanessa asked.

"I don't know what to think about that. Is it true that someone wrapped that manuscript around that pottery? Yes, it is. Do we have any evidence at all that their intent was to mislead us? No we don't. Quite the contrary, it seems as if someone was trying very hard to give us a leg up on the search."

"But, who could have done it?"

"We may never know, and for the time being anyway, we can't spend any more energy than we already have trying to sort it all out."

Werner unrolled a large map of the Middle East and spread it out on his desk. Carefully placing a compass onto the map's surface, he inscribed a perfect circle around an area dominated by a central lake.

Looking up, he tapped the map and said, "Elliot and I have narrowed things down to this general location."

I glanced at the map and didn't recognize a single thing.

"And, where is this location?"

Elliot answered, "At the center of the circle is a town called Beyşehir, on the shores of Lake Beyşehir in south central Turkey. In antiquity, the city was called Pisidia."

A latent, seminarian memory sprang to the surface of my mind.

"'But when they departed from Perga, they came to Antioch in Pisidia.'"

"Excuse me?"

I said, "It's from the New Testament book of Acts—probably somewhere around the middle. The apostle Paul and his traveling buddy, Barnabas, made a couple of trips through Pisidia on Paul's first missionary journey."

"Oh...right. Right you are. Our interest is focused on the years immediately following the Crusades. Specifically, 1206. At the time Renaud and Everard would have arrived in Rodosto, the city would have been completely devastated by war. It, therefore, makes no sense for it to have been any more than a stopping off point."

"Forgive me," Paddy said. "When who, and who arrived where?"

"Oh, sorry. The manuscript mentions two men who arrived at a city called Rodosto on St. Martin's Eve in 1206. We believe it was these two knights who carried the remnant of the true cross from the holy land...not Helena Augusta."

Werner picked up the narrative.

"Politically, Rodosto, at the time, was a hotly contested piece of real estate. As such, two weary knights carrying what they perceived to be precious cargo in the form of the remnant, would have perhaps stayed long enough to re-provision, but then they would have been on their way."

Elliot said, "Now if you look at the map," he indicated a place near the top. "You can see that Rodosto—in modern times called Tekirdağ—is relatively close to Constantinople, or modern-day Istanbul. Our belief..." he began tracing a route, "...is that these two men fled to Constantinople; found no suitable respite there and continued on their way eventually arriving at Beyşehir—

Vanessa asked, "How are you spelling the name?"

"Beyşehir?"

"Yup."

"Oh, it's B,e,y,ş,e,h,i,r."

Vanessa laughed, "I never would've gotten that. It sounds like you're saying *Bayshaits*."

"Yes, well, the Turkic Oghuz contains some quite challenging pronunciations for those of us unfamiliar with the language. And, to be honest, I'm not sure I'm even getting it right. But it's what a native speaker told me, so I'm going to just go with it."

"How far is it between those two cities?" Paddy asked.

"Roughly seven hundred-sixty kilometers."

I traced the hypothetical journey and said, "While I respect your expertise, gentlemen, I find the notion of two battle-weary knights carrying the remnant of the cross on a four hundred and seventy mile overland journey through often hostile territory to be implausible."

"Right," Elliot countered. "However, if you think about it for a moment, I believe you will see the logic."

"Okay, try me."

"At the time, Beyşehir was devastated from the crusades. So much so that it was renamed the *Desolate City*."

Vanessa said, "But, wasn't Rodosto in the same shape? Why go from one desolate city to another?"

"Because it doesn't make sense," he beamed.

"Old son, you're gonna have to help this ol' country boy with that one," Pete replied.

Werner interjected, "Look, if you had something precious in your possession, and your goal was to get it to a place of safety…"

It suddenly made sense to me.

"I get it. It was almost a hiding in plain sight sort of thing."

"Yes," Elliot exclaimed. "That's exactly it. We believe they took it there because everyone else was fleeing the area."

Cassie mused, "Yeah, and why run in to a place others are running *from*?"

The jangling of Werner's desk phone broke the silence that followed.

"Yes?" he answered. "Oh, right. Here he is."

He handed the phone to Elliot.

"Elliot Spencer here." He listened for a few seconds, his already pale complexion going ghostly white. "I see. Yes. I will tell him."

As he handed the phone back to Werner, his hand was trembling visibly.

"What's going on, Elliot?" I asked.

"They…uh…" he began. "They have my mum."

I nodded slowly.

"And so it begins."

CHAPTER TWENTY-SEVEN

Mrs. Fiona Spencer had been in Gérard's custody for a mere ten minutes before he concluded that taking the woman hostage had been a terrible tactical error. Partly, because she was feisty. But also, because...he *liked* the fact that she was feisty. And Gérard didn't like many people. If you developed feelings for someone, it complicated things when it came time to carry out orders.

Take Delilah, for instance.

How she haunted his thoughts and dreams. Her face. Her form. Her laugh. Her sheer grit and intelligence. How often he had imagined them together, doing things that lovers do.

He had been in love once. So long ago now. Long before Nathaniel Prince and The Nine. Long before his soul had begun shriveling under the relentless and cumulative onslaught of the horrors committed on behalf of the great man he served.

But he told himself that he would give it all up for Delilah...if she would have him.

It was a complication when Nathaniel ordered Delilah terminated. At first Gérard hadn't understood. Assassinate Delilah? She was one of them. Family. He had stopped just short of questioning his employer's command. But, if there was one thing about Nathaniel Prince that those in his employ learned quickly, it was that orders were not to be questioned. Ever. Orders were to be carried out regardless of how ludicrously insensible they appeared to be. The man's greatness was such that he saw things that others failed to comprehend. And if he desired something to be done, it was because there was a greater good to be gained.

Besides, who was he, a mere servant, to question the decisions of Nathaniel Prince?

But because of the depth of his feelings for the girl, he simply couldn't bring himself to even consider causing her harm. It troubled what was left of his soul. So much so that he had contracted with two Seattle locals to carry out the deed. When the call had come that they had botched the job, he was at once both relieved and furious. Relieved because she yet lived; furious because he knew that Nathaniel would now demand that he do it himself.

And then there was the knowledge that Emily was not alone. An advocate—a protector—had arisen. Jake Moriarity. And while Gérard had never met the man, he knew about him. Who didn't? Moriarity was a veritable legend among the tactical community and global criminal underground. He supposed a confrontation was inevitable. It was no matter. Gérard would win.

He always won.

Mrs. Spencer interrupted his thoughts by asking, yet again, why he had felt it necessary to remove her from her comfortable home right in the middle of *Last Tango In Halifax*—her absolute favorite series on BBC.

It made him smile. Here was this old woman who had been taken against her will, and rather than manifesting fear—as he absolutely would have expected any normal person to do under the same circumstances—she was complaining about missing her favorite show on "telly."

"Aren't you afraid?" he asked, sitting beside her in the back of the transport vehicle on their way to the private airfield where Nathaniel's private jet awaited.

"Of you?" she exclaimed with a derisive laugh. "You've got to be joking. Why should I be afraid of you?"

He smiled his most evil smile.

"Many people are afraid of me. And for good reason. You see…I am a killer."

She appraised him for several seconds before saying, "You won't kill me. Not while my Elliot has something you want."

"And, what does he have that I want?"

"Well I don't know. But it must be something big, 'else you wouldn't have snatched me from me home."

She was right, of course. About him not killing her.

At least for now.

"And then, of course, there's Jake," she said smugly.

"Jake?"

"Moriarity. Me 'n him are pals."

"And, why should that concern me?"

"Because if he was to find out that you took me against my will, he would come after you, he would."

Why did it seem that everywhere he turned in this operation, the man's name kept coming up?

"Even so," he said. "Where we are going, no one will ever find us until I wish them to do so."

She smiled confidently.

"Jake can find us. He can find anyone anywhere. He's famous for it, you know."

The private airfield came into view. He stared at the waiting jet and pulled a cell phone from his blazer's inside pocket.

After dialing a number, he spoke quietly but authoritatively in his native French, "There has been a change of plans."

Nathaniel Prince, although not accustomed to being dictated to, was nevertheless attentive to what Gérard had to say.

"Okay. Tell me."

"I am taking the woman to Seattle."

That made Nathaniel smile.

"I like it. Go right at them rather than waiting for them to come to us. And what about this Moriarity?"

Gérard said, "He will present no problems."

"That is not what I have heard."

"I have never let you down before, sir, and I do not intend to start now. Whatever his strengths, he has never before encountered one such as I."

"Just the same...take care, Gérard. One does not develop a reputation as formidable as Jake Moriarity's without at least some of it being true." After a pause, he asked, "And how about our guest? Is she cooperating?"

Gérard glanced at Viola Spencer sitting beside him—her face betraying not even the slightest trace of concern.

He found it...unsettling.

"She is fine. All will be well, sir."

Nathaniel nodded silently and disconnected the call.

He believed in Gérard and in his unique abilities. But, he also believed the reports and rumors about Jake Moriarity.

And then there was the American FBI, for whom Moriarity worked. It was an unforeseen complication.

And Nathaniel Prince did not like complications.

Back in the car, Viola Spencer gave Gérard a sidelong glance and said, "I speak French, you know. So I understood every word you said to whoever it was on the other end of that call."

Gérard replied, "It is of no importance. We will go to Seattle. Who knows, you may even get to see your son. You would like that, no?"

"Oh..." Viola replied, "...I'll see Elliot, all right, and Jake will be with him. Just you wait and see."

Seattle.

Where Delilah waited.

How he would loathe killing her.

Perhaps it wouldn't come to that.

But, the great man had given the orders. And he had always followed orders.

He dialed another number on his phone.

"Make the plane ready for a flight to Seattle with a brief stopover in New York."

He ended the call and said, "There are many things to be seen, Madame Spencer. Many things indeed. I look forward to the days ahead with great anticipation. It has been a long while since I have been truly tested. It will be good for me."

"I quite disagree. If you know what's good for you, young man, you will take me back home and not provoke Mr. Moriarity. It won't turn out well for you."

"We shall see, madam. We shall see."

CHAPTER TWENTY-EIGHT

"Why would they do that?" Elliot asked, his voice thin with fear. "Why would they take my mum?"

"Leverage," I said. "By having her in their custody, it's a bargaining chip. You do what they want, or—"

"Or what? They kill her?"

I wanted to tell him that could never happen.

I wanted to tell him that even a man as ruthless as Nathaniel Prince wouldn't kill a helpless, innocent old woman.

But…the man had been willing to have Emily killed—a virtual family member.

That's cold.

"I hate to say this, Elliot, but that's a distinct possibility."

"Good Lord," he moaned while sinking into a chair and covering his face with his hands.

"I said it's a possibility…not a *reality*. Let's not get ahead of things here."

Paddy said, "Make any demands, did they, Elliot?"

Elliot shook his head slowly.

"No. The caller just said, 'We have your mother. You know what to do.' But, I don't have the slightest idea what that means."

Emily cleared her throat.

"I think it means that they want you to give me the manuscript so I can deliver it to them."

Werner slammed both hands down on the desktop causing nearly everyone to jerk.

"So that's what this little charade is all about."

"Werner, what are you talking about?" Emily asked.

"All this talk of The Nine—if they, in fact exist—and their purported attempt to have you killed, it has all been a clever ploy to get us to hand the manuscript over to you!"

"My God, Werne," Elliot exclaimed. "Get a grip, old boy."

"Get a grip? Think about it, Elliot. How do we know she didn't have someone pretend to call and say they have your mother? Call her! Call your mother's cell. I bet she answers."

I said, "In the spirit of covering all the bases, that might not be a bad idea."

Elliot nodded wearily and glanced at his watch.

"11:00 a.m., which will make it 8:00 p.m. in Manchester. She's probably watching telly."

He pulled a number up from his favorites menu on his phone and stabbed the screen with a finger.

"It's ringing," he announced.

I watched as his expression grew ever more worried. Finally, he pulled the phone away from his ear.

"It's no good. There's nothing for it…they have her, Werner. She's never without her phone and always answers on the first ring. Emily had nothing to do with this."

"He's right," Emily said. "You have to believe me, Werner. And you have to believe that this is real or they *will* kill her. I know these people."

I said, "At this point, I'm inclined to believe Emily."

"So, I'm supposed to just hand the manuscript over to her and watch the little turncoat walk out of here with it?" Werner replied.

"Werner, please," Emily pleaded.

"I trusted you," he bellowed. And then more quietly, "I…I…loved you."

His confession, coming as it did in the midst of the tension of the situation seemed to catch everyone off-guard.

"You what?" she replied.

"It's true. God help me, but it's true. I have fallen completely and helplessly in love with you, Emily. And…you have broken my heart with your perfidy and duplicity."

"Werner...I..."

"And I think it goes without saying that whatever else happens at the conclusion of this sad little drama, your services are no longer needed or desired here at the university."

Ah, yes. Unrequited love. It can cause the heart to turn on a dime, so to speak. All that pent-up emotion denied an avenue of expression in one area can quickly recoil and be released with equal passion in another. As someone once said, *"No one can hate you more than someone who used to love you."*

I said to Werner, "Not to be insensitive, but at this point we have far more pressing issues to deal with than your feelings for Emily. Elliot's mother is in mortal danger."

Werner nodded and wiped a hand across his face as if removing some form of offending substance.

"You're right, Jake." After a pause he added, "Please forgive my outburst, everyone."

Cassie said, "There's nothing to forgive, Werner. So, what happens next, Uncle?"

I thought it through for a few seconds and then replied, "I can't explain why...but I think whoever took Elliot's mother is on their way here."

"To Seattle?" Elliot exclaimed.

"Yes."

Paddy asked, "Pardon my sayin' so, Jacob, but that doesn't make any sense at all."

"I know. And that's precisely why I think it's going to happen."

Pete said, "You know...from a tactical perspective I can see your point. They say they have Elliot's mom, and we go flyin' off to find and rescue her, when all along, they're on their way here. And when they roll in, there's nobody to stop them from takin' the manuscript."

"That's right, Pete."

"It sounds *exactly* like something Gérard would do," Emily said. "He's like that—totally unpredictable. Probably why he's never been beaten."

Vanessa grinned broadly.

"But, he doesn't stand a chance against Jake, because Jake's got something that will beat unpredictability every time."

Emily replied, "Yes, I read that about him. Almost a sixth sense thing. Am I right?"

I said, "Oh, I don't know about that. But let's just say that I have been known to display a certain prescience about things from time to time."

Cassie rolled her eyes.

"Oh please, Uncle. From time to time? How about every single time?"

It's true. I do seem to have an extra something when it comes to knowing things that others do not. Whatever it is, I have benefitted greatly over the years from having it.

"So, how are we playin' this, boyo?" Paddy asked.

It was a good question.

And I hadn't the slightest idea how to answer.

"Well...for the time being, there's not much we can do. Even if they were already in route when the call was placed, they're still a good eight to ten hours out depending on the equipment they're flying. And my sense is that they will stop off in New York. Don't ask me why, but that's just how I'm feeling it."

"So," Cassie said. "If they *do* stop in New York, that gives us until tomorrow to make preparations."

"Yes, I've been thinking about that."

Cassie's gaze narrowed.

"I don't like the sound of that."

"Me either," Vanessa added darkly.

"Look," I said lamely, "The complexion of this case has changed drastically since we first became involved. And given that this man, Gérard, is now involved, the potential for danger is very high and I simply cannot put you two in harm's way. So...I'm sending you back to San Diego."

"Uncle," Cassie moaned. "That's not fair. Things are just starting to get exciting and you want to send us home."

"Yeah," Vanessa agreed. "Not fair at all. I mean we could stay in the background well away from the...umm...action and stuff. We'd be safe. Cassie wouldn't let anything bad happen to me."

"No, I wouldn't."

Never a match for my girls when it came to topics being hotly contested, I wilted under the pressure.

"Okay. Fine. You can stay." As they began to celebrate, I cut them off with a curt, "But, you go where I say you go and do what I say you do without contention or your collective bottoms will be on the first flight out of town. Understood?"

They both stood to full attention, shouted, "Yes sir," and snapped off a crisp salute, which they apparently found hilarious.

"Very funny," I chided. "But I mean it."

"I know, Uncle," Cassie said, as she wrapped her arms around me. "We'll be fine. Just give us something to do away from the fray."

I thought for a few seconds and said, "Okay. How about when things start getting dicey—and they will—you stay with Werner, Elliot and the manuscript."

"Oh, now wait a second," Werner protested. "You're going to leave us and one of the most important archeological documents on earth in the care of a...a girl?"

Pete said, "Excuse me for sayin' so, Dr. French, but that there little girl could pert near kick my butt if I wasn't payin' attention. Believe me, she's fierce."

I added, "She's also an expert marksman and is highly trained in a variety of martial arts." Werner was staring at Cassie skeptically, so I suggested, "Pete...attack her."

Without missing a beat, Pete lunged toward Cassie, who easily sidestepped his initial thrust, grabbed his outstretched arms and executed a perfect judo hip throw landing Pete on his back on the floor where she immediately maneuvered into position to execute a Brazilian jiu-jitsu arm bar, which, had she been serious, would have resulted in his elbow joint being completely shattered.

The entire exercise had taken less than ten seconds.

Cassie and Pete stood, bowed to each other in the martial arts tradition and resumed their former positions with neither one of them breathing hard.

"Uh," Werner said. "That was…impressive. Okay. I'm good."

Elliot was simply beaming.

"Oh, I say. Good show. Bloody good show."

CHAPTER TWENTY-NINE

Cassie was attempting to explain to Werner and Elliot how she had been able to toss a man over her shoulder that outweighed her by more than a hundred pounds, when my phone started buzzing.

It was Aaron.

I stepped out of the office to take the call.

"Aaron," I said in greeting.

"Hey, sugar. Miss me yet?"

"You have no idea. How's it going back there?"

"Well, it's interesting. I mean here I am getting ready to perform for the President of the United States, so you'd think that the focus would be on technological excellence, right?"

"Sounds reasonable."

"Yeah, well, according to Muriel and Eddie, the front of house sound is marginal at best."

I said, "Interesting. So, what's the problem?"

"You mean besides having a front of house sound engineer who can't even spell 'frequency' let alone hear one?"

Aaron has a real hard time with sound engineers. In his opinion, jazz shouldn't be reinforced electronically, but rather experienced in intimate gatherings without the intrusion of electronics. Hard to pull off when you're the premier jazz pianist on the planet and routinely sell out venues in excess of five thousand seats.

"Oh, come on, Aaron. It can't be that bad."

"No man, I'm serious. We'd be better off if they just turned off the damn PA system and just let us play. The Kennedy Center has incredible acoustics. Everyone would hear the music as it's meant to be heard without some joker behind the mixing console messing it all up."

"I'm guessing Snake didn't come with you?"

"Snake" was Theo Brown, Aaron's long-time sound guy who typically went everywhere with him.

"He didn't make the trip. Daughter had some big thing goin' on at school. I told him to stay home and be a dad because surely the Kennedy Center would provide a quality sound engineer."

"Oops."

"Nah man, it'll be all right. If I have to, I'll just have my manager raise all kinds of holy hell and go straight acoustic."

"So, when do you go on?"

"Show starts at 8:00 p.m. So I've got some time to kill… and maybe an engineer or two."

I laughed.

He continued, "Now, tell me what's happening in Seattle."

I filled him in as concisely and expeditiously as I could, but it still took close to fifteen minutes to get it all out.

When I was through, he said, "Damn, Jake. Sounds like some serious stuff goin' down. Want me to head up there tomorrow and lend a hand?"

"Well, yeah, but aren't you guys going to tour the Capitol or anything?"

"Did all that yesterday. Truth of the matter is, neither Muriel nor Eddie is really all that into it. I could send them on back to San Diego in the morning on our scheduled flight, book a flight to Seattle and probably be there by mid-afternoon."

Paddy and Pete together should be sufficient to handle anything that might come up, but the thought of having Aaron alongside of me bolstered my courage and lifted my spirits in ways I can't really explain.

I said, "Okay, but only if this doesn't impose on your plans."

"Impose on my plans? Who you think you're talkin' to?

Impose on my plans? That's a hell of a thing for you to say to me!"

"All right, already. Come. Get here as soon as possible. Sheesh."

He laughed.

"Yeeeaaaah man. Now that's more like it. You gonna hook me up with a heater?"

"Heater" is slang for firearm.

"Oh, I might be able to scrounge something up."

"Be good to see Paddy again. I haven't seen that old S.O.B. for years."

"He'll be glad to see you too. Okay, so let me know what time to expect you and one of us will be there to pick you up."

"Sounds good. And Jake?"

"Yeah?"

"Try to stay alive until I show up. I got me a feelin' about this one."

"I know. Me too."

He disconnected the call and I returned to the office.

"Was that Aaron?" Vanessa asked.

"Yeah. And he's flying out tomorrow to join us."

Paddy said, "Ah, ya don't say. That's a good thing, and so it is. I haven't seen the boy for, probably five years now."

"He's looking forward to seeing you too, Paddy."

Emily asked, "Who are we talking about?"

I explained, "Aaron Perry. My best friend, frequent companion on various cases, and the best jazz pianist on the planet."

Her eyebrows arched upwards.

"That Aaron Perry?"

Cassie giggled, "Yeah, *that* Aaron Perry."

Pete added, "Don't let the man's musical credentials fool you. He's a straight up lethal operative: former combat Marine, sharpshooter and master of multiple forms of martial arts. He's also six-four and around two hundred and sixty pounds, none of which is fat. Strongest human I've ever worked with. I'd pick Aaron to stand beside me in a tussle over almost anyone I know, Mr. Moriarity here being the lone exception."

Emily flattened her mouth into a straight line and nodded her head slowly.

"Sounds very impressive."

Vanessa said, "It almost sounds like you're assembling a dream team to take on these guys."

"Yeah," I replied. "Well, if they are anywhere near as capable as I imagine them to be, it's going to take everything we have and then some to prevail."

Elliot asked, "Since my mum was kidnapped, are you going to involve the FBI?"

Ordinarily, kidnapping is the absolute purview of the FBI. But in the case of International incidents wherein a foreign national is kidnapped on foreign soil and then transported to the United States...while it might be clear to some of my colleagues at the Bureau, if you want to know the truth, it all starts to look like the underside of an embroidered cloth to me.

I said, "My very basic understanding is that since she is a British citizen—and that the kidnapping happened on British soil—it's a bit of a gray area. Technically, if in fact this Gérard guy actually brings her here, then the FBI would assist in apprehension, but the British authorities would have to extradite and prosecute. It's all about sections and sub-sections of the law and very difficult to get anyone to speak authoritatively on the matter."

"So," he said. "For the time being you're going to do this on your own?"

"For the time being. And, honestly, I'm comfortable with that."

"Then...so am I."

Werner asked, "What next, Jake?"

I glanced at my watch.

"Well, since it's 12:15...I'm thinking lunch."

Paddy said, "Now there's a fine idea, and so it is."

Since everyone was in agreement that it was, indeed, a fine idea, we all headed out to find an appropriate place to have lunch, which, predictably, turned out to be a matter of some discussion. In the end, we settled on a pizza place that was, apparently, a favorite of the local student population.

The pizza was good, and the beer was cold.

The day was looking better and brighter, at least until we got the call that someone had broken into Werner's office.

CHAPTER THIRTY

We crammed the remaining pizza down our throats and ran for our cars, committing more than a few moving violations in our haste to return to the university.

The university police were already there when we arrived at 1:30 p.m. and doing a passable job of examining the crime scene. I had a bit of a standoff with their sergeant until I flashed my FBI credentials and told him that it was my case, had been my case prior to the break-in and that if he didn't back off I'd have the place swarming with agents. After a bit of needless posturing, he relented and told his officers to stand down.

The office was a wreck. It looked as if a mini-tornado had swept through leaving chaos in its wake. Books had been pulled off shelves. Desk drawers emptied. Papers strewn everywhere.

I said, "Werner, where did you leave the manuscript?"

Sweating profusely, his face ashen with worry, he marched across his office to one of the bookshelves. Triggering a hidden button of some sort, the shelf swung outward to reveal a hidden safe set into the wall. Squatting down, he keyed a code into the electronic pad and opened the heavy steel door. Breathing an audible sigh of relief, he stood holding the precious manuscript in his hands.

"Good Lord," Elliot said. "That is a beautiful sight to see."

Paddy pulled me aside.

"Jacob, with this break-in it is readily apparent that we can't relax our guard even slightly."

"I agree. But, short of posting guards on this office 24/7, I'm not sure how to proceed."

He jerked his head toward the campus police sergeant and his officers who were hovering around the doorway and outer office.

"Have laddie-buck there and his boyo's put a guard on this place. Give them something important to do."

I thought about it. On the surface, it made sense. But there was something bothering me.

I called the sergeant over.

"Do you know who called in the crime?"

His head swiveled toward one of his men and he jerked his thumb in his direction.

"That would be officer Woodley over there."

"Okay, and how did he discover the break-in?"

"He was on routine patrol and noticed that something was off. So he came inside and found the office as you see it."

The story stunk like three-day-old fish.

I said, "I'm going to need to interview officer Woodley."

"Sure," he replied before shouting, "Woodley, Mr. Moriarity needs to talk to you."

Woodley looked up from a conversation he'd been having with another officer. I saw a flash of something in his eyes. Fear? Concern? He hesitated only slightly and then made his way over to where the three of us stood.

Woodley was a younger fellow, perhaps twenty-five or twenty-six; 5'8" or 5'9" tall and stocky, after the manner of guys who spend a lot of time in the gym.

"Yes, sir," he said very politely.

I asked, "Officer Woodley, I hear that you are the one who discovered the crime scene."

"Affirmative. I was on my usual patrol when I noticed the outer office door open to the hallway."

"And that's unusual?"

"Yes, it is. Dr. French and Dr. Spencer are real sticklers for doors being closed and locked when no one is in the office."

Paddy said, "So, it made you suspicious, did it?"

Pete moved over to join the conversation, taking up a position a step behind officer Woodley.

"Like I said, if they aren't here, those doors are never open," Woodley replied.

"And is it your usual practice to come by durin' the lunch hour?" Paddy continued.

He hesitated slightly, and then said, "I wouldn't say it's unusual. It's kind of a timing thing. I have a particular area that I'm responsible to patrol. So depending on what's going on in other places—conversations I may have with staff and students—I could be delayed by five or ten minutes. But given that it is Dr. French and Dr. Spencer's practice to go out for lunch every day, along with their assistants, I try to swing by here between twelve and one on the days that I work."

I said, "So, walk me through it. You're on patrol; walking down the hallway, I assume, and...what...you notice the outer door standing open?"

"That's affirmative."

"And then what did you do?"

"I called the Sarge and told him what I was seeing and that it made me suspicious. He told me to go ahead and check it out and get back to him. So I entered the outer office and saw Dr. French's door standing open. I called out his name and received no reply, so I drew my service weapon and entered the office where I found it as you see it."

"And you didn't see anyone either in the office or fleeing the scene?"

"No sir, I didn't."

Pete asked, "About what time was this, officer Woodley?"

Woodley turned to glance at Pete, seemingly surprised to see him there.

"Uh, I'm going to say it was about 12:30."

I made eye contact with Pete and Paddy and then said, "So...we all left for lunch at 12:15; I personally watched both doors being locked behind us; you came by fifteen minutes later and found Dr. French's office in this condition. Tell me, officer Woodley...how is it possible that someone could have broken in and in a mere fifteen minutes, create the level of destruction you see around you?"

He blinked rapidly a few times without saying anything. A dead give-away that an answer was being formulated that would be anything *but* truthful.

The sergeant said, "That's a fair question, Woodley. You have an answer?"

His answer was to turn and attempt to run through Pete.

Big mistake.

Besides outweighing Woodley by a good sixty pounds, Pete is just one tough son of a bitch. Woodley never had a chance. He was on the ground in under twenty seconds.

I said, "Sergeant, I need you to take officer Woodley into custody for us and hold him for further interrogation."

His face as hard as stone, he replied, "It will be my pleasure. Harris! Banks! Hook Woodley up and take him back to the holding cell."

The other two officers did as instructed and marched Woodley out of the office with him fighting them every step of the way.

The sergeant was shaking his head.

"That's a real surprise. Woodley has been one of my best officers."

I said, "Well, we are dealing with very wealthy, ruthless and influential people here, sergeant. They will stop at nothing to achieve their goals."

"And, what are their goals?"

"I can't tell you just yet. But let's just say, that it involves a matter of profound historical significance that could involve billions of dollars."

He nodded his head curtly.

"Fair enough. And listen...about our initial meeting, I

apologize for my attitude. I tend to get a little territorial. Please know that moving forward, you have the full cooperation of my department."

I shook his hand.

"Thank you, sir. I really appreciate it."

"Now, if you'll excuse me, I'm going to go kick Woodley's butt around the station for a while. Let me know when you need access to him and he'll be available."

He left and instructed the other two officers to stay behind and assist us in whatever manner we deemed appropriate.

Cassie asked, "So, that officer did all this?"

"Apparently."

Werner was shaking his head.

"I can't believe they got to officer Woodley. He always seemed like such a good guy."

I said, "Well, even good guys can be turned if the price is right."

Emily added, "And, trust me, Nathaniel would have made sure that the price was right."

"So, you're sayin' he made him an offer he couldn't refuse?" Paddy asked.

"Something like that. I'm sure that along with the bribe there would have been subtle, or not so subtle, threats of bodily harm or death to him or someone he cared about."

Vanessa said, "I have a question."

I indicated for her to continue.

"How did this Nathaniel dude even know to reach out to Woodley?"

Paddy chuckled.

"Now that's an interestin' question, and so it is."

He was right.

I said, "I don't know, Vanessa. I mean did they work their way through the entire campus police force until they found someone who bit? Or did they have prior knowledge about Woodley that made him a prime candidate?"

Emily cleared her throat.

"If I may…Nathaniel has resources that rival any intelligence gathering agency on the planet. My guess is that he went through the campus police roster and found something out about officer Woodley that could be used as leverage against him either in the form of a threat or perhaps a certain proclivity toward something unsavory…or perhaps he was just greedier than his colleagues."

"Well, whatever the case, we have just been given an example of just how extensive Nathaniel's reach really is. And as Paddy reminded me a few minutes ago, we cannot afford to relax our guard. We got lucky this time. Next time might not work out in our favor."

Elliot's cell phone rang. He glanced down at the caller ID.

"It's my mum."

CHAPTER THIRTY-ONE

I took the phone from him and answered.
"Yes?"
A deep, male voice spoke in heavily accented French.

"Dr. Spencer?"

"No. This is Jake Moriarity. May I assume that I am speaking with Gérard?"

"Moriarity," he breathed. "Yes. I have been expecting to speak with you. I suppose this is fortuitous."

"Well, if ever we meet, I assure you that you will change your opinion."

"Ah, is that a threat, mon ami?"

I said, "I do not threaten. I merely inform. If you have taken the time to check out my reputation—and I am quite sure you have—you will have noticed that I have never lost, nor do I intend to start."

"Yes, but reputations can be bought and sold. Who is to say what is real and what is…how would you say…yes, a product of overactive imaginations."

"Cut the crap, Gérard! You and I both know it's real."

"Whether it is real or not will be determined soon enough. You see…I too have never—"

I cut him off, "What do you want?"

"What do I want? I thought that was obvious. I want the manuscript and you are going to give it to Emily."

"And?" I prompted.

"And she will take it where I direct her to take it."

"And then, I suppose, you will kill her."

"Whether I do or do not is of no concern of yours."

The guy was really starting to tick me off.

I said evenly, "You're out of your league with me, Gérard. I know you think you're a really bad guy, but you can't win this time. Period. Furthermore, if Emily so much as sustains even a bruise, I will take you apart piece by piece until there is nothing left to identify."

He pressed on as if I hadn't spoken.

"You will give the manuscript to Emily or suffer the consequences."

"And what might that be?"

"I have Dr. Spencer's mother. And I am prepared to cause her a great deal of suffering if my wishes are not met."

I decided to let him know that I knew his plans.

"Well, I guess we'll see about that when I, along with agents from the FBI meet you at Boeing Field in Seattle."

I heard a slight intake of breath and then, "How very clever you are, Moriarity. How very clever, indeed."

"It didn't require cleverness to figure out your play, you piece of shit! It's so amateurish a schoolboy could've done it."

I could feel the tension beginning to build, which was exactly what I wanted.

"Do not underestimate the resources of Nathaniel Prince."

I said, "Is this the part where you tell me how powerful he is? Well, don't bother. Because when it comes to resources...I have the United States Federal Bureau of Investigation at my disposal. It is *you* who should not underestimate me. Oh, and, by the way, there will be agents at every possible landing site in the Seattle area, so good luck setting that bird down without getting swarmed by law enforcement officials."

Of course, I hadn't even discussed the case with my friend, Zack Hastings: Special Agent in Charge of the Western United States. But I knew he'd go along with whatever I needed.

I could hear Gérard's breathing tick up a notch.

He said, "And what if we set down just long enough to throw whatever is left of Mrs. Viola Spencer onto the tarmac? How would you like that, you smug bastard?"

With Elliot standing three feet away, I couldn't really call Gérard out without sending Elliot into complete panic.

So, I replied, "You won't do that. Because real men don't hurt women."

Silence.

Then, "We will speak again shortly."

And the line went dead.

Elliot said frantically, "What's happening? Is my mum okay?"

I handed his phone back to him.

"My sense is that at present she is fine. Gérard was making some very unsettling threats regarding her safety, but I don't think he will go through with it."

"Don't be so sure," Emily warned. "You have no idea how evil the man can be."

I stared at her for a few seconds before asking, "And how was he with you, Emily? Was he ever rough? Cruel? Degrading?"

"Well…no. He was always very polite…" she paused as a small smile stretched the corners of her mouth. "At times, he almost seemed flirtatious."

"And have you ever heard of him hurting a woman?"

She thought for a moment and then replied, "Come to think of it…I have not."

"Then, I think Mrs. Spencer is safe for now."

Paddy asked, "So, what is the lad goin' to do, Jacob?"

"His task is to secure the manuscript. I'm pretty sure right about now he's feeling all kinds of stupid for kidnapping Elliot's mother because, A) I don't think he has the emotional capacity to harm her, and, B) we didn't panic and immediately acquiesce to his demands. So, with all the effort he's expended thus far, he is no closer to accomplishing his goal. Which could produce some interesting dynamics."

"How so?"

I said, "When you are hyper-focused on one thing like he is—and the thing seems to be getting further from your grasp instead of closer—it tends to make you sloppy. Taking Elliot's mom is a perfect example. He didn't think it through." I suddenly had a very intrusive thought. "You know…"

When I didn't say anything else, Cassie prompted, "Is there something that goes along with that?"

"Oh, yeah. I was just thinking that we should go get the wood."

Werner said excitedly, "You mean…go to Turkey? Just like that?"

"Sure. Why not? You claim to know where the remnant is. So, let's go get it."

Werner and Elliot looked at each other, a combination of panic and elation warring for dominance on their faces.

Pete said, "I like it. When that ol' boy rolls in, we'll already be gone and he won't have the slightest idea how to find us."

I asked, "Werner, how long do you need to make preparations?"

He was shaking his head back and forth, opening and closing his mouth as if he couldn't bring organization to his thoughts.

Finally, he replied, "Okay, let's see…we've already applied for entrance visas. We have the funding. We would need to book flights, secure ground transportation and lodging once we are in-country. So…" he paused and glanced at his watch. "It's 2:15 p.m. The main thing will be the flights and just the chore of packing. So, let's say…we could potentially be ready to go day after tomorrow."

"Not good enough," I said more tersely than I intended. "We need to be on our way by tomorrow afternoon at the latest."

"I just don't see how that's possible. I mean the packing of our equip—"

"Forget the equipment. If necessary, we'll acquire what we need once we're there. In fact, we need to take carry-ons. Nobody checks luggage."

Pete said, "What about firepower? You got a hook-up over there?"

I grinned and replied, "Oh, there's always a hook-up for the right price."

We were all gathered around Werner's desk.

Except Emily.

I glanced around the office.

"Anybody know where Emily went?"

"Possibly to the restroom?" Vanessa suggested.

Werner suddenly swore loudly and prolifically.

"The manuscript is gone!"

I wasn't prepared to believe what my eyes were seeing. The safe, standing open, just as Werner had left it when the call from Gérard had come in, was now missing its most important item.

Which meant that Emily was every bit as crooked as Werner had suspected.

"She can't have been gone long," I said as I moved into the outer office to question the two campus police officers. "Did you see Ms. Young come through here?"

The one with a nametag that read, "Barnes" replied, "Yes sir. She ran out of here about five minutes ago like the devil himself was after her."

I felt like a fool.

I don't like feeling like a fool.

"Cassie, Vanessa, stay here with Werner and Elliot in case she decides to double back. Pete, Paddy...with me." To the two officers, I said, "Can you two assist us?"

Barnes replied, "We'll have to call it in, but I don't see why not."

As the officer radioed his sergeant, Elliot asked, "Jake, do you think this was her plan all along, or was this something spontaneous?"

"I don't know, Elliot. I just don't know. But for some reason, it feels more like a spontaneous move. But we won't know for sure until we catch her. Speaking of which..."

Barnes gave me a thumbs-up, and the five of us left the office in pursuit of the perfidious Ms. Young, who had some serious explaining to do once we found her.

And we *would* find her.

CHAPTER THIRTY-TWO

Emily Young was in total panic. She hadn't planned to grab the manuscript out of the open safe, but when everyone had been crowded around Werner's desk and discussing the trip to Turkey, she couldn't resist.

It had been spontaneous.

It had been reckless.

It had been...necessary.

She did not want to die, and having survived one attempt on her life, she had little reason to believe that she would survive a second. Nathaniel Prince was not accustomed to failure. And if, indeed, he had determined that she was now a liability, he would keep coming for her until she was dead. Of that she was certain. She also didn't want Werner and Elliot to be exposed to Nathaniel's relentless pursuit, for he would find them eventually. And when he did...their lives would be snuffed out with no more thought than he would give stepping on an ant that had strayed into his pathway. And then there was Elliot's mother. She was a sweet, innocent lady. If she handed over the manuscript, Nathaniel would have nothing to gain by killing her.

Ducking into the women's restroom of the arts and science lab, she pulled out her cell phone and dialed a number from memory.

"You are calling quite late. This better be good," Nathaniel said in greeting.

"Nathaniel, I have the manuscript."

"Yes, I know you have the manuscript. Which is exactly why you are in the trouble you are in."

"No," she countered. "I mean I took it. I have it...Dr. French does not."

Her pronouncement was greeted with silence.

"Well now," he said finally. "This is interesting. Most interesting indeed. And, where are you, child?"

She nearly gave away her location, but something checked her.

"I'm...in a safe place. For now."

"I see. Fair enough. And, how do you wish to proceed?"

She hadn't really thought anything through. What was she supposed to say?

"I...well, I am hopeful that this demonstrates my loyalty to you to the extent that you call off Gérard or any other goons in your employ. It was unsettling to realize that you think so little of me that you ordered me terminated." She added for emphasis, "Uncle Nathaniel."

"Yes...I can see how it would be. It wasn't personal, my child."

"First of all...stop calling me that. I am *not* your 'child.' And secondly, it's hard to get more personal than having someone killed."

She could hear the anger in his voice when he replied, "Careful, Emily. You forget your place."

"No, just the opposite. I am now quite well aware of my 'place.' I have the manuscript, and you do not. I am open to negotiation, but I must warn you that the cost will be high."

"And, what makes you think you can trust me? After all, I *did* try to kill you."

Now fully immersed in the process known as stream of consciousness, she continued to make the narrative up as she went along.

"Because you want the manuscript more than you want to end my life. You see, I have it memorized and I intend to destroy the original. Oh, and there are no copies."

He hissed, "You wouldn't dare."

"Really? Remember who it was that provided the primary influence in my life. It was you. All of that ruthlessness you have practiced throughout your life, well…it rubbed off on me. So, don't test me, old man. If you want to find the remnant of the cross—and, trust me, it does exist—I am the only one who can lead you to it."

In the resulting silence, she could hear his breathing quicken. She had him hooked. She was sure of it.

He said, "For the sake of discussion, let's say that I agree to go along with this…this extortion. What will it cost me?"

She just blurted out the first figure that came to mind.

"Thirty million euros."

He laughed.

"I see you haven't lost your sense of humor. Now, let's try again, only this time with a more reasonable number."

"You're right. That was just off the top of my head without giving it any thought. The real number is fifty million."

"Preposterous! Unthinkable! I don't have that kind of—"

"You can dispense with the feigned outrage, Nathaniel. You and I both know that your net worth is in the billions. Fifty million is, as the Americans say, chump change to a man with your resources. Oh, and Mrs. Spencer will be released unharmed and you will stay away from Dr. French and Dr. Spencer."

"Of course," he hedged, "I could agree to everything you say; allow you to lead me to the remnant…and then kill you."

"Oh," she said putting a brightness in her voice that she did not feel. "Didn't I tell you? You will deposit the money in an offshore account in the Cayman Islands. As soon as I have the routing numbers and security codes, I will send you the coordinates. And with fifty million euros at my disposal… I can completely change my identity—my appearance, if I so desire. In short, Nathaniel, you will never see me again."

He chuckled darkly.

"I know you think you are being so clever. But if I want to find you, I shall."

"Okay," she replied. "Then the deal's off. Goodbye, Nathaniel."

"Wait!"

After a few seconds silence, she prompted, "Yes?"

"As much as it pains me to say so…you have bested me. Okay. It will be as you wish. Fifty million euros in exchange for the coordinates to the location of the remnant. Give me a day to arrange the—"

"You have two hours."

"Two hours! Impossible!"

"Nathaniel," she chided, now feeling as if she were in complete control. Her knees had even stopped shaking. "Please. Can we dispense with the pretense? A man with your connections could get it done in half that time. Two hours. I will await your call."

She pulled the phone away from her ear and stabbed a finger toward the "end" button.

"Oh, Emily," she breathed as she buried her face in her hands. "What have you done?"

CHAPTER THIRTY-THREE

Realizing that Emily couldn't have gotten far, we split up and first began clearing the three floors of the building that housed the department of anthropology and archeology, although in my heart I knew she wouldn't be found. So, after about five minutes, I broke away from the others and walked outside where I stood stone still in one spot, just breathing and feeling.

Where would she have gone? Unless she had the hidden physical skills of a world-class sprinter, the radius would be fairly small. My eyes settled on an adjacent building across the quad. The sign read, "Department of Arts and Sciences."

"Bingo," I said out loud to no one in particular before setting off at a quick jog.

Once I was in the lobby, I stopped again and surveyed the immediate surroundings. There was a large foyer from which three hallways originated. One directly in front of me, and one to the right and another one to the left. Just to the right of the center hallway was a staircase, which I assumed led to the second floor.

She wouldn't be there. She would have stayed on the ground floor.

And where would she hide? Where is the one place a woman can be universally assured of privacy from the eyes of prying men?

The women's restroom.

Consulting the directory posted between the center hallway and the staircase, I found arrows pointing in opposite directions for the men's room and ladies' room. The ladies' room was down the hallway to the right.

I started confidently in that direction.

I never saw the man coming.

He came charging out of a classroom on the right-hand side of the hallway shoving me hard into the wall.

He was a big guy.

Bigger than me.

And strong.

But the problem with a lot of big, strong men is that they assume that strength and body mass are an advantage. I suppose there are instances where that would be true, for example, a 275 pound man going against one that only weighed 150 and the smaller man had no self-defense skills.

However, that was not the case this time.

Whatever advantage he had in weight—perhaps 25 or 30 pounds—I more than compensated for by being quite advanced in street fighting skills. In short, he didn't have a chance.

Following the initial collision, he attempted to get his arms around me, supposedly to attempt some form of crushing maneuver. But I managed to snake my arms up through his and get my hands locked around the back of his neck. I immediately began brutalizing his lower abdomen with knee strikes, one or more of which must've hit home in a very sensitive area because all the air whooshed out of him and I could feel his legs start to give way. Since he was falling anyway, I used the momentum to pull his face into a particularly brutal knee strike that broke his nose and sent him into unconsciousness.

Once he was on the ground, I made sure his airway was clear and that he was breathing before I called Pete to let him know where I was and what was transpiring. He said he'd bring the campus police with him and take the man into custody. Fortunately, I had some zip ties in my tactical trousers, which I employed liberally in securing the man's hands behind him.

Leaving him in place, I continued down the hallway until I came to the women's restroom whereupon the question arose, "How do you surreptitiously enter a women's restroom at a major university without scaring the crap-weasels out of an innocent party who may be inside doing their business?"

I don't know. I figured if there were anyone inside besides Emily Young, I'd just have to rely on my FBI credentials.

With my ear to the door, I listened carefully for signs of movement. Hearing nothing, I eased the door open, fully prepared to hear the sounds of shrieking females. But, I didn't see anyone.

I said, "Emily? If you're in here, you need to come out."

Silence.

I tried again, "Emily. It's Jake. You're not in trouble. Just come out and let's talk about how to resolve this."

Still nothing.

Okay, so there was nothing for it but to check each one of the six stalls. Squatting down, I peered under the partitions but didn't see anything. Which didn't necessarily mean anything. She could have drawn her feet up when she heard me come in. So, I went down the row, opening each door slowly. When I got to number four, although it was also empty there was a lingering fragrance.

Emily's perfume.

I was certain of it, for it was very unique.

I had just finished off the other two when the door opened and two chatty coeds entered. They took one look at me standing half in and half out of the last stall and one of them began to scream. I fumbled around for my credentials, finally managing to hold them up where they could see them, and attempted to calm the terrified girl down.

Pete, having heard all the commotion, came charging in behind them prompting another round of shrieking, this time accompanied by jumping and flapping of arms.

Apparently, Pete is a far more scary prospect than I.

When we finally got the two calmed down and I explained why we were in there, the one who had been doing the most screaming said, "What does she look like again?"

"She's mid-thirties; medium height with short brown hair; expensive cut; slender frame, but looks like she works out. She has sort of hazel colored eyes and was last seen wearing jeans, a white sweater and black leather jacket."

Pete added, "And she's right purdy."

The girl screwed up her face.

"What did he say?"

I translated, "He said that she's pretty."

"Oh, okay. I think I saw her come into the building about twenty minutes ago. I had just come down the stairs when she ran through the entrance and down the hall out there. She was in such a hurry, she almost ran me down."

I said, "You sure it was her?"

"Well, no. But that woman definitely matches your description."

"Thank you for your cooperation. It has been very helpful."

"By the way," she asked. "What's up with the cops out in the hallway? Does the guy they're taking into custody have anything to do with this?"

"Possibly. Now if you'll excuse us..."

I let the sentence trail off and pulled Pete out into the hallway with me, the girls staring after us in confusion.

"So what's up?" he asked. "Was she here?"

"I'm sure of it. You know that scent she wears?"

"Yeah, buddy. Never smelled anything like it."

"Well, she sort of left a scent trail behind in one of the stalls."

"Huh," he said. "And how about the big dude you took out? Do you think he was another guy sent to eliminate her?"

"Has to be. There's no other explanation."

"But, how did he know where to find her?"

I thought about it for a moment.

"My guess is that she called someone from the stall—probably Nathaniel—to strike some sort of deal to deliver the manuscript to him and get him to call off the dogs." Something else occurred to me. "She won't give him the manuscript. That would play right into his hands. What she must've done is…yeah…I bet she asked for a sum of money—enough to go somewhere and start over with a new identity—and once the money was delivered, she'd reveal where the remnant is located."

"That right there is a bold move. They must've been tracking her cell signal, and the dude out in the hall was supposed to take her out and retrieve the manuscript."

I said, "That is certainly a plausible explanation."

"But…?" He prompted.

"I don't know. There's something that bothers me. Something having to do with Gérard. Something Emily said about him."

"You talking about what she said about him sorta havin' a thing for her?"

"Yeah. And if he did—does—there's no way he'd allow anyone to put their hands on her. If she had to be taken out, he'd do it himself."

"That's cold."

"It is. But it all depends on the level of control Nathaniel has over him. Does that control override matters of the heart?"

Paddy came up behind us.

"Jacob, there's somethin' you'll be wantin' to see."

"What is it?"

"Just come with me."

As Paddy led us out of the building, across the quad, I asked, "Can you at least tell me what this is about?"

He stopped walking and faced me.

"I'd rather you just have a look first without any preconceptions."

"Okay. Fair enough."

We resumed our trek, which seemed to be leading toward a building that housed several administrative offices.

Paddy blew through the front entrance without hesitation, walking quickly past three young receptionists, all of whom appeared to have recently seen a ghost.

It made me very nervous.

Down a short hallway and then into an office with a temporary sign reading, *"Emily Young: Research Assistant."*

The campus police sergeant was in the office, standing by the side of a desk...behind which sat the apparently lifeless form of Emily Young.

CHAPTER THIRTY-FOUR

Upon closer examination, I realized that her eyes were open and filled with fear.

Paddy said, "The young lady appears to be sufferin' from some form of induced paralysis."

I moved around the desk to stand beside her, turning the chair around to face me.

"Emily, if you can hear me, blink your eyes."

She immediately complied.

"Okay, good. I'll pose yes and no questions. One blink for yes, two blinks for no. Do you know who did this to you?"

She blinked once.

I asked Paddy, "Who found her?"

Paddy said, "After the officers hustled off to help Pete with the situation in the other buildin', I continued searching. When I came into the outer office there, the three young lasses were just comin' out of Ms. Young's office, cryin' and carryin' on somethin' terrible. When I asked what was wrong, they just pointed to the open door. I looked in; saw her sittin' here; and after callin' for the sergeant to watch over things, I went lookin' for you, and so I did."

"I don't see any evidence of struggle."

"Nor did I," Paddy confirmed. "But there is this."

He pointed to a small, pinprick on the side of her neck about two inches below her left ear.

I bent in for a closer look, her eyes tracking me.

"Emily, did someone inject you with something?"

She blinked once.

Glancing around the office, I spotted her purse, upended and emptied of its contents.

"Did they take the manuscript?"

Another blink, followed by a tear.

Pete said, "So, maybe that fella back there wasn't a lone wolf. Maybe they had a team tracking her, just waiting until she surfaced so they could take her out and retrieve the manuscript."

I was feeling quite emotional. And I don't know why. Probably because in the short time I had known her, I had grown very fond of Emily Young. Not in a romantic way. More along the lines of admiring who she was as a person—her drive; her passion; her intelligence. The way I had it figured, taking the manuscript was a desperate attempt to save her life.

I said, "Emily, did you take the manuscript in an attempt to get Nathaniel to withdraw the order to have you killed?"

More tears and another blink.

"And to save Mrs. Spencer and direct attention away from Werner and Elliot?"

One blink.

I cupped her face in my hands and kissed the top of her head.

"Okay, listen. You're not in trouble…at least not from me. You did what you had to do. I'm sure that Werner and Elliot photographed the manuscript and—"

She blinked twice.

"You're saying that they did *not* photograph the manuscript?"

One blink.

I glanced at Pete and Paddy.

Emily's tears began falling freely and she began struggling to breathe.

I instructed the sergeant to summon medical and said quietly to my colleagues, "The paralyzing agent is working its way toward her lungs. Without knowing exactly what it is, the only thing we can do is help her breathe. Help me, Pete."

While Paddy cleared the way, Pete and I picked Emily up and gently laid her inert form on the desktop.

Paddy said, "Probably Ketamine. She'd be able to hear, feel...but remain completely paralyzed. Based on my recollection, the short cycle would be around twenty minutes."

Pete asked, "And it'd affect her breathing?"

"Not typically," Paddy replied. "But it's been known to happen."

Leaning in close, I said, "Emily, whatever they injected you with is affecting your breathing. I'm going to have to help you breathe until the EMT's arrive.

She blinked once in understanding as the tears continued to flow.

I tilted her head back, pulled her jaw open and began doing what I could to help her breathe. It was an interesting experience performing mouth-to-mouth resuscitation on someone who was fully conscious. Kind of like a one-sided, quite awkward form of making out.

The sergeant said, "Medical is about ten minutes out."

"Thank-you." To Emily I whispered, "Hang in there with me. Help is on the way."

As I continued the process, I felt her lips move of their own accord and noticed in her eyes that she was trying to get my attention.

Leaning in so my ear was right next to her lips, she managed to whisper, "I have been wondering what it would be like to kiss you."

It made me laugh.

"That's just the drug talking. But the fact that you are able to vocalize even slightly tells me that the paralysis is beginning to wane. This is good, Emily. This is real good."

Pete asked, "Is she speaking?"

"Yeah. It seems she's on the downside of the cycle."

Through more tears Emily struggled to say, "I thought I was going to die."

"Not today, my friend. Not today."

"I'm so ashamed, Jake. This isn't—"

I placed my fingers gently over her lips.

"Don't worry about anything, Emily. We'll sort it all out later. Do you think you can breathe on your own now?"

She attempted a smile.

"Well, if I say yes, does that mean you'll stop kissing me?"

"That's funny." To the others I said, "She's able to breathe on her own again."

"Saints be praised," Paddy exclaimed while crossing himself.

"Emily, you indicated that you know who did this to you. Can you tell me who it was?"

"Yes," she whispered. "It was Ramón."

"Okay. Who is Ramón?"

"He's Nathaniel's other assistant."

"You mean, besides Gérard?"

"Yes. Gérard may be ruthless, but Ramón is heartless. The only reason he didn't kill me is because he fears Gérard. He…told me he wanted to. And he…he touched me. Everywhere."

A commotion in the reception area and then four paramedics rolled in accompanied by their Captain.

I said, "This young woman has been injected with a paralyzing agent. Probably ketamine…" Something occurred to me and I added, "Possibly front loaded with dilaudid. She seems to be coming out of it, but she's still critical."

"Trouble breathing?" the fire Captain asked.

"Yes, which is why I suspect the addition of dilaudid. But it seems to be subsiding."

"Okay. We'll take good care of her."

I glanced over at Emily, whose fear-filled eyes were brimming with tears.

She blinked her eyes rapidly. Trying to tell me something. I excused myself and shouldered through the group of EMT's gathered around her in a frenzy of activity.

Leaning in close, I asked, "Something you want to tell me?"

She said, "Ramón will meet Gérard wherever he decides to land. You need to find him before he can pass the manuscript off." More tears and then, "I...memorized the manuscript. But, maybe something in whatever I was injected with...I don't know...but I can't remember anything about it. Everything is just gone."

One of the EMT's tapped me on the shoulder.

"Sir, we've got to roll."

I nodded and patted Emily's face.

"I'll see you at the hospital. And don't worry, we'll get this sorted out."

I backed away and the young firefighters carefully lifted her onto an EMT stretcher, strapped her in and rolled it out the door.

I said, "Paddy, you packing?"

Patting a hidden appendix holster, he replied, "Always."

"Then, would you mind accompanying her to the hospital? I don't think she's in any further danger, but I'd rather err on the side of safety."

"It would be my pleasure, Jacob."

Pete and I watched him lumber over to the truck and inform the EMT's that he was going with them. Climbing through the open rear doors, he sat down close to Emily's head, patted her shoulder and told her he was going to be with her and not to worry, as he'd keep her safe.

Pete said, "That old fella seems like one tough sum'bitch."

"You have no idea. But the thing is...the toughness is mainly mental. I'm sure he has his moments—we all do—but I have never known the man to fear anything. I've seen him in some pretty extreme situations, and he just taps in to something deep inside and wills himself forward."

The doors slammed shut, and the paramedic ambulance roared out of the parking lot—lights flashing and siren wailing

—with the firetruck close behind.

Pete asked, "What's next?"

People keep asking me that. And…I never know what to say.

The thing is, life is unscripted. Never is this truer than in situations like the one we were facing. Even if I had a clue about what to do—and I most assuredly did not—who's to say that by the time I executed said plan the dynamics would remain the same? The manuscript was gone and Dr.'s French and Spencer, for reasons known only to themselves, didn't think to photograph it. And even though Emily claimed to have memorized it, some weird drug interaction was messing with her memory and it was anyone's guess as to whether she'd recover the memory. And Pete wanted to know what happens next?

I said, "We need to go back to the office and talk to Werner. If this Ramón guy really is in possession of the manuscript, we've got a lot of work to do to catch up." I paused, mulling over a thought that had suddenly presented itself. "But, I don't think he plans to hand it off to Gérard, like Emily suspects."

"Why not?"

"Think about it. What's the fastest way to get an image to someone?"

"Ah, yeah. He'd just snap a photo on his phone and text it to that Nathaniel feller."

"Right, My guess is that he did that immediately, and even if he does give the manuscript to Gérard, Nathaniel will already be well on his way to prepping an expedition to fetch the remnant. In fact, my guess is he's already told Gérard to turn the flight around and return to base."

"Well, shit."

"My thoughts exactly."

CHAPTER THIRTY-FIVE

Nathaniel Prince stared at the enlarged image of the manuscript on his computer monitor, attempting to decipher the obscure references and vague directions. He had to admit to feeling let down. His expectation had been that once in possession of the manuscript, the truth would unfold before his eyes clearly marking the pathway to the object of his desire. However, he now knew it was going to take monumental effort. But, it would come, of that he was certain. In the meantime, he had things to do, not the least of which was summoning Gérard back from the now unnecessary flight to Seattle.

He dialed the number on his SatPhone and waited while the call connected.

"Yes," came Gérard's immediate reply.

"Where are you?" Nathaniel asked.

"Somewhere over the Atlantic. Approximately three hours from New York."

Nathaniel said, "Turn around and head back. The situation has changed."

"Changed? How?"

"Ramón has the manuscript."

"Ramón? How did—"

"He has been in Seattle for two days."

Gérard felt the first tickling of fear.

"Delilah?"

"Don't worry. She is alive…for now. Although I can't say for how long."

Gérard said, "He obtained the manuscript from her? How?"

"It seems she stole it from Dr. French and then called me with an outrageous demand, which I agreed to meet in order to buy time. Ramón has been tracking her movements at the university, and it was a simple matter, really, to take it from her."

"Simple?"

"He injected her with a paralyzing agent."

Gérard decided that the next time he saw Ramón, he would kill him in the most painful manner he could devise. Maybe paralyze him first so he could see and feel but not be able to move. Just like he had done to Delilah.

He said, "That was a mistake."

"What? Taking the manuscript?"

"No," Gérard growled. "For Ramón to touch her. It was a mistake."

"Ah, yes," Nathaniel said. "I forget. You have feelings for the girl. Well, so do I. She's like a daughter to me. But there are times when one must do what must be done regardless of the cost." After a pause, he asked, "Are you still with me, Gérard?" When there was no answer, he prompted, "Gérard?"

Something switched in Gérard's brain. Something on a primal level. What he said next was arguably driven by emotion, but it was emotion he'd kept pent up for far too long.

"I have served you well, Nathaniel Prince," he said evenly. "I have carried out your wishes precisely, expeditiously and without questioning."

"Is there a 'but' coming?"

"Call it what you will. I am serving notice that Delilah is now under my protection. If any harm comes to her, I will reciprocate in kind. Are we clear?"

Nathaniel was taken aback. No one spoke to him in that manner or in that tone of voice. Especially not Gérard. He found himself temporarily at a loss for words. At once both flummoxed and fuming.

He said finally, "Are you…threatening me, Gérard?"

Was he? He supposed he was. And it felt good.

"Think of it more along the lines of a promise. And before you begin to imagine how you can retaliate, keep in mind that you have no one to carry out your threats. Everyone fears me, for I am the best there is."

He was, of course, correct. Gérard *was* the best; it was why Nathaniel had hired him in the first place these long years ago. But if he allowed anyone—even Gérard—to threaten him and get away with it, control would begin to slip away. And once it began, trying to regain it would be like trying to grasp water with your hands.

Nathaniel said, "I am disappointed in you, Gérard. I thought our relationship was stronger than this."

"Relationship?" Gérard replied around a dark laugh. "You have just revealed the extent to which you value relationships. Your coldly calculated decision to have Delilah eliminated exposed your true character."

"Fair enough. So, how do we proceed?"

Nathaniel Prince knew exactly how he would proceed, but he was attempting to buy time by posing the question.

Gérard, for his part, *also* knew exactly how his employer would proceed and, in that regard, had already thought several moves ahead.

"I will continue on to Seattle; pick up Delilah and keep her safely in my custody until this thing with the remnant is settled."

"And, what if I decide to send Ramón to take her from you?"

"Ramón," he said derisively. "Ramón is a child compared to me. He would be no more trouble than a gnat. If you did, in fact, make such an ill-advised decision…it would cost you more than you can possibly imagine."

"So," Nathaniel countered. "We now find ourselves on opposite sides?"

"Not on opposite sides, Nathaniel. We are on the same side but with contrary agendas. Mine is to protect Delilah. Yours is to eliminate anyone perceived to be standing in the way of you possessing the remnant. I believe in the end, I will prevail."

Nathaniel couldn't remember a time when he had experienced the level of anger he now felt. Of all the things in life he despised, betrayal was at the top of the list. He had had people killed for far less than what Gérard was doing. Many people. Then again…Gérard had been the one doing the killing. He hated to think about the possibility of his own weapon being turned against him. Time to lay aside his pride and embrace expedience.

"Gérard, my good friend, I do not wish to be at odds with you. Let us do this…let us lay aside our grievances—our disagreements—and finish what we began these long years ago. I need you to be with me, mon ami. You have always been my strong right arm. So, what do you say? Can we work together?"

Gérard was not a stupid man. He neither believed a word of what Nathaniel proposed, nor did he think for one second that he, operating on his own, could withstand the might of Nathaniel's resources. So, he did what Nathaniel had suggested: he embraced expedience.

"I will remain in your service on one condition."

"Name it."

"Delilah is off the playing field. She is no longer a consideration."

Nathaniel would agree to the demand simply because in the end, they would both be dead anyway.

"It will be as you desire," he replied in his most winning tone of voice.

Gérard knew it was a lie, but perhaps it would give him the time he needed to do what he had in mind.

First on the list…kill the bastard Ramón with his bare hands.

CHAPTER THIRTY-SIX

We were gathered back in Werner's office, attempting to come to grips with the reality that the manuscript and all the intricate clues contained within—along with our hope of capturing the remnant—was gone forever.

Werner sat behind the desk, his elbows planted on the desktop, head buried in his hands.

"It never even occurred to me to photograph it," he moaned.

Elliot concurred, "Nor I. And I cannot provide even the slightest, cogent reason."

Pete said, "So basically, we're screwed, glued and tattooed."

Vanessa kept fidgeting, so I asked her what was wrong.

"Well," she replied. "Are you saying that if you had a picture of the manuscript that you could find the remnant?"

Werner said, "That may be an oversimplification, but… yes."

She nodded for a few seconds before saying, "Okay. Well…I can make that happen."

"How?" he asked.

"I have a photographic memory."

My head jerked toward her with enough velocity to crack several vertebrae in my neck.

"You what?"

"I have a photographic memory," she replied matter-of-factly, as if it were common knowledge.

I appealed to Cassie who shrugged and said, "First I've heard of it."

I stared at Vanessa.

"And, you don't think that this was something you should have shared with us?"

She frowned.

"No. I mean why would I? It's not like it's a big deal."

"Well, right now it is." I paused and then said, "Just to be clear, you're saying that you could reproduce the manuscript with all the detail?"

She pondered the question for a second or two before replying, "So, I'm not saying that I can draw the map because, well, I'm not an artist, but as far as the written portion, yeah. I can see it clearly in my head."

Elliot said, "With all the details?"

She smiled and nodded.

"Yup. All of it."

We all sort of stared at each other for a bit before Werner slapped a blank piece of paper onto the surface of the desk and said, "Show me."

Vanessa took the proffered pen, sat down at the desk, bent over the blank sheet of paper and started writing.

My phone started buzzing.

It was Paddy.

"Paddy, what's happening?"

"Just callin' to report that the young lass is goin' to be fine. She's regained movement in her extremities—stiff, but it's comin' along."

I said, "That's good news. Has she said anything about remembering details from the manuscript?"

"We were just talkin' about that very thing and, I'm sad to say that she continues to draw a complete blank."

"Well, that's okay because, come to find out, Vanessa has a photographic memory."

"Jesus, Mary and Joseph! You're puttin' me on."

"No, it's true. I didn't know anything about it and neither did Cassie."

"Huh. Should I tell Emily?"

I said, "Not just yet. It'll be better if she keeps trying to remember. Because, if she's forgotten the details of the manuscript, who knows what else the drugs caused her to forget?"

"That's a good point, Jacob. Okay, then, I'll keep an eye on her and stay in touch."

Paddy rang off and I updated the others on what he had reported.

Werner shook his head slowly, a deep frown etching his ruddy features.

"Part of me wishes that she'd just stay paralyzed."

"Werner," Elliot exclaimed. "What a simply awful thing to say."

"I know...I know. But what she did was unforgivable."

I said, "And what if I told you that a big part of the motivation driving her actions was to draw attention away from the two of you and to secure the release of Elliot's mother? How would you feel about her then?"

"Is that true?" he replied.

"Yes. All of it."

"Well...I..." he sputtered.

Elliot said, "What my dear friend is trying to say is, he now understands that Emily did what she had to do in order to save lives—hers included. Because in the end, lives are more important than anything the manuscript represents."

Vanessa lifted her head, a triumphant smile lighting up her pretty face.

"Okay. I'm done."

Werner and Elliot bent over the page, closely scrutinizing what Vanessa had written.

"Good Lord," Elliot breathed. "It's accurate down to the most minute details. Well done, young lady. Well done."

"This...this is remarkable," Werner added. "I've always heard about photographic memory, but I've never actually encountered someone who had it."

Vanessa shrugged.

"Like I said, it's not a big deal. I mean I've always had it."

With a wink she continued, "Gotta' tell ya', it really helped in school."

I asked, "With what Vanessa has provided, can you find the remnant?"

Werner replied, "Without question."

"Then, make the plans because Nathaniel has a one hour head start on us, and I have a feeling that every minute counts."

"Right," he said and immediately dialed a number on his phone.

"While he's doing that, we need to make some plans of our own, not the least of which is getting you two girls back to San Diego."

"Hold on a second," Vanessa challenged. "So, you're telling me that even though I single handedly saved the whole expedition…you're sending me back to San Diego?"

Cassie stomped over and stood next to her.

"Yeah, what about it?"

Now, I must tell you that in the realm of male to female negotiations I am a notorious loser. There's just something about it that turns me into a sniveling ten-year-old boy.

"But, the danger will be unprecedented. I cannot in good conscience—"

Cassie interrupted, "We can take care of ourselves. Besides, what if you get into a situation where you need Vanessa's memory for clarification?"

She even batted her eyes for emphasis.

Vanessa joined her.

I appealed to Pete, who held his hands up in surrender.

"Don't look at me, Mr. Moriarity. I got no dog in this fight."

Sometimes in conflict, discretion most definitely *is* the better part of valor.

I said, "This is a terrible idea. I just want everyone to remember that I said it. But…okay. You can come."

The girls jumped around like high school cheerleaders

at a homecoming game where the home team has just scored the winning touchdown.

My phone buzzed.

It was Aaron.

"Aaron, what's happening?"

"Well, we're going on in about an hour, but I wanted to tell you that I'm on a 7:20 a.m. flight tomorrow that will get into Seattle around 10:00 a.m."

"Great, that should work out perfectly. But, be prepared to jump onto another flight as soon as you land."

"Really? Things moving along, huh?"

"I'll explain everything when you get here, but circumstances have changed and we're in an accelerated timeframe."

"If it's accelerated, wouldn't it make more sense for me to just get on a flight and meet you…uh, where we goin' again?"

"Istanbul."

"Okay, meet you in Istanbul? I mean seems like a waste of time to crisscross the country like that when I could—"

"Nah," I said, interrupting him. "I don't like it. Can't really tell you why, but I want you to be with us whenever we move out."

"All right. Then I'll make sure I catch a few hours sleep."

"Be good to see you, bro."

"You too. Didn't feel good from the beginning about not being a part of this."

I said, "Me either. Well…see you tomorrow."

"Yes, indeed."

As I stabbed the "end" button on my phone, I was suddenly filled with a renewed sense of hope.

Aaron was coming.

Everything was going to be all right.

It was a good thought.

A hopeful thought.

Too bad things don't always turn out like we hope.

CHAPTER THIRTY-SEVEN

The rest of the afternoon and evening were filled with a chaotic mix of intense planning and visceral reaction to the events set in motion by Nathaniel's procurement of the manuscript.

He was closer than we were by half a world.

His resources were virtually without measure.

Ours were limited by departmental budgets, special endowments and grants.

He was already well on his way to Beyşehir.

We were stuck in Seattle desperately trying to get our act together.

It didn't help that Werner and Elliot were bickering. At the core there seemed to be a pitched struggle for control. Thus far, Werner was winning.

Finally, I'd had enough.

"Hey," I hollered, causing both men to jump. "You two are acting like a couple of schoolboys who have the hots for the same girl. If we are going to have even a prayer of getting to the manuscript before Nathaniel, you need to knock this shit off and concentrate. Do I make myself clear?"

Werner brushed a strand of stray locks behind his ear and said, "Sorry, Jake. Truly I am. It's just that Elliot and I have always—"

"Been competitive," Elliot interjected. "It started long ago and, as you can see, continues to this day. For my part, I will attempt to curtail my need to be in charge."

"But," Werner added. "Someone has to be in charge. I vote that you be in charge, Jake."

"Hear, hear," Elliot seconded.

I said, "Okay. But if I am in charge, it's one hundred percent or nothing. Do we have an agreement?"

They both nodded their acquiescence and we left them to their planning and headed over to the hospital to check in on Emily.

Once in the car, Cassie asked, "So, give it to me straight, Uncle. What kind of odds are we facing?"

I said, "Well, if I were a betting man...I'd give up betting."

"That good, huh?"

"Look, it's not that I doubt our abilities as a team, especially with the addition of Aaron."

Vanessa exclaimed, "Aaron's coming?"

"Oh, yeah. I sort of forgot to tell you. He'll be here around 10:00 a.m. tomorrow."

More shrieking erupted from the back seat.

Pete said, "It'll sure be good to have the big guy along."

"Yes," I agreed. "Yes, it will. To my point...I don't doubt our abilities. I mean we have a pretty stellar track record of prevailing against whatever is thrown against us. And the people we've gone up against haven't exactly been lightweights."

"But?" Cassie prompted.

"But, Nathaniel Prince is a whole different animal. Ruthless and resourceful."

"How is he different from, oh, say, The Persian?"

She was referring to Bahar Ghaznavi, aka "The Persian," who, along with Hayato Momotani—Oyabun of the Yakuza crime syndicate—were ringleaders of a global cartel specializing in the theft and resale of Holocaust art. We not only destroyed their syndicate and sent Ghaznavi to prison for the rest of his life, but were also instrumental in helping to return many works of art to the families from whom they were originally stolen during World War II.

I knew what she was asking: *"If we took those two down, then how could Nathaniel Prince be a problem?"*

On the surface of it, it was a fair question. And I suppose answering, "You're right. He won't be a problem," wouldn't be out of line. But...even though I had yet to meet Nathaniel Prince face-to-face, there was something tingling in that special sense I had that said we needed to proceed guardedly, circumspectly and all the other adjectives that would describe one's comportment when in the presence of a black mamba.

I pulled the rented SUV off to the side of the road, put it in park and turned in my seat so I was facing everyone.

"As you all know, I don't do a lot of planning when working a case. Plans, in my view, can become their own form of bondage, if you follow my meaning." Based on their nods of understanding, I continued, "But that doesn't mean you shouldn't be prepared for what you are likely to face...and I've got to tell you...I think in Nathaniel Prince, we are facing a foe the likes of which we've never seen."

Pete asked, "Can you be a little more specific, Mr. Moriarity?"

I thought through what I wanted to say and then replied, "My sense is that the man is pure evil."

"Evil like Paul Morgan?" Vanessa said.

"Yes and no. Morgan was evil—consummately so—but he had no resources. Nathaniel Prince is everything Morgan was with the addition of nearly limitless resources. I mean, think about it: he literally wants to rule the world, thus his desire to clone Christ and through him launch a global theocracy with him and his cronies at the head and Jesus as their puppet."

"That's sick."

"Yes, it is. More than that, though, it's evil...on many, many levels."

Pete said, "But, he can't do anything unless he gets his hands on the remnant, right?"

"That's right, Pete."

"Which," Cassie added, "...is why we have to get there first."

I eased the vehicle back into the traffic lane.

"Yes. And even though we're fighting against Nathaniel's time advantage, I believe there's still a chance that we can do that."

The rest of the way to the hospital, everyone was lost in their own thoughts, alternately checking their phones and staring vacantly out the windows. There was really nothing left to say until we had some actionable information from Werner and Elliot. Then again, perhaps when we got to the hospital, Emily would be more conversant and would be remembering things more clearly.

My phone buzzed.

It was Gabi.

"Ms. Marcus."

"Mr. Moriarity," she replied. "Any further developments since last evening?"

I laughed humorlessly and said, "Oh, you could say that."

"Okay. I'm intrigued. Care to fill me in?"

"Yeah, uh...where to start. So, I suppose the biggest development is that Emily Young stole the manuscript."

"She what?"

"Yeah. Stole it, and then got ambushed by one of Nathaniel Prince's operatives who injected her with some kind of paralyzing agent and then stole the manuscript from her."

"Oh, goodness, is she all right?"

"I think so. We're actually on our way to the hospital to check in with her."

She said, "But, what about the remnant? How are you going to find it without the manuscript?"

"Well, as it turns out, our little Vanessa," I flicked my eyes to the rearview mirror to see her smiling at me, "has a little secret she's been keeping from us."

"Oh, do tell."

"She has a photographic memory."

"Seriously?"

"And she proved it by reproducing the manuscript word for word, nuance for nuance."

"I'm...stunned. I've never known anyone with a legitimate photographic memory."

"Me either," I replied. "She said she's always had it."

"Well, okay then. So, where does that leave you?"

"Nathaniel's operative—a real piece of work named Ramón—undoubtedly took a photo of the manuscript and texted it to his boss immediately. And a man like Nathaniel Prince doesn't have to wait around for things to happen. He snaps his fingers and makes things happen."

"So, he's probably already well on his way with preparations."

"Indeed. Werner and Elliot are hustling, trying to get things together so we can leave for Turkey tomorrow afternoon."

"After Aaron arrives?"

"How did you know he was coming?"

She laughed.

"Muriel and Eddie are flying here to Vegas and are going to stay with me while our men are off saving the world."

"Ah, that's great. That's really great. I'm so glad to hear it. Pete will be thrilled as well."

She was silent for a few beats before saying, "I still don't feel good about this, mister."

"I know what you mean. But...it has to be done because these people have to be stopped."

"And you're the only one who can do that?"

"Something like that."

"Be safe, Jake. I need you."

It took me a couple of seconds to reply given the wad of cotton someone had just shoved down my throat.

"The feeling's mutual. I love you, Ms. Marcus."

"And I love you, Mr. Moriarity. God help me, but I do."

As we ended the call, I felt girlish arms encircle my neck from the backseat, as Cassie said, "It never gets any easier, does it?"

I patted her hand.

"No...no it doesn't."

"Don't worry, Uncle. We'll be okay. Aaron's coming."

And there it was—the sudden and strong realization that I had been feeling less than adequate without my friend's presence. And I wondered...when had that happened? Whenever it was, the feeling was far more deeply entrenched than I cared to concede.

"You know it, kiddo," I finally replied.

Of course, there was no way in hell I'd ever let the big guy know how I felt.

CHAPTER THIRTY-EIGHT

The members of The Nine, minus one, sat in a hastily arranged meeting at Nathaniel's chalet. They did not have far to come as most of them were permanent year-round residents of the chalet itself, or one of the several lavishly appointed outlying buildings that made up the compound.

Affixed to the northernmost wall of the conference room—and covering the entire wall—was the latest and best ultra-high definition monitor. Projected on its surface was the photo of the manuscript Ramón had sent to Nathaniel. And even though most of the men in the room wouldn't have been able to tell you what it all meant to save their souls, they were, nevertheless, to a man excited, for it represented one of the final elements of the plan they had worked so hard to birth and nurture.

Nathaniel stepped up to the monitor and pointed to a section nearly obscured by the poor lighting.

"Note the variance in the lettering just here." He moved his hand and continued, "And here…and here…also…here."

"What does it all mean, Primus?" Number Two asked.

Turning to face his colleagues, Nathaniel answered with a zealot's glee, "It means, my friends, that we now know *exactly* where to find the remnant of the true cross. I have already taken the liberty of assembling a ground crew and arranging for all the financing this expedition will require."

"And," Number Two continued, "do you have a reasonable expectation of how long this will take?"

"Actually, I do. We plan to have our operatives on the ground tomorrow before sundown. After they are in-country,

I believe it is *reasonable* to expect that the remnant will be in their possession by no later than two days from now."

Number Five asked, "And what about this Moriarity fellow? Are you concerned at all about the potential he represents to impede or even thwart your plans?"

"While Jake Moriarity is a formidable opponent, we have directions to the remnant. He does not. And even if, by some stretch of the imagination, he had a copy or a photograph of the document, we will have a considerable time advantage. I find it impossible to believe that a counter expedition could be launched in less than three days' time. After all, Dr.'s French and Spencer are just department heads at a medium sized American university. Their resources pale in comparison to ours. No, my friends, I do not fear Jake Moriarity."

Number Six asked, "And what about Delilah? Is it your intention to have Ramón, as they say, finish her off?"

Emily Young's face suddenly filled Nathaniel's imagination—a memory from when she was still a little girl...innocent, pure, absolutely lovely...the light of his life.

"Dear Number Six, I know the source of your query. It comes from the deep well of affection you have for the girl. Don't forget that she is my niece. I too have great affection."

"But, you ordered her execution."

"Yes...yes, I did, and I regret the decision. But...to your original query, I believe she will pose no further hindrance to our goals. My choice is to simply let her be at this point."

Number Two asked boldly, "Is that due to Gérard's reticence to do her harm?"

Nathaniel turned swiftly toward the source of the question and shouted, "It is due to my decision to let her live. That and nothing more."

"So, you're saying that if you gave Gérard the order to kill the young woman that he would carry it out without hesitation?"

He thought back to the last conversation with Gérard and his statement that Emily—or Delilah—was now under his protection. The traitor.

He said very evenly, "I am still in charge here and everyone who works for me carries out my wishes, or they suffer severe consequences. Now, if there is no more discussion on the matter, can we please move on? We have many details to work —"

"And who will carry out these consequences?" Number Two said brashly, cutting him off.

"Excuse me?"

"Gérard is gone. Ramón is gone. In short, your henchmen are nowhere to be found. So, I repeat, who will carry out these consequences you so direly referenced?" He hurried along without waiting for a response. "I will tell you who…no one! You are all alone, Primus and we can do whatever we so desire."

Primus smiled.

It was not a pleasant sight.

"So, it would appear that the mutinous thread of DNA I had believed snuffed out along with Number Eight's miserable life has found another host. A willing vessel so to speak."

Nathaniel pulled a sleek, nickel plated Walther PPK from his right coat pocket and calmly shot Number Two where he sat. The bullet caught him exactly in the center of his forehead causing the unfortunate man's body to splay awkwardly, his sightless eyes staring into infinity.

Clearing his throat lightly, Nathaniel said, "Now, as I was saying…if there is no further discussion on the matter, can we please move on? There are many details demanding our attention."

In the midst of nervous and horrified glances, the rest of the members nodded or voiced their acquiescence leaving Nathaniel wondering if there was anybody left within their ranks that he could trust.

He thought not.

Just as well. He had been on his own his entire life. Some things never changed. And he was fine with that.

Two men appeared from a panel concealed in the wall to the right of the video screen. Hard men. Men with scarred faces and cold eyes. They moved without a sound to where Number Two's body sprawled ingloriously, hoisting him to their shoulders and carrying him out the same portal through which they had just entered.

The remaining six members sat stone still and staring, pondering what had just transpired. Two of their number summarily executed one day apart. But even though their minds were reeling, no one wanted to draw attention to himself by voicing a question. Better to be quiet, circumspect, for it had become quite obvious that their leader had tipped completely over the edge of sanity into the cold depths of madness.

As the panel slid seamlessly back into place, Nathaniel turned to the men and asked collegially, "Anyone care for a cognac?"

CHAPTER THIRTY-NINE

When we arrived at the hospital, to our complete surprise we found Emily Young almost fully recovered from the effects of the drug, which, as we suspected, had in fact been ketamine frontloaded with dilaudid. She was doing well enough that the attending physician said that as far as he was concerned, she could be released. While I wasn't certain I *wanted* her released, short of remanding her to police custody, there was really no compelling reason to keep her in the hospital. Following a quick conference with Pete and Paddy, we decided all would be better served if she just came along with us. At least that way we could keep an eye on her.

The ride back to the apartments was…strained; conversation was muted; no one was in a very good mood. I mean even though I understood the dynamics driving Emily's actions, in my mind she was still not to be trusted.

She had fooled me.

I don't like to be fooled.

If you want to know the truth, I hate it.

But, after another hastily consumed meal, a practice that was becoming far too common, we arrived at our lodgings about 8:00 p.m. and immediately began to make plans for the next day's trip. I say "make plans", but really, there wasn't much for us to do except show up with our luggage and the weapons we had brought along with us.

Which brought up another issue: firepower. There was no way in hell I was going to engage Nathaniel and his goons without some serious weaponry.

It was time to call Zack.

That would be Zack Hastings, the FBI's Assistant Director In Charge of the Western United States and my direct supervisor. He's kind of a big deal, but we're pals and his friendship and loyalty to me has never wavered.

It was 9:15 p.m., the time when guys like Zack were just getting going.

I dialed his number and he answered on the second ring.

"Jake Moriarity," he said. "How the hell are you?"

"Doing well, Zack. Are you home or out making some poor agent's life miserable?"

"Ha. I'm actually in Salem meeting with the Oregon SAC's. Just standard departmental stuff. We just broke up for the night and are on our way to a late dinner." After a pause, he asked, "So, can I assume that this isn't a social call?"

"Right. I've got a situation I could use your help on."

"Okay. Give me the details."

"I'm working with a couple of archeology professors at a university up here in Seattle: Werner French and Elliot Spencer."

"You've worked with Spencer before, right?"

"Good memory. So, they got their hands on a manuscript from the thirteenth century that they claim contains detailed directions to the remnant of the true cross."

"As in, Jesus' cross?"

"That's the one."

"Hasn't that already been done...finding the remnant, that is?"

"According to their research, it's all very suspect. It's a long and complicated story, but they believe—and they have some pretty compelling evidence to back it up—that they know where the actual remnant resides."

He said, "And I suppose they want you to go get it?"

"Yeah, which wouldn't be a problem except that they aren't the only ones going after it."

"What a shock."

"I know, right? There's a group somewhere in Europe

calling itself The Nine—"

"Stop it!"

"I'm not kidding. The Nine are led by an honest to goodness piece of shit named Nathaniel Prince. These people have virtually unlimited resources and they also want the remnant, but not for archeological purposes. These men are ultra-orthodox Jews who, while rejecting Jesus as Messiah, have never given up on their hope that Messiah would one day come with military might, wipe the earth clean of their enemies and set up a global theocracy with, you guessed it, them at the center. And to pull this off, they intend to extract DNA from the remnant and clone Christ."

Zack was silent for a few seconds and then said, "Well, damn. It's like a science fiction version of an Indiana Jones movie."

"Oh, it gets better. They had a plant inside of the archeology department at the university. A young woman named Emily Young. She was Dr. French's personal research assistant and a legitimate doctoral candidate with all the credentials. Turns out she's Nathaniel Prince's niece and was sent to work undercover so French and Spencer could be tracked all the way to the remnant's location. Well, for reasons known only to her, she had a change of heart last evening and confessed everything to me, shortly after which, a couple of local thugs—working in The Nine's employ—tried to kill her. After that, she promised to help us stop her uncle."

"But…?" he prompted.

"But…this afternoon she stole the manuscript. We caught her, but not before one of Prince's operatives got to her, injected her with a paralyzing agent and took the manuscript from her."

"So," he asked, "did she survive?"

"Yeah. It was a ketamine/dilaudid cocktail, so the effects were powerful, but with a short shelf-life."

"Okay, the manuscript is gone. May I assume that they had photographic backup?"

"Believe it or not...they didn't."

"You're joking!"

"Sadly, I'm not. But, get this...unknown to any of us, Vanessa has a photographic memory."

"What?"

"Yeah. She sat down and in about thirty minutes reproduced the manuscript in flawless detail."

"That little girl is just full of surprises. So, how can I help?"

"Well," I said. "We're leaving tomorrow afternoon for Turkey—the location of the remnant...south central Turkey, to be exact. Nathaniel will have had several hours head start on prepping a team; his resources are vast; and geographically he's much closer. His flight time to Istanbul is about three hours, and from Seattle it's close to sixteen. So, we're really hustling to get our shit together. Where I could really use your help is hooking us up with appropriate weapons and ammo."

"Okay. We talking the usual Jake specials, or do you need something more robust?"

"If I were to compose a wish list, it'd include a Barrett M82 sniper rifle; two Sig Sauer P226 Tacops .357 pistols with four twenty round magazines each; two suppressed HK G36's along with a *Standard* DP-12 tactical 12-gauge shotgun and an HK416. Oh, and the standard body armor for four burly men."

He laughed, "That's it? That's all you want? No armored vehicles or anything like that?"

"I know it's a big ask, Zack, but this is scary stuff. The whole cloning thing sounds like a long shot, but with the kind of money Nathaniel Prince has at his disposal, he can hire the top geneticists on the planet. Publically, the scientific community is being pretty coy, but I know cloning of mammals—large mammals—has been going on for quite some time."

"Yeah, in fact I just read an article addressing the whole human cloning issue. Apparently, the scientific community feels that the path forward has less to do with the actual process of cloning than it does with—hang on, I actually wrote this part down in my notes..." I heard him fussing with his phone and then he said, "Here it is, and I quote: 'The biggest hurdles facing us may have less to do with the process and more to do with its potential consequences, and our collective struggle to reconcile the ethics involved.' In other words, we can do it...we just don't know if we should."

"Yeah, that lines up with what I've heard as well. But, there seems to be a consensus that by the mid 2020s, it'll be happening. And if they are projecting that timeframe, then you know it's already possible."

He said, "All of which supports your contention that this is a very scary scenario you're facing. So, yeah...whatever you need, Jake. I'll just call the Seattle SAC and you can coordinate with him."

"It's a new guy, right?"

"Oh, that's right. You two haven't met. He's actually only been there about six months. Terence Press. He's a good guy. You'll like him."

"Great. Just have him call me."

"Roger that." He paused and then added, "Be careful on this one, Jake. I don't like the feel of it."

"People keep telling me that, so I suppose I should listen. Okay, I will be as careful as a naked man in a cactus garden."

"Thank you for that nightmare image. Hey, is Aaron going with you?"

"Yeah, he'll be in tomorrow morning. Pete, Cassie and Vanessa are going as well. Oh, and Paddy Quinn."

"Paddy? How'd you rope that old rascal into helping you?"

"Wasn't hard. Seriously, his life doesn't amount to much since Maggie died. He was grateful for the distraction."

He blew out a long breath of air and said, "You know... I of all people get it about budgets and bottom lines and such, but to let a guy like Paddy go from the force—"

"Especially with his closed case rate," I interjected.

"Yes, exactly. It just doesn't make sense on any level. Hell, for a guy like Paddy, what he did was so much a part of who he was that I can't imagine him feeling like he's worth much without it."

"Which is exactly why I reached out to him. Well, that and the fact that the old bastard is still the smartest investigator I've ever worked with."

"I'm not sure you ever knew this, but about five years ago, he bailed my butt out on a case that had all the potential to produce a very negative effect on my career. He just walked in, looked the situation over, said to do this, go there, talk to that guy, ask these questions…and, boom, case solved."

That made me laugh.

"That's Paddy."

"Well," Zack said. "That's a good crew you've got there. Okay, Jake. Let me know if there's anything else you need."

"Thanks, my friend. I owe you."

"More than you could ever repay," he replied with a laugh before ringing off.

I was just about to tell the others about my conversation when my phone started buzzing again. I thought it was Zack calling me back with something he had forgotten, but when I looked at the screen, I saw "Désirée" in the caller ID.

CHAPTER FORTY

"Désirée," I said in greeting. "To what do I owe the pleasure of this call?"

"Bonsoir, Jake. I heard that you are preparing for an epic adventure and I thought to myself, *Surely this cannot be true. My dear friend Jake would not do something of this nature and not ask for Désirée's help.* So, I decided to call and tell you that I am on my way."

Désirée is a very close friend whom we met during our rescue of Gaspard Ducharme. A 5'9" bundle of beauty, brains and fierce lethality, she now serves as Gaspard's pilot and personal bodyguard.

Yeah, she's that tough.

I said, "Wait…wait a second. How do you even know what I am doing?"

She laughed quietly.

"Non, mon ami. A girl must have some secrets. Let us just say that I keep track of those who are important to me. And you are very important to me."

"Okay, so how much do you know about what I am currently doing?"

She spent five minutes telling me about the mission as if she were reading from a script.

When she finished, she added, "Oh, and Monsieur Ducharme has generously made his jet available to you while he is in LA visiting Simone. He will be there for two weeks. Is enough time, no?"

My head was spinning.

"Yes, uh…really? Gaspard said that?"

"Mais oui. What do you expect? He loves you and your

family, Jake...as do I."

Désirée and I had shared a moment during the effort to rescue Gaspard. It had been early on in my relationship with Gabi and, well, let's just say that had Gabi not been in my life, I could very easily have a French girlfriend today.

"Well, I don't know what to say, Désirée."

"I can help you with that. Say, *Désirée, mon chér, I accept your generous offer of assistance and will look forward to seeing you at*...what time should I be there?"

Few women leave me feeling absolutely flummoxed. Désirée was one of them.

"Uh...well..." I stammered. "10:00 a.m.?"

"Très bon. I will be there. And, approximately what time do we need to leave for Istanbul?"

"Well, we were planning to go commercial, but if we're using the G650, I don't know."

"Okay. I have performed some calculations, and it is 6068 miles from Seattle to Istanbul. That is the equivalent of about 5272 nautical miles. The aircraft has a range of 7000 nautical miles, so we can fly non-stop if needed."

"It is *definitely* needed."

"So, we should plan anywhere between ten-and-one-half to eleven hours flight time."

"Well, that definitely beats the commercial schedule all to hell."

"Of that there is no doubt. Given those specifics, what time should I have the plane ready to go?"

I said, "We were planning on an early afternoon departure and I can't think of a good reason to change those plans."

"Bon. And, what about arms and ammunition?"

"Zack Hastings is setting me up with the new SAC here in Seattle. He will—"

"Oh, Jake, Jake. You dishonor me and our friendship," she said with a pout in her voice.

"What? How?"

"Do you think so little of me that you would even

for one second imagine that I would offer to help and come empty handed? Do you not remember Monsieur Ducharme's armory?"

Indeed I did. It was where I first fell in love with my current stockpile of weapons.

I asked, "Are you telling me that you have some of those weapons with you?"

"Not *some,* mon ami. Most."

"So, you're saying that you have a Barrett M82 sniper rifle; Sig Sauer P226 Tacops pistols; suppressed HK G36 416 *and* a DP-12 with enough ammo to outfit a small attack force?"

"Oui," she replied simply as if it were of no more consequence than packing a makeup bag.

"Come on. Seriously? Even the Barrett?"

"Assuming that the very impressive Mr. Tolles will be the one called upon to do suppressing fire, I brought an MSSR instead."

"Of course," I said. "Marine Scout Sniper Rifle. It's what he's used to."

Pete Tolles holds one of the highest scores ever recorded in the Marine Scout Sniper School. Once in the field, he turned their motto, "One shot, one kill," into a living reality. He has never told me how many kills he was credited with. Only that it was enough to, "Keep me talkin' to Jesus."

Désirée said, "The MSSR doesn't have the range of the Barrett, but it is twenty pounds lighter. "

"Thus, more portable." I was impressed. "It sounds like you thought of everything."

"One tries. In all seriousness, Jake…Monsieur Ducharme and I keep track of where you are and what you are doing. It is the least we can do when you have done so much for both of us. So, when we learned of what you were facing, and who, I tried to choose what I considered an appropriate level of weapons."

I was touched by their concern. Truly.

"Well, I thank you and look forward to seeing you tomorrow."

She said something in French that I couldn't translate, given my meager understanding of the language, and then disconnected the call.

I shoved my phone into my pocket and stood leaning against the wall outside of the apartment, pondering what had just transpired. A sound made me turn. Vanessa was walking toward me.

"Hey," she said as she came and adopted a similar pose right next to me.

"Hey, yourself."

"I have a question for you."

"Okay."

"I've been thinking about this thing tomorrow."

"And?"

"And…it's gonna be really and truly dangerous, isn't it?"

I paused a beat before answering, "Yes, Vanessa. It is."

She nodded silently for a few seconds.

"Okay. Well…I hope you don't think less of me, but I think maybe I don't want to go."

I put my arm around her and pulled her into a hug.

"There is nothing you could ever do that would change the way I feel about you. If you want to know the truth, I'm ecstatic that you don't want to go."

"You are?" she said quietly, her face pressed against my chest.

"Absolutely. I mean I was never knocked out with the idea in the first place."

"So, you'll let me go home?"

"Well, I'll let you go to Las Vegas and hang out with Gabi—that's where Muriel and Eddie are going as well."

She pushed back, her eyes suddenly lit up with excitement.

"Seriously? I can go hang out with Gabi?"

"Yes. I'll get the flight booked tonight and call Gabi so she can be prepared to pick you up."

She stood on her tiptoes and kissed me on the cheek.

"Oh, thank you, Jake. I feel like I'm a hundred pounds lighter."

"I know what you mean."

She went skipping back toward the girls' apartment. I stayed in place, but in my heart, an equivalent action was taking place.

I pulled my phone out and texted Gabi with the news. Her response consisted of a string of text emoji's, the sense of which baffled me, but I assumed it represented joy.

CHAPTER FORTY-ONE

Morning.

And another meal consumed in record time.

This was getting very old. I don't appreciate having to wolf down my food. I've spent far too many years doing that while pursuing various cases. It's bad for the digestion. It's bad for relationships. It's bad for your sense of well-being. Hell, it's just a crummy way to consume one's necessary nourishment.

I think if I am forced to ingest one more Egg Mc-something I may just lose it.

It was 9:00 a.m. and I was driving to the airport to pick up Aaron and drop off Vanessa. Aaron was coming in at 10:15 and Vanessa's flight left at 11:07. We were about fifteen minutes out and traffic wasn't horrible, so getting there on time wouldn't be a problem.

Vanessa said, "You know, part of me still wishes I was going with you."

"Part of me wishes that as well. But, as we discussed, this has all the ingredients to develop into a very dangerous situation."

"I know. I mean I'm not a coward. But I'm also not stupid."

"Right. There have been a lot of very brave people who have lost their lives simply because they didn't take the time to think things through and make wise choices."

"Well, even though I feel like I'm going to be missing out on the adventure of a lifetime, I still think this is the best choice for me."

"Most definitely."

"Will you have time to keep us updated on what's happening once you're on the ground?"

I said, "I will try. But it's always sketchy once you become engaged in the process. Things don't always progress in a manner you deem appropriate."

"I get that. It's just that I feel sort of invested and would like to know what's going on."

We rode a little ways in silence and then she said, "I can't believe my life right now."

"Uh...is that in a good sense or bad sense?"

"Oh, good. Definitely good. I mean look at my life today compared to what it was just eighteen months ago."

Eighteen months ago, Vanessa was living on the streets of Pacific Beach in San Diego, running for her life from crooked Las Vegas politician, Harry Olivetti, and being pursued by none other than Pete Tolles and his pal, Buddy Bracken. After Olivetti's son, the late Colin Olivetti, had married Vanessa's sister Laurie, he had almost immediately begun physically and sexually abusing Vanessa. This after having her mother and best friend murdered. When Vanessa found evidence to bring down the Olivetti empire, Harry 'O had put a contract out on her.

When Aaron and I had found her, she was in pretty desperate shape. But, eighteen months of love and—dare I say it—tons of grace, she was a completely different person. I glanced over at the proud young woman sitting next to me and was overwhelmed by the transformation.

I reached over and grasped her hand, giving it a little squeeze.

"I love you, kiddo."

"I love you too, Jake," she replied around a sob. "And I can't wait to officially be your daughter." After a pause, she asked in a small voice, "I know it's not, like, official and everything yet, but would it be okay if I, you know called you dad?"

My heart nearly exploded in my chest.

I couldn't speak. The best I could manage was to

squeeze her hand a bit harder and nod, hoping like hell the tears wouldn't exceed the boundaries of my eye sockets.

We rode the rest of the way like that. Not talking. Simply holding hands.

Once we arrived at SeaTac, I left the car with a valet attendant and did the Vegas thing, you know, giving him a twenty to "keep it close." I walked with Vanessa as far as the TSA security line, which, to my eyes, appeared to be the approximate length of a soccer pitch.

"Well," I said. "This is where I have to leave you."

"I know." She threw her arms around my neck, hugging me fiercely. "Stay safe...dad. I can't lose anyone else."

"You know it, sweetheart," I mumbled, trying with all my might not to allow the break that was lying in wait to hijack my normally quite manly voice.

She stepped back and joined the queue and I backed away, giving her a little wave when she turned around to see if I was still there.

After a few more seconds, I moved on to find a suitable cup of coffee and wait for Aaron to arrive.

I had just found a stand selling Seattle's most famous brand when I heard, "Hey there, sugar. Did you miss me?"

I spun around to see Aaron walking toward me, a huge grin plastered across his not unattractive face.

"Aaron. What are you doing here? Your flight isn't supposed to get in for another thirty minutes."

"Why, I'm fine, thank you. So nice of you to inquire." After I responded with an epic eye-roll, he said, "Found an earlier flight. I've actually been here for a minute."

"Defined as...?"

"Oh, like...forty-five minutes. Been in a lounge catching up on some text messages."

"When will Muriel and Eddie arrive in Vegas?"

"Umm...like...midafternoon-ish."

"That will work out great. Vanessa's flight gets in around 2:30 p.m. so—"

"Vanessa is going to Vegas?" he asked in surprise.

"Yeah. She decided that this situation was getting just a bit too perilous for her age and experience."

"Good choice."

"I thought so. And, the three girls will have fun with Gabi."

"They all love her."

"And she loves them back."

I aborted my coffee mission and started walking with him toward baggage claim.

"So," he said. "On a scale of one to, I might want to update my will…how dangerous is this thing we doin'?"

"Pretty darned."

"That bad, huh?"

"It's just that this guy, Nathaniel Prince, is unlike anyone we've ever encountered. He's incalculably wealthy. But even beyond that…he's a zealot."

"Those are some crazy-ass dudes, bruh."

"Yes, indeed. And if that weren't bad enough, it's just the whole issue of finding the remnant of the true cross. At the end of the day, it's a piece of wood. A very old piece of wood, but it's *just* a piece of wood."

"That purportedly has Jesus' DNA all over it."

"Right. Thus, the cloning thing. But think about it: a piece of wood from 33 AD that we are supposed to believe has been carried by hand almost twelve hundred miles across some of the most unforgiving real estate on the planet. And now it resides somewhere in south central Turkey and we're supposed to find it."

He said, "Sounds Sisyphean if you ask me."

I looked sideways at him.

"Seriously, bro?"

"What?"

"You gonna roll that vocab out on me at a time like this?"

"Sisyphean?"

"Yeah, Sisyphean."

"Why not?"

"Because," I said. "It sounds pretentious. Like something a…I don't know…a writer would use just to bolster his word cred."

He gave me the side-eye. No one can give a side-eye like Aaron Perry.

"Look," he explained patiently, "why say, 'Wow, Jake. This sounds like a task that is so difficult that we never gonna complete it,' when I can just say Sisyphean?"

"Have you had coffee yet?"

"No!"

"Well, then, that explains it."

"Explains what?"

"You always adopt an air of etymological superiority when you haven't had coffee."

"Etymological? Now who's being pretentious."

"I'm not being pretentious. I'm just stating an obvious fact."

"It's pretentious."

"It's not."

"It is."

I laughed and threw my arm around his burly shoulders.

"Good to see you, bro."

CHAPTER FORTY-TWO

"You seem troubled," said Mrs. Viola Spencer as she stared across the cabin toward her captor. "Are you all right?"

Gérard turned a steely gaze toward her.

"What I am and am not is of no concern of yours."

"Oh, well excuse me for asking. Excuse me for showing a bit of humanity. Excuse me for trying to show some concern even though you have done nothing to deserve naught but my utter contempt."

As she turned her head and stared out the window, Gérard was caught in a maelstrom of rampant emotions, none of which had anything at all to do with her. No, it was all about his employer—soon to be *former* employer if things worked out the way he imagined—and Delilah, the object of his desire. And if he cared for her to the extent that he had become convinced, why did he persist in calling her by the ridiculous, made up code name? Because, in his fantasies it was always Delilah in the starring role. Not Emily Young.

Staring once more at Mrs. Spencer, who had done no wrong and, thus, deserved none of his acrimony, he said sincerely, "I must ask your forgiveness, Madame Spencer. You did not deserve such an acerbic response, nor do you deserve these present circumstances."

Turning warily toward him, she replied, "Why don't you tell me about it? Perhaps I can help."

In spite of his best efforts to contain it, a short laugh erupted.

"You? Help me? But…what could one such as you offer one such as I in the form of assistance?"

Smiling sweetly, she said, "I'm a mother, I am. And mothers know about things that trouble young men's souls. So, what is troubling your soul?"

The notion was absurd bordering on farcical. Ludicrous. He, a trained killer baring his soul to a matronly, middle-aged woman whose qualifications seemed to begin and end with the fact that she was a mother?

Suddenly, his ears heard his voice saying, "Well, I don't know where to begin."

She reached across the aisle and patted his hand.

"Just tell me where it hurts, dear."

The simple, caring gesture nearly left him undone, for try as he might he could call to mind no memories from the recent or distant past where he had been touched lovingly by a woman.

"I..." he struggled for words. "I love a woman."

"Well, I figured that much out on 'me own, I did. Doesn't take much insight to see that. What is her name?"

"Del—" he began, before changing it to, "Emily. Emily Young."

"Emily is such a pretty name. I bet she's a real looker."

"Que veux-tu dire?" he said with a puzzled expression.

"Oh, sorry. It's English slang for, she's a real beauty."

"Ah, mais oui. She is all of that, and more. She is the most beautiful woman I have ever...how do you say it...put the eye on?"

"Laid eyes on?" she prompted.

"Oui. From the first time I saw her, my heart... it was not my own."

"Have you ever been in love before, dear?"

"No. Never. Because of...because of what I do—who I am—I have kept myself at the distance. In my line of work, it is inconvenient to...feel anything. When you feel, you become careless, and when you become careless...that is when you and those you are sworn to serve can be hurt."

"And who do you serve?"

Her questions. He had never experienced anything like it. She seemed to know the exact point in his heart where the fiercest battles were raging.

"I serve…"

"Yes?"

He turned his head and stared into her bespectacled gaze.

"If you had asked this question of me yesterday, I would have told you that I serve Nathaniel Prince."

"And now?" she asked.

"Now, I fear that I am serving my heart."

"And, you think it is a bad thing? To serve your heart?"

"Ah, but this is the énigme…the conundrum that I am in. I do not know if it is good, or bad because it has never happened to me before. I have always been loyal to Monsieur Prince. All these years I have served him; never once questioning his orders—his decisions. And when others would dare such a thing, I meted out harsh retribution. And now…"

She said, "What has brought you to this?"

He sighed and shook his head sadly.

"He asked, no, required me to…" he struggled to even form the words. "To kill Emily."

Viola gasped, "No he didn't. Why would he ask you to do such a terrible thing as that?"

"Because it is what I do. It is who I am. I make difficulties go away, whether in the form of circumstances or…people."

"So, you're telling me that you are an assassin?"

"J'ai honte de te l'avouer."

"I understand," she replied. "I suppose if I'd killed people, I'd feel shame too."

"It is not so much over what I have done—although there were many shameful acts—but more over who I am… who I have become as a result, n'est-ce pas?"

"Yes, I do understand, but the man talking to me right now is not a killer. He is just another poor bloke in love."

Gérard sighed, "It is as you say. But, what do I do?"

Viola glanced out the window and asked, "Where are we?"

"We are on our way back to Nathaniel's private airfield outside of Zurich."

"I see. And why are we going there?"

"Because—" Gérard suddenly realized that he had no credible answer. "Because that is where I always go."

"Is the pilot and staff loyal to you?"

"Completely. Unquestionably."

"So, they will go where you tell them to go?"

"Mais oui…within the limits of the aircraft's range. Why are you asking these questions?"

"Would it be possible to call my son?"

Gérard blinked rapidly before replying, "That can be arranged. But, why?"

"Because what you are attempting to do, young man, cannot be done on your own. You need help."

Gérard laughed again.

"And, what form of help can an archeology professor provide to one such as I?"

"Oh, it is not Elliot you need. It is Jake."

Gérard rocked back as if he'd absorbed a stiff left jab.

"Jake Moriarity? What do I have to do with this man? He is my enemy."

"Really? And, why do you say that?"

"Because…because…"

He stopped speaking and thought about it for a few moments. Why indeed? What dynamics were in play that pitted one man against the other? Nathaniel. It was all about Nathaniel. If he were no longer serving the man, then why should he and Moriarity be foes?

Digging the satellite phone from the inside pocket of his sport coat, he handed it to her and said, "Make your call."

CHAPTER FORTY-THREE

It was 11:45 a.m.

Aaron and I had just arrived at Werner and Elliot's offices when Elliot came running out, waving his phone in the air and shouting my name.

"Oh, Jake," he said breathlessly, "you're back. Thank the good Lord."

"What's happening, Elliot?"

He thrust his cell phone toward me.

"It's my mum. She wants to talk to you."

I took the proffered phone and said, "Mrs. Spencer, it's Jake."

"Hello, Jacob. I have someone here who wants to talk to you."

"Okay...but—"

"Moriarity?" came the deeply burnished tones of Gérard's voice.

"Gérard? What game are you playing at?"

I left the room and stepped back into the hall as he said, "It is no game, monsieur. Things have changed since last we spoke."

"Care to enlighten me?"

There was a quickly spoken exchange between he and Viola, and then, "I am no longer in the employ of Nathaniel Prince."

"All right. Go on."

"He...instructed me to...eliminate Emily Young."

"I see. So, you refused?"

"Oui. It is, as you say, what I did for love."

Suddenly it all made sense. Emily had been right about

his feelings for her.

"Where are you now?"

"We are heading back to the continent, but Madam Spencer thought that maybe you and I should talk before we decide on our final destination."

"I'm listening."

"Nathaniel Prince has a small army at his disposal. He has but to snap his chubby fingers and they come running. Hard men. Mercenaries. All of them highly trained former commandos from various branches of military; from countries all over the world."

"Okay," I said. "And…"

"You will be hopelessly outnumbered."

"Can you bottom line me, Gérard?"

"Bottom line? Je ne comprends pas bien?"

My command of French wasn't great, but I knew what he was asking.

"Uh…cut to the chase. Get to the point."

"Ah, oui. What I am saying…is that I make myself available to assist you."

I did *not* see that coming.

"And how do I know that I can trust you? How do I know Nathaniel didn't put you up to this to get you inside?"

"I suppose…well…I give you my word that you can trust me."

About as far as I'd trust a viper.

"Trust is something that has to be earned, Gérard. Emily is terrified of you—thinks that you are a stone-cold killer without a heart, without conscience."

"Yes, it is as she says. I have been all of those things and more. But now…"

"Go on…" I prompted.

"I find there is something in life that is more important than serving Nathaniel Prince."

"Emily."

"Oui."

"And, what if this emotion you feel for her is not returned? What if she—"

"Recoils from me?"

"Yes."

He took a long time to say, "It is enough for me to love her."

"Even if she offers nothing in return?"

"Even then."

This was shaping up to be one of the most bizarre conversations I'd ever had. Listening to this man speaking so tenderly about the object of his affection was right up there on the weirdness scale of listening to Adolph Hitler gushing about his love for Eva Braun after giving the order to have another hundred thousand Jews exterminated.

I said, "Fly to Istanbul. We will find you there."

"And what about Mrs. Spencer?"

"There isn't time to take her back to London. We will make sure she is taken care of."

"Bon. I have grown very fond of her during our brief association. And, what about Nathaniel?"

"As you said, he will be bringing a substantial number of operatives along—"

"That is not what I mean."

"Okay. What?"

He paused and then said, "When the time comes to kill Nathaniel, you will allow me the pleasure?"

"Because he ordered Emily's death?"

"Oui."

"And all the years of your association with him mean nothing at this point?"

"Less than nothing. The man is not deserving of the air that fills his lungs. Do you know that in the past two days he has had two of The Nine killed?"

"Because...?"

"Because they displeased him."

"And, who killed them?" I asked, feeling I already knew

the answer.

He hesitated only slightly before saying, "I was responsible for the first. The second one...he did himself."

I said, "When the time comes—*if* it comes—I won't stand in the way of any retribution you feel is deserved."

"Merci. Then...I suppose we will meet soon, Mr. Moriarity."

I disconnected the call and stood in the hallway, leaning with my back against the wall wondering how much weirder this case could get.

Aaron stuck his head out and said, "You okay, bro?"

"Yeah. I just had a call from Gérard."

"Okay. Who 'dat?"

"Nathaniel Prince's enforcer and personal assassin—or I should say, *former* enforcer and personal assassin."

"You don't sound convinced."

"I'm not." We walked back into the outer office. "A couple of hours ago, the guy was threatening me with great bodily harm."

Aaron said, "What changed?"

"Oh, the superior negotiating skills of Mrs. Viola Spencer regarding Emily Young."

"And who is Emily Young?"

"You'll meet her in a minute. But, she is Nathaniel's niece and, apparently, the object of Gérard's desire. For reasons known only to himself, Nathaniel ordered her to be executed."

"Dude, that's harsh. Why would the man order his own flesh and blood killed?"

"Well, for one thing, she's not his flesh and blood. Nathaniel and Emily's father were best friends; Nathaniel was always over to their house when she was a child; over time, she just began calling him uncle."

"Okay," he said. "But that's still all kinda harsh."

"It is. If you want to know the truth, I haven't come close to sorting out all the dynamics, but for now all we need to know is that Gérard has taken a dim view of Nathaniel ordering him to kill Emily and wants to join forces with us. If I were Nathaniel…I'd be watching my back because Gérard has vowed to kill him."

"You gonna let him?"

"Actually," I said. "I am."

"And what does Emily say about this dude."

"Gérard?"

"Yeah."

I laughed, "Oh, let's see…she said, 'He is the worst man I have ever met. He is cruel. Evil.' Or something along those lines."

"Well, all right. I can see why you want him along," Aaron said sarcastically. "Always use a trustworthy dude like that."

"I know, I know. But…there's just something about this situation that has me concerned."

"And, you thinkin' we can use all the help we can get?"

"Yeah, which is why Désirée is joining us as well."

"What? Seriously?"

"Yeah. And get this: Gaspard insists that she fly us to Istanbul in his Gulfstream."

"Well, if the man insists, I suppose we could lower our standards just this once."

"Just this once."

CHAPTER FORTY-FOUR

We walked into Werner's office and six heads immediately swiveled in our direction.

"Well?" Elliot inquired expectantly.

"First off, your mom is fine."

"Oh, thank God!"

"It would appear that she has won Gérard over, to the extent that he is now willing to abandon Nathaniel and join us."

"What?" Emily spat. "That's impossible. No one is more loyal to Nathanial *than*—"

"But," I interrupted. "Nathaniel ordered you killed." I let that settle for a few seconds, and then continued, "Whether you know it or not, Emily, Gérard is deeply in love with you and didn't take kindly to that."

Her eyes widened almost comically.

"In love? I mean I knew he sort of had a crush on me when I was younger, but...love? How can he be in love with me? He barely knows me."

"The heart has its reasons, et cetera, et cetera," Aaron growled.

"What does that mean?"

I said, "It's from Blaise Pascal. He said something like, *'The heart has its reasons which reason does not understand.'*"

"Wait," she said, holding her hands in front of her like a traffic cop, "so you're saying that Gérard is choosing me over Nathaniel? That's impossible."

Cassie asked, "Why do you say that?"

"Because. He's...he's completely loyal to Nathaniel. He has done terrible, inhuman things for him—all without the slightest vestige of conscience, I might add."

"Yes, but…love," Cassie said with a smile.

"I wish you guys would stop saying that word in relation to Gérard. It's creeping me out."

I said, "Look, we don't have time to debate the finer points of Gérard's love life. We have other developments to discuss." After a brief pause, I continued, "For instance…Désirée will be joining us."

Pete and Cassie responded enthusiastically as the others turned puzzled expressions my way.

Aaron explained, "Désirée helped us out big time on a case a while back. Saved our butts, if you ask me."

I added, "That's a fact. She's a highly skilled operator and also a very good pilot. Which brings me to the rest of the news. Gaspard Ducharme is insisting that Désirée fly us to Istanbul on his private Gulfstream. Oh, and Gaspard is also supplying all of the weapons and ammunition we will need for defense—including an MSSR for you, Pete."

"I say," Elliot breathed as the others reacted.

Paddy asked, "And what would be their interest, if you don't mind me askin'."

I replied, "Their interest is in helping out good friends. And, to be clear, they want nothing in return."

"I'm confused," Werner said. "These people, whoever they are—friends of yours, I gather—are willing to help us out…" he snapped his fingers, "…just like that at tremendous cost to themselves, and they want nothing in return? Pardon my cynicism, but nobody does that. And, quite frankly, I find it hard to believe in their altruism."

"Now Werner," Elliot chided.

"It's okay," I said. "I understand the skepticism. But, look around the room, Werner. I need to remind you that none of us are getting paid. We're here at our own expense."

He sat back as if rocked by the realization, an embarrassed blush crawling up his ruddy face.

"I, uh…hadn't thought of it like that. Sorry, Jake. The

events of the day past…" he paused to pierce Emily with a disapproving stare, "…have left me mistrustful and out of sorts."

"I'm sure we can all identify," I said. "But we haven't the luxury of pausing to sort out our feelings at present. Now, I received a text from Désirée a short time ago and she is on schedule to arrive at Boeing Field somewhere around 12:30 p.m. Once she has the plane on the ground, we need to be ready to load. Where do we stand with procuring the equipment you require, Werner?"

"It is all assembled and loaded into a van."

"So as far as you and Elliot are concerned, you're ready to go?"

"Yes."

I turned toward the others.

"And everyone else is also packed and ready to roll?"

I received a chorus of affirmations in reply.

"Okay, then…here's what I want to do." I looked at my watch and tried to do some quick figuring. "It's 12:15 p.m. and Désirée is landing at Boeing Field at 12:30. I want us to be there by no later than 1:30."

"How long will the flight be?" Cassie asked.

"Désirée figures the G650 can make it to Istanbul in ten to eleven hours. Istanbul is ten hours ahead of us, so if we take off at, oh say…2:30 p.m., that'll be…" I appealed to my niece's superior mathematical skills. "Help me, Cassie."

"12:30 a.m. there."

"Right. So, figuring eleven hours for our flight, we should arrive in Istanbul by…"

"Approximately, 11:30 a.m. tomorrow."

"That just plum makes my head hurt," Pete said.

"Werner, do you have ground transportation all lined up?"

"Yes, we have two Land Rovers and a cargo van at our disposal."

"Drivers?"

"Yes, for the Land Rovers. But for obvious reasons…" he

paused to cast a withering glance in Emily's direction, "Elliot and I are driving the van ourselves."

"Okay. So, Pete, I want you and Paddy to stick with them."

"Roger that," Pete replied simply.

I continued, "We won't need the drivers. Aaron, you, me and Gérard will drive one Land Rover and Cassie, I want you, Emily and Désirée in the other."

"Girls rule, boys drool," she said around a smile.

Emily appealed, "You can't be serious about allowing Gérard to come along."

"I am completely serious."

"But he's...he's..."

"One of the better operators on the planet, from what I've heard. Aside from your issues with the man, why wouldn't I want an elite operator like him as backup?"

"Yes," Werner interjected. "And what, pray tell, makes this Gérard fellow any more untrustworthy than you, young lady?"

She stared at Werner without speaking, before dropping her gaze and giving her head a little shake.

I said, "Moving along, once we're on the ground, we need to leave immediately for..."

I turned to Elliot.

"Oh, Beyşehir."

"Yes. And, approximately how far is it from Istanbul?"

Werner said, "Umm...about six hundred and twenty kilometers, so given decent driving conditions...seven or eight hours travel. But, I'd plan on nine."

"Okay, and once we're in Beyşehir, how far to the location of the remnant?"

"Well, that's a bit more difficult to predict."

"Because...?"

"Because we've got improved roadways between Beyşehir and Istanbul. But from Beyşehir to the spot that houses the remnant, it gets a bit sketchy."

"How sketchy?"

Werner and Elliot shared a glance, and Elliot said, "You see, the thing is, Jake…"

He paused, and when nothing followed for a good five seconds, I prompted, "Yes…the thing is…?"

"The thing is…we are no longer completely certain that the remnant is where we have believed it to be."

That was *not* good.

"This is a hell of a time to share that bit of news. And, how long have you felt this way?"

"Umm…since approximately three hours ago."

"And when were you going to let the rest of us in on it?"

My tone was growing harsh, but I didn't really care. I hate it when people conceal things from me.

"Now, it isn't like that," Werner argued. "It's simply that when we were studying Vanessa's copy of the manuscript, there seemed to be irregularities."

"Right," Elliot said, picking up the narrative. "And these irregularities have led us to believe that there were errors in her recall."

Emily raised her hand as if requesting permission to speak.

"Yes, Emily?" I replied.

"Can I see Vanessa's copy?"

"Absolutely not," Werner exploded. "How stupid do you think we are?"

I said, "Give it to her."

"You can't ask me to do—"

"I'm not asking, Werner. I'm telling you. Give it to her!"

My tone had now progressed beyond harsh all the way to right-royally-pissed.

He attempted to stare me down. A foolish waste of effort on his part. No one can stare me down.

Opening a battered briefcase that was sitting on his desk, he rummaged around inside and came out with a slim binder that he grudgingly surrendered into Emily's waiting hands.

After studying the copy for thirty seconds or so, she said, "She didn't make a mistake."

"How could you possibly know that?" Werner asked haughtily.

"Because, before I...stole it, I committed the entire thing to memory."

"Which, if you don't mind me sayin', young lady, you claim to have forgotten," Paddy said.

"I know, but my memory is suddenly crystal clear. I suppose if you wanted to get technical you could call what she did a mistake, but it's grammatical and has nothing to do with the content." Placing the folder on the desktop, she tapped a section and continued, "I won't go into the details, but the reason you began to doubt the location is due to this phrase right here. I'm sure you've heard about the debate in literary circles regarding the Oxford comma?" After several nodded heads and verbal affirmations, she added, "The way Vanessa copied this down is loosely the equivalent of an Oxford comma."

"So," I said. "You're saying that the remnant is right where Werner and Elliot believed it to be?"

"Without question."

"Then...let's go get it."

CHAPTER FORTY-FIVE

"How much longer until we are ready to depart?" Nathaniel Prince inquired impatiently of his pilot.

"Sir," he replied. "I realize your eagerness to depart, but we cannot go until the load is finalized and secured in the hold. Additionally, there are pre-flight checks to log, and fuel to take on. In short, this is a process than cannot be hurried. To do so is to flirt with certain disaster."

Stepping toward the man, Nathaniel said, "You have thirty minutes to get us airborne, or disaster will fall upon you. Certainly."

Startled by the outburst, the man blinked rapidly, started to make a reply and then seemed to think better of it, choosing instead to simply walk away and continue his tasks.

A large, brutal-looking man approached Nathaniel and said in an accent reminiscent of the San Fernando Valley area of Southern California, "The team is assembled and ready to board, sir."

"Weapons and ammo?"

"More than should be required, actually."

"Very good. We are facing an opponent who is, by reputation, infinitely resourceful."

"Nothing that we haven't faced before, sir."

Nathaniel couldn't decide whether to lambast the man for his arrogance or laud the man for his confidence.

In the end he settled on, "While I appreciate your enthusiasm, I have learned that it's best to not underestimate one's opponent."

"Duly noted, sir," the man replied respectfully before

walking away to join his squad, which consisted of eight other men, each one seemingly as hard as their leader.

They were mercenaries, or MERC's—soldiers of fortune, whose loyalty and service were available to the highest bidder. Nathaniel had employed such men many times throughout the years. He found them useful when things needed to be done where a conscience would get in the way.

The squad leader, Dagnar, was a 6'7", three-hundred-pound blonde, Nordic giant who had once competed in the World's Strongest Man competition. Born in Moorpark, California to Norwegian immigrants, Dagnar had spent the first eighteen years of his life in that city. But something in his soul kept calling him back to his ancestral land. Following his eighteenth birthday, he left his family and the country of his birth behind and enrolled in the University of Oslo where he would eventually earn undergraduate and graduate degrees in ancient philosophy.

With a facile intelligence that seemed incongruous with his barbaric appearance, Dagnar was, as they say, the whole package. Brutal and efficiently deadly, he had answered Nathaniel's call on more than one occasion and had proven himself worthy of the exorbitant fee he charged for himself and his squad of killers. There was only one scenario where Nathaniel wouldn't bet on the man winning a head-to-head confrontation. And that was against Gérard. Even though Dagnar was nearly a head taller and a hundred pounds heavier, Gérard possessed a level of lethality that transcended anything Nathaniel had ever seen.

And then there was Moriarity. On the basis of some hastily conducted research, Nathaniel had learned enough of his reputation to consider him a legitimate threat, thus the acquisition of Dagnar and his team, who were more than a match for Moriarity. At least until you got to the part where Gérard had vowed to help Moriarity, a bit of distressing news that had come to Nathaniel in the past half-hour. That's where things could definitely go sideways in a hurry. It all depended on whether Moriarity was as good as his legend said he was.

The First Officer announced that it was time to board and everyone began moving in the direction of the stairs while Nathaniel hung back feeling a strange hesitation. And why was that? Could it be worry? He had never worried about anything in his entire life. And if it were true, what was he worried about? Gérard or Moriarity? Both, perhaps. While he had never seen Moriarity in action, he had seen Gérard plenty of times. And if Moriarity were even a fraction as good as Gérard, his level of worry was well founded.

By the time he had ascended the stairs and stepped into the main cabin, he had shaken off his disquiet and was feeling more himself. Taking his seat, he immediately began to run over the details of their mission in his mind, worry now a thing of the past. The first thing on the agenda was to ascertain just how much of a head start he would have on Moriarity. He calculated that it would be substantial. Somewhere on the order of ten hours. In ten hours, they could get in, recover the remnant and be on their way before Moriarity's flight even landed—knowledge that produced another strange set of emotions.

Did he want to avoid confronting the man? Was that what he was really after? Or did he anticipate the confrontation the way a heavyweight champion anticipates a championship fight with the top-rated challenger. Top-rated? Only time would tell.

"Dagnar," he said across the aisle to the giant mercenary.

"Yes, sir?"

"I am rethinking the plans we discussed and finalized."

He swiveled his overly large head in Nathaniel's direction.

"Very good, sir. Do you wish to make alterations?"

"Yes," he replied. "I believe I do." A pause, and then, "I have every reason to believe that we will be successful in acquiring the remnant. But, if we fail to deal with Moriarity in a manner that produces finality, I have a feeling that he will track us, as they say, to the ends of the earth."

Dagnar nodded and replied, "Understood. Then, are you proposing we secure the remnant and remain on site until Moriarity arrives?"

"Yes, I am." Nathaniel paused and then said, "Tell me, Dagnar, what have you heard about this man?"

Dagnar stared at him in silence for a long moment before replying, "Permission to speak freely, sir."

"Permission granted."

"I have heard much about this man. He is one of those men that people in my profession talk about."

"And what do they say?"

"His fame is almost legendary. To my knowledge, he has never been beaten. He is feared."

"And, do you fear him?" Nathaniel prompted as the plane began taxiing for takeoff.

"That is not the term I would use. Every mission requires a thorough knowledge of your enemy, and I have gathered enough knowledge to have come to the conclusion that Jake Moriarity is a man deserving of my respect."

"Are you saying that he intimidates you?"

"Once again, sir…not the term I would use. In acquiring the database we used to develop a profile, I learned of his strengths."

"I hear that they are considerable."

"Indeed they are, sir. However…"

"Yes…go on."

"Even the strongest, most capable individual has a source from which he derives his power—the glue that holds everything else in place."

"Kind of like gravity?"

"Yes sir."

"Fascinating. But I don't see how this helps us."

"If you strike at that source, the entire structure will collapse."

"Are you telling me that you know his source of power?"

Dagnar said carefully, "As I mentioned, we were able to gather a considerable amount of intel on Moriarity. His weakness can be found in those he loves."

"I'm not sure I understand."

"Classic military strategy states that once you determine what your enemy cherishes and protects, striking them there will produce a level of pain sufficient to make them vulnerable to attack."

Nathaniel nodded in understanding.

"And may I assume that you have plans to strike Moriarity where it will really and truly hurt?"

"Yes, sir." He paused to pull two printed photos out of a valise, which he then handed across the aisle. "Striking him here will leave him helpless."

Nathaniel stared at the photos.

"Mr. Aaron Perry, I know. But who is the other?"

"Cassandra Harvey…Moriarity's niece; wife of the famous novelist, Charleston Hawthorne."

"So…are you saying that when the engagement begins, you intend to concentrate your efforts on taking these two out?"

"That's affirmative."

"But, how do you even know they will be with him?"

"We know."

They stared at each other in silence for a few moments before Nathaniel said, "Very well. Do what you must."

"Very good, sir."

The Bombardier Global 7000 made the turn onto the runway and the pilot gave full throttle to the powerful GE Passport engines, sending the jet screaming down the runway. Nathaniel was feeling very good. Soon, he would have the remnant; Emily Young would be dead, taking the dreaded secret with her to her grave; Jake Moriarity would be eliminated as a threat; and the greatest coup in human history would propel him into the position of world leadership he was born to have.

And nothing could stop him.
Not even the mighty Jake Moriarity.

CHAPTER FORTY-SIX

I was sitting in the cushioned comfort of Gaspard Ducharme's Gulfstream waiting for Désirée to complete the pre-flight check. Pilots take things like that seriously, which is probably why there aren't more airliner disasters than there are. I read once that the odds of a plane going down are about one in eleven million. In other words, there's a greater chance of being struck by lightning or being eaten by a shark than dying in a plane crash. I was, therefore, willing to give Désirée all the time she required to complete her tasks.

I decided to use the down time to call Gabi.

I tapped her name under my phone's favorites section and waited for the call to connect. It rang once...twice...and kept ringing all the way until my ear was filled with her deep and dusky-hued voice telling me that she was so glad I called but was unavailable at the moment and to leave a detailed message. Well, actually, that isn't what she says on her voicemail message. She says, "This is the number you dialed. You know what to do." Which is a damn sight better than my, "Before you leave a message, ask yourself...can this be handled by a text?"

After the beep prompted me to begin speaking, I said, "Hey...sitting here on Gaspard's jet waiting to take off. I don't know when I'll be able to talk to you again...so...anyway... uh...just wanted to tell you that I love you. Hope you're having a great time with the girls, which is probably where you are right now—out doing girl stuff. Umm..."

I stopped speaking because I didn't know what else to say. I never know what to say on voicemail. If you want to know the truth, leaving a voicemail message is one the most frustrating and awkward experiences I encounter on a regular basis. I mean you don't want to go on and on, but you at least want to leave enough information to let them know why you called. Complicating the experience is the fact that fully half the time people don't even bother to listen to the message and simply text you back with, "You called?" To which I always reply, "Yeah. There's a voicemail. Listen to it."

I finished off with, "So…yeah…wish I could talk to you. You guys are probably at Green Valley Ranch watching a movie, or something. Anyway…okay. That's really all I wanted to say." Then there arose a social etiquette conundrum. I had already said, "I love you." Would it be proper or improper to say it again as a valediction?

"I know I already said I love you…but in case you've forgotten…I love you, Ms. Marcus. I'll talk to you soon."

And then I ended the call, and sat back in my seat and thought about how much I had wanted to talk to her and tell her just how much she had come to mean to me…and how very afraid I was in the deepest part of my soul that this mission wasn't going to work out well and that, perhaps, I'd never see her again.

Paddy's huge bulk sliding into the seat next to me derailed the runaway train of my emotions.

"Jacob," he said in greeting.

"Paddy. You ready to go?"

"Sure, and I'd be a damn sight more ready if there was a wee spot o' whiskey to take the edge off."

"I'm sure that's a possibility." I paused and then asked, "Tell me the truth—how do you feel about this case?"

"Well now, that's a matter I've given some thought to." He glanced around the cabin before continuing, "This is a talented crew, Jacob. Hell, boyo, if it was just you and Aaron I'd give you odds of prevailin'. But when you add in the rest of us…"

He let the sentence trail off, as it didn't really need completing. We were good. We were better than good. We were the best.

He said, "You worryin' about it, Jacob?"

"I wouldn't say worrying. Just thinking through all of the possible scenarios; factoring in that Nathaniel is gonna come loaded for bear, so to speak."

"Meanin' that he will hire some MERC's?"

"He'll have to. One of his main enforcers is either still in Seattle or in transit, and the other has jumped ship and will be working alongside of us."

"And, how do you feel about this fella?"

I said, "I don't know how to feel. He's good, I know that. But he's also disloyal. He proved that much by leaving Nathaniel and joining us. Not that I'm complaining because, from what I've heard, he's not the kind of guy you want to be facing off against."

"And neither are you, bucko. Neither are you."

Aaron wandered down the aisle.

"Any idea what the holdup is?" he asked.

Paddy gestured toward the cockpit.

"The darlin' Désirée, God love 'er, was distracted in her pre-flight preparations by a lumberin' old fool who was so smitten by her beauty that he just had to spend some time talkin'."

"Flirting, Paddy?" Aaron asked. "You are already flirting with our pilot?"

"If that's what you want to call it. Myself, I prefer to think of it as exposin' the young lass to the best that Ireland has to offer."

Désirée chose that moment to come out of the cockpit. She had her hands behind her back; her lovely face brightened by a genuine smile.

"You should have warned me about this one, Jake," she said, nodding toward Paddy. "He is very sly."

"Yeah, I suppose that was an oversight on my part. But at least now you know."

"He tried very hard to get me to compromise my principles. But, there are certain things a girl just can't do and maintain her integrity." She let the moment play out before adding, "But, I have decided to give you what you want, monsieur."

Aaron said, "Now wait a damn minute! What the hell are we talkin' about here?"

Her hands came around her sides, one of them holding a bottle of Jameson's Whiskey."

"Jesus, Mary and Joseph!" Paddy exclaimed while reaching for the liquorous palliative. "God love ya', lass. God love ya'."

"Whiskey?" Aaron exclaimed in confusion. "We were talkin' about whiskey?"

Paddy frowned and replied, "Sure 'n what else?" as he cradled the bottle with the same reverence a mother would show toward a newborn.

Cassie came up behind Aaron and said, "Everything's squared away in the back, Désirée."

"Thank you, Cassie. We should be ready for takeoff in ten minutes."

"Y'all are a bunch of jokers," Aaron mumbled as he walked back down the aisle toward his seat.

"What's wrong with him?" Cassie asked.

CHAPTER FORTY-SEVEN

I may have mentioned this before, and if so…it bears repeating. I don't like flying. I don't like it at all. So, to compensate I typically fall asleep as soon as the plane reaches its cruising altitude and don't wake up until the pilot announces that he is beginning his initial descent.

Not everyone can do this. It takes a special skill, and I feel sorry for those who are forced to stay awake. It must be torture.

This flight was no exception. I fell asleep and didn't wake up until we were just outside of Istanbul.

I stood, stretched and headed for the Gulfstream's onboard lavatory, which, for the record, is nicer by far than the ones typically found on commercial airliners. After performing a few essentials, which included brushing my teeth to rid my mouth of a taste that can only be likened to a cadre of camels jointly and severally defecating with great gusto in my mouth, I exited in search of coffee.

As I made my way to the galley—where I found Cassie and Aaron huddled around the coffee maker, looking like addicts awaiting a fix—I heard Désirée announce from the cockpit that we were about thirty-five minutes out from Atatürk Airport. I glanced at my watch, did some quick adjustments to compensate for the time zone and figured that we'd be landing around 11:15 a.m. Istanbul time.

"Did you sleep?" I inquired of my niece.

"Yeah, I did. Probably six hours."

I turned to Aaron.

"And how about you?"

"Oh," he growled. "You know how I am. A little here.

A little there. Patch it all together and it equates to a decent night's sleep."

We each poured a cup of coffee and stood with our hands clasped around the cups, savoring the smell and taste of the special Full City Roast, Nicaraguan coffee Désirée had brought along just for me and Aaron.

It was our favorite.

Paddy eased past on his way to the lavatory, grumbling, "Damn prostate! Even when I don't have ta' pee, it feels like I do. If Gulfstream really wanted to own the title of being the world's most advanced business jet, they'd offer catheters for their elderly passengers."

"Ew," Cassie said, making a face, as Paddy entered the lavatory, closing the door behind him.

Given our proximity we couldn't help but hear him through the door.

"Come on now, give us a drop. Just a drop, you right bastard!"

"Who's he talking to?" Cassie asked.

I glanced at Aaron who rolled his eyes as if to say, "You got this, bro."

"Umm…" I said. "It's…a…guy thing. As you get older, your prostate gland swells and, uh, swollen prostates often, uh…"

Aaron picked it up, "Uh…make it difficult to, uh…pee?"

"Yeah. Pee."

We heard the toilet flush and the sound of water running in the sink and the rip of paper towels being torn from the dispenser and then Paddy opened the door and stepped into the aisle.

"Well," he announced. "That was a frustratin' experience, and so it was."

Cassie said, "Umm…I'm just gonna… go back to my seat."

Paddy watched her walk away and asked, "What's wrong with her?"

Pete came down the aisle, looking as if he were ready for action.

"Mornin' gents," he said brightly. "I smelled the coffee."

Paddy stared at him and jerked his head toward the lavatory.

"Don't ya' have to use the facilities, boyo?"

"Why, no sir, I don't. I mean I went before we took off, so I'm good."

"But, that was eleven hours ago!" Paddy shook his head and looked back and forth between the three of us. "How about you, Aaron?"

"Nah, I'm good."

"Jacob?"

I shook my head no.

"None 'o ya, huh?"

Pete started laughing and said, "I was just kiddin'. Man, oh man, I gotta pee like a racehorse!" as he maneuvered around us and into the lavatory.

Aaron slapped Paddy on the back.

"Me too, bro. I was just waiting my turn."

I said, "And I already went."

Paddy grinned.

"Ah, that's funny. That's a real funny joke to play on the old fella. If I weren't a good Catholic I'd wish that you be plagued by an itch and lack the nails to scratch it!"

I laughed and said, "We probably need to sit down and go over a few things before we land. Head on back to the front when you're finished here. Tell Pete."

About five minutes later, all eight of us were assembled around the front seats, some sitting, some standing, all tired of being in the air and looking forward to being back on terra firma.

I began, "We've got about twenty minutes before we land. Once we're on the ground, things need to happen very quickly. We have a ground crew lined up to transfer our gear from the hold into the various vehicles. Pete, I'd like you and

Werner to supervise that process." As they nodded their agreement, I continued, "Elliot, I'd like you and Emily to plot out a roadmap to the site where the remnant is housed. Use your phone's GPS, get an actual map, I don't care. Just figure out how to get us to where we're going. Désirée, you hearing this?"

"Oui, monsieur," came her reply over the intercom.

"I need you and Cassie to come up with some basic provisions for the trip. Given that we have no clear idea of where we're going, we need to make sure we have food and water."

"It would be my pleasure, monsieur," she said, a sentiment that Cassie readily echoed.

"Nathaniel will have had a considerable head start on us, and if I were in his shoes, I would have left someone behind whose sole purpose is to frustrate and delay our progress, so Aaron and I are going to post up and act as guards."

Elliot said, "I must say that in my wildest dreams, I never anticipated this effort turning into a...a military situation."

"Excuse me for sayin' so, Professor," Pete replied. "But that's just plum naive. I mean how did you think this was gonna go? That we was just gonna waltz in there and relieve those people of their treasure without a fight?"

It was as if Pete had punched Elliot full in the face.

"Good Lord," Elliot said. "In my zeal to acquire the remnant, I never thought about the fact that those who are in possession wouldn't want us to have it."

"Neither did I," Werner confessed.

"Yeah," I said. "I was wondering when you were going to get around to that."

"I suppose at the end of the day, it would be enough for me to just see the remnant—perhaps, touch it," Werner mused. "Photograph it; catalogue it; perhaps offer the people, whoever they are, a fee to bring it to the university as a display piece for a period of time."

Emily said, "If it is where I believe it to be, we will be dealing with a religious hierarchy who may or may not be zealots, and zealots, by nature, are largely unreasonable."

"Well," Elliot averred. "It was never my intention to simply take it from them by force."

I asked, "Then, how did you intend to get it back to the university? I mean this is a little late in the game to be talking about all of this."

Werner sank back into his seat, his face a mess of conflict.

"How could I have been so arrogant. I suppose in my mind's eye, I saw us finding the remnant, announcing who we were and the people just offering it to us for the sake of getting it to a place where more people could view and benefit from it."

"Sure 'n that's not gonna happen," Paddy said. "Like as not, they will put up a considerable resistance to the idea of it bein' removed."

Emily replied, "I agree. You have to understand that the area we are going to is economically distressed. This remnant —if indeed it exists—most likely represents the only thing of value the village has ever had. It's ancestral. Generational. That's why I fear Nathaniel getting there before us. He has a habit of just taking what he wants without regard for consequence."

"And how likely is it that he will get there before us?" I inquired.

She grinned.

"Not very."

"And why is that?"

"For the same reason that threw professor French and professor Spencer."

Cassie said, "You talking about that grammatical thing?"

"Exactly. Unless they have a top notch palaeographer working with them, I can almost guarantee that they will be sidetracked for a good, long while."

"A palae-what?" Aaron inquired.

"Palaeographer. Someone who studies ancient writing."

Aaron said, "So, we have a chance of getting there before them?"

Emily nodded.

"Yes, we do. Given the head start Nathaniel has had, it's a slim chance, but a chance nonetheless."

Désirée announced, "We are beginning our final descent. Please take your seats and engage your lap restraints."

I did as instructed and sat back, staring through the window at the vast, emerging landscape below.

Istanbul.

Byzantium.

Lygos.

Constantinople.

Three thousand years of history. So much of it covered in blood.

Cassie leaned across me to see out the window.

"I wasn't expecting it to be this beautiful."

"Really? And what were you expecting?"

"I don't know," she said, as she sat back in her seat "Maybe something not quite so modern."

"Well, straddling Europe and Asia as it does, there are both modern and ancient parts."

"Yeah, but I see skyscrapers and incredible architecture."

I chuckled.

"There are fifteen million people who live here, Cass. Not exactly a primitive society."

She said, "It's funny the impressions you form of places where you've never been."

"I know what you mean. I'm actually looking forward to our drive today. I think we're going to pass through some beautiful country. Tons of agriculture; cities that are every bit as modern as anything you'd find in America."

"Mountains?"

"Yeah. We basically have to climb from sea level in Istanbul to almost four thousand feet to get to Beyşehir."

"How about the roads?"

"From what I've been able to gather, they're not exactly goat trails."

If you want to know the truth, I'd actually prefer goat trails. It's harder to move a large company of armed MERC's around on goat trails.

CHAPTER FORTY-EIGHT

Atatürk Airport's runway gradually emerged as we banked in on our final approach over the Sea of Marmara. It was truly an impressive sight. I remembered reading somewhere that a new airport was under construction in Istanbul that, when completed, would make it the largest in the world with a capacity of somewhere around two hundred million passengers per year. Viewed from the air, I couldn't imagine why anyone would need an airport bigger than Atatürk. It was massive. Désirée circled twice before being given clearance to land, which she did deftly and flawlessly. She then began the process of taxiing—a process that went on long enough that I probably could have taken another nap.

I'm not kidding.

We dodged and wound our way in and out of jets and jumbo jets like a halfback going for the goal line and finally arrived at the General Aviation terminal and the waiting Airmark ground crew. As the marshaller directed us into position I could see a black Land Rover with four men standing beside it in a semi-formal arrangement. At first I thought perhaps they were part of the crew that Werner had contracted to handle our ground operations, but then I noticed the nearly identical black suits that each one wore and changed my assessment.

My next thought was that they were operatives Nathaniel had dispatched to intercept and neutralize us before we had a chance to get started. I dismissed that notion as well, thinking that there was no way in hell even a man as ruthless as Nathaniel would risk an open-air attack in broad daylight.

I got Aaron's attention and pointed through the window.

"Looks like we've got company."

"Any idea who they are?" he asked, bending over Cassie to peer through the window.

"None whatsoever. But, if body language is any indicator of intent, they definitely don't look like they harbor ill will toward us."

"Yeah, well...just the same..." he pulled a nasty looking pistol from a shoulder holster and racked the slide.

Being the consummate professional that I was, I decided that was probably a good idea and alerted the others as to the potential threat represented by the four men.

Désirée came out of the cockpit and saw us prepping our weapons.

She said, "Should I be aware of something?"

I gestured toward our welcome committee and said, "We're not sure what their intentions are, so we're just being prepared."

Emily rose up from looking out the window, a funny half smile on her lips.

"It is Gérard," she explained, gesturing toward one of the men. "I didn't think he was serious, but...there he is."

The man she indicated was standing in the middle of the group, his hands clasped comfortably and non-threateningly in front him.

"Interesting," I replied as Désirée opened the cabin door, triggered the control that lowered the AirStairs and stood back to allow our exit while at the same time pulling out a suppressed MAC-10 machine pistol chambered for .45 ACP rounds and slamming home a thirty-two-round magazine.

Werner and Elliot, seeing all of the firearms, were understandably nervous, so I took a moment to explain the situation and that, as we had discussed previously, it is far better to have a gun and not need it than it is to need a gun and not have it. I also told them that it would be better for them to stay on the plane under Désirée and Cassie's protection for the time being than to accompany us. They agreed, and we exited the plane.

When Aaron and I reached the tarmac, Gérard walked purposefully toward us and stopped when he was about three feet away.

"Monsieur Moriarity, it is a pleasure to meet you," he said as he dipped his head and offered his hand.

I shook his hand.

"I must say that your present attitude is far different than a few hours ago when we were discussing mutual destruction."

He shrugged and made a face as if to say, *"It is of no importance."*

Aaron asked, "Has anyone ever told you that you bear a striking resemblance to Jean Reno?"

A wry smile and then, "You are the first one today, monsieur."

It was true. He definitely looked like a young, Jean Reno. There was the same short, black hair and scruffy beard Mr. Reno is fond of wearing. Not slender, but certainly not muscular either. All in all, his appearance seemed to belie what I knew him to be: a ruthlessly efficient, coldly remorseless killer. And yet, even though we had briefly been enemies—and the possibility existed that we would be so again at some point—I found it impossible to dislike him. I sensed that we shared a kindred spirit, for we were each, in our own way, a barbarian. Even though historically, barbarians have been feared and shunned by polite society, there are times when they can prove useful.

When I was in seminary, I wrote a paper on a guy named Jephthah, one of Israel's judges, who lived about 982 BC. But he didn't always have that rank. The son of a prostitute, Jephthah was an outcast. Driven from his home in Gilead by his half-brothers—with the backing of the town elders—the historical account states that he settled east of Gilead in a city called Tob, where, according to the book of Judges, "Outlaws collected around Jephthah and went raiding with him."

In short, he became a barbarian.

But, when the hated Ammonites attacked Gilead, guess who the town elders turned to for protection and leadership? You guessed it. The barbarian. Because there are times when nothing short of a barbarian will do. Which is why men like Gérard and me will never be out of work.

While we were going through the introductions, Emily walked up behind me and I saw her presence reflected in Gérard's face. It was an amazing thing to behold. All of the hard lines disappeared, replaced by a softness only made possible by deep affection.

"Emily, mon chér," he said softly. "It is good to see you—to see that you are okay, and that the fool known as Ramón caused you no harm."

"Gérard, we need to get something settled right away."

"Oui?"

"Whatever you are feeling, or think you are feeling for me is not now, nor will it ever be reciprocated. I don't love you. I *can't* love you. I don't even like you. Given what I know of you, it is going to be difficult for me to even find a way to keep from despising you. And I need to know you understand that."

He shrugged again.

"Oui. Of this I am well aware. And I would never do anything to make you uncomfortable..." he stopped speaking and smiled. "Unless protecting your life makes you uncomfortable, in which case I will insist on continuing regardless of your feelings."

She almost returned his smile.

Almost.

"Yes, well, I just needed to get that out there," she said before stepping back to join Pete and Paddy.

I signaled that it was safe for the rest to exit the plane. As I did so, Gérard snapped his fingers and one of the other men opened the passenger side rear door of the Land Rover. Viola

Spencer stepped out, looking none the worse for wear. In fact, she appeared to be rather enjoying the experience of being ferried around in a luxury SUV with four burly men as her protectors.

Elliot was just coming down the AirStairs when he saw her.

"Mum!" he shouted, elbowing his way past the rest of us and running to embrace his mother. "Are you okay? Did they hurt you?"

"Oh, now Elliot," she said in faux complaint. "There's no need for all that. These men were perfect gentlemen. In fact, Gérard and I are fast friends now. Aren't we, Gérard?"

He smiled and shook his head slowly, ironically.

"It is as the lady says. She, unlike anyone before her, has bested me."

When everyone was off the plane and standing in a tight group around Gérard and his men, I said, "Do you have any idea of Nathaniel's plans?"

"Oui," he replied. "He will have hired a squad of mercenaries—"

"An actual squad?" Aaron asked, interrupting him. "Or is that a figurative term?"

"Eight men, plus Dagnar, monsieur."

"Dagnar?" Cassie said screwing up her face. "That's a real name? It sounds more like a character from Masters of the Universe, or something."

"Oui, mademoiselle. Dagnar is his name. He is the leader of Nathaniel's MERC's. He is formidable."

"I have heard of this man," Désirée said. "And he is, indeed, formidable."

"To my knowledge, he only fears one man."

"And who would that be?" I asked.

He hardened his face and replied, "C'est moi."

Not surprising.

"Okay, so he has nine mercenaries, and I assume they are very good."

"They are the best," he confirmed. "And Dagnar is better than all of them."

Paddy stepped forward.

"And what would be makin' the lad so good, if you don't mind me askin', sir?"

Gérard seemed to consider his answer before replying, "He has no conscience."

Emily barked out an ironic laugh, "Well, neither do you."

"Tout à fait, mon chér. But the difference is that Dagnar enjoys the pain and suffering he causes. He even studies ways to enhance the experience for his victims. As for me? Suffer, don't suffer...it is of no consequence to me. It is merely a job to be done."

Emily gestured emphatically in his direction as if to say, *"See what I told you?"* before heading into the terminal with Elliot and his mother.

I said, "Knowing Nathaniel as you do, will he have left anyone behind to attempt to sabotage our efforts?"

"Mais oui, monsieur. Which is why my men and I have been here for the past two hours awaiting your arrival."

"I see. And, did you observe anything during that time?"

"Non, monsieur. Nothing. But that doesn't mean that they are not close by, just waiting for the right opportunity."

I turned to Pete and Werner and said, "We probably need to get the gear offloaded and into the vehicles."

"We're on it, Mr. Moriarity sir," the ever-deferential Mr. Tolles replied as he and Werner walked toward the cargo hold and the waiting ground crew.

"Now," I continued. "About the provisions—"

"It has been taken care of, monsieur," Gérard said.

"Excuse me?"

He gestured toward a van that I hadn't seen earlier parked behind and parallel to the Land Rover.

"We have everything we will need for the trip."

I raised my eyebrows in surprise.

"Really? And, who paid for that?"

He grinned slightly and said, "Nathaniel was gracious enough to provide us with all the provisions we will require."

"You have a credit card?"

He wagged an American Express Centurion card in front of me.

"Oui, monsieur. So, whatever you need, simply let me know and…"

"Okay. Got it." I gestured toward his men. "And these men?"

"Nathaniel is providing them as well. They will be at your service for the duration."

"That's very generous of him," Aaron replied with a grin.

Emily, Elliot and his mother returned carrying several maps between them.

"Find anything?" I asked.

"I believe we did," Emily replied. "It'll take us a bit to plot a route, but I am confident of being able to do so."

The normally taciturn and conservative Elliot surprised us all by muttering, "Shit just got real," and gesturing toward a vehicle that was headed toward us across the tarmac at a high rate of speed.

Through the front windshield I could clearly see the driver and at least three passengers, and the man sitting in the front passenger seat appeared to be a blonde giant.

CHAPTER FORTY-NINE

Inclining his head in the direction of the vehicle, Gérard said, "It would appear that Dagnar has come to offer his greeting."

The vehicle screeched to a stop and five men spilled out, each one heavily armed. They assumed an expertly arranged tactical formation, seemingly surprised to find themselves facing so many weapons.

One of them stalked toward us by himself. I assumed it was Dagnar. He truly was a giant. One of the largest men I have ever seen, as a matter of fact. He made Aaron appear small, and that is not easy to do. I noticed this because he completely ignored the rest of us and stopped directly in front of Aaron. He had at least three inches in height and forty or fifty pounds on him.

He didn't say anything, but just stood there staring.

Aaron stared back.

He's good at it.

It was an interesting situation, those two very large men just facing off and staring at each other without speaking.

After about a minute had ticked by, Gérard said sharply, "Dagnar!" causing the big man's head to snap toward him. "What game are you playing at?"

Dagnar turned his attention back toward Aaron before replying, "It is not a game, Gérard. I have business to attend to with this man. And I ask you to stay out of it."

Aaron moved a step closer and growled, "The only business you will have with me, son, is pain."

Dagnar responded in kind and moved in until there were mere inches separating them.

"Yes, there will be pain, but I will not be the one experiencing it."

"You sound very confident for a piece of shit. In fact, I think this may be the first time I've ever heard a piece of shit talk. You ever heard a piece of shit talk before, Jake?"

"Can't say as I have," I said enjoying the game. "But, we really don't have time for this. So, Dagnar, or whatever the hell your name is, you need to run along and stop annoying us or I will personally take you apart."

He turned as if seeing me for the first time.

"You must be Moriarity."

"Your powers of perception are truly staggering."

He sneered, "I will deal with you as soon as I am through with your friend."

Désirée said, "Should I shoot him?"

"Not just yet, but Pete, Paddy...if blondie here makes any aggressive moves, kill all his men."

"With pleasure," Pete replied.

Dagnar had to know that he was outnumbered better than two to one; that he had no chance of prevailing should it come down to a firefight. And yet he chose to take decisive action.

I should say that he attempted to take decisive action.

Without warning, he tried to head-butt Aaron.

I may have mentioned that Aaron Perry—besides being the world's premier jazz pianist—is also highly skilled at several forms of martial arts. Among them Hapkido, Aikido and Brazilian Jiu-jitsu. He is also the most brutally strong human I have ever encountered. He weighs two hundred and sixty pounds and can easily bench-press twice his bodyweight.

In addition, he is just ridiculously fast.

I was about to say for a man his size.

Forget that.

For a man of *any* size.

By the time Dagnar had begun his movement, it was as if Aaron had anticipated the move and was three or four moves ahead of him. I won't bore you with the technical details, but I will tell you that if I had not seen what happened with my own eyes, I would've had trouble believing it had happened.

As Dagnar snapped his head forward, Aaron somehow sidestepped the blow and kicked his feet out from under him while at the same time grabbing his right arm in some form of Hapkido mumbo-jumbo, the result of which was Dagnar doing a face-plant onto the tarmac and Aaron standing over him with his right foot planted firmly in the middle of the man's back.

Then we heard a sharp crack and Dagnar crying out in pain.

It seemed as if Aaron had dislocated the man's shoulder.

But he wasn't through.

I forgot to mention that Aaron also has the largest, strongest hands I've ever seen on a man. They're about the size of one of those big, competition Frisbees. While he still had control of Dagnar's arm, he went ahead and snapped his thumb, followed by a complete mangling of his wrist. It was only then that he stepped back and resumed his original position.

The entire sequence of events had taken no more than ten seconds.

And he wasn't even breathing hard.

Dagnar's men didn't seem to know what to do, so Gérard stepped forward and helped the man to his feet, brushed a bit of debris from his clothing and said, "You are very fortunate, mon ami, that it was Monsieur Perry you were facing. Me? I would have killed you. And should you ever be so stupid as to try something like this again…I promise you that will be the final outcome."

Dagnar was obviously in excruciating pain, but he attempted to stand tall, mustering as much dignity as possible given the circumstances.

"Now crawl back to Nathaniel and tell him that he cannot win against me…" Gérard swept his arm in a broad circle,

"...against us. He is out-classed and out-manned." He turned slightly as if starting to walk away, and then, "Oh, one more thing."

Almost faster than my eye could track, Gérard punched Dagnar in the nose, shattering it into multiple shards of bone, causing the man to shriek in pain and drop to his knees clutching the crimson ruin with his good hand.

Nathaniel's champion, completely and utterly destroyed.

Two of Dagnar's men ran toward us causing everyone on our side to draw down on them. They stopped with their hands raised and explained that they only wanted to help their fallen leader. Gérard, hands clasped casually behind his back, nodded for them to continue and they attempted to lift Dagnar to his feet. After three failed attempts, they finally settled on dragging him toward their vehicle.

The sudden display of brutality seemed to have left everyone in shock. Viola stood with her hands covering her mouth, Elliot's arm stretched protectively across her shoulders; Emily stood with mouth agape, visibly trembling; Werner, leaning against the AirStairs railing for support, kept wiping his hand across his eyes as if attempting to banish what he had just witnessed.

As for the rest of us—Désirée and Cassie included—we were no strangers to bloody and brutal violence. And as unpleasant as it was to observe, it was nothing we hadn't seen before.

As Dagnar's men loaded him carefully and with great difficulty into the front passenger seat, I said, "What was that about?"

Gérard said, "We have a history together...this man and me."

Cryptic, but I decided not to press it further.

"Well, I suppose that takes him out of the game,"

"Only partially, monsieur. He is left handed. So, he will still be able to shoot. Only now, motivated by revenge, his decisions will be compromised."

It was sound, battlefield logic. Brutal, but sound.

Cassie said, "Why did he do that? Why just walk up to Aaron and try to attack him? I mean he doesn't even know him!"

I deferred to Gérard who replied, "It is something I have seen him do before. He follows a strategy of determining what your opponent cherishes—the thing that is under his protection—and then attacking them at that point, believing that in so doing you will demoralize them, making them susceptible to attack. I am only surprised that he chose Monsieur Perry and not you, mademoiselle."

I said, "Perhaps he determined that Aaron was the strongest, and if he could take him down, the rest of us would lose heart."

Aaron replied, "If the boy would've done his homework, he would've known better than to tussle with me."

Gérard smiled, saying, "Oui, but that is not the way Dagnar thinks. I believe he did, indeed do his homework, as you say, and that is the very reason he chose to attack you."

Dagnar's vehicle roared to life and sped off. As it moved by I could see him slumped back against the seat, a towel pressed against his ruined nose.

I clapped my hands and called for everyone to gather around.

"What you just witnessed was unpleasant, but necessary. There may very well be more of that level of violence, and worse, to come. So, I need everyone to focus and set aside any emotions you may be feeling." I paused for effect, and continued, "This is a serious, brutal business we are involved in here. With everything that is at stake, Nathaniel will have justified any action...including the taking of life to accomplish his goals, and we have to be prepared to meet whatever he throws at us head-on. With that in mind...Cassie, I need you to find a nice hotel—a *very* nice hotel—where Mrs. Spencer can stay for the duration...and I want you to stay with her."

She asked, "And, how should I pay for it?"

Gérard smiled slightly and pulled a thick wad of cash from an inside coat pocket.

"Monsieur Prince would be most happy to accomodate you."

In the midst of the ensuing laughter, I continued, "The rest of you need to understand that moving forward will place you in harm's way. I cannot force this upon you. It has to be a decision you come to on your own."

I made eye contact with each of our team and received non-verbal assent from each.

"Good. Now…" I glanced at my watch, "it's 11:50. I want to be loaded and on our way in thirty minutes, which means we've got to hustle."

Gérard said, "If you will allow it, monsieur, my men and I will secure a perimeter just in case Nathaniel has any further ideas of preempting our endeavor."

"Thank you, Gérard. That will be very helpful."

As he moved off to consult with and position his men, Aaron walked up beside me.

"Something weird about that Dagnar dude."

"What do you mean?"

"I don't know. Hard to explain. Just…maybe like…he wasn't giving it everything he had, or something."

"That doesn't make any sense at all."

"Yeah," he said. "I know. But that's the way it felt."

"You realize that you're basically suggesting that the man took a dive, right?"

"I know…I know. But, I'm just sayin'."

"His nose sustained multiple fractures, Aaron. Why would a guy deliberately—"

"Nah, man. He wasn't planning on that happening. I'm talking about before…when he took me on. After you've been in hand-to-hand combat as much as I have, you get a feel for various opponents. Like, knowing when someone is overconfident, or hesitant or just plain scared shitless."

"And Dagnar?"

"Like I said...felt to me like he was holding back. I mean, hell Jake...'man that big should've been able to buck me right off his back, but he just laid there and took it."

"Yeah...I'm not buying it. You beat the shit out of him and there was nothing he could've done to stop you."

He shook his head slowly, and then said, "I'm not so sure. Not sure at all."

"And this is troubling to you?"

"Not necessarily. It's just that it's something worth noting, is all."

"All right. Duly noted."

He nodded and sauntered off to help with the unloading leaving me standing there wondering what in the bloody hell was going on, because if what he was suggesting was true...it made me very nervous. I don't know why...but it did.

CHAPTER FIFTY

Nathaniel Prince was angry. One might even say the man was seething.

In point of fact, there were only two or three times he could recall in his entire life when he had felt the level of rage that now roiled his emotions.

Staring at his fallen champion where he lay on the hastily improvised gurney—right arm immobile and a local physician attempting to set the remains of his nose—he said, "Tell me again what happened."

Dagnar moved the doctor aside and answered through gritted teeth, "You know what happened."

It had been roughly three hours since the humiliating, excruciatingly painful incident. Three hours to think it through. Three hours to experience every single detail over and over again in his mind. Dagnar turned his head and nodded for the doctor to continue, his eyes flitting around the cluttered warehouse Nathaniel had secured for their staging area.

Nathaniel prompted, "No, before that. I want to know *how?* How could you have put yourself in harm's way like that? I find it so very unlike you that it makes me suspicious. We had specific intel regarding Mr. Perry's prowess, but you chose to ignore it."

"It wasn't like that."

"Then, please…enlighten me," Nathaniel prompted, his rage barely held in check.

"It's simple. At the last second, I decided to change tactics."

"You're going to have to explain that to me."

The doctor finished up and seemed like he wanted to give Dagnar instructions on how to care for his nose, but one of the MERC's spun him around and hustled him from the building.

Dagnar probed the area tenderly with his fingers while saying, "I held back, thinking that by doing so, I could entice Perry into acting in an overconfident manner and turn that against him."

"But…?"

"I learned that with this man, there is no overconfidence. There is no need. He is…formidable. The strongest man I have ever encountered—and the fastest."

"Stronger than you?"

A hesitation, and then, "Yes. Stronger than me."

"And so he bested you…you who could not be beaten!"

"I never claimed that distinction."

"But it was implied," Nathaniel shouted. "It must have been, or else I never would've hired you." He let his rage subside, and then said, "And what happens now? You are a cripple."

Dagnar moved his right arm and wrist gingerly, testing for range of motion.

"No, not crippled. Merely impaired."

"But, you now only have one arm and a nose you cannot possibly breathe through."

Dagnar suddenly smashed his left hand down on top of a wooden table that had been dragged over to the side of the gurney, crushing it into several pieces causing everyone, including Nathaniel to jump and back up a few paces.

"As you can see," he said calmly, "I have more strength in my one hand than most men have in two. And I am left-handed. I can still shoot and I can still think. I will finish what I started with this Mr. Perry. Celebrity or not, I will kill him, Moriarity and everyone with them."

"Including Gérard?" Nathaniel prompted.

Dagnar thought through the encounter with his hated

rival.

"Including the traitor, Gérard."

"Whom you have also never bested. And now you have an injured arm and a brutally broken nose." Nathaniel paused and then added, "In spite of your contentions to the contrary, Dagnar, it seems to me that you are running more on bravado than reality; that you are not thinking clearly; that, perhaps, your motivation at this point has more to do with seeking revenge than in carrying out the task for which you were hired and paid an enormous sum of money."

Dagnar seemed to consider Nathaniel's words before replying, "While I will admit to harboring feelings of revenge, I can assure you that my thinking is as clear as it ever was."

Nathaniel pressed in, "Are we speaking of the same level of thinking that caused you to grossly overestimate Mr. Perry?"

"That was different. That—"

"And then there is Jake Moriarity. From what I have heard, Aaron Perry pales in comparison to him, and Aaron Perry made you look like a rank amateur. If you couldn't handle Perry, what makes you think you can handle Moriarity?"

"It will not be a prob—"

"It's already a problem!" Nathaniel exploded. "I am staring at the evidence of just how great of a problem it is. Nathaniel turned and stalked around the room angrily, pausing to kick over a couple of wastebaskets in passing. Stopping at the doorway, he turned and glared in Dagnar's direction. "I will give you some time to get your thinking right, Dagnar. I do not want to replace you…but if it comes down to that or failing in our mission, I will not hesitate. And when I say, 'replace,' I am sure you understand that I mean *eliminate*. Are we clear?"

Dagnar stared at the man, his expression inscrutably blank.

"Perfectly. I will not disappoint you."

"Ohhh…" Nathaniel breathed, his voice dripping with

irony, "You have *already* disappointed me, Dagnar. Now, you just have to work on not doing it again."

And with that, he stormed out of the room, followed by his four personal bodyguards.

Dagnar allowed his head to fall back heavily onto the cushioned comfort of the pillow the doctor had provided, his mind awash in a deluge of emotions.

The mission no longer mattered. All that was left to him was exacting a terrible vengeance and restoring a reputation that was now in tatters.

And what of this Moriarity? While he had largely ignored the man during his disastrous encounter with Aaron Perry, he had felt his life force. It emanated from him in waves. He always felt a similar sensation when in Nathaniel's presence. It was something that transcended physical strength, although from the intel he had been provided, Moriarity was nearly as formidable as Perry in that regard. It was more a force of will. And he found that he was compelled to admit that it intimidated him. Then again, that could be his ragged emotions exerting undue negative influence on his ability to formulate rational thoughts.

He signaled one of his men for assistance and stood to his feet.

The man asked, "What now, Dagnar?"

He stood, one hand on the table attempting to gain some semblance of balance.

"Now, we do what we were hired to do."

"And what of—"

"Moriarity?" He paused for effect, and then, "Moriarity should pray that we do not see one another again."

"But, Gérard is with him, and the other man—"

Dagnar slapped the man across the face, sending him sprawling onto the filthy floor.

"You will not speak that name again!" Turning to regard the rest of his squad, he added, "None of you will speak his name ever again. Are we clear?" As they nodded affirmation he said, "Bring me my weapon. It is time to go."

The men began loading into the two waiting SUV's as Dagnar struggled to fit the weapon's strap over his head with one arm, thinking all the while that he would use it to strangle Aaron Perry the next time he saw him.

CHAPTER FIFTY-ONE

It was 4:47 p.m., and we were a little over four hours outside of Istanbul, our five vehicles running in a tight formation down D200.

Five.

It was a ridiculous number of vehicles, but even with Cassie staying behind to watch over Mrs. Spencer, there were still eight from our original party plus Gérard and his three men. One van contained our provisions—couldn't really do without that. Another van was reserved for armaments, ammo and transporting the remnant and whatever other relics we came across. And the other three vehicles were SUV's. So, two of Gérard's men were in the "chuck wagon", as Pete had dubbed it; he and Werner rode in the other van; Paddy, Emily and Elliot were in one of our SUV's, Gérard and his driver in another, while Aaron, Désirée and I were in the third.

After more discussion than I felt warranted, the travel order was like this: Gérard and his driver were in front; Emily and Elliot were the official navigators of the expedition, so Paddy's SUV was next; Aaron and I were third; then came Pete and Werner's SUV with the chuck wagon bringing up the rear.

Like I said...too many damn vehicles.

Cassie hadn't been exactly thrilled with my decision to leave her behind with Mrs. Spencer, but she understood the need and accepted the assignment with grace. I wasn't worried about either one of them for Cassie was more than capable of holding her own against anyone Nathaniel might send against her. Not that I thought that there was even a remote chance of that happening. Still...it was good to know Mrs.

Spencer was safe.

We had just sped through a formidable looking city called Eskişehir and were approaching the turnoff to merge with D675. Based on the level of traffic we were seeing, I figured we had a minimum of three and a half to four hours to go before reaching Beyşehir, which would put us in well after dark, a situation not to my liking. But the dustup with Dagnar and company had set us back close to an hour, and at this point there was no making up for lost time.

Gérard texted that we were going to be taking the exit right before the merge so that we could make a rest stop at the Gulf Oil gas station and also take on fuel for the duration of the journey.

I've got to tell you that as I've gotten older, rest stops seem to occur with much more frequency. Time was when I could easily go eight hours without feeling a pressing need to relieve my bladder. Not anymore! My doctor tells me that it's a prostate issue. Prostate issue? I'm not old enough to be even *thinking* about prostate issues let alone having them, which he assures me I do not.

Have prostate issues, that is.

Nevertheless…I do find myself having to pee more often than when I was a younger man. Probably too much information, but there you go.

We pulled off the freeway looking like a damn military convoy and quickly took care of our business and were soon back on the road.

After the merge with the D675, the country really began to open up. Everywhere we looked there seemed to be agricultural fields in various levels of planting, harvesting and tilling. It was an impressive sight, and one that took me completely by surprise. My estimation of Turkey had been that it was a dry and desolate land fit more for camels and scorpions than abundant agriculture.

Aaron said, "Wasn't expecting this."

"Me either. I guess it shows how ignorant most of us

Americans are of world geography."

"Yeah, man. We pretty narrow in our focus. As in, if it ain't happenin' here, it ain't happenin' at all."

Désirée added, "It is not just Americans, monsieur. We French are notorious for believing that we alone are superior among all mankind."

We rode in silence for a time, just watching the landscape roll by.

Finally, Aaron said, "Let me ask you a question."

"Ask."

"You feel okay about this Gérard dude?"

"I don't know. I suppose. Why do you ask?"

He sighed.

"Hard to explain, but I keep getting this idea that maybe he isn't what he appears to be."

"So, you're saying that he isn't a stone-cold killer?"

He flapped his hand at me and said, "Nah, man. Not that. I'm talkin' about the man not being entirely forthcoming with us."

"As in he's not really on our side?"

"Yeah."

"Well, he's not."

Out of the corner of my eye, I could see his dreadlocked head snap toward me.

"You know that?"

"Of course. Look…he's not *for* us. He's *against* Nathaniel. The two are not the same thing."

A pause, and then Désirée said, "The enemy of my enemy is my friend?"

"Something like that."

"And you're good with that?" Aaron asked.

I thought about it for a few seconds and said, "In this instance, I see us as co-belligerents."

"That another way of saying what Désirée said?"

"About my enemy's enemy?"

"Yeah."

"I guess it is. And the bottom line for me is that I'm good with whatever will help Elliot and Werner secure their remnant and get us all home safely."

He asked, "But what if the dude gets greedy and decides to take the remnant for himself?"

"I don't think he'd do that."

"Why not?"

"Emily."

"What about her?"

I explained, "Gérard has a thing for her. I don't think he'd do anything that could potentially cause her harm."

He grinned and said, "As long as she's working with us."

He had a point.

"Yeah, there is that."

We rode for another bit in silence, during which time I thought through the conundrum presented by Ms. Emily Young. She was definitely a wildcard. Having already demonstrated a proclivity toward disloyalty—even though it appeared that, partially at least, she had been acting in the best interest of others—if it came right down to it, I would have a tough time giving her my complete trust. And yet, I had no choice but to trust her, at least for the time being.

I finally said, "While it is true that both Gérard and Emily are demonstrably untrustworthy, they are by no means allies. She has made it quite clear that she despises the man."

"Yeah, but…that remnant represents the potential for tremendous financial gain. People have done some weird shit for money."

Aaron was right. I hate it when he's right.

Désirée said, "Gérard and his men could pose some problems should they be so inclined."

"No…I get that. But it would represent a needless distraction."

"So, what 'chu gonna do?" Aaron asked.

I checked my watch.

"Given that we're within two and a half hours of Beyşehir, there's not a whole lot else we can do at this point besides just roll with it and keep our eyes wide open."

"Heard that."

Once again, silence descended and we rode the rest of the way with each of us lost in our own thoughts. This was becoming very complicated. And we hadn't even found the damn thing yet. Because once we did…there would be another level of complications arising out of our hope to procure the remnant and its owners desiring to keep it. It made me wish I was sitting on my back patio, looking out over the Las Vegas valley with Gabi by my side; sipping a really good New Zealand sauvignon blanc and talking about how gorgeous she looked in the moonlight.

Suddenly the lead vehicle—the one with Gérard in it—braked and pulled off to the side of the road, prompting the rest of us to follow.

"Could be nothing," Aaron observed as he racked the slide on his P226. "All the same, though."

CHAPTER FIFTY-TWO

We pulled over behind Emily and Elliot and parked, and the passenger side door of the lead SUV opened and Gérard stepped out and began walking toward us with a purposeful step with Aaron gripping the pistol where it couldn't be seen from the outside.

When he got closer to us, he indicated that I should roll down my window. Which I did.

He said rather breathlessly, "We do not need to go through Beyşehir in order to reach our destination."

"Okay, I'm listening."

He held up his phone and tapped the screen revealing a map of the area.

"We are here…and where we are going is approximately…there."

I took the proffered device and did the two-finger thing on the screen to expand the Google Earth image, noticing immediately that a place called Altinapa Dam had been highlighted.

"Altinapa Dam?" I queried, as Désirée leaned in from the back seat to observe.

"Keep looking," he replied.

I followed a long river valley stretching southward from the dam and saw a tiny village called, İsa'nın haçı."

Emily arrived, standing beside Gérard with about as much enthusiasm as one would expect from someone being forced into proximity to a rabid dog.

She said, "I apologize for not noticing this earlier. Gérard called me and pointed out the alternate route. I agree.

We need to change. It's the only way to get to İsa'nın haçı without wasting time—time we don't really have."

"What does İsa'nın haçı mean?"

"Basically, Jesus' cross," Désirée explained, and then off of our surprised looks continued, "Turkish is one of five languages in which I am fluent."

I said, "Impressive." Then to Emily, "So, you're telling me that the place we're going is actually called Jesus' Cross? That's a little obvious, isn't it?"

"Well, without going into a lot of explanation, which I'd rather not do standing by the side of a busy highway..." She paused as a large tractor-trailer blew by, shaking our SUV in its backdraft, and then continued, "It has been officially called by that name for centuries. The locals, however, call it, Mucizelerin Portalı...the portal of miracles."

I checked my watch. 6:15 p.m.

"We have arranged for accommodations in Beyşehir. Are you suggesting that we blow those off and head directly for this place?"

Gérard said, "That is exactly what I am suggesting, monsieur. Nathaniel is most likely there, or very close. And I fear for the people in possession of the remnant if he gets to them before we do."

Pete jogged up.

"What's goin' on, fellas?"

Gesturing for Pete to give me a second, I asked Emily, "What are the chances of Nathaniel figuring out the mistake in grammar in the manuscript and getting there ahead of us?"

"Very slim. There are seven experts in this field, and three of them are with us on this expedition. And the other four are so far under the radar that even a man as resourceful as Nathaniel would be severely challenged to find them."

To Pete I said, "We're changing things up a little. Taking a different route and going straight to the village housing the remnant."

"Sounds good to me. Let's ride."

And with that, he turned and ran back to explain the situation to Paddy before climbing back into his van.

Aaron got my attention and pointed down to his phone, where he had written, *"Could be they're in collusion. Different route because of trap?"*

I thought about it. Looked each of them in the eyes. Glanced back at Aaron. Decided that the change was legit.

"Okay, Gérard. Where do we go?"

He tapped the map on his phone and said, "As you can see, in only five miles, we need to merge onto D300. From there it is, how do you say…a straight shot to the dam and the village beyond."

"And, how long will it take to get there if we bypass Beyşehir?"

"No more than two hours," he replied confidently.

"It's 6:20 now, so between 8:30 and 9:00. It'll be full dark. Not the ideal time to be entering unfamiliar territory."

"Oui. But, it is necessary, monsieur."

Aaron leaned toward the open window and said, "What if Nathaniel gets there ahead of us and sets up an ambush? In the dark, we'll never see it coming. I say we continue on as planned into Beyşehir and wait until the morning to head out."

Another big rig blew by nearly taking Gérard and Emily off their feet.

"This is impossible, Monsieur Perry," Gérard replied. "There is no time to lose."

I said, "Look, we can't stay here arguing about this on the side of the road. If one of those damn big rigs doesn't take us out, sooner or later a member of the local constabulary is going to show up and want to know what five vehicles are doing lined up on the side of his highway. If he decides to search Pete's SUV, we're all screwed." I paused…thinking. Then, "I know it's risky…but given what's at stake, it needs to be done."

Aaron shrugged, "Well, it's not like we're undermanned

or outgunned. So…I'm in."

I caught Désirée's eyes in the rearview mirror and she gave a quick, non-committal shrug that I took as affirmation.

I said, "All right. Let's roll."

With a curt nod of his head Gérard jogged back to his SUV with Emily following a little behind, her expression set with hard lines.

As we pulled slowly out into the travel lanes, I said to Aaron, "So, you still thinking those two are in collusion?"

"No, I'm not. Hard to fake that level of contempt."

"I know what you mean. It feels as if she genuinely despises the man."

"Oh," Désirée replied "she definitely despises him. She told me all about it before ou,r flight. The issues between them are numerous and very deep. What you are observing is genuine."

We were following the queue onto the D300 turnoff when my phone buzzed.

It was Cassie.

"Hey, little girl. Everything okay?"

"It is now!"

She sounded a bit winded and disgusted.

I put the phone on speaker.

"Aaron and Désirée are here with me. Want to tell us what's going on?"

"Well, Mrs. Spencer and I started feeling, in her words, 'a bit peckish,' so we ordered room service. A *lot* of room service. Like…two hundred dollars worth." She added, "I did the currency conversion. Anyway, when it was delivered, the guy bringing it in had a weird vibe about him."

"One of Nathaniel's goons?" Aaron asked.

"No, nothing like that."

I said, "Then what?"

"He was looking at me like I was looking at the steak on the tray."

"Oh boy."

"Yeah. And after he got the trays settled on the table and the plates arranged, the kid made a pass at me."

"Explain pass."

"Umm…while I was distracted getting Mrs. Spencer settled at the table, he comes up behind me and wraps his arms around me and actually grabs my boobs."

Aaron chuckled, "Can't imagine that worked out too well for the boy."

"No, it didn't."

"That is unbelievably random."

"Not really. I saw him eyeballing me when we checked in, so when he brought the food in and I recognized that it was the same kid, I was sort of expecting him to try something. He just had that look about him."

I asked, "And, is he hospitalized or merely feeling contrite?"

"Definitely feeling contrite and perhaps considering visiting the hospital when he starts peeing blood in the morning."

"Damn! What'd you do to him?"

She said, "As you are aware, I really don't like people grabbing me from behind or, as Viola put it, 'touching my lady bits.' Brings back too many memories of my time with Paul Morgan."

"The late Paul Morgan," Aaron reminded.

"Yes, well…this kid grabbed me, so I spun—just like you taught me, Aaron—and threw him over my shoulder onto the coffee table. Then, I flipped him over onto his stomach and started dropping elbows onto his kidneys. After reminding him how tender a man's genitals are, I broke his nose for good measure."

Aaron feigned being choked up.

"I'm just…so proud."

I said, "And is it safe to assume that he left after that?"

"Well, yeah…after I helped him recover a little bit."

That was my girl.

"You're the only person I know who, after beating the living hell out of someone sticks around to make sure they're okay."

"Oh, come on, Uncle. You do the same thing."

"And, how did Viola take the sudden display of violence?"

Cassie laughed.

"She was standing on the sofa screaming for me to, 'Bust his bollocks!'"

"So, what happened afterwards?" Aaron asked.

"I let him go."

"You let him go?"

"Yeah."

"Let him go like Arnold Schwarzenegger's character let Sully go in Commando?"

She laughed and said, "No, no…nothing like that. I actually let him go and told him that if I saw him anywhere around the hotel during the rest of our stay that I'd tell the manager what happened and have him arrested. Where are you guys anyway?"

"Well, we're on a highway called D300 and we're on a route that will completely bypass Beyşehir and get us to the village that houses the remnant by later this evening."

"Night, huh?"

"Yeah. Can't be helped."

"Well, be careful, Uncle—you too, Aaron, Désirée."

"I love you, little girl."

"Love you too, Uncle."

She rang off and Désirée said, "She is quite amazing."

"Always has been. I saw stuff in her at the age of seven when she came to live with me that is in full bloom now."

"It must make you very proud."

"Yeah, it does."

Aaron yawned and stretched, and said, "You know…I'm actually feeling pretty good about the decision to get this thing done tonight."

"If you want to know the truth, so am I."
And then it started raining.

CHAPTER FIFTY-THREE

Now, when I say raining, you need to understand that I'm not talking about a wimpy, Southern California drizzle. It was a level of rain that my very southern mama would've referred to as a gully washer. The windows of heaven seemed to have been torn open in diluvian fashion. Even on the highest speed, the Land Rover's wipers were no match for the sheer volume of water cascading down upon our hapless vehicle from a tattered sky.

"Bro," Aaron said, shouting to be heard over the din. "This sucks!"

I stabbed out Gérard's number on my phone and waited for the call to connect, only to realize after several seconds of silence that we had zero connectivity.

"Something must've taken out the nearest cell tower, or something," I hollered.

Aaron held his phone up for me to see.

"I got nothing."

"Nor do I," Désirée echoed.

"And I'm sure no one else does either."

We needed to pull over and ride out the squall, if indeed that was what we were experiencing. Anything more than that, and I feared for our ability to get to where we were going. Glancing through the side windows, because they seemed to be a bit freer from water than the windshield, I couldn't see anything in any direction except darkness. No lights. No sign of civilization. Nothing.

"This is not good."

I looked in my rearview mirror just in time to see the chuck wagon spin out and come to rest against an embankment facing the opposite direction.

"Well, shit," I muttered under my breath and started honking my horn and flashing my lights to alert the two vehicles in front of us as I slowly pulled over to the side of the roadway, which at this point had narrowed down to one lane in either direction due to the sheer volume of water

Aaron said, "If one of those big rigs comes along right about now..."

There was no need for him to finish the sentence.

Pete pulled in right behind me, but there was no sign of Paddy or Gérard's vehicles.

I said, "We've got to go see if that van is drivable. If not, we're going to have to leave it behind."

"Yeah. Given the situation, provisions are the least of our worries," Aaron agreed.

"Désirée, can you haul our tactical bags out of the back, please?"

"Mais oui, monsieur."

Fortunately, we had been possessed of the presence of mind to include rain ponchos and boots when assembling our provisions, which we hurriedly dug out and pulled on over our clothes.

I said, "Désirée, I need you to stay here with the vehicle in case we need to move."

"Oui."

Aaron and I threw open our respective doors and stepped out into the downpour. It was like jumping into the deep end of a swimming pool. The incessant rain seemed intent on filling every cranial and facial orifice.

"Now I know what it feels like to be waterboarded!" Aaron hollered as we slogged our way toward the disabled van, with Pete exiting and joining us along the way.

"Man, oh man!" he yelled as we ran toward the van. "I haven't seen rain like this since the last time I was home."

When we got closer to the van, we could hear the driver trying vainly to start the engine.

"What happens if it won't start?" Pete asked.

"We leave it," I said. "There's no other choice."

"Maybe we could get enough food outta here and into our van to at least get us through the next day or so," he suggested.

As I approached the driver's side window, the man lowered the window enough to communicate and said in very heavily-accented French, "It is no good. The engine, she is flooded."

"Along with everything else," Aaron grumbled.

Seeing's how Aaron is fluent in French, I asked him to communicate Pete's suggestion to the men regarding offloading some of the food as Pete and I hustled back to his van.

As we clambered inside, Werner shouted, "What's happening?"

I said, "The chuck wagon is out of commission and we're going to have to leave it behind. But first we have to transfer as much food as possible into here."

"I mean…I live in Seattle and I've never seen rain like this."

With the chuck wagon turned and facing the wrong way, Pete was able to back up so that the rear of his van was within six or eight inches of the rear doors. With Werner holding a tarp over the remaining space, we were able to get a significant amount of provisions transferred with a minimal amount of soaking.

After we had salvaged everything we could, I had Aaron tell the men to lock the van up and get in with Pete and Werner so we could be on our way.

I have to tell you, though, that it concerned me that neither of the two lead SUV's had come back for us.

It concerned me quite a lot.

Pete said, "We gonna just keep driving in this mess, or sit here and ride it out?"

Aaron added, "Do you even have an idea of where we're going without GPS?"

I did not, and told him so.

"But, we can't just sit here on the side of the highway, either. It isn't safe," I added, glancing up at the sky that seemed, in the last several minutes, to have found a new reservoir of water to unleash.

Désirée started honking the horn, so Aaron and I hurried forward.

Once inside and out of the deluge, she said, "I have just heard from Emily."

"You have cell service?" I exclaimed.

"Oui. It was brief, but long enough for her to get a call through to me."

"Where are they?"

"She does not know. They are broken down somewhere ahead of us."

"Broken down? What happened? Did she say?"

Désirée said, "Only that they are stranded."

Aaron asked, "Is Gérard with them?"

"No, monsieur. They have become separated with no way to communicate."

"Okay," I replied. "We're going to move ahead and try to find them."

Aaron said skeptically, "How you gonna do that?"

"Look, we know that they are ahead of us. The traffic isn't heavy because, I mean, who in bloody hell would be out driving in this mess unless they absolutely had to? So, we drive as quickly as caution will allow until we find them. We can't leave our friends stranded."

"Heard that."

I ran back and explained the situation to Pete and Werner and then returned to our SUV, threw it in gear and pulled out carefully through the flooded outside lane, thanking my lucky stars that Werner had had the good sense to rent Land Rovers, whose four-wheel drive capabilities and ability to withstand liquid assault are nearly legendary.

A mile went by.

Then two.

At approximately 9:00 p.m., we passed a very bad wreck involving three cars and a two-ton box truck. All four vehicles were off the roadway with one of the cars on its roof and the other drivers and passengers attempting to extricate at least two people trapped inside.

"Now that right there is what worries me," Aaron growled.

"Doesn't do a whole lot for my confidence level either," I concurred.

Five miles and still no sign of Paddy's SUV.

"Is it possible we could have passed them?" Désirée inquired.

"I was going to say no, but with visibility what it is and given the almost complete absence of light...I can't really say. I'm going to give it ten miles and then, well...I don't know what we'll do. Turn around and come back, I suppose."

"Perhaps by that time our cellular service will have been restored."

Aaron huffed, "Yeah, and maybe monkeys will fly out my butt."

Désirée frowned.

"I'm afraid I do not understand the connection between cellular service and monkeys, monsieur."

Aaron rattled off a few phrases in French, causing Désirée to laugh and say, "Mais oui. Now I see. It is sarcasm."

Suddenly, a shape emerged in front of us out of the midst of the liquid darkness.

It was our missing SUV.

"There they are," I said.

I parked directly behind it, with Pete pulling in behind me. Aaron and I exited and ran forward to check on our friends.

It was empty.

CHAPTER FIFTY-FOUR

"What the hell!" Aaron hollered over the roar of the rain.

A quick scan of the interior revealed nothing except copious amounts of water where the rain had intruded through the open doors.

"The amount of water on the front and back seats looks like someone pulled all three of them out."

Aaron had the rear hatch open and was saying, "All their stuff is gone. Luggage. Tech bags. Paddy's weapons. Everything."

I jerked my thumb toward our SUV and we rushed back to get in out of the torrent.

Désirée looked a question at me and I answered, "It's empty."

"But…how?"

"I wish I could tell you."

"I didn't see any blood," Aaron observed. "So, it doesn't look like Paddy even had time to put up a fight."

The passenger door behind me opened and Pete threw himself inside.

"So, what's goin' on?" he asked.

Aaron answered, "The SUV is empty. They're gone. Their stuff is gone."

I said, "Obviously, someone from Nathaniel's crew was following us and when Paddy's vehicle broke down, they were close enough to move in and make the abduction."

Pete replied, "Man, in this weather, if a vehicle even looked similar to the one you're driving, there's no way they would've been able to make the distinction."

Désirée said, "And if someone came up to the driver's window..."

I continued her sentence, "...especially if they were wearing rain slickers like ours, Paddy would have rolled down the window without even checking their identity."

"So now they got three of our people," Aaron said, shaking his head slowly. "They gonna pay for this."

Pete asked, "You think there's gonna be a ransom demand?"

"No," I said. "This is to keep us away from the remnant."

"But, there's no way in hell they could'a planned this weather. How'd they pull it off?"

"Just got lucky, I suppose. Dagnar obviously had a vehicle ghosting our movements—"

"And when the storm hit they just sorta took advantage of the situation?"

"Yeah, Pete," I said. "That's exactly what happened."

Désirée asked, "What do we do now?"

A slow moving big rig came past leaving a wake in the foot of water that had accumulated at the side of the roadway, a line of six cars following in quick succession taking advantage of the tractor-trailer's mass to carve a way forward.

"First thing...Pete, you need to get back there and let Werner and Gérard's guys know what's happening." Which he was well able to do, given that he was nearly as fluent in French as Aaron. "Secondly...we need to keep moving forward—see if we can find a logical place to pull off and ride out the rest of this storm. Because every storm passes eventually, and we need to figure out ahead of time what we're going to do after the storm."

"Roger that," Pete replied and jumped out, running back to his van through the rain.

"So," Aaron queried. "How we fixed for shooters?"

"Well...there's you, me, Désirée, Pete and Gérard's two guys. And between us, we're packing some serious heat."

"I'm liking our odds."

"Me too. But first things first…"

Désirée said, "Jake, do you want me to drive? I am well able, and it would leave you free in case something were to come up."

She had a good point.

"Okay. But the first place that seems even remotely accessible, pull over."

We traded places, and she eased out into the flooded travel lane making sure that Pete was close behind in the van.

There were no cars moving in either direction except for our two vehicles. The effect was a surreal isolation. We couldn't see more than a few feet in front of us.

Couldn't see anything off to the side.

Couldn't hear anything except the roar of the rain on the SUV's sheet metal roof.

Couldn't go more than five, or at the most ten miles per hour.

Désirée said loudly, "Monsieur, at this rate, I'm afraid that even if there were a place to pull off and shelter, we would never see it."

Aaron was in the front passenger seat and I was right behind him in the rear. Both of us had our faces nearly pressed against the glass straining our eyes to see what, apparently, could not be seen.

Suddenly, we heard Pete honking and saw his headlights flashing. Désirée brought the vehicle to a stop and we turned to see what Pete was trying to communicate.

He exited the van and ran toward us through the water that was now mid-calf deep.

As Désirée rolled down her window, he said, "We drove right past a turnoff about a hundred yards back."

Aaron shook his head, "No way, bruh. Me and Jake both never took our eyes off the side of the road and we didn't see anything."

He insisted, "It's there, I swear it is. Let's just back up a piece and check it out."

I said, "We've got nothing to lose at this point. But, just so we don't become completely disoriented, why don't you back up and have a look-see while we stay here. If there's something there, flash your headlights twice."

With a curt nod of his head, he jogged back to the van, threw it in reverse and began backing up carefully while we remained in place, swiveled around in our seats watching his progress. When his headlights flashed two times, I could've wept for relief.

Désirée began backing up until we were even with the van, and we followed him onto an exit ramp that was completely flooded over with at least a foot and a half of water. The only thing that even indicated it was there were reflective markers on either side marching off into the obsidian blackness like spectral wraiths beckoning us to our doom.

Okay, melodramatic, but I was in a mood.

The Land Rover was built for situations like this, but I was concerned with the van's ability to navigate the high water. To my surprise, however, it handled the challenge like a champ, and in five minutes or so, we found ourselves sharing a bit of high ground with about fifteen or twenty other vehicles seeking shelter from the storm.

One of which was Gérard's SUV.

He saw us pull to a stop and came running across the parking area, a hastily contrived poncho—consisting of a blue tarp with a hole raggedly cut into the center—providing insulation from the incessant inundation.

Throwing open the left, rear passenger door, he climbed inside.

"I am happy to see you, Monsieur Moriarity."

I cut right to the point.

"Nathaniel, or Dagnar, has taken Paddy, Elliot and Emily." In response to his shocked expression, I continued, "We found their SUV abandoned by the side of the highway a little ways back."

With a hard expression, he replied, "It is Dagnar's doing.

He must have been following us."

"Yeah, that's what we figured, because there is no way anyone could have predicted this mess."

"I should have killed him when I had my hands on him," he spat, and then proceeded to swear with surprising proficiency.

I don't speak French well, but I know enough to have picked up something about Dagnar being a fatherless child with Oedipal tendencies.

I said, "Our guess is, they were taken to get us to back off."

"Oui. That is logical. But, they cannot see any more clearly than we, monsieur. They will not be far."

I'm not sure why I didn't think of that...but I didn't.

"You have any ideas?" I asked, feeling like a rank amateur.

"Oui. Between here and our destination, there are only two more, how do you say it...rest areas? Oui, rest areas. No one, not even a deranged individual such as Dagnar, would attempt to continue traveling in this weather. If they are not here—and they are not; I already searched—then they will have to be at one of the other two."

Aaron said, "He makes a good point."

"Yeah," I replied, not wanting to sound as stupid as I felt. "So, if Dagnar is thinking like you're thinking—that only a 'deranged individual' would attempt to travel in this weather—then, we should move out. Maybe catch them by surprise." I paused, and then asked, "Do you have a general idea of how far these rest areas are?"

"Oui. This," he swept his hand around where we were parked, "is not a rest area. It is merely a place to pull off the roadway. The rest area is approximately five kilometers from here. It is where they will be."

I was liking this guy more by the minute.

"Okay. Then, we should head out. If we stay in a tight formation, we should be all right."

"Oui. I will lead. You will follow."
I didn't like the implications, but...what the hell.

CHAPTER FIFTY-FIVE

We had been following Gérard for approximately thirty minutes with no letup in the storm.

It was unlike anything I had ever seen. This was truly Biblical in proportion. Which, I suppose, made perfect sense given that Biblical historians and scholars traditionally place the beginning of humanity somewhere within Turkey's borders.

"Gettin' late, bruh," Aaron growled as he held his phone up for me to see.

10:50 p.m.

I saw Gérard's brake lights flash up ahead and sensed his SUV slowing.

Désirée said, "And, what will we do if we pull in to this rest area and find Paddy and the others? Will there be a…what do you say…a shoot up?"

"Shootout. I don't think so. Too great a risk of killing or wounding one of our people or, worse yet, an innocent bystander."

"But, if we cannot take them from this Dagnar person… what will be the point?"

I had no idea what to say, and it made me feel, well… dumb, and if you want to know the truth, I was getting damn tired of the sensation.

I said, "Maybe if we just explain the situation to Dagnar he will let them go."

Désirée replied—with a wink to Aaron—"And maybe the monkeys will take flight from my bottom."

She and Aaron fist bumped.

We followed Gérard into the rest area.

A very crowded rest area.

It felt as if there were at least a hundred cars, none of which could be seen clearly.

An immediate problem presented itself—I mean besides the nearly total lack of visibility: We had no idea what we were looking for. And as long as the downpour continued, doing a car-by-car search would prove challenging.

After driving past several dozen cars, we found space for our three vehicles to park and, since the van had the most room, we all gathered inside its suddenly very tight confines.

Werner said, "It's good to see you, Jake. Been difficult to just sit here and not really know what was going on."

"Well," I replied, "if it makes you feel any better, we don't have a clue what's going on either. Not really."

Pete asked, "So, how we gonna proceed, boss?"

I thought about it for a moment or two, and then replied, "They have to be driving an SUV—"

"Or two," Aaron interjected.

"Right. Or two. So, we eliminate all of the passenger cars."

"How about box vans?" Pete asked.

"They could definitely be in a box van."

"Or two cars," Désirée suggested.

"No, I don't think so."

"Why not?"

"It just doesn't make any sense. Passenger cars don't have the same room as SUV's—"

"Or vans and box vans," Pete reiterated.

Werner said "Poor Elliot."

I replied, "I think Elliot will be fine. It's Emily I'm worried about."

Gérard uttered another string of curses.

"If the dog known as Dagnar harms her, I will cut him into tiny pieces, every one of which will beg for death—but death will not come. I will keep him alive for a month or more, begging for release—"

"Let's focus, here," I said. "Revenge is one thing, rescuing our friends is quite another."

"My apologies, monsieur," Gérard replied after a pause to collect himself. "So, we will concentrate our search to SUV's, vans and box vans?"

"Yes. But, if you find anything that looks promising, come back and report it so we can make our move together."

Désirée suggested, "What if we all went together, monsieur? It would save the time spent attempting to communicate. Getting separated in this weather would prove challenging."

She was right.

"Okay, so we'll move in a tactical formation: two, by two, by two. Aaron and I; Pete and one of Gérard's men; and then Gérard and his driver. Désirée, I need you and one of Gérard's men to stay here and guard Werner and our ammo."

"Oui monsieur," she readily agreed as Gérard designated one of his men to join her.

"Since visibility is limited to about six feet, we need to move in a strategic pattern." I was shouting to be heard over the constant roar of the rain on the roof. "We'll begin with the perimeter and work in concentric circles inward."

Werner said fearfully, "If they're here, isn't it possible that they've already seen us and could actually be moving in right now?"

"While that is definitely a possibility, it would be unlikely. Remember, as Gérard noted…they can't see any better than we can, and if you look around the parking area, no one has their interior or exterior lights on."

"Afraid of running down their car battery," Aaron said.

"Exactly. So, even if they are here, they are in their vehicles and can't really see outside. I mean…check it out. Look through the windows. What do you see?"

Everyone checked it out. We couldn't even see the car right next to us.

"But," Gérard said. "If they can't see out...neither can we see in."

Désirée cleared her throat politely.

"Excuze moi, messieurs. But, if it is Dagnar who has taken Emily and the others, I will recognize his car."

Heads snapped toward her in unison.

I said stupidly, "You will?"

"Oui. I saw it at the airport. It had a distinctive—"

She rattled off a question in French to Gérard who replied, "Dent."

"Ah, oui. A Toyota Land Cruiser with a dent in the right front fender."

"Then again," Aaron mused. "Dagnar could still be so jacked up from our little dustup that he's not capable of doing much 'cept layin' flat."

"With all due respect, monsieur," Gérard replied, "this will not be the case. Dagnar, he is here. Of this I am certain."

I said, "That is good information, Désirée. But, I still need you here with Werner."

"As you wish, monsieur."

I glanced around the crowded confines of the van, meeting everyone's eyes.

"Okay. We need to move out. Remember...stay close to the man next to you, and no more than five feet between each two-man team." Following their nods of affirmation, I opened the door, and with the others in close formation behind me stepped out into what felt like the spin cycle of a front-loading washer

It was ridiculous. Added to the relentless rain and the foot of water on the ground, there was now a vicious wind that drove the downpour straight into our faces.

"Did I mention previously that this sucks?" Aaron shouted over the din.

"Only a couple of times, so I didn't know whether you were sincere or not."

We began to move as unobtrusively as possible toward

the outer ring of cars, trucks, campers, passenger and utility vans and SUV's and eventually made one loop around the perimeter, with zero results. So, we moved inward a ring and started again.

We were about a third of the way through that ring, when out of the corner of my eye, I caught a flash of light.

It was only momentary.

Coming from an SUV to my left.

An SUV with a peculiar dent in the front fender.

A Toyota Land Cruiser.

We had found them.

CHAPTER FIFTY-SIX

Paddy Quinn sat in the back seat of the smelly SUV, directly behind the giant known as Dagnar, truly the largest human being he had ever seen. Although he was no midget himself at 6'2" and better than two hundred and seventy-five pounds, the man made him feel positively tiny. Emily was in the middle seat and Elliot to her left. At least, he believed they were still there. The darkness was so profound, and visibility so limited, it had gotten nearly impossible to see anything beyond the proverbial hand in front of your face.

That they had been taken at all was a bitter pill for him to swallow. He, the decorated NYPD Detective Sergeant, bested without even putting up a fight. It was a disgrace, that's what it was. The way the man had just walked up to the driver's window and Paddy—thinking it was a fellow traveler in need—had rolled it down for him without even a hint of suspicion. And here they were and there was nothing he nor anyone else could do about it. He felt about as impotent as an eighty-year-old eunuch.

The only thing that gave him hope was the fact that Dagnar was in bad shape—horrible shape, if the groaning and cursing were any measure of his discomfort.

"How long will ya' be keepin' us here, boyo?" he asked.

Dagnar replied through clinched teeth, "As long as it takes, old man. Now shut-up."

Old man, huh? He hoped to be offered a chance to redeem himself; to prove that he wasn't washed up; that he wasn't just another old man put out to pasture.

Emily said, "By now, Jake has certainly discovered that

we're missing and will be attempting to find us."

"Fine," Dagnar answered, "let him. In fact, I hope he finds us. I've got business with Mr. Perry."

"If I were you," Paddy replied. "I'd be prayin' that don't happen."

Dagnar suddenly yelled to his driver, "The next one who speaks...shoot them in the head."

"Ah, you'll not be doin' that," Paddy said confidently.

"Why not?"

"In a small, enclosed space such as this, the concussion from the shot would deafen you, not to mention the fact that everyone would see and hear it—includin' the local authorities who are almost certainly lurkin' somewhere in the midst of all these cars. Plus, you've already lost an arm and yer nose is so busted up ya' can't breathe. You don't want to lose your hearin' as well. So, nah, you'll not be shootin' no one, although, now that I think about it, you may be shootin' yourself when this is all over for the shame of it."

Dagnar hollered, "Shut up!"

Elliot said placatingly, "Mr. Quinn, perhaps we should—"

Paddy rolled right over him.

"Oh, I'm just gettin' started, and so I am. Yeah, I can see how it will all play out: you're not a man used to losin', Dagnar. Imagine when word gets around in the tactical community that Jake Moriarity bested you. What do you think that will do to your reputation? I can't imagine there'll be a lot of calls comin' in." He scoffed, "I mean...who wants to hire a loser?"

Dagnar tried to turn in his seat to take a swing at Paddy, but only succeeded in jamming his injured shoulder against the seat restraint and crying out against the pain.

"I'm gonna kill you, old man," he thundered, "and I'm gonna take my time doing it."

"Sure 'n if I had a dollar for every time some two-bit tough told me that, I'd be a wealthy man. Nah, you'll not be killin' me...'cause you'll already be dead."

Emily suddenly grabbed onto Paddy's left knee with a claw-like grip, nodding silently to their right through the window. When Paddy turned his head to follow her gaze, at first he couldn't see anything through the implacable torrent. Then, someone opened a car door in the next aisle providing just enough ambient light for him to notice people moving in what appeared to be a tactical formation through the crush of cars.

Fumbling in his inside pocket for his phone, that for some reason he'd been allowed to keep, he stabbed frantically at the touch screen only to realize that he'd turned his phone off when it had become obvious that there was no signal to be had. Emily picked up on the idea and dug around in her coat pocket coming up with her phone that, thankfully, was *not* dead. She handed it over to Paddy who then subtly and quietly moved the phone against the window.

He pressed the home button triggering the lock screen; turned it off; triggered it; turned it off again hoping that if it was Jake and his team moving through the lot, the momentary flash of light would be enough to draw his attention their way. He saw Dagnar turn his head toward the sudden intrusion of light, but he quickly returned the phone to Emily. He didn't think he had gotten his head around far enough to pick up the fact that the light source had been directly behind him.

But his driver did.

"Boss," he said. "I think one of them turned their phone on."

Dagnar's size combined with his injuries prohibited him from turning around. Even if he could, the darkness was so profound that he couldn't really see anything.

"That true?" he asked, turning his head slightly to the left. "Did one of you turn their phone on?"

Emily replied, "Umm...I did. I, uh...I wanted to see what time it was. Sorry. I didn't know it wasn't allowed."

Dagnar backhanded the driver across the side of his head.

"Why didn't you confiscate their phones, you stupid bastard?"

"You didn't tell me to, boss."

"What? I have to tell you everything? You want me to tell you when to take a dump too? Idiot!" He fumed for a few seconds before thrusting a huge left hand back over his shoulder. "Give me your phones. Now."

After his three prisoners grudgingly complied, he shoved the phones into the SUV's glove box, mumbling something about how if you wanted something done right you have to do it yourself.

Then he said, "We're not always going to be confined to a vehicle and this storm will pass and the sun will come up and when it does, and when we're all someplace nice and private… I am going to have my way with you. All of you. I am going to introduce you to pain sources you never even knew existed. Especially you, old man. When I get through with you I—"

"Jesus, Mary and Joseph!" Paddy exclaimed, cutting him off. "Would ya' listen to that big lug go on. Blab, blab, blab. All talk and no action. It's just pathetic to see a man reduced to such a level of impotency. Speakin' of which, he probably can't get it up either, from all the steroid use. I hear it shrinks a man's dangly bits. Is that it, Dagnar? Is that what's made you such a weak, pathetic creature?"

Dagnar screamed, slammed his fist into the dashboard and threw open his door in a full rage and started to get out only to be confronted by a DP12 shotgun being shoved up under his chin, and Jake Moriarity's voice saying, "Hello Dagnar."

CHAPTER FIFTY-SEVEN

What I wanted to do was to pull the trigger and send Dagnar on his way into whatever afterlife awaited one such as he.

But, he had valuable information.

So, for now, at least...I allowed him to live.

"Moriarity," he spat, his voice nasally from the broken nose.

"And a pleasant good evening to you as well, Dagnar. You don't seem all that pleased to see me."

I reached forward and grabbed Dagnar by his bad arm and yanked him out of the SUV.

It was a lot of bulk to yank.

To his credit, he didn't scream. But I knew it hurt.

It was supposed to hurt.

I *wanted* it to hurt.

He said, "You take advantage of my weakened condition. Exactly what I would expect from a coward like you."

It made me laugh.

"You know, I've been called a lot of things in my life... but coward isn't one. I'll tell you what...should you survive this—and from where I stand, that is an idea that is becoming more remote by the second—I will meet you in a place of your choosing; one-on-one; and we will settle this. Fair enough?"

He stared for a few seconds before replying, "Or, we could do it now."

I laughed some more.

"Dagnar, I know you are feeling humiliated and you're desperately trying to regain face, but taking me on when you are a hundred percent would not result in a favorable outcome for you. What do you think would happen going up against me with one arm?"

I'll give him this—the man was relentless.

And stupid.

"Why don't we find out?" he replied doggedly.

Having tired of the pissing contest, I said, "Pete, can you take Emily and Elliot back to the van? Dagnar and I have a few things to discuss relating to his future health, and there's no reason for them to suffer through any further boredom."

"Sure thing, Mr. Moriarity, sir," Pete replied, as he opened the rear doors and ushered them out.

I suddenly noticed that the storm had abated, to the extent that there was now only a steady rain falling. Persistent as opposed to spiteful. A few cars had their headlights on and the drivers were seemingly waiting for a window of opportunity to be on their way. Given that reality, it simply wouldn't do for prying eyes to see me attempting to extract information from an injured man, regardless of how oversized his proportions.

What I had to do...had to be done quickly.

"Aaron," I said, while continuing to hold the shotgun close to Dagnar's face. "Perhaps you could have a conversation with the driver and request his assistance in finding Nathaniel."

"Be my pleasure," he growled in reply as he started around the SUV's front end.

I heard the driver's door open and then the driver's gasp of pain, followed by gurgling sounds one would typically associate with an individual in the throes of tremendous distress. The darkness was still sufficiently profuse as to make vision limited. It was just as well, for what we were hearing did not sound pretty. Understand, that Aaron does not enjoy causing pain, neither does he ever do anything that causes skin to rupture and bleed. He is an expert in the field of nerve manipulation.

Gérard said, "He is very efficient, your Mr. Perry."

"He is nothing if not," I replied as the troubling sounds came to an end.

Aaron reappeared, saying casually, "Boy says he'd be happy to take us to Nathaniel."

Dagnar exploded, "I will kill him for—"

Gérard backhanded him across his injured nose before I could stop him.

Not that I would have tried all that hard, mind you.

"You will keep silent unless requested to speak. N'est-ce pas?"

Dagnar pressed his left hand hard against his nose in an attempt to stem the fresh tide of blood, his gaze fixed on Gérard malignantly.

I said, "What are we looking at in terms of head start?"

Aaron replied, "According to my new best friend over there, Nathaniel is already in the village where the remnant is housed, and has been there for at least two hours."

"Which..." Gérard replied, "...does not bode well for the keepers of the remnant."

However," I mused. "Nathaniel will have been dealing with the same storm that has kept us grounded. So, if he is, in fact, there...he will still be there for as long as this storm has a mind to stick around."

"Oui," Gérard agreed. "And we must not forget the dam."

"The dam?"

"Oui, monsieur. The Altinapa dam."

"Oh, yes. I had forgotten all about it. You said that, İsa'nın haçı, the village of the remnant is downriver from it, right?

"Oui. And given the amount of rainfall we have experienced over the past several hours, I am quite concerned that the dam's structural integrity will not be able to withstand the increased water levels."

I hadn't thought about that and wondered out loud about the chances of the dam bursting.

"This I do not know, monsieur. But it is a simple matter

of physics, no? The water rises, it has to go somewhere. Either the dam breaks, or the keepers of the dam release some water downriver. And if that happens, I fear for the people of İsa'nın haçı. The damage would be terrible."

Paddy said, "Sure 'n it would. But better a bit of damage than the dam burst and the poor wretches lose everything."

I quickly thought through our options.

"All right, it's…12:40 a.m. and I have no idea where we are or how to get where we're going. But, we have people with us who do. So, we'll leave Dagnar's vehicle here and I want him with you and two of your men, Gérard. Your other man will be with me and Aaron to keep an eye on Dagnar's driver who, I'm sure, will be more than happy to navigate for us."

Paddy said hesitantly, "What would you like me to do, Jacob?"

There was something in the way he asked the question that revealed the nature of his query. He was feeling old and stupid for having let Dagnar get the jump on him so easily. And I couldn't let my good friend remain in that state of mind.

"Well, I was sort of thinking you'd be with me and Aaron. That is, unless you have other plans."

I couldn't make out his facial expression, but in the ambient light, I could see him stand a little taller.

"It'd be an honor to go with you, and so it would."

"That's good, because I'm going to need your help before this night is over."

"Jacob," he began…struggling for words. "About the thing with the big fella there. I—"

"You handled it like a true professional," I said, cutting him off. "The phone idea alone was pure genius. We never would've found you if you hadn't thought of that. Keeping your wits under pressure is exactly why I need you with me, Paddy, old friend."

He nodded his head once, and shook my hand.

A couple of Britt's wandered by, arms around each other's shoulders; three sheets to the wind, by my reckoning.

One of them said, drunkenly slurring his speech, "Oy, what's goin' on over here. We been watching out the window and it looks like somethin' is goin' on over here because watching out the window we saw that somethin' is goin' watching out the—"

Aaron walked over and stood in front of the dopey pair.

"Nothin' to see here fellas. Why don't you be on your way."

The chatty one leaned in, staring up at Aaron's size.

"Bloody hell, but you're a big one, ain't you? Look at 'em, Alf. He's a right big bastard, ain't he?"

Aaron dipped his head and glanced around conspiratorially.

"Can you two keep a secret?"

The one called Alf, snapped off a sloppy salute.

"We're the soul of discretion, we are, mate."

"Good, then I need to tell you a secret." He beckoned them closer. "This is a top-secret military operation and I need you to pretend you never saw anything."

Chatty guy said, "Are you an American?"

"Yes, I am."

"So, is this, like, a CA...uh...IA...CAI operation?"

"I could tell you...but then I'd have to kill you."

They thought that was hilarious until they saw Aaron's face and determined that he wasn't kidding.

"All right, mate. Your secret's safe with us," Alf said and attempted another salute, nearly landing himself on the ground in the process.

As they stumbled back to wherever they had come from, I said, "Let's see: lying; misrepresenting yourself; threatening. You should've run for Congress."

"Very funny." He glanced at Dagnar who was now seated in the back of Gérard's SUV, his good arm zip-tied across his body to the handgrip over the door. "Dude's planning something, or knows something. Probably both."

"Why do you say that?"

"Way too calm."

"Maybe he's on a bunch of pain killers. I know I would be."

"Nah, man. It's not that. I don't think he's had anything. The pain energizes him."

"Well, tell Gérard to keep an eye on him."

"Roger that."

I could see Dagnar's face.

He was smiling—a truly frightening sight.

CHAPTER FIFTY-EIGHT

The drive to Altinapa took the rest of the night and we arrived shortly after sunrise, exhausted and feeling out of sorts. The roadway had been an absolute horror, filled with more wrecks than we could count—two of which almost certainly involved fatalities and at least a half-dozen with serious injuries. Added to that sad tally were dozens of cars stalled in high water, spun out or simply parked littering the shoulders awaiting the storm's passage. As a result, our progress had been accomplished in fits and starts, as they say; queued up behind other victims of the storm's fury, at times inching along at a proverbial snail's pace with brief periods where we barreled along at a whopping fifteen or twenty miles per hour.

There were places where the highway had been nearly impassable due to the sheer abundance and depth of water. It was during those times that I was once again grateful to be in a Land Rover.

The ammunition and armaments van that Pete was driving hadn't fared quite as well. About 3:00 a.m. we had been forced to abandon it, transferring the pistols, rifles and boxes of ammunition into our three remaining SUV's. When you added fourteen passengers—more than half of whom were men in excess of six feet tall and two hundred twenty-five pounds—it was a tight fit.

But we made it work.

Barely.

We decided that the only thing that made sense was for Dagnar to ride with us. Aside from the occasional mumbled threats, and in spite of Aaron's apprehensions, the man had behaved himself on the journey. Nevertheless, we continued to keep an eye on him.

Ours was the only Land Rover with four passengers. I mean it simply wouldn't have worked to attempt three people in the back seat when one of them is 6'7" and over three hundred pounds. During the transfer of equipment and passengers, we had settled on me, Aaron, Gérard and Dagnar in the rear SUV; Désirée, Emily, Paddy, Werner and Elliot in the middle; with Pete, Gérard's three men and Dagnar's driver in the lead. Not an ideal situation, but there was nothing else we could do.

Sunrise over Altinapa Dam Lake was a multihued wonder courtesy of the patches of clouds left over from the storm. However, my attention was not on the sky, but on the Meram Deresi, or Purport Creek below that had been turned into a raging torrent due to the overflow from the dam. Just watching the ferocious flow of water clawing its way through the narrow passage gave me little hope that there would be anything left of the small village downstream.

What we needed was speed.

What we *had* was another nearly impassable road. Only this time, it wasn't a state highway, but a rough, two-lane road nearly washed out in places due to the storm's savagery.

We were stopped, standing outside our vehicles—Gérard, Pete, Paddy, Désirée, Aaron and myself—and staring at a particularly challenging section that, had we not been driving reliable four-wheel drive vehicles, we never would have attempted to navigate. Two of Gérard's men had been left behind to watch over Dagnar, with his other man babysitting Dagnar's driver.

Paddy said, "Sure'n we never had to deal with anythin' like this in the City."

"Yeah," I replied, "well, I live in the desert where we get flash floods. And I've never had to deal with anything like this either. It's like something you'd see in the Amazon basin or something."

Werner, Emily and Elliot joined us.

"Can we make it?" Elliot asked.

"I don't know." I pointed to an area about fifty feet from where we stood where a three-foot-wide channel of water was running laterally across the road. "If the issue were only deep water, I'd say our chances were good, because these vehicles are built to withstand a fording depth of around thirty-three inches. But it's not. As you can see, the water has carved a channel across the road and the current is quite swift."

Werner countered, "Surely we could simply back up and blast through?"

"Well, sir," Pete said, "these here vehicles have a curb weight of around forty-five hundred pounds. Now, bein' from the hill country of central Texas—also known as flash flood alley—I've seen many, many flash floods. So, I've had to study up on situations like this. The rule of thumb is, for every foot of water, you knock off around fifteen hundred pounds of your vehicle's weight. That water is at least two feet deep, so now we're in a fifteen hundred-pound vehicle. Also, water flowing at only six miles per hour has a force equivalent of air from an EF5 tornado. That there water looks to me to be flowing at about twelve miles per hour."

"Good Lord!" Elliot exclaimed.

I knew that everything Pete was saying was spot on. And yet...we had to keep moving forward. Obviously, we couldn't go around. And we couldn't go back for there was nothing to go back to.

I said, "Pete, if we could get one vehicle across, do you think we could set up and winch the others across if needed?"

He walked forward to get a closer look at the water. Bent down and stuck his hand in, letting the murky liquid swirl around his fingers. Stood up and walked back to join us.

"The channel seems to be sloped on each side."

"Which means?" I prompted.

"Which means that if you got a good run at it, and didn't mind jacking up your frame a little, I think that one vehicle could possibly make it across."

Aaron teased, "Why, you just a fountain of hope, aren't you?"

We all stood in place just staring for a few seconds before Désirée said "Monsieur, please allow me to make the attempt. I have spent my life driving these vehicles in extreme off-road conditions. This is nothing I have not encountered previously. I am well able to do this."

I considered her request briefly before replying, "Well, all right, Désirée. You're on."

With a curt nod of her head, and a barely audible, "Merci," she walked back to the lead vehicle, opened the door and quickly explained the situation to the two men inside, who exited and moved over to stand by our group.

Gérard said, "If she loses that vehicle in the attempt, we are, as you Americans are fond of saying, screwed."

"We're screwed anyway if we can't find a way across," I replied.

We all cleared out of the way as Désirée revved the engine and began moving toward the channel. As she picked up speed, spontaneous cheers of encouragement began to erupt from the group and if I had to guess, I'd say that she was going at least twenty miles per hour when the front wheels hit the ditch. There was a long, agonizing moment when it appeared that the wheels had stuck and the current began to rock the vehicle, nudging it slowly, but surely, downstream. But like the expert driver she purported to be, she didn't remain static. She began to work the gears, playing with the four-wheel drive, giving it just enough power to keep the tire treads engaged with the surface, but not allowing the loss of traction.

The front wheels finally cleared the opposite edge, putting the Land Rover in an even more vulnerable position with the much lighter rear end now in the water. Suddenly, the rear end was picked up by the current and began to swing slowly around. But, she still didn't panic. She simply kept doing what her experience and training had taught her to do. And when the front wheels finally pulled the vehicle free from the grip of the current, we cheered like the winning country at the World Cup; jumping around like fools; fist bumping and high fiving. In response to our acclaim, Désirée got out of the car and gave a little bow before beginning to unspool the forward winch line.

Pete jumped over the channel, took the winch and guided it back across, and in short order, the other two vehicles had passed over and we were once again free to be on our way.

And we would have been, had Dagnar not chosen that moment to fulfill Aaron's prophecy.

CHAPTER FIFTY-NINE

We were just preparing to climb back inside our Land Rover when, in a tremendous show of strength, Dagnar pulled the overhead hand grip out of its moorings and clubbed Gérard on the right side of his head, knocking him immediately senseless. He then bolted from the vehicle and stood outside, bellowing for me to come and fight him.

I remained in place for a few seconds wishing I could just shoot him—like in the original Indiana Jones movie where Jones is confronted by a giant Moroccan dude with an even larger sword and, instead of fighting him, just pulls out a gun and shoots him after mugging to the camera.

But I couldn't.

And don't you want to know why?

It's because I have morals.

Sometimes I hate that fact.

I said, "This is gonna hurt," and started to step out of the vehicle.

Aaron reached over and grabbed my arm.

"Don't do it, Jake. Let me. I'm the one he's really pissed off at."

"Come!" Dagnar bellowed maniacally. "Come to your death, Moriarity. Come and let me tear you to pieces with only one arm."

The sad thing was, I was quite sure he could make good on his claim.

"Doesn't sound like it to me," I replied to Aaron.

"Yeah, well…I should still be the one who goes."

"No. It'll be fine. I've faced guys bigger than him."

"Seriously?"

"Uh...well...no. But it makes me feel better saying it."

I got out and walked slowly around the front end and stood about ten feet away, staring at him.

He was big as a house.

But, he had a badly broken nose and a recently dislocated right shoulder and a messed-up wrist. That should go a long ways toward evening out the odds.

"I will tear your head off and—"

"And crap down my throat? Really? That's the best taunt you can come up with?"

I don't really do the smack talk thing when facing a situation where a physical encounter is inevitable. I mean, what's the point? Two guys stand there and throw taunts back and forth. Yak, yak, yak. Just get on with it and may the best man win.

He was just starting to formulate what I am sure he imagined being a brilliant retort when I charged him. Most huge men are not used to being charged by much smaller opponents. Judging by the expression on his face, he seemed to be no exception. He didn't seem to know what to do, which was exactly the outcome I had intended.

I feinted as if I were going to throw an overhand right toward his nose. It is a natural human reflex to protect areas of our bodies that are injured. It's called a flinch. It can be trained out of us, but only through years and years of experience. He obviously had not gone through that training, for his immediate response was to cover up. Exactly what I had expected and wanted him to do. Adjusting the trajectory of my punch, I continued the forward motion, only rather than landing it, I grabbed his right arm—his badly wounded arm—planted my feet and twisted it as if attempting to create a pretzel.

He bellowed in pain and attempted to pummel me with his left. Again, it was what I wanted him to do, for in order to throw punches, he had to turn his head toward me, thus leaving his face wide open and unprotected. Having ducked my head to avoid the massive blows raining down, I timed my movement and let go of his arm with my right hand, rearing backward and stabbing my fingers toward his eyes. I felt them make contact, and he staggered backward bawling in pain and pawing at his eyes with his good hand.

Dirty move? Probably. But, remember…he had planned to tear my head off and use my neck as a latrine. I need my head. In fact, I'm rather fond of my head, and so is Gabi.

As one of my former fighting gurus had drilled into me, "If a man can't see, he can't fight. If a man can't breathe, he can't fight. If a man can't stand, he can't fight." Dagnar couldn't see, so, technically he couldn't fight. But I wanted to up the ante. So, while he was attempting to recover his sight, I took my time and stabbed two fingers into that hollow in the throat right below the Adam's apple. It's called the episternal notch. Struck at the right angle and with a modicum of force, it causes you to feel as if you are going to choke to death. You won't, but it feels like it for five to ten minutes.

As he was staggering around, attempting to see and breathe, I kicked his feet out from under him. I figured that in the shape he was in, there was no way he'd be getting back up on his own.

It worked.

Dagnar was on the ground, writhing in pain; he couldn't see and was having difficulty breathing. The fight was over.

I turned to see Gérard moving slowly toward me.

"Very impressive, monsieur."

"Thanks. But I wasn't going for impressive. I was going for effective."

"Mission accomplished. What are we to do with him now?"

That was a really good question. If you want to know the truth, I had been wondering about the exact same thing.

"I don't know. Any ideas?"

We both stared at the man on the ground. He was a pathetic sight, really. A once proud champion reduced to nothing.

Gérard suddenly pulled a pistol and shot Dagnar in the head.

I heard retching behind me and turned just in time to see Emily bent over and vomiting, with Werner and Elliot collapsed back against the side of the vehicle, their mouths agape.

As Gérard calmly returned the pistol to his shoulder holster, he explained, "I told you that there was a history between us. This man...he..." He seemed to struggle, and then, "...my sister; she was only fourteen when he raped and tortured her to death. Just for something to do. I vowed that I would avenge her and have waited these long years. And now...I have."

I stared down at the body on the ground.

"I understand, and I shed no tears for Dagnar. But now we have another problem: what do we do with his body?"

Gérard whistled and his three men came running. After a flurry of instructions given in French, they hustled over and began dragging the body toward the rapidly swelling river.

Emily shrieked, "What are you doing? You can't just throw him in the river! He's a human being, for God's sake."

"No, mon chér," Gérard replied calmly. "Not a human... but a monster."

"If he's a monster," she spat. "What does that make you?"

"My sister's avenger."

We heard a loud splash and turned in time to see the current pick Dagnar's body up and carry it swiftly downstream.

"It is finished," Gérard intoned solemnly and walked slowly back toward the Land Rover.

Emily stalked toward me, her face a mask of rage.

"You can't possibly be considering allowing this...this madman to stay on with us!"

"I am, and I will," I replied simply.

"Then you are no better than him!"

I took a deep breath and said intensely, "Emily...you have just experienced a tremendous shock. Now, I encourage you to step back and not say anything you will regret later. Because—as I am sure you already know—I do not suffer fools lightly. And you, young lady, are acting like a fool."

With that, I turned and walked back to the SUV leaving her standing in place, her once pretty face now stretched into a rictus of hate and anger.

She screamed loudly, angrily and stalked back to the Land Rover she had been riding in. I did not envy her fellow passengers.

Having transferred Dagnar's driver to our vehicle, we took the lead and drove with as much speed as seemed safe, which is to say we proceeded at a crawl. While we didn't encounter any further areas that were washed out, there were plenty of sections containing low points that had one to two feet of standing water across the road. But it was standing water, so the Land Rovers conquered the challenges like the off-road champs that they were.

I had Aaron inquire of Dagnar's driver as to where we were in relation to our destination. Seemingly still in shock from seeing his boss gunned down in cold blood, Aaron had to repeat the question three times. When he was finally able to formulate an answer, his voice sounded flat and entirely lacking in inflection.

Aaron said, "He's pretty much out of it, but his best guess is that if we continue on at this speed, we should be there in a little over an hour."

I checked my phone for signal. It was weak, but I was connected.

I called Gérard.

"Oui, monsieur?" he answered.

"Our guy here says we should be at the village in about an hour or a little more. What do you expect to find once we arrive?"

He hesitated slightly, and then said, "This is the only roadway in or out, so unless Nathaniel has arranged for aerial transport—which I would absolutely expect him to do—

he is still there. If the remnant were, in fact, housed in the church, as Dr. French and Spencer contend, then we can expect that everyone associated with the church will be dead and the remnant in Nathaniel's hands."

"And, how about support personnel?"

"Dagnar began with a squad of eight men plus himself. That number is now down to seven. As I said previously, they will be highly skilled MERC's—every bit as good as my men."

"If that is the case," I said, "then we have him outmanned and outgunned."

"Oui, unless, of course, he has managed to recruit someone from the local talent pool."

"Local talent pool?"

"Monsieur, surely one such as yourself knows that in every city, town, village and hamlet there are hard men who will do almost anything for the right amount of money. I assure you, in spite of the village's religious sounding name… such men will be there, and Nathaniel will have hired them."

A fact I had not included in my calculations.

"So, if he is still there, there will be—"

"Entrapments. Oui. This will happen even if he is gone."

"Thank you, Gérard," I said and stabbed the end button on my phone.

Aaron asked, "Heard your end of that. What did Gérard have to say?"

I turned my head to see him.

"Basically that we're rolling right into a trap."

"Good to know."

CHAPTER SIXTY

We paused on the outskirts of İsa'nin haçı, or what was left of it...which, if you want to know the truth, wasn't much. Think Indonesia in 2004 following the earthquake and tsunami, or Hurricane Katrina, or Harvey. It was bad. People wandering the streets, their faces bearing expressions only observed on those whose eyes have seen what their minds cannot rationally process. Somewhere in the inner reaches of my cynical brain rattled the thought, *"If there ever was a magic portal...it sure did these people a lot of good."*

We all exited our vehicles and formed up in a loose semi-circle, just staring at the horror in front of us.

Emily mumbled, "These people are in desperate need of humanitarian aid, and we're here to steal away their most precious possession."

"I wouldn't worry too much about that," I said. "Nathaniel almost certainly has already been here and gone."

"But, it's just the thought that we—"

Paddy took her shoulders in a firm grip and spun her around so they were facing each other.

"Listen, Emily, darlin'...I need you ta focus. I know you've been terribly upset by everythin' that has happened—hell, lass, we're all upset. But you'll be doin' no good to yourself nor anyone else if you allow your mind to continue slidin' down that slope. Now, shoulders back; head up; eyes straight ahead...there's my girl."

The only thing I could figure is that something must've transpired in the van before we arrived—something of a relationship building nature—because Paddy's words had an immediate and profound effect on Emily. She gave her head a quick nod, and allowed Paddy to pull her into a hug, which, in my experience, was somewhat akin to being mauled by a friendly bear.

Over the top of her head, he mouthed, "She'll be fine."

Pete tapped me on the shoulder and pointed toward the bell tower of a church that seemed to have escaped much of the damage, given its position on relatively high ground.

"If I was that Nathaniel fella, I'd have someone up there with a scope and a suppressed rifle."

The words had no sooner left his lips when we heard the trademark "slap/thud" of a high velocity bullet striking a body center mass, followed a nanosecond later by one of Gérard's men falling lifelessly to the ground.

"Behind the vehicles!" I hollered and grabbed Emily protectively, literally dragging her along beside me as she screamed like a child on her first trip through a house of horrors, which, apparently, our adventure was about to become.

With everyone behind a wheel well or engine block, I said, "Pete, can you get inside and retrieve that MSSR without getting your head shot off?"

"Well, Mr. Moriarity sir, I don't rightly know. But, only one way to find out." Without further discussion, he opened the rear door and yanked a bag out of the rear footwell. Grinning slyly, he explained, "I thought we might be needing this, so I prepared in advance."

"Good man," I said. "Think you can take that joker out?"

"Give me a second and I'll let you know."

His hands flew through a quick weapon's check before slapping in a STANAG 30 round magazine and bringing the rifle up into firing position. At the same time, he opened the front driver's side door, lowered the passenger window and sighted in.

He said, "I'm not seeing…hang on."

Even with a sound suppressor attached, the report of the rifle startled everyone.

"One shot, one kill," he intoned, citing the Marine Sniper code, his cheek still pressed hard against the body of the rifle.

I asked, "You seeing any other hostiles?"

"Not from this position, but you can bet your booty that they're out there."

"All right. Gather 'round." I waited for our crew to move over behind the SUV while Pete kept up surveillance on the surrounding area. "We have a few things to accomplish, and none of them are going to be easy. First of all, we have to get Werner, Elliot and Emily into a secure situation and Dagnar's driver tied up so he doesn't get any ideas of bravery. Second, we have to eliminate the remaining hostiles—and I seriously hope this doesn't turn into a situation like the Army Rangers and Delta Force encountered in Mogadishu."

"Was that the Black Hawk Down thing?" Werner asked.

"Yeah. Because, as Gérard so astutely observed, it is highly likely that Nathaniel has secured the services of some locals. Be that as it may, it doesn't change what we're here to do. Thirdly, if it still exists, we need to find and secure the remnant. Fourthly...we need to neutralize any further threat Nathaniel may pose to us."

Emily said in a small voice, "By 'neutralize,' do you mean kill him?"

"Not unless he is trying to kill me. What really needs to happen is that he stand trial in open court so the world can be aware of his evil, because there are others besides him who are members of The Nine."

Gérard said "I believe the number is now down to seven, monsieur."

"Still too many." I turned to Paddy. "Old friend, I need you..." I paused to nod toward Désirée, "...and Désirée to shelter in place here and provide protection for the other three. We'll move the vehicles into a triangle so you'll have plenty of room in the center."

"Fine (he pronounced it 'foine') with me, laddie buck.

These old knees are no longer fit for tactical exercise...or any other kind of exercise for that matter. Désirée and me will keep your people safe, and so we will."

Désirée voiced her agreement and we began getting the vehicles into formation, strapping on body armor and preparing weapons and ammo for a serious tactical assault.

"Pete," I hollered. "Anything moving?"

"Got some locals tryin' to get up their courage to make a run on—hang on." The gun spit three times. "Now there's three less of 'em. The rest are divin' for cover."

"Boy can shoot," Aaron said admiringly.

"Good job, Pete," I affirmed. "Now listen...when we move out, five of us will pursue a classic combat assault formation while Pete provides suppressing fire. In fact...Pete?"

"Yes sir?"

"Just do what you do. I don't even care if I see you again until this is all over."

"Roger that," he replied.

"All right. Any questions?"

Aaron asked, "Do we even know where the church is?"

Pete gestured toward the bell tower.

"I think we're lookin' at it."

I shot a glance at Dagnar's driver.

"Is that true?"

He started to shrug, only to be slapped in the back of the head with the barrel of Désirée's pistol, after which he rattled off something in French that, if body language were any indicator, seemed to be of a positive nature.

"I'll be damned," Werner exclaimed. "We are so close, Elliot. So close."

"Indeed we are, old chap," Elliot agreed.

"Pete, check that place out top to bottom. If you've got cell service, call me and leave the line open."

He pulled out his phone and glanced at the screen.

"Got...one bar. It'll have to do."

"All right. Form up. Give him some cover fire."

Keying off of movement about a hundred yards to our right, seven of us opened up and were gratified to see about a half-dozen men running for the hills, weapons tossed aside and hands in the air.

"Go Pete," I hollered and watched as my 6'3" two hundred-fifty-pound friend suddenly became a Ninja.

In short...he disappeared. It was uncanny.

"The hell he go?" Aaron asked in amazement. "Dude's almost big as me. I can't move like that. Can you move like that?"

"Not on my best day, bro. Which is why Pete is out there and you and me are here."

Through my earbuds, I could hear Pete grunting with exertion, but I still couldn't see him.

Then, "Okay. I'm in. Moving through the main entrance...and...clear. Into the sanctuary." The gun spat and he continued, "Another one of those bastards down. Headed for the narthex—is that what you call it? Hell, I don't know. Sounded good." He was silent for a few seconds, then I heard the gun fire three shots in rapid succession. "One more local, and two of Nathaniel's MERC's down."

"What's happening?" Werner asked.

"Pete's clearing the church. Four hostiles down so... make that six hostiles down so far."

Pete said, "Near as I can tell, the main floor is clear. Come on up and I'll waste anyone who tries to stop you. It's good to have the high ground."

I hollered, "Okay, move out!"

We ran in a loose wedge with Gérard and his two men in the center, Aaron on the left wing and me on the right. It took us about a minute to cover the one hundred yards, and, in spite of Pete's assurances, we entered the church cautiously.

Pete was posted up just inside of the small lobby, sighting through one of the windows.

He said "I'm gonna clear the bell tower," and hustled back through the front entryway toward a free-standing tower located to the right of the main building.

In a surprisingly short amount of time, he yelled from the top, "We're clear."

"Dude's half monkey," Aaron said in amazement.

After Pete rejoined us, I said, "Now we need to find this chamber, if, in fact, it exists. Any idea where to begin, Gérard? Nathaniel ever say anything?"

"Oui. I believe it is directly below the altar in the front."

"Okay. Lead the way."

CHAPTER SIXTY-ONE

We followed Gérard toward the altar area and watched while he stomped around, bending down at several points to pry at a tile that seemed to be loose. After this had gone on for about ten minutes, and he had covered nearly the entire area, he suddenly stopped, and stomped more gingerly around a specific area.

"I believe it is here," he announced while bending down and beginning to pry at the corners of the old tile while yelling for his men to join him.

It was no easy task as the tile looked to be two feet by three feet and roughly four inches thick. But it also seemed to have been recently moved.

As they struggled to lift it, Gérard said, "We are not the first ones here, mon ami."

He beckoned me over and I could clearly see boot tracks in the layers of dust that had accumulated on a narrow series of steps descending downward into utter darkness.

We turned our weapon lights on and carefully began the descent with me in the lead.

"Pete," I said with my foot on the second step. "Post up behind the altar and keep us safe while we're down there."

"Roger that."

You might as well know that I don't like small, enclosed spaces. And I like small, pitch black enclosed spaces even less. If you want to know the truth, I hate it. Probably has something to do with a residual memory of my battle with Yves Barreau in the subterranean blackness of the former Wonderland Amusement Park in San Diego.

The stairway seemed to be chiseled out of solid stone and was narrow enough that we had to go down sideways. At any moment I half expected to see an ancient Knight Templar spring up, wheezing, "None shall pass!" or something to that effect while waving his rusty sword at us. But that didn't happen and shortly we found ourselves in a smallish chamber that bore the signs of great age.

I cannot fully explain what I was feeling in that moment. Probably about as close as I've ever come to a sense of reverence. For across the small room—which measured roughly eight by ten—there was a secondary chamber with a doorway that seemed to have recently been desecrated. Brutally so. Hammered with absolutely no consideration to the archeological treasure this chamber represented.

Aaron said, "Well, looks like Nathaniel beat us here."

"It does at that. But...I think he isn't far."

"Why you think that?"

"The only way he could have escaped is by land, water or air. The river is too turbulent for a watercraft; there is no way in hell a chopper could have flown through that storm last night, and even if he called for one this morning, where would it come from? And we came in on the only road."

"Then, where is he?"

Gérard was standing by the portal, with a look on his face that I can only describe as being one of pure awe.

He said, "This...this is where the cross of Christ sat for more than one thousand years." Rubbing his hands gently over the remaining surface, he almost whispered, "I can still feel its power. Nathaniel was right."

"So were Werner, Elliot and Emily," I added.

He ducked inside, stooping to account for the extremely low ceiling; shone his weapon light all around and returned, saying, "There is nothing left inside. Nathaniel took everything."

We heard Pete's rifle firing rapidly and turned back toward the stairs as I heard him saying through the earbuds, "I might could use a little help up here, Mr. Moriarity sir."

"On our way, Pete. Hang on."

We charged up the narrow staircase, slowing down as we neared the top. Poking my head over the rim, I saw muzzle flashes coming from the area around the entryway. I really hated to tear up such a beautiful old house of worship, but I had no choice. So, I put my weapon on full auto; emptied a full clip before heaving a fragmentary grenade in that general direction. As soon as it exploded, we stormed out of the opening and began strafing the back of the sanctuary.

Four men went down and Pete said loudly, "That's all of 'em. I got the other two."

It must have been true because a deathly quiet descended over the space. So much so, we could hear each other breathing.

Suddenly, we heard the sound of a gunshot from the direction of our vehicles.

"Come on," I hollered and began sprinting down the center aisle and didn't stop until we had reached our friends.

Paddy was down. Désirée was tending to him. Werner and Elliot were completely paralyzed with fright. And Emily was nowhere to be seen.

"What happened," I asked, dropping down beside Paddy, whose face was the color of gray slate.

"The little bitch," Désirée spat. "She took my pistol when I laid it down to secure the bonds on Dagnar's man. Paddy tried to take it away from her, and…she shot him."

"Paddy…Paddy," I said, my lips close to his ear. "You're going to be fine. Just hang on. We've got a triage—"

His large, strong hand reached out and gripped mine.

"Now, don't ya' be tryin' to pull a fast one on old Paddy, boyo." A sudden spasm stopped him, contorting his face. "It's all right. Now I know how my story ends."

"I'm not going to let you die today, old friend."

A far-away look settled into his eyes.

"Ah, Maggie, dear. You're lookin' so lovely, darlin', and so ya' are."

"Paddy!" I hollered.

His eyes regained focus and he said, "I don't suppose you've got a spot of whiskey for an old soldier."

"Sorry, friend. We left everything in the other van."

He closed his eyes and breathed sharply as another spasm of pain rocked him.

"I know that...this is it for me, Jacob. Although, I wouldn't mind one 'a those fentanyl pops I know you've got in there."

"Aaron!" I hollered. "You heard the man. Give him a pop."

"On it," he replied having already pulled the triage bag from the back of one of the SUV's.

He handed one of the magical little painkillers to me and I tore off the wrapping and shoved it into Paddy's mouth between his cheek and gum.

He sucked on it a few times.

"Ah, now that's better, and so it is."

I asked Désirée, "Where is he shot?"

She gestured to the area around his liver. The entry wound was quite small, but I knew that there would be a fist-sized hole in his back, as evidenced by the copious amount of blood pooling under him.

Paddy took a deep shuddering breath...and then he was gone.

I stood, barely containing my need to express my grief while at the same time launching another tirade toward the God in whom I no longer believed, and yet continued to blame for virtually every misfortune of my life and the planet in general.

I spun around, scanning the ruined village as if by doing so I would catch a glimpse of the little traitor.

"Did any of you see which direction Emily went?"

Werner gestured toward an area to the right of the church and toward the river.

"I believe it was that way, Jake. Although, to my shame I could only see from where I was cowering on the ground."

"It is true," Désirée confirmed. "She went that way." She stood. "And now, I will go and kill her."

"Not without me, you won't."

Gérard drew his weapon and pointed it at my forehead.

I said, "That, my friend, is a terrible mistake," as his two men also drew down on us."

From behind us, Pete drawled, "Ya'll might want to drop those weapons. I can drop all three of you before you take your next breath."

I could see the struggle on Gérard's face as he turned to his men and rattled something off in French that resulted in them tossing their weapons at my feet where Aaron quickly confiscated them.

With great pleading in his voice, Gérard said, "Please, monsieur, allow me to accompany you. It is Emily. She is ma chère amie. Even though she despises me, I cannot help the fact that I love her."

"Fine," I answered after a moment's hesitation. "But you leave your weapon behind."

He handed it over immediately, grip first.

"Aaron, Pete, stay here with our friends. We will be back."

And with that we left, jogging in the direction Werner had indicated.

I had never seen Désirée as worked up as she was. Her countenance was fierce. The only thing that had come close was when I had watched her encounter a man known as The Persian the year before—a man who had routinely abused her; a man who had attempted to execute her current boss, Gaspard Ducharme.

But this was even worse than that.

I said, "Gérard, I need to know that if Emily fires on us, you will not attempt to stop us from defending ourselves."

"I give you my word, monsieur."

When we had gone perhaps three hundred yards, we came upon a scene that was surreal. For there before us were Nathaniel Prince and Emily Young.

I could hear her hollering, "Give it to me, Nathaniel, and I will pull you to safety." And him replying, "Just how stupid do you think I am, Emily?"

Nathaniel was in the river with his arms locked around what was obviously an ancient piece of wood...the remnant. He was being battered mercilessly by the raging current. Two of his men lay dead in crumpled heaps at the river's edge. Emily stood knee-deep in the river with her right arm wrapped around a jutting tree limb—Désirée's pistol gripped tightly in her hand—while holding desperately to the collar of Nathaniel's jacket with her other hand.

Quite obvious was the fact that the river's current was going to win that particular tug-of-war unless someone intervened.

The intervention came in the form of Gérard yelling Emily's name and plunging into the river with absolutely no regard for his safety.

She turned her head toward the sound of his voice, yelling, "No! Get away from me! Get away! I don't need your help! The remnant is mine!"

He reached her and began attempting to pull her to safety with his arms locked around her waist. In response, she shifted the angle of the pistol and shot him through the neck. His eyes went wide in surprise and shock and he lingered upright, swaying, his eyes gradually losing their focus before being caught away like a piece of carrion, spinning in the swiftly flowing current.

Nathaniel reached toward her with one arm, his eyes wild with fear; all of his billions worthless to him now.

"I don't want to die. Save me, Emily," he pleaded.

"Hang on, uncle. Hang on. I have you."

But she didn't.

His jacket ripped and he began slipping away, but not

before she wrested the wood from his grip, holding it aloft like a trophy. Whether it had been her intent all along, or things had just worked out that way, I cannot say.

The current caught the great man, tumbling him over and under. The last we saw of him, the force of the river propelled him headfirst into an outcropping of rock. The result wasn't pretty. Then he was lost to view.

As Emily turned toward us with a triumphant smile on her face, Désirée raised her gun and took aim.

"That is for Paddy, salope," she hollered and would have shot her had I not slapped the gun aside.

"Jake!" Emily hollered desperately.

I turned to see her being pulled under by the current. Covering the ten feet separating us I dove toward her, grabbing a fistful of her coat, but I knew it wouldn't last for long, the current was too strong.

Fighting the current, her eyes locked on mine, she managed to say, "I'm...so sorry about Paddy. I...the gun...it just went off...he was...my friend...he...so sor..."

And then her coat tore free. With a last desperate lunge, I managed to grab the wood before she was spun away by the raging waters and was lost to sight.

I must confess that I cannot adequately explain what happened to me in that moment, except to say that...scenes began flashing before my eyes in a rapid-fire sequence. And I began to feel things: a broken nose; flagrum stripping the skin from my back; a crowd of people shoving me; something about thorns; eyes swollen nearly shut from repeated blows of many fists. So intense was the experience, I involuntarily lost my grip on the remnant and could only watch in horror as the wood was picked up by the flow and carried off along with the other detritus.

"Jake," Désirée hollered. "Jake, are you all right?"

Then she was helping me to my feet. I turned to regard my friend, my mouth working wordlessly in an attempt to describe what had just happened to me.

"Jake, what is it? What is wrong?" she asked, concern coloring her face.

"I...I don't know. I saw..."

And what had I seen?

A vision born out of stress, exhaustion and an overactive imagination?

Or by touching that ancient piece of blood-soaked timber...had I touched the wood between the worlds and as a result, experienced some sort of mystical, supernatural encounter with the man whose blood had flowed so freely over that roughly hewn patibulum?

"Come, mon cher," Désirée said, linking her arm through mine for support. "Let us get you back to the others."

With a final glance toward the raging cataract, I began to doubt my experience. And then I realized that I had been a doubter throughout most of my adult life.

But the thing about doubt...is that it makes you wonder.

EPILOGUE

We were somewhere over the Great Plains, cruising at forty-one thousand feet in Gaspard Ducharme's Gulfstream. Two days had passed since the tragic culmination of our expedition to Turkey. If you want to know the truth, I was still struggling. With all of it. So much death and destruction. So much loss, both personal and otherwise. It was difficult to recall an experience that had left me feeling so…I don't know…"less than" upon its completion. Less than I was when I began. Less than I should have been for those who had depended on me. Less than Paddy had needed me to be.

Prior to our departure, the bulk of our efforts had been directed toward helping to coordinate humanitarian aid for the village of İsa'nin haçı. Their losses were profound: forty percent of their agricultural fields were gone; close to sixty structures—including barns, commercial buildings, and private residences—had been declared a total loss; forty-eight men, women and children had lost their lives. They were an ancient people, visited often by tragedy. This was just one more in a long series of devastating occurrences. They had survived worse than this.

When we had gone back to collect the bodies of Nathaniel's men and those he had hired locally…they were gone. No one seemed to know a thing. "Men with guns? We didn't see any men with guns." Our suspicion was that Ramón had gotten there ahead of us; had hidden out during the conflict and had arranged for the bodies to be removed ahead of the authorities' arrival.

The only casualty we had to deal with was our dear

friend Paddy Quinn.

Paddy's death had affected me deeply. After all, had I not invited him to accompany us, he would still be living...well, to hear him tell it, the life he had was no life at all, but merely an existence. An existence he resented the hell out of. Perhaps he was in a better place. Perhaps he was walking through Elysian Fields with his beloved Maggie. Perhaps...

Werner and Elliot were disconsolate over having come so close to gaining that which they had so desperately sought; grief stricken over the deaths of Paddy and Emily Young.

Even though Emily had proven herself to be a rank traitor, she had, nevertheless, been a bright and beautiful young woman filled with promise and purpose. I believed her "deathbed confession" about Paddy's shooting being an accident. And now she was gone, along with all her hopes and dreams.

And Werner had loved her.

The two professors had stayed behind in İsa'nin haçı, having organized an expedition to search the banks downstream, hoping against hope that they would find the remnant lodged somewhere accessible. It was a long shot, though, for the banks that I saw were littered with enough wood to make it look as if a tornado had torn through the village. Nevertheless, they assured me that they wouldn't sleep until every possibility had been exhausted. And I believed them. It's an archeologist thing.

The plane ride home had been a somber affair, what with carrying Paddy's body in the hold and contemplating everything we had just been through. Aaron and Pete had slept most of the way; Cassie had spent a considerable amount of time on the phone with Michael in conversations that, judging by her fallen countenance, hadn't gone particularly well. It was a situation that concerned me greatly, but left me not knowing what, if anything, I was to do. It's that intrusion thing, again. I had always been there to rescue my beloved niece. It was damn hard to sit by, watch her suffer and struggle and just wait for her to figure stuff out on her own. And yet, I knew it was what I had to do.

I had called Gabi after the conflict just to let her know that I was all right, and we'd had another conversation somewhere over the Atlantic. She and the girls had been having a wonderful time. I didn't tell her about what had happened when I touched the wood, mainly because I simply didn't have a clue what to say.

Zack Hastings had called me to let me know that Interpol had raided the headquarters of The Nine—now The Six...not nearly the punch, if you ask me—and had arrested all of them, including Ramón on more charges than I could possibly articulate. At the very least, the lives of those men would be tied up in legal affairs for years to come, hopefully culminating in their imprisonment. But the thing about guys with money is that they rarely suffer the same consequences as us mere mortals. Truthfully, the chances of the whole lot of them wriggling out from under anything more severe than finding their bottom lines reduced by a considerable sum were quite low.

Cassie sat down in the seat next to me.

"Hey, Uncle."

"Hey yourself, little girl. You good?"

"I was about to ask you the same thing. I know you're struggling with something. Don't forget...I can read you like a paperback novel."

"That obvious, huh?"

She linked her arm through mine and laid her head on my shoulder.

"Well, I know something happened at the end back there in the village—something that has had a profound effect on you. Might be good to talk about it, you know."

"I...don't know if I can," I said, my voice breaking on the last word.

Sitting up, she stared at me.

"Okay, this is now officially freaking me out. You need

to tell me what's going on."

How could I?

I said lamely, "I...I just...experienced something in the river when I had my hands on the remnant."

Her eyes grew wide.

"Like, what?"

"I don't know. Like...flashes of memories. Only they weren't *my* memories."

"Whose, then?"

Whose indeed?

"I couldn't begin to tell you."

"Do you remember anything specific?"

I said, "Horror. Pain. Someone whipping my back with a flagrum. Having a broken nose. Eyes nearly swollen shut from multiple beatings. Feeling sharp objects being jammed into my skull."

"Dang, Uncle," she breathed. "That sounds like—"

"Don't say it! I know what it sounds like. I'm just not ready to give mental assent to that particular reality."

She giggled and said, "Sounds like you need to have a chat with Father Jack."

Father Jack Mahoney is one of the good guys. He lives in San Diego and runs a small parish but spends most of his time feeding hungry people. For years now he has been my go-to guy for matters too deep for me to wrestle through on my own.

"Yeah," I agreed. "You're probably right."

"There's no probably about it," she countered. "Promise me you'll call him as soon as we get back and before you head back to Vegas."

"Okay, okay." I let a few seconds tick by before saying, "I'm actually glad we didn't secure the remnant."

"Really? How come?"

"I don't know. Maybe this is part of what happened to me, but...it just feels sort of...sort of wild. Untamable. Like, if someone were to attempt putting it on display somewhere—"

"What? Lasers would shoot out and start melting people's faces?" she teased.

"No, nothing like that. It's just that...I think maybe some things are meant to remain hidden. You know?"

She nodded slowly.

"I do know. So, are you suggesting that there was, umm, a bit of divine intervention in that wood being swept away?"

Was I?

"I'm not prepared to go that far."

"How far will you go, then?" she prodded.

I turned my head and stared out the window at the world so far below me. So indistinct. Such a hodgepodge of fields and cities and mountains and lakes and people just living their lives and...dying, some before their time.

I turned back to face Cassie and said, "I will go so far as to say that there are things in this world that transcend intellectual dismissal or explanation; things that exist in the realm of wonder that we may never fully understand; faint reflections of riddles...mysteries that are meant to stay mysteries."

She linked her arm through mine and returned her head to my shoulder.

"I'm good with that."

"Me too, kiddo. Me too."

*****

The two young boys had been sent out by their father to search the banks of the Meram Deresi with instructions to not come back unless they had found something valuable. Being nine and eleven respectively, they possessed only the most basic understanding of what constituted value. But, being obedient sons, they set out to fulfill their father's wishes.

He was not long for this world. The cancer. They weren't sure what cancer was, but they knew enough to know that people who had it didn't live very long. And so they dutifully searched through the accumulation of debris along the banks of their typically friendly little creek—the creek that had been turned into a frothing, foaming, raging monster over the past few days; a hungry gap-mawed beast whose insatiable appetite had devoured nearly everything in its path.

The elder brother called to his younger sibling, "Come look here."

When the younger brother arrived, he found his big brother bent over and staring at what appeared to be a waterlogged, old timber with a splintered end.

"What is it?" he asked.

"I don't know. But...I think it might be valuable."

"Why? It's just an old piece of—"

The elder brother slapped the youngster upside the head.

"No. It's not just an old piece of wood. There's something about it."

Rubbing away the sting from the blow, the younger brother replied, "Look, if we take that back to father, he will beat both of us. He said to bring back something valuable."

The older brother reached down and began attempting to dislodge the wood from its resting place there in the mud and rubble.

"Help me," he hollered as his younger brother dropped down and began attempting to pry it free.

Suddenly, with the wet sound of suction breaking, the wood came free sending both of them stumbling back to land on their haunches.

"Should we clean it up before taking it home?" the younger asked.

"No. It's perfect just the way it is."

The younger brother stared skeptically, but shrugged his shoulders and went along with his older sibling. Like always.

And so, they took it home.

Their father didn't beat them.

He thought it was the perfect piece to complete the

doorjam that had been destroyed in the flood.

He congratulated them on such a wonderful find.

Two months later, he no longer had the symptoms from the disease attempting to steal his life away. Two months after that, friends and neighbors, and even a few strangers, were dropping by simply because they just felt better when they were in that humble abode.

Six months after that, on any given day, you could find a line of halt and lame waiting their turn to simply walk through that front door and spend a few minutes speaking with the man—who had developed the reputation of being a sage; someone who seemed to know the answers to hard questions—and then walking away whole.

And four months after that, word reached the cloistered congress of six men in a sixteenth century chalet, hidden away in the Swiss Alps, that something very interesting was happening in a tiny village in south central Turkey.

AUTHOR'S NOTES

There has been much written, discussed, speculated and scoffed at over the years regarding the existence of remnants of the true cross. Whether the Emperor Constantine's mother, Helena Augusta, in fact, carried back anything of legitimacy from her trip to the Holy Land in 326-28 AD is open for debate. For the purposes of this novel, I chose to regard her findings negatively.

As to the authenticity of historical records regarding the crucifixion of one Jesus of Nazareth, the phrase, "hotly debated" comes to mind. There are those who accept the canonical records as historical fact. There are others who reject those records, yet have trouble reconciling non-Christian historical records such as the report of the crucifixion by Roman Senator Tacitius, historian Flavius Josephus and a letter written by Mara bar Serapion to his son. There are others, still, who reject the notion that Jesus existed, or that Romans actually carried out crucifixions.

As to whether Jesus existed or is a fabrication of someone's overactive imagination, I suppose that is something the reader will have to settle on his or her own. Sadly, there is no debate regarding the existence of crucifixion. Preponderance of historical evidence—and since 1968 archeological evidence—exists to confirm the horror. While it was carried out in many forms, the specifics described by the character of Professor Spencer in the novel were not dramatized.

To my knowledge there is no Northwest Pacific University, nor is there a village downriver from the Altinapa Dam called İsa'nin haçı.

As always, heartfelt thanks to my amazing support

team without whom I could not accomplish the task of novel writing: my advance readers, Bob Book, Sharon Walling, and Steve Betz; art director and cover designer, Sarah Wagner; and my editor, Cheryl Gollner, who ever lives to shape the ravings of this mad scriblerian into a form and substance suitable for mass consumption.

Thank you for reading my work. Jake and friends will soon be back as *A Faint Reflection Of Riddles* continues with Book Two: *The First Stone*.

> R.G. Ryan
> August 2019
> Ocean Beach, California